D0757292

CHASING DOWN THE MOON

CHASING DOWN THE MOON

CARLA BAKU

LOOK MA NO HANDS
EUREKA
2015

ISBN: 978-0-9861717-0-3

Chasing Down the Moon is a work of fiction. Names, characters, businesses, places, events, and incidents, including those of a historical nature, are products of the author's imagination or are used fictitiously. Any resemblance to actual persons, living or dead, events, or locales is purely coincidental.

The following lyric and poetic excerpts are from works in the public domain:
"To a Mouse." Robert Burns, 1785
"Blessed Assurance." Crosby/Knapp, 1873
"Hanson Place." Robert Lowry, 1864
"Our God, Our Help in Ages Past." Isaac Watts, 1719
"Barbara Frietchie." John Greenleaf Whittier, 1864

Translation of poem by Zhou Xuanjin from scholarly resources and multiple translations, copyright 2015 by Carla Baku. For more poetry by Zhou Xuanjin, see *Immortal Sisters: Secrets of Taoist Women,* edited and translated by Thomas Cleary (Boston: Shambhala Publications, 1989)

Cover design by Tara Mayberry (teaberrycreative.com)
Copyright 2015 Carla Baku

Look Ma No Hands Publishing
P.O. Box 84
Eureka, California 95502
lmnohpub@gmail.com

To Brian, first and last.
Funny how things work out.

THE CHARACTERS
(First-name alphabetical order)

Bai Lum: Proprietor of the Chinese mercantile in Eureka.

Billy Kellogg: Troublemaking friend of Byron Tupper

Byron Tupper: Teenage son of Garland Tupper.

Clarence and Cora Salyer: Married couple, hoteliers in Eureka. Clarence also runs a brothel where four Chinese women are held as indentured prostitutes.

Daniel and Annabella Briggs: Well-to-do next-door neighbors of the Kendalls.

David and Prudence Kendall*: Known around town as 'Captain Kendall' David is an admired businessman and Eureka city councilman. Prudence is his wife, and they have an adult daughter, Phoebe, whom they dote on.

Elsie and Charlie Dampler: Elsie is a self-important busybody; Charlie is her obedient husband.

Francis Jane Beebe: Close friend of Elsie Dampler, and former classmate of Byron Tupper.

Garland Tupper: Bullying and brutal father of Byron Tupper.

Hazel Cleary: Rose Allen's paternal aunt. An Irish immigrant, she is housekeeper to the Kendalls. Mentor and landlady to Matilda Gillen.

Hong Tai: Ya Zhen's six-year-old brother.

Ivo: German cook at the Salyer's Hotel.

Jacob Weimer: Deacon at the Congregational Church and friend of the Huntingtons.

Joe and Mary Reilly: Joe is proprietor of a livery; wife Mary is a member of the Women's Christian Temperance Union.

Li-Lau: Naïve young prostitute at the Salyer's Hotel.

Louis Baldschmidt*: Twelve-year-old painter's apprentice on the newly-constructed Carson Mansion.

Matilda 'Mattie' Gillen: Lives with Hazel Cleary and Rose Allen. She emigrated from Ireland to escape family problems; employed as a girl-of-all-work at Salyer's Hotel.

Molly 'Old Mol' Blevins: Manages the everyday "back business" for Clarence Salyer.

Reverend Charles and Lucretia 'Lucy' Huntington*: Elderly pastor of the Congregational Church, and his wife.

Robert Allen: Widowed father of Rose Allen. A wainwright and master craftsman in Paw Paw, Illinois.

Rose Allen: Raised by her father in Illinois, she moved to the coast to escape the stifling life expected of her in the Midwest. Lives with her aunt Hazel Cleary and works as a housemaid and part-time children's tutor.

Shu-Li: Young girl living with Bai Lum.

Thomas Walsh*: Mayor of Eureka.

Tom Brown*: Local sheriff

Wei Lum, Chen Ma, Dong-Li Ha: A few of the men who make up the hard-working population of Eureka's Chinatown.

William Carson*: A wealthy timber magnate who has kept many men working during hard times by employing them to build his extraordinary Victorian mansion.

Wu Lin and Wu Song: Sisters indentured to Clarence Salyer many years ago.

Ya Zhen: A teenage girl from the mountains of Hunan China, where she lived with her parents and her little brother. Now an indentured prostitute at Salyer's Hotel.

*Indicates actual historical persons. To learn more about them, see "A Note to the Reader" on page 336.

PART I

SPARKS

Ignorance is the night of the mind, but a night without moon and star. —*Confucius*

For man is born unto trouble, as the sparks fly upward. —*Job 5:7*

BEFORE

September 23, 1881

Dearest Father,

At long last, I have stopped moving long enough to pen a legible letter to you. The steamship from San Francisco made port in Humboldt Bay early yesterday morning, and before I even had time to realize where I was, Aunt Hazel had me settled into my own upstairs room, a cup of tea on the night table and a bath drawn to wash away the soot, sweat, and salt of the past nine days. Whether I'll ever launder it all out of my traveling skirt remains to be seen.

You were right, Papa, that it would be hard travel, but I did love it, even the stark expanses of Utah and Nevada. There were reminders along the way that many had come before us, and under far more wearying modes of travel than a modern rail car. At one place I saw a chifferobe that had long ago fallen from some passing wagon, the wood bleached white as bone. I had to wonder what sorts of creatures were now at home in those shattered drawers— scorpion, spider, snake? Miles on, the whole lot of us were in a grim temper—no surprise, hot and dusted with cinders as we were—and as the train toiled up into the Sierra Nevadas, there commenced some especially black jesting about the Donner Party. I confess to having joined in, which made a woman sitting near me cover the ears of her little boy. I sigh even now to remember her expression and my realization that I had (once again) trampled the invisible line of female propriety that has always been so elusive and troublesome. Will I ever learn?

When we dropped into the Sacramento Valley, there were, as far as we could see, fields of wild sunflowers, their faces no larger than the palm of a man's hand, spread out on either side of the tracks. Our entire company actually broke into hurrahs to see it— California!

Papa, I've nearly emptied the inkwell, and not even begun to tell you about Eureka—it is a rough place, and glorious. I'll write soon and tell you how I'm settling into my adventure. What I miss most, already: brushing the sawdust off your shoulders right before supper. My best love to my best fellow.

Your prodigal,
Rose

CHAPTER ONE

Hunan Province, China, 1883

THE STARVING TIME. Each spring, this is what the people in the village called the lean months, when the best mushrooms were gone from the woods and spring greens had not yet come up. Ya Zhen was sixteen, a slender girl, tall like her father. Her hands and arms were strongly corded from a great deal of physical work. Today she huddled under a blanket, trying to keep her small brother distracted so that he would stop complaining of hunger. She could not stop thinking about an egg, how the yellow yolk would coat her tongue. But the last hen had stopped laying and gone into the pot long ago, feeding them and feeding them, first with parceled bits of flesh, then smoky traces of marrow, and finally broth, diluted a little more each day until it was a sip of hot water infused with the memory of chicken.

The rain was relentless. For weeks, the unbroken wall of water between the river and the clouds had sent the fish into hiding. Their mother sat by the ashes of her cooking fire, hands resting in her lap, palms up. Earlier in the morning she had raked through the cold char, looking for a bit of fish or rice that might have fallen in the fire days before, something she could feed her son. There was nothing. The night before, she had fixed a last bit of porridge and given it to the boy. But there had been no breakfast and now the afternoon mealtime was long since passed.

"Pretend you are a tiger," Ya Zhen said. "You are in your den, hiding from the hunters. Shh," she whispered. "They are so near."

Hong-Tai crouched under the blanket with her, his pupils large in the dark. "I am going to eat the hunters," he said, baring his small, square teeth. He was six years old, tall for his age with a long face and prominent cheekbones, like their father.

"Oh no, it's too dangerous," said Ya Zhen. "There are too many, and they have long arrows. You have to wait. I'll tell you when to come out."

"But I'm hungry, *Tǎ jà*. I want to eat." He pulled the blanket off his head. Before she could catch him, Hong-Tai jumped off the bed and ran to their mother. "*Mā*," he shouted at her. "Give me food now."

Their mother turned her head slowly, face blank, as if she could not hear him.

"Give me food!" He raised a hand as if to strike. Ya Zhen grabbed his arm and led him outside. The yard was boggy with mud, but the clouds had thinned enough that she could judge the sun's position low in the sky, a luminous gray spot behind the darker gray overcast.

"Let's find worms and try fishing again," she told Hong-Tai. She didn't want to leave her mother alone, but an empty belly compelled her. Their father had left five days ago, down the mountain to try to sell the meager remnants of last year's millet crop. It was the last bag, saved back for seed, but the fields were too wet to plant and he feared the seed would mold if he waited any longer. He had promised to bring back food and should have returned after three days.

"Tigers don't dig for worms," Hong-Tai said. He folded his arms over his chest.

"That's true," said Ya Zhen. "They can't hold a line and pull the fish up, either. Or cook the fish. Tigers never cook."

"Mā will cook the fish for me." He ran to the maple tree at the corner of the hut, broke off a small branch and handed it to his sister. "I'm not really a tiger," he said. "Are the fish hungry now?"

She tapped a finger on top of his head. "Maybe they are."

After a few minutes digging with the branch, they had a writhing ball of red worms in a reed basket. While Hong-Tai gathered damp grass to cover them, Ya Zhen returned to the house for their tackle, a plain bamboo pole strung with twine and hook. Her mother had gone to the bed and curled on her side, facing the wall. Most of her hair had come loose of its knot at the nape of her neck and it trailed out on the bed behind her like weeds floating at the riverbank.

"Mā," Ya Zhen said. She touched her mother's shoulder. "We're going to fish." Her mother did not stir. It had always seemed to Ya Zhen as if her frail mother had one foot in the ghost world. "We'll be careful. I'll keep Hong-Tai with me." She went to the door. "*Bà* will be home soon," she said, almost in a whisper. Her mother's back looked thin as a child's and she did not reply. Ya Zhen could hardly make out the rise and fall of her breathing.

Normally she would cast bits of rice onto the water to tempt fish to the surface, but she had no rice, no millet. She didn't need it. The long rains had indeed made the fish ravenous. She baited her hook and had a fish on the line immediately. The live thrum quivered into her palms and she drew it to shore with the utmost care. After landing three small trout, she let Hong-Tai take a turn. In seconds, he had a strike. "Tǎ jà," he shouted, jumping from foot to foot. She helped him pull the fish—a big one, easily twice the size of hers—onto the bank and showed him how to retrieve the hook. He was so excited he cast in again before baiting the line and nearly tossed their pole into the river. They pulled the line in and he turned the fishing back over to his sister, squatting to admire his own catch. After she pulled in a fifth silver trout, Ya Zhen cleaned them on the riverbank, throwing the entrails back into the water and wiping her bloody fingers on a hank of moss. Hong-Tai, still squatting, watched.

"This one for me." He pointed at the largest and smoothed its tail with a grimy finger.

She opened her mouth to tease, to tell him the fish was hers, but his nose ran and his teeth chattered. "Of course," she said. "You can eat it up and get a big belly."

This high in the hills the river ran fast and cold; the flesh of the trout was firm, pink. Ya Zhen's mouth watered and she wanted to bite into the fish raw. She knocked the few remaining worms onto the dirt, wrapped all five fish in clean leaves and tucked them into the basket.

The thin spring sun had dipped behind the peaks, throwing the small valley into early twilight. Her fingers were bright red, numb from the water, and Hong-Tai shivered. She rubbed his arms through the thin fabric of his jacket and proposed they race to see who could get home first to start the fire. He sprinted ahead of her, pigtail bouncing from shoulder to shoulder.

She was ten years older than Hong-Tai and had been a second mother to him from the beginning. Her father, always distant with the girl, had been transformed when his son was born. She could perfectly recall how animated his face became when the midwife brought him news of a male child. It seemed to Ya Zhen that overnight her taciturn father became young, as if his face was lit from inside. He had showered Mā with small affections and gifts and had carried Hong-Tai around so much that the women in the village began to call him *nán yín pú*: little mother.

Climbing the hill, Hong-Tai saw his father first, standing in the open door. "Bà ba!" He ran hard and was caught up into the air, laughing. "I'm hungry, Bà. My belly is angry and Mā wouldn't feed me."

His father set the boy on his feet and smiled down at him. "Go to the table now and see what's there. Your mother has a surprise."

Ya Zhen was right behind Hong-Tai. "Hello Bà," she said. "We have fish for dinner."

His eyes skimmed her face and then looked past her, at the mountain. "Come and eat." He turned and she followed him inside.

A cooking fire now warmed the hut. Ya Zhen's mother poured hot tea, and she had made porridge. On the table were opened parcels of food her father had carried home: rice, with which her mother had made the porridge, and pickled radish to eat with it; strips of salted herring; and sticky buns with bean paste, as if they were celebrating the new year again. Ya Zhen gave the basket of trout to her mother, who was busy filling Hong-Tai's bowl, smiling.

It seemed impossible that she was the same woman, earlier left in the bed with her face to the wall.

"See what your father has brought us," she said. "Eat now and I'll cook the fish."

Ya Zhen put food on her plate, her mouth watering when she smelled the pickled vegetable. She went to a low stool near the hearth. The porridge was hot and creamy, and she felt it warming her, filling her belly while she watched her father and brother eating at the table. Hong-Tai tore a dumpling open and licked out the creamy paste. He stuck out his tongue and crossed his eyes trying to see it. Ya Zhen covered her mouth and laughed. She waited for her father's reaction; it seemed she had spent all of Hong-Tai's life, six years, trying to learn something about her father by watching him watch Hong-Tai. She was surprised. He was not looking at the boy, but at her, leaning back in his chair, his unshod feet stretched toward the fire. When she caught his gaze, he looked away, scratching his head.

After they had eaten and the table was clean, her father brought more packages out. The first he gave to Hong-Tai. It was a suit of clothes, the pants and tunic made of heavy brocade, dark blue, and a new jacket, thickly padded with a tall collar that reached the boy's chin.

"Look, Tǎ jà," he said to Ya Zhen. He ran to her and turned slowly, holding his arms out stiffly to his sides, face solemn and pleased.

"You look like the son of the great north wind," she said, running her palm over the satiny brocade. "Very strong and powerful."

Hong-Tai broke into a grin and began to run around the table. "I am the wind. Watch out, I am blowing my cold breath on you!"

"Come here zǎi," their mother said. She drew Hong-Tai close and held his face between her palms. "My handsome boy." Hong-Tai leaned against her, looking down at his new clothes. "So much money for the seeds," she said to her husband. "You were shrewd to make such a bargain."

He looked at her levelly, then at Ya Zhen. He pushed the last parcel across the table toward her. "Take this," he said.

Ya Zhen was so stunned by the offer of a gift that she had to look at her mother first, thinking she must be mistaken. Her mother's eyes were large and surprised in the firelight. She nodded at her daughter.

She opened the thin paper carefully, so that it could be used again. There was a garment, brilliant scarlet. Ya Zhen stood and held it up. It was a wedding robe, embroidered with gold thread, peonies and cranes. The fire glimmered on the patterns. Ya Zhen felt thunderstruck, as if every thought had been swept from her mind. But somehow her body knew; her hands began to tremble and tiny reflections shimmered on the walls of the small room. When her mother moaned, Ya Zhen's knees buckled and she fell back onto the stool hard enough to make her teeth click together.

"This girl is to be congratulated," her father said loudly. "She will soon have a rich husband."

Ya Zhen's mother shook her head in tiny arcs, no no no. She looked from father to daughter, father to daughter, tears beginning to slide down her cheeks. Then she looked at Hong-Tai in his beautiful new clothes.

"No," she said, and caught her son by the arm. "Take it off. We have to give it back."

"Bà!" Hong-Tai howled, pulling away from his mother, stumbling and landing on the floor. He started to cry. "You made me fall," he wailed. "My clothes are dirty."

Ya Zhen's father made two long strides across the room and slapped his wife hard on the face. He was a tall man, as were many men from the north, and Ya Zhen's mother staggered and fell onto the bed, blood on her mouth. Ya Zhen felt rooted to the earthen floor, like an old cypress holding her place in the world by habit. Their father had often spoken roughly to them, but Ya Zhen had never seen him strike their mother. Hong-Tai saw his mother's blood and screamed. He ran to Ya Zhen, buried his face in her neck, weeping.

Her father stood panting, and looked back at Ya Zhen. "Tomorrow you will travel to meet your husband in the south. Take some of this food for your journey." Without looking at her, he told his wife to get up, to help Ya Zhen prepare to leave. "It will be at first light," he said. He picked up Hong-Tai. The boy tried to hold onto his sister, but his father spoke sharply to him. "We will take care of night business now." This meant carrying a last bucket of water from the well, splitting some kindling for the morning fire, and going to the latrine. Hong-Tai looked at Ya Zhen over his father's shoulder as he was carried out. His wet eyes were large in his face.

"Mā," Ya Zhen whispered. Her mother had curled up, just as she had earlier in the day, weeping quietly. The girl stood, fighting the ragged, wobbly sensation in her legs. She found the cloth her mother used to wipe the dishes and wet it in the drinking bucket. "Mā," Ya Zhen said again, pulling gently on her mother's shoulder. Her mother let herself be rolled onto her back like a child. Ya Zhen brushed the hair out of her face and winced at the deep gash on the corner of her mother's mouth. The flesh of her cheek was smeared with blood and was swelling, the perfect outline of her father's hand rising there.

Ya Zhen wiped at the blood as gently as she could. Her mother did not flinch or pull away, but her eyes opened. When Ya Zhen rinsed the cloth and reached out to wipe her face again, her mother gripped her wrist and took the cloth. She sat up and pulled Ya Zhen to her. Ya Zhen could not remember her doing this since she was a tiny child. The strength in her mother's arms surprised her, and she relaxed into the embrace. Her fear filled her like a raw tide, and she allowed herself to weep.

"No, Mā. No, Mā." She said it over and over, and her mother rocked her back and forth. She cried until her throat was raw and she was no longer making real sound, just a keening that she felt in the center of her head. When she had no more strength to weep, she sagged against her mother and simply breathed in the light, earthy smell of her.

"It is not a lucky thing to be born a woman," her mother said. "Your fate will be in the hands of your husband now."

By the time her father brought Hong-Tai back into the hut, nearly asleep on his feet, Ya Zhen's mother had wrapped the girl's few possession in a bundle: a wooden comb, a second shirt, a small pile of sunflower seeds twisted in a corner of the paper her father had packed the parcels in. She also wrapped the bits of food left over from dinner, and finally the wedding robe. Before she tied everything up, she went to the bed and got on her hands and knees. From far underneath she pulled a small wooden box. It was plain, no scrollwork of any kind, but the finish gleamed like pooled honey. Her mother set the box on the table and lifted the lid. She brought out a pair of chopsticks, polished ebony. On the end of each one was a jade inlay, a meticulous dragon with a small seed pearl eye.

"My mother gave these to me when I married," she said. "They have fed all your grandmothers." She tucked the chopsticks into the bundle and tied it in a snug roll. "This will bring luck," she said.

"But I don't want to go. Please. Don't let him."

"Your husband has already paid."

"I want—"

"You must learn to want differently." Her mother leaned her head close to Ya Zhen's, her face grim. "Now you are the daughter of your husband's mother." The words were so simple, the way she said them, and each one fell like a stone onto Ya Zhen's heart. Her mother took up the broom, swept ashes back into the hearth with her back turned. It seemed to the girl that her mother grew smaller, receding even as she stood in one place, while the little sounds of the stiff bristles making their *whist, whist* raised an impenetrable hedge between them. After what might have been a very long time, or only moments, there were footsteps outside. Ya Zhen's mother touched her own bruised and swollen face.

"Your father is coming. Get in your bed."

All night she lay awake and shaking beneath her blanket. Her father had said she would marry a wealthy man. No wealthy families lived in this village, nor in the village where her mother's aunt lived, most of a day's walk to the east. All her life she had known that her parents would arrange her marriage, but she imagined there would be some warning, that perhaps she would know the family of which she was to become part. In no scenario had she imagined being far from Hong-Tai. What would happen to him when their mother got lost in the ghost world, as she had during their father's absence, which she often did during the dark months of winter? All her life, Ya Zhen had acted as a buffer between Hong-Tai and the temper of their father, distracting the little boy when his demands became wearisome and irritating to the adults. She kept remembering her father, standing over their mother after striking her, panting while his wife bled into her own palm. Would he strike Hong-Tai? Ya Zhen felt as if some vital part of her belly had torn loose from the fear trampling inside her.

Her mother wept off and on during the night, small sounds like a kitten. Once her father spoke softly, and her mother had stopped crying. Long before the first cockcrow, her mother rose, built the fire and put the kettle on. Ya Zhen feigned sleep when her mother shook her shoulder.

"You must wash now, daughter," she said.

Ya Zhen opened her eyes. "I am not your daughter."

Her mother blinked and drew back. Her mouth was less swollen than it had been the night before, but a dark bruise mottled the side of her face and her eyes were puffy from crying. She smoothed the hair back from Ya Zhen's forehead. "Just for this last morning," she said. "Come and wash for the journey."

She got up, her joints stiff from lying awake all night. The reflection of the small flames leapt up on the earthen walls of the house. Hong-Tai and her father still slept, the little boy's arms and legs flung wide across his mat, his face smooth and careless.

While she poured hot water into a bowl and undressed to her thin undergarments, her mother tied her bedding into a roll. She placed this with Ya Zhen's other small bundle of belongings next to the door. Ya Zhen watched all this from the corner of her eye. She felt that perhaps it was a dream, that she really had fallen asleep in the night and would soon wake to find her mother cooking more rice porridge, Hong-Tai pulling one of her eyelids open as he loved to do when she slept longer than he did. But the rough rag on her face and arms, her own breath steaming from her lips, and now the sound of a rooster from the village—these were not a dream. Her mother stirred millet into a pan, a sense of hurry in all her movements.

Then there were voices and the sound of horses on the road. Her mother looked toward the closed door. She dropped the stirring spoon and rushed to wake her husband.

Later, Ya Zhen remembered the last moments with her family in disjointed blocks of motion. Her father opened the door and went into the yard and Hong-Tai ran out with him. Her mother combed and braided her hair, whispering advice. "Be submissive to his mother. If she likes you, your life will be easier. The first time…after the wedding, you must try to stay calm. There will be a small pain, but a calm spirit will bring you a strong son." She went on and on like this, but Ya Zhen could hardly hear any of her words. All she could hear was the sound of men talking, rough voices, her father placatory and cajoling in a way she had never heard him before. Then he called to her mother to bring Ya Zhen out.

Her feet were so heavy and without feeling, they seemed to have turned to clay. When she crossed the threshold into the early morning, there were two men on horseback. Another man drove an oxcart filled with sacks of wheat and millet, and a barrel of fish, salt bleeding out and coating the sides in crusty white streaks.

One of the horsemen, a lean and muscular man whose expression was flat as slate, dismounted. He motioned at Ya Zhen with one hand. "Bring her here."

Her father clasped her arm and led her forward. The other mounted man and the ox driver looked on, silent. The first man took Ya Zhen by the shoulders and turned her around, looked at the back of her, ran his hands down her back, over her buttocks, and down the length of her legs. Ya Zhen could hear her mother crying again. "Peasant feet," he grunted, for her feet were not bound. He grasped her chin. "Open your mouth," he said quietly. Was this her husband? She tried to catch her mother's eye, until he gave her jaw a small jerk. "Open," he said, scowling. People spoke to misbehaving dogs in such a voice. She opened her mouth. The man hooked a finger inside and pulled, looked at her teeth. Hong-Tai, who had been standing behind his mother's legs, roared and ran at the man.

"Don't hurt my sister!" he shouted. Before their father could stop him, Hong-Tai had thrown a punch at the man's arm. The man knocked him aside and he sprawled in the dirt of the yard.

"Hong-Tai." Ya Zhen lurched toward her brother, but the man had her by the arm, twisting just enough to keep her from breaking free. Their mother lifted Hong-Tai, wiping the dirt off his face with the edge of her sleeve.

Suddenly someone grabbed Ya Zhen from behind and hoisted her, the other horseman. Though not much taller than she, he was powerfully built. He slung her astride his horse and climbed up, clamped an arm around her waist. The first man mounted his own horse and turned for the road.

"Wait," cried Ya Zhen's mother, "her things, her bed." She pointed at the door of the house. Ya Zhen's father, whose face had gone as white as milk, ran for the bundles, even as the group moved out of the yard.

"Throw it in the wagon," said the first man, not looking back.

Ya Zhen's father tucked the two bundles among the sacks of grain, walking alongside as the oxen gathered speed, but did not look at Ya Zhen. This done, he turned his back, shoulders bowed. Hong-Tai bellowed, screaming her name. Her father tried to subdue him, but Hong-Tai slapped his face. Ya Zhen's mother stumbled under the weight of the flailing boy and lost her hold. He tried to run after them, but they were already far down the road and his father caught him and carried him, howling, back to the mud house.

Ya Zhen felt each of his cries like a stroke of lightening in her belly, in the place where the horseman had clamped his hand. She tilted back her head and a cry rose from her gut that sounded like an animal.

"You should save that voice for your wedding night," the horseman said in her ear. "You will be the wife of a hundred men. So much pleasure will surely make you sing." He and the other men laughed. Ya Zhen closed her mouth and tried to stop the violent shaking in her arms and legs.

Two hours outside Ya Zhen's village, the lead horseman ordered them off the road and announced he would be the first to congratulate the new bride. He told her to take off her clothes. When she only stood still, shaking her head, he pulled out a short blade. He grabbed her wrist and made a shallow gash between her fingers. Ya Zhen cried out and held her bleeding hand to her chest.

"This will heal quickly and your new owners will never see the scar," he said. "There are many places on your body like this. I will show you each one unless you do as I say." He waited.

Their faces registered only a species of impassive hunger. All around her the day looked as she might have expected, bright, the sun just skimming through the eastern peaks, the up-and-down song of little yellow-throated birds. In that moment, she understood the nature of her life: an outlier.

They wiped themselves clean with her clothing, and when she couldn't stand or walk, the cart driver pulled her by one arm and heaved her in with the bags of grain. He threw her stained clothes on top of her and climbed into the front of the cart. The ox grunted and the wagon lurched forward. She was so grateful for the air in her lungs, so relieved to be off the ground, her body, even in its pain, belonging to herself again, that she lay silent, heavy as stone. There was no birdsong now, only the sound of grit passing under the wagon's wheels and her breath in, then out.

Come nightfall she was feverish, by turns shaking and burning. The men stopped and made a camp, leaving her in the cart. She had pulled her clothes back on and dragged her bedroll on top of her without the strength to open it, and before she lost consciousness the men argued over her. The lead horsemen said they must be careful or risk losing the rest of their pay when they got her to Guangdong.

"That demon will not pay for her if she is dead," he said in his quiet voice, and that finished the argument.

When the cold shaking swept her, her teeth rattled together like the sound of pebbles in a gourd. This roused her and she stared through the slats of the cart at the fire, wishing she could get closer to warm herself. Then a vast heat ran through her, starting deep in her body, creating a terrible thirst. The lead horseman came to the cart and looked at her lying among the sacks. He gave her a bowl of tea, which she gulped until she choked. When she coughed, she felt more blood soak her trousers and a wave of dizziness knocked her backward. She fainted then. He must have opened her bedroll because she woke some time later with her blanket spread over her. It smelled like the inside of her home, of her mother's cooking fire and the sweet, woody smell of *huo xiang*, the strong herb used to discourage moths. Ya Zhen was surprised to find that this did not make her cry. Perhaps she was too ill or too exhausted. She thought she might be dying and found that even this did not upset her. Her whole body felt hollow as a gallnut because her spirit was ready to fly into the night sky with the sparks rising from the campfire.

She rose and fell through consciousness all night. At one point, she found herself back in the village, sitting above the river in the old camphor tree. Hong-Tai was fishing and she called to him from her place on the branch. But her voice was the small bleat of a cuckoo. He picked up stones and threw them at her, laughing. She burst through the branches and the tiny white camphor flowers showered into his hair. Then it was dark again and the fire gone out, the men asleep. There was deep breathing near the side of the cart and at first she was afraid one of the men watched her in the dark. Then she realized it was the ox, staked nearby. She could see its flank through the slats. She tried to put her hand through and touch the warm hide, but she couldn't reach it. She fell asleep that way, hand and wrist stretched through the staves. Finally there was a trace of light in the sky, but she could not so much as lift her head to look around. Everything in her belly and deep inside where the men had hurt her was a roaring fire.

When the men woke, the lead horseman brought a bowl of water to the cart. Ya Zhen just looked at him and closed her eyes again. He lifted her head and told her to drink. She did as he said, and the water was like cool silk going down her throat, but moments later she vomited it up again. The force of this caused a great searing pain through her lower body that made her want to scream, but she could only gasp like a fish pulled out of the river, clutching her belly, which was hard and hot.

The man's face looked tight and worried. He spoke to the others over the fire while they drank their tea. The second horseman frowned and shook his head; they were engaged in another argument, but Ya Zhen couldn't make sense of what they said. She drifted out of the world again.

The next time she opened her eyes, she was out of the cart, inside a dark room and lying on a pallet. She was naked again and an old woman washed her, dipping and rinsing the rag in a wooden bowl that smelled of red elder flowers. Her skin felt cool. When she tried to lift her head, the woman put her palm on Ya Zhen and pressed her back.

"No, little bud, *mò qǐ lái.* Don't try to get up." This was an *ēn mā*, a granny shaman from some village. She took a cloth from Ya Zhen's forehead and rinsed it in the bowl, replaced it. The smell was light and sweet and she wished she could drink something that smelled like that. As if reading her mind, the woman brought a cup to her lips. The tea was not sweet, but deeply bitter. She was thirsty, though, and took several deep swallows. Immediately, her body broke out in a hard sweat.

"Good," the woman said, nodding and wiping Ya Zhen's skin again. "This hot wind must blow through you." She rinsed the rag and smoothed it over Ya Zhen's face, the way her mother had when she was very small. Large tears formed at the corners of her eyes and rolled into her ears and hair. The woman nodded again. "You have come to great pain," she said, "and you will have to bear this burden for a long time." Her gray hair was pulled back severely and was so thin her weathered scalp showed through. The ēn mā smiled. "You are lucky, though." She laughed at Ya Zhen's expression, showing a few worn-down teeth. "Oh yes," she said, as if the girl had contradicted her. "You will not die. You will slide through the bars of your cage, like the shadow of an eel sliding through the water. Here, open your mouth." She held a smooth piece of wood as long as her finger. "Put this between your teeth."

With great care, the woman bent Ya Zhen's knees. Her thighs began to shake and she gripped the edge of the pallet. Slowly, the woman extracted a matted bundle of herbs from inside Ya Zhen's body. The girl ground her teeth into the stick. "Now I put fresh medicine inside. This will draw the fire out." She packed a wad of damp herbs into a thin cloth, wetting it with the elderflower water. "You bite the stick," she said, and Ya Zhen did, until her jaws ached. When the woman finished, the sweat poured off Ya Zhen. The woman wound a soft rag between the girl's legs and around her hips and covered her with a loosely woven sheet of homespun cloth.

"They will take you tomorrow," she said. "I told them I would buy you. I have an extra pig and some chickens—good laying hens. I need help here." She poured the elderflower water into a bucket and threw the fouled bolus on the fire, where it sizzled. "They won't sell. They want gold, and I don't deal in anything I can't eat or grow."

"I have some food," Ya Zhen said. "Where are my things?"

"Everything is right here," said the woman, patting the little bundle under Ya Zhen's head. "I've already eaten your food. You won't be able to take anything solid for a day or two." She tamped something into a small pipe, leaning close to the fire to see. "They didn't bother with it, I know, because they'll take the chopsticks if they see them. Don't let anyone see them."

She lit the pipe and took a breath, blew smoke out her nostrils. Then she took another, and before Ya Zhen realized it, had gently clamped her old lips over Ya Zhen's nose and exhaled. The girl inhaled reflexively. She felt a sensation like warm water break over her, spread into her limbs.

"You'll mend," said the woman, "if they stay off you." She took another speculative draw on her pipe, watching Ya Zhen sleep. She sat on a bench by the fire and stretched her feet out, farted, scratched herself. She pulled a knife from the old pigskin booties she wore, laid it in her lap and began to hum an unnamed cradle song her grandmother had sung to her long decades ago, a song about a foolish man who got into his boat to try and catch the moon. Thinking it was a huge pearl that would make him rich, he chased the moon all night, until it set in the west, and he was forever lost at sea.

They took her in the morning. Before they did, the ēn mā closed the door in their faces so she could speak to Ya Zhen alone. The lead horseman was furious, but when he made threats, she made sport of him.

"You almost killed your treasure here, didn't you?" She laughed and did a little dance in the doorway, thrusting her hips back and forth. "I've doctored her, but you'll probably fool yourself anyway, take her all over again, this one who could weigh your pockets with gold. Probably do her in with your pecker, because that's how it goes with little roosters. Makes you feel fierce, almost like a man." She laughed again, spat into her palm and rubbed her hands together briskly.

"I have miles to make up," the man said. His voice was calm, but Ya Zhen, who had managed to sit slightly on the bed, could see his pulse pounding in a fat vein that branched like lightning across his forehead.

"What I have to show this child won't slow you much." She closed the door. When she turned to Ya Zhen, all the caustic humor had left her face. "Listen to me, now," she said. "You must change that dressing once every day."

"Keep me here." Ya Zhen's voice was a dry croak.

There was a long silence. Ya Zhen, propped on the mat, watched the woman stare into the corner as if something was written there. Finally, she sighed and took Ya Zhen's hand. Into it, she folded a rag pouch the size of a big turnip. "This is what I can do for you. Change the dressing. Do it the way I showed you before, yes?" Ya Zhen nodded. Her fear sat like a stone on her chest, making it hard to breathe. The woman had dressed her in an old tunic and trousers that were soft with age and frayed at the cuffs, but otherwise sound. She tucked the pouch into her pocket.

"Those three," the woman said, tilting her head toward the door, "are dogs. Sometimes a dog can run a tiger into a corner, but this never works out well for the dog." A tear ran down Ya Zhen's cheek, and the old woman brushed it away. Her fingertips felt stiff as tanned hide. "It is better to be the tiger, little girl."

She went to the door and pulled it open. "Carry her," she ordered the ox-driver. "As if she were your own grandmother."

He ducked into the room and lifted Ya Zhen. She closed her eyes, not wanting to see his face so close to hers. Back she went into the cart among the bags of grain, clutching the tiny bundle of her belongings to her chest. Her bedroll had been spread, and she lay back on it, thankful for the small comfort. The ēn mā shuffled out and passed a gourd of broth to Ya Zhen, stoppered with a piece of moss.

"Help her out into the bushes midday and when you stop at night," she told the ox-driver. She ignored the two horsemen altogether. Ya Zhen could see the ox driver was afraid of the old woman. "Otherwise, keep your hands off her, and you might outrun your own sorry luck." She turned without further comment and stalked into her small hovel.

When the door closed, Ya Zhen felt as though any hope of kindness in her life had been extinguished, like spitting on a candle. She lay back, feeling the humped shapes of the grain bags under her, and watched the sky pass as they started down the road again. The winter sun had come out, low in the sky and lacking real warmth, but strong enough to cast a few narrow shadows. She spread her thin blanket over her, trying very hard not to make movements that strained her belly. Lying flat with her belongings tucked under her head again, the pain faded somewhat and the movement of the cart lulled her into a shallow doze that lasted all afternoon.

The men did not help her into the bushes, and she did not ask for help. When they stopped, Ya Zhen inched herself out of the cart and squatted to piss, holding onto the wheel. Her hot urine burned and she chewed the inside of her cheek to stifle a cry. The second horseman came around the wagon and watched her, and there was nothing she could do but relieve herself and crawl back into the wagon. But the men did not interfere with her again, not on the rest of the long trip out of the hills and into Guangdong Province, not once for the next eleven days. The ox-driver brought her tea and food when they stopped for the night, and after the men were asleep Ya Zhen wet a fresh mass of the ēn mā's herbs to pack around her wounds.

When they reached the port at Guangdong on the morning of the twelfth day and turned Ya Zhen over to the broker who had purchased her, she was able to walk by herself. Even thin as she now was, she was deemed acceptable and herded onto a steamship with fifteen other girls. Some seemed as young as Hong-Tai. Several wept, but most wore the shocked and hollow face that Ya Zhen saw when she caught her own reflection in the water. The ship's crew shouted and hectored until the girls were below deck. They all crouched there in the dark, and now the weeping became a tide of broken voices, almost all of them calling for mothers. Ya Zhen kept her own mouth closed and would not cry.

One month they stayed on the ship from Guangdong, girls packed into the lower hold like salted fish in a barrel. Rough seas and no latrine, no way to clean the feces or vomit. Ya Zhen learned during the second week that a young sailor would look the other way, allow her to sit huddled into a corner on the upper deck, if she first let him run his hands under her shirt and between her legs and rub himself furiously against her. It didn't last long. She understood that the hour or two she could stay out in the fresh air, clutching her few belongings, might save her life. Three young women had already sickened and died; their bodies hauled out and tossed into the sea like spoiled vegetables. Many more were too ill to get up off their soiled mats.

Ya Zhen began to know that she would not die and the knowledge brought no relief. One day, while squatting above decks, men began to shout and point over the rails. Faint on the horizon there were dark smudges. This was land, finally. The men called it by name and Ya Zhen tried to repeat the two strange words, but could not: San Francisco.

CHAPTER TWO

THEY FORCED TEN GIRLS into a long, low building. Three had died on the trip from Guangdong and two were so ill that they stayed behind, limp on their meager pallets. Ya Zhen's legs shook during the short walk from the docks. Other girls couldn't seem to make their feet work properly and were half carried by the ones who could help. Only one girl cried, her tears steady and silent and her face expressionless. They all smelled like shit and old meat.

Ya Zhen, at the back of their trembling assemblage, craned her neck, trying to understand something about the city bursting up on all sides. The brief glimpse only confused her. To what could she even compare what she saw? Not even the busy port city where she had gone onto the ship in China looked anything like this. The roads were filled with people and wagons and horses, creating a tumult of sound. Chimneys, smokestacks, steamships and locomotives added hazy layers to the smutty skyline. The cobbled hills seemed to rise straight into the chilly air. Huge, ornate houses sat almost on top of each other and she couldn't imagine how many families must live in each one. A woman walking nearby glanced in her direction but turned her head strenuously away when she saw the girls. It seemed to Ya Zhen that the woman was being swallowed by her clothing. The garment was severely constricted at her waist, yet ballooned out and trailed behind in voluminous swathes of fabric. On her head was a gigantic hat, sprouting so many feathers it looked as if a large brown bird had settled there and built a nest.

"Get inside." A burly man took Ya Zhen by the upper arm and gave her a push. He shut the door behind him and stood in front of it, feet spread and arms crossed over his great hanging gut.

The room was large and tall-ceilinged, and although it was nearly empty, there was a strong smell of heavily-greased machinery. Men stood in several small groups. Some were Chinese. Some were white, with faces the color of a duck egg. They chatted among themselves, eyed the girls who huddled in the center of the room. It was cold enough that their combined breath rose over them in a small cloud. Three women stood by, faces flinty. Their clothes were similar to the woman outside, but coarser. None wore hats.

One of the men, dressed stiffly in spotless black clothing, pulled a gold watch from his pocket, clicked it open, and nodded at the women. They began to shout at the girls, harsh and unintelligible, pushing them into a single line. Marks were chalked onto the floor—numbers, Ya Zhen thought—and each girl was jostled into place behind a mark. A tall woman with a beaky nose walked down the line barking words, pulling up the chins of girls who looked at the plank floor. The crying girl let her face bow again when the woman passed; the woman turned on her heel and yanked the girl's hair, jerking her head back. This time, the girl kept her chin raised and the tears dripped steadily from the line of her jaw onto her slight bosom.

When the tall woman passed near the end of the line, Ya Zhen stood erect and stared at the opposite wall. This was a way station and these men were another version of the three men with the oxcart. The woman put her hands on Ya Zhen's rolled belongings, and Ya Zhen stepped backward. The woman wrenched the bundle from Ya Zhen and tossed it to the floor, then grabbed her by one earlobe and yanked her back into line.

"You don't want to get fresh, little girl," she said. "I'll take you out back of here and teach you to be pert." Ya Zhen didn't understand the words, but the woman's meaning was clear. She stood straight; when the woman walked away, she maneuvered the bundle closed and pressed it between her feet.

"Now, gentlemen," the finely-dressed man announced. "I expect some decorum here. Do not touch the young ladies. If you have questions about a particular girl you may address it to Mrs. Caruthers or one of her assistants." The sharp-faced woman nodded her head once. "In the interest of time they've come straight from their journey. But not to worry—I guarantee they'll clean up fine." This elicited a bit of laughter from the men. "When you make a decision," he said, smiling, "see me."

The waiting men converged on the line of girls, looking them over front and back. The sharp-faced woman called Mrs. Caruthers, and her helpers, scurried back and forth as men called out or crooked their fingers. Three men looked at Ya Zhen, two Chinese and one white man. The Chinese men whispered together, too low for Ya Zhen to hear. When they gestured, one of the women went behind Ya Zhen and pulled her hair out of its braid. She gingerly ran her fingers through Ya Zhen's hair, which fell almost to her knees, and turned her around for the men to see.

"No lice," the woman lied. "Her head is clean." She made Ya Zhen face forward again.

The white man leaned so close that Ya Zhen could smell whatever grease he had used to comb back his own dark hair. The smell was acrid yet floral, a combination that made Ya Zhen's empty stomach churn.

"You'd best check the rest of her for vermin," he said. "Pull those britches down for us."

The woman curled her lip at him like an agitated dog. "You have to pay earnest money before we do that."

"How much?"

"Ten percent and you can step behind that curtain and have a good look. But no refunds."

Ya Zhen recognized the flat greed in the man's eyes. Her hands and feet prickled. Although her body had healed well after the ēn mā poulticed her, she felt an echo of that burning, low inside. Meanwhile, the two Chinese men, seeing the seriousness of the smelly man's intentions, moved on.

Up the line, someone burst out in sobs. Everyone looked. A slender girl, perhaps twelve years old, wept while a white woman yanked the girl's trousers down to reveal her nearly-naked lower body. The other helper lifted the girl's tunic, exposing tiny breasts set above a wasted ribcage.

"Convinced?" said the man with the round hat.

The interested shopper took his time looking at the girl. "That's fine," he said, in an odd, high-pitched voice. "I just heard that sometimes you fellas try to pass off a pretty boy. I didn't want to put no money down on a boy."

They pulled the girl's clothing back in place. She put her forearm over her eyes and keened a single word, *Maaa*, a high, piercing note that seemed to cleave the air in the cold room. The girl next to her began to cry as well and Mrs. Caruthers hissed at them both to be quiet.

The man who had wanted to see the crying girl's body fished in his pocket and tried to poke something into her hand.

"Here's a little sweet. That's not so bad, is it?"

She kept her arm over her face and let the hard candy fall through her fingers onto the floor. The girl next to her picked it up, smelled it and put it in her mouth. Some of the men laughed.

The man interested in Ya Zhen smirked. "Earnest money, eh? Why'd he get a free peek?"

"Mr. Salyer," said Mrs. Caruthers, "we've done business in the past. You know you'll get your money's worth today. Have you made a decision?"

The man nodded. "She'll do."

Mrs. Caruthers looked over her shoulder at the finely-dressed man and snapped her fingers. He sauntered over, a small smile flickering on his clean-shaven face.

"You've chosen well, Clarence." He cupped a hand under Ya Zhen's chin. His touch was gentle and his hand warm and soft. Ya Zhen could smell a trace of mint on his skin. "She's a treasure. I'm sure you'll have a lucrative association."

"Let's get down to it, Bishop. I have a ship to catch at noon."

"Plenty of time." The finely-dressed man clapped the man called Salyer on the shoulder. "Step over here and we'll have you on your way. Mrs. Carruthers," he said, nodding at a desk near the back of the room, "bring the girl."

The woman took Ya Zhen by the elbow and they all walked to the desk. The men sat and began thumbing through a thin sheaf of papers. They conversed over the tiny figures printed there, stopping now and again to argue some point.

Ya Zhen didn't need to understand their clipped and throaty speech to know she was the merchandise in question. She felt nothing. There was nothing to be done, nowhere to run, so she stood still, waiting for the next thing to happen.

She could hardly have been more surprised when Mrs. Carruthers turned her beaky profile around and began to speak Mandarin. The words barely resembled anything Ya Zhen had ever heard, the speech flat and toneless, but she comprehended something that sounded like "papers by your hand." The men looked on, the fancy man smiling amiably, while Mrs. Carruthers placed the smooth barrel of a pen into Ya Zhen's right hand.

Ya Zhen looked at the three of them. She could neither read nor write, so she stood very still, holding the pen loosely at arm's length.

"You," Mrs. Carruthers said. She tapped the bottom of the paper where Salyer had just signed. When Ya Zhen made no move, she grasped the girl's hand and guided her into scrawling a large **X** on the page. Then they pressed her thumb onto a black pad covered in ink and pantomimed that she should press her mark. This done, Salyer pulled an envelope from his coat.

"Five hundred," he said. Things have gotten damn steep, Bishop."

The finely-dressed man riffled through the envelope, then put it into a locked drawer in the desk.

"Worth every penny, Clarence. Best wishes in your collaboration." He shook Salyer's hand, then turned and lifted Ya Zhen's hand to his lips. He touched his warm mouth to her dirty fingers and let them linger there, then strolled back to the business at hand.

Ya Zhen looked over her shoulder at the other girls as Clarence Salyer shepherded her to the door. They all stood in line, mute as penned rabbits as the men walked up and down.

She had hardly gotten her feet on dry land when Salyer had her aboard another steamship. When they left the place where he had purchased her, he walked just slightly behind, pointing the way and jerking the shoulder of her shirt if she didn't maneuver quite as he intended.

Her hair still hung loose, whipping around her in the damp onshore wind, and she longed to tie it out of her way. The cold bit through her thin clothes and she hugged the bundle of her belongings between her breasts. Salyer walked her roughly parallel to the harbor where dozens of ships sat at anchor, their masts and smokestacks like a forest filled with bare tree trunks. Seagulls circled everywhere, calling or jostling for purchase on pier posts streaked white with guano. They passed a short row of food vendors and the smells of hot bread and boiled meat made Ya Zhen dangerously lightheaded. Saliva poured into her mouth and she wiped her sleeve over her lips repeatedly to keep from drooling. Salyer was in a hurry and rushed headlong without giving the vendors so much as a glance.

At last he moved them onto a crowded pier. Here he indicated that she should follow him, giving her an ugly threat that needed no interpretation. As they passed into the crowd, people parted around her like fat melting away from a hot knife. They turned their heads away or stared with disgust. Ya Zhen thought they must smell her. She let her hair fall on both sides of her face, a dark, unwashed shield.

Once aboard, a man in dark pants and a rough jacket hailed Salyer. His beard was so heavy and his brows so thick, it seemed to Ya Zhen that he peered at the world through of a mask of hair. They approached a hatch, the squat door forcing them to stoop as they passed. A narrow set of metal stairs led into a deep cargo area crammed with luggage and crates. In one corner, a spot had been kept clear. Salyer pointed.

"You'll sleep here," he said. He looked around briefly and yanked loose a length of padded material tucked around an upholstered footstool. "This should be warm enough. It's not long." He stood close, his eyes roaming over Ya Zhen's face. "Hell, you don't understand a thing I'm saying, do you?"

She stared at the floor in front of her, willing herself not to tremble. This is where he will hurt me, she thought. Right here.

He didn't, though. Not then. He pushed the makeshift blanket into her hands and motioned that she should sit on the floor. "Much as I'd like to try you right here on the floor, that woman who said you're clean was quite a storyteller. Stay put." He made for the stairs.

"Salyer," Ya Zhen blurted. His name did not sound the same when she said it, but it got his attention. He smiled, showing a neat row of pretty little teeth, one of which was covered in gold and glinted in the light falling from above.

"Got my name already. Aren't you quick."

"*Sà dì qīa de ba*," she said, hating the pleading sound in her voice. But she hadn't eaten for two days and rations had been slim at best on the ship from Guangdong. Her midsection hurt as though her stomach had collapsed against her spine. The hunger she sometimes faced at home was nothing compared to the desperation she now felt to fill her mouth, to chew. She pantomimed eating and put a hand on her empty belly.

"I'll be back with something later. But probably nothing until supper time. They won't serve a noon meal." He put one foot on the stairs and looked back at her. "This is a locked door. There are plenty up top who'd as soon throw you overboard as look at you."

"*Wǎ hǎ o è*," she shouted at his retreating feet, *I'm hungry*, but he went out and the hatch shut with a metallic thud.

There were tiny windows widely spaced, throwing just a silver hint of daylight near the high ceiling. She could hear water lapping against the ship's hull near her and the sound of footsteps overhead. Despite all the cargo, there was a cavernous, echoing quality to the hold. Ya Zhen could make out the shapes of stored items nearby, their corners dimly lit, like hunched shoulders. She could not shake the sense that the girls with whom she had traveled from Guangdong were with her here, all of them now silent, waiting.

Feeling her way in the near-dark, she spread the ragged piece of quilting out beneath her, doubling it so she could slip between the layers. The fabric felt gritty under her fingers and smelled of mice. She tied her hair back with a length of thread pulled loose from the hem of her pants. Thinking of rodents, she tucked the braid inside her shirt. She settled between the musty layers and watched the feeble light from the high windows until she began to drift.

She entertained the thinnest semblance of sleep, rising and falling with the ambient sounds above and below. Fragments of sight and sound ticked past her consciousness. In one, a little girl stood before her, hair parted on one side and caught in a red ribbon. The child stood on tiptoe, holding out a torn fragment of paper, but when Ya Zhen tried to see what was marked there her fingers smeared the character into a blur. When she looked up, the little girl was gone. Now she was walking down a path that wound through trees, the sun flickering through a tall canopy, illuminating the ground in scattered piebald patterns.

Hours later, she came fully awake when the porter returned. She squinted up at him. It was full dark outside and he carried a small kerosene lantern. He held it high, so that it lit only one side of his bearded face and showed heavily pock-marked skin in the few places not covered by wiry whiskers. One eye, pale as a winter sky, stared at Ya Zhen. Then he lowered his lamp a little, showing the plate of food in his hand.

"Just a bit of supper here," he said. His voice was low and musical. "It ain't much account, but it's hot and maybe you hungry." He crossed about half the distance between them and set the plate on the floor. She could smell it and felt as though her belly was trying to turn itself inside out. She waited, though, afraid to get too close.

He went up the stairs, carrying the lamp, but was back immediately. When he bent this time it was to leave a fat-bellied glass jar of water. He stepped away then, taking his light. "Sorry to leave you in the dark, miss," he said, "but they have my job if I give you this light." When he was halfway to the top, she scurried over to the food. He climbed the last few steps, talking to himself. "No way to treat a dog."

The plate held a fatty cut of ham and potatoes covered with thin gravy. There were also peas, everything swimming together. Ya Zhen couldn't see any of it, but she felt it into her mouth, swallowing in large gulps. She coughed on the potato, choked it down, and picked up the water. It was cool inside her, and she felt it push the lump of food past her throat and into her hollow gut. In a few bites, the plate was empty and she licked it clean, then licked her fingers.

She sat for a moment, breathing hard. The jar didn't have much water left, so she forced herself to take just a small sip, saving some for morning. With one hand on the wall, she worked her way into the corner and placed the jar there, on the floor, so as not to knock it over. Then she moved as far from her crude bed as possible, inched herself between two boxes, and squatted to piss.

She found her way back to her things and crawled under the mildewed blanket. The food had warmed her and she was soon deeply asleep. For a mercy, she didn't dream at all.

She woke just after dawn, hearing people moving around above her. She could see a little now and retrieved the water jar, emptying it in a single swallow, then wished she had saved a little to wash her face. She opened her bundle, undid her hair, and worked the comb through it a little at a time. The lice made her head itch madly, especially around her hairline and behind her ears. She pulled the long greasy hank of her hair into the tightest braid she could manage and tied it at the end.

The sound of footsteps increased above her and then the hatch door opened, letting in a dim bar of early light.

She collected her few things and crossed to the steps. When she looked up, the silhouette of the porter was above her, muscular and still. Behind his head the sky slowly brightened. She lifted a hand to greet him and he waved, just a slight flick of his fingers. Then another figure moved into the doorway, Salyer, smiling, his gold tooth glinting in his freshly shaved face. He looked to Ya Zhen like some maladapted child next to the bearded porter.

"Here we are," he called down. His voice echoed around the cargo hold. "Home sweet home."

BISHOP BROKERAGE CO.
SAN FRANCISCO, CALIFORNIA

THIS INDENTURE made the sixteenth day of May in the Year of Our Lord One Thousand Eight Hundred Eighty Three.

Witness that Mr. Andrew Bishop, Proprietor of the Bishop Brokerage Company of San Francisco, California, does, for valuable consideration in the amount of Five Hundred Dollars, bind over to Mr. Clarence Salyer of Eureka, California, the woman Ha Chin whose consent hereto is indicated by her signature or mark, below.

By these presents said servant will be placed to dwell and serve in the establishment set forth here, The Hotel Salyer, in a capacity to be determined by Clarence Salyer that provides for the comfort of all patrons of said establishment. Servant shall her master well and faithfully serve in all business according to her wit power and ability and shall honestly and orderly in all things behave and demean herself during the term set out below.

During said term, Clarence Salyer shall provide to his servant Ha Chin competent and sufficient meat drink apparel washing and lodging and other things necessary and fit for such a servant.

The term of this indenture shall be from the day of these presents and for a period of five years. In addition, any days of illness, indisposition, or poor behavior that prevent said servant from serving in the capacity set out herein shall be added to the total length of time served.

WITNESSETH these signs pertaining hereto

Andrew Bishop   Proprietor and Broker
_____

Clarence W. Salyer   Indenturor
_____

X Indentured
_____

PART II

EUREKA

POLICE COURT – The vote of the Chinese bill is already bearing
fruit. John O'Neil was before Judge Tompkins Wednesday on a charge
of battery, the victim being a Chinaman. It seems that O'Neil had
imbibed a little whiskey about the same time that he learned of the fate
of the Chinese bill, & the mixture so worked upon his mind as to
overcome his better judgment. While entertaining a few men on the
street corner with his views on the Chinese question, he hailed a
passing celestial & promptly knocked him down. This was an act that
brought O'Neil to grief. He informed the court that if the president
would furnish no relief he would undertake the job on his own account,
& intimated that those who "stood in" with the heathen had better look
a little out. The court thought he needed a little rest, & prescribed
thirty days at the county jail.   *Daily Humboldt Times*
                                                  Friday, April 7, 1882

Such a race of people can only prove a detriment in any community
that lays claim to civilization, progress & truth. Age only seems to
steep them deeper in their degraded filthy mode of life.
                                                  Daily Humboldt Times
                                                  February 1, 1883

If we could read the secret history of our enemies, we should find in
each man's life sorrow and suffering enough to disarm all hostility.
                                                  —H. W. *Longfellow*

CHAPTER THREE

EUREKA HUNCHED AT THE EDGE of Humboldt Bay, where a few sparse and widely-situated settlements worked at survival. Set on a remote and rocky scrim of Pacific coastland, arriving there by any means was a feat of some endurance. Large ships disappeared with shocking regularity in the rough waters north of San Francisco. On dry ground, terrain in every direction was mountainous in a way that defied road-building. While the rest of the country became connected by networks of rail lines, Eureka simply held tight, with little to recommend it save a great deal of lumber and the idea of having arrived in a place that proved one's mettle by the very act of having attained it.

The late February afternoon was bitter. People kept their hearths burning all day to hold back the damp; steady wisps of chimney smoke faded into the overcast sky. To the west, low clouds and mist hanging over the bay merged into a curtain of cold murk that made the water almost invisible. The hills to the east looked black in the February afternoon. This was dense northwestern forest, muscular Douglas fir and coast redwood that grew over three hundred feet tall, dwarfing even the most ambitious buildings in Eureka. Fog lay in tattered skeins in the upper branches. For nearly a week storms had pounded the coast, finally bringing down the telegraph lines.

Bai Lum, proprietor of the Chinese mercantile, took up a broom and made another careful circuit of his store, sweeping traces of mud, now dried, and other street detritus out the door. On the sidewalk he did a quick sweep, too, brushing the boards in front of his door as clean as he could.

The day was draining off, though the transit of the sun had been indistinguishable all day. Finally, now, a burnished streak showed behind the clouds to the west. Despite the cold, it was fine to be outside after a busy day in the store. Business was good, steady. His reputation among his Chinese neighbors and the white townspeople was impeccable. The primary way he had established this trust was by honing his instinct about the town's desires: what sorts of goods were wanted, when, and by whom. For seven years he cultivated a silence that implied acquiescence and cooperation. This tactic had worked seamlessly and allowed him the tremendous flexibility of the nearly invisible. Then Rose Allen had moved to Eureka.

Rose had one day charged into the mercantile, wet from a wholly expected rain shower for which she had prepared not a whit. She didn't notice that she was dripping onto the painted floor of his store, nor did she seem to realize that she had left the door slightly ajar. It was clear, though, that Rose Allen saw Bai Lum—she saw him very well.

On this cold afternoon, old Chen Ma was on the sidewalk too, also with a broom. The old man, though, had been sweeping most of the day—as he did every day, day after day—and would only quit when his son came out to fetch him. The fellow was too intent on his toil to notice Bai Lum, and Bai Lum would be a stranger anyway, despite their lengthy acquaintance. Such was the way time robbed us, but Chen Ma was kindly content and happily surprised by life, so who was a victim after all?

Bai Lum turned to brush down the front of the building, where the industry of small spiders was revealed, with stunning regularity, by the fog. Lifting the broom as high over his head as he could reach, he noticed the curtain at the upstairs window—his living quarters—twitch. There was the girl's face, peeping out at one corner of the narrow window, only the top of her face showing, but quite plainly visible to any passerby. When she realized he was looking, her eyes widened and the white curtain dropped back into place. He kept at the little cobwebs, knocking them askew with particular vigor and tamping back his dull anger at the girl. How many threats would it take, how many warnings of a terrible fate, before she obeyed him? One fat spider made a hasty scramble across the wall; Bai Lum slapped it down and crushed it underfoot. It was while he scraped the dead mess off the sole of his shoe that he heard Rose Allen's footsteps and his irritation melted like late frost. Another customer was approaching, too—Fang Chai, a saw in hand. Bai Lum followed Fang into the store and re-tied his apron, still able to hear Rose three blocks away, whistling some rollicking tune, her boots making their confident *thump, thump, thump.*

She strode along the plank walk in her usual headlong posture. Rose Allen was marked by a disposition both serious and practical, and a certain angularity of face and body: narrow waist and broad shoulders, square chin, straight eyebrows set in a calm line above her eyes. Her dark jacket and skirt, though pressed and fitted, hung a bit askew. She had forgotten her hat (again) and springs of tightly kinked red hair frizzed out around her face and nape. A thin line of mud from the street clung to her hem, but mud was the nature of things in February. A transplant to Eureka—as was virtually every adult in town—Rose had grown up in Illinois among pig farms and wheat farms, between vast stands of native hardwoods and the tropical-looking paw paw trees for which her hometown was named. She was only twelve when her mother died, and the ladies of Paw Paw had done their level best to close staunch ranks around her. A female raised by only her father, Charles Allen, wainwright and widower? Motherless girl? Absurd! Despite the best intentions of those venerable ladies, though, the older Rose got, the less likely it seemed that she would make a success of courting—what with her apparent high expectations of male intelligence and her desire that a buggy-ride conversation could advance beyond the generalities of the week's past weather and swine farrowing practices. She dreamed of escape, and finally—with her father's full collusion—she set out for California. She arrived in Eureka at age twenty-three to live with her father's eldest sister, Hazel Cleary. For almost four years it seemed she had made a perfect bargain: though she missed her sweet father, she relished her plain bedroom at her aunt's house, with its tall windows that faced east and south, and the dark shelves she was slowly but surely filling with her own books, purchased with the money she earned working with her aunt at Captain and Prudence Kendall's house, and occasionally working as a children's tutor. All week she made beds and dusted knick-knacks and watered Mrs. Kendall's houseplants, and on Sundays she stayed in her room, curled in her comforter with a book—no buggy rides, no pig-centric small talk. For company she had her aunt, and right across the hall she had Matilda Gillen—Mattie, she was called—another stray soul that Hazel had rescued. She was a wispy, freckled young woman whose mother, a neighbor of Hazel's in Limerick, had fallen on desperate times and sent her daughter to the states. She worked at Salyer's Hotel nearly every day, serving food in the dining room, mopping up after meals, and washing dishes in the hotel kitchen. Rose, who had never mastered what she considered the invasive intricacies of female friendship, loved that Mattie craved her own privacy, and was mindful of Rose's.

For four years Rose had been ridiculously happy. In fact, life seemed nearly ideal. Until she fell in love.

So here she was, once again headed for Bai Lum's mercantile in the Chinese block. Tonight Rose and Hazel would help Prudence Kendall host the Women's Christian Temperance Union in the Kendalls' fine front parlor. Rose didn't care a fig about temperance, having been raised to embrace moderation. Aunt Hazel herself was not above using spirits for medicinal purposes and imbibed a small glass of wine every Christmas Eve. The real reason to belong to the WCTU, according to Hazel Cleary, was to be certain of having the ear of the "right people." So tonight Rose would not only help prepare but would help with hostessing duties. This morning she had convinced Mrs. Kendall that they should serve chrysanthemum tea and rock sugar—the look of the delicate flowers in each cup was such a charming surprise and the ladies would love it. And where in Eureka could she get such a treat?

Only at Bai Lum's store. Nearly every day it occurred to her that there was something at Bai Lum's she could not live without.

In reality, it was Bai Lum that Rose wanted. Which was, of course, impossible.

She stopped just short of the mercantile, pulled at her coat and ran her palms over her hair in a fruitless attempt to smooth the stray curls that pulled loose from her hairpins and corkscrewed in the damp weather. The westering sun suddenly slanted through a thin place in the clouds and lit the summit opposite, turning a triangular section of mountainside bright green. The highest ridge, Berry Summit, was still jacketed in snow. The weather had been gray for so many weeks that Rose felt like some burrowing animal, squinting and blinking above ground. Standing still, she heard the ringing whine of some nearby sawmill and, under everything, the ocean. The years she had lived in Eureka had not altered her sense of being dwarfed by the raw landscape. While the gentle slopes and prairie woodlots of Illinois had been enveloping, a community nest, it seemed to Rose that people had to cling tenaciously to this cold, scraggy bit of Pacific coast. It suited her.

She paused on the threshold, then went into the mercantile with a familiar lifting-off sensation, wanting to find Bai Lum with her eyes, wanting not to seem like she was looking.

The market smelled like ginger and lard and old paper. On the far wall, a large woodstove set into a deep brick mantel fought the chill, and Rose hovered near it a moment to warm herself. It gave off a strong, steady heat. A large pipe, almost four inches in diameter, ran out the side of the brickwork, up the wall and across the ceiling. The store was packed with merchandise, but all the wares were displayed precisely. The plank floor was immaculate.

Rose saw him immediately, tall and lean, dressed in black as always. He spoke with a Chinese man who held a small hand saw and gestured at the cutting edge. There were no other customers. Bai Lum made eye contact with her and nodded slightly. She smiled and nodded in return. The sense of lightness washed over her again, awful and wonderful, completely out of her control.

The sugar and tea were behind the counter and he would get them for her, so she took time to wander the store. She walked past pyramids of tinned food—mackerel, peas, condensed milk. These things were set up at the front so that a non-Chinese shopper could spot familiar items first. Rose walked behind the carefully stacked cans to look at the tables and shelves situated near the rear of the store.

Here were bolts of satin brocade and polished cotton in rich, saturated green, red, and royal blue. Narrow boxes held piles of lacquered chopsticks. Paper kites—dragons, lions, and a dazzling vermilion carp with a curved tail—hung from the exposed pipe running across the high ceiling and swayed minutely when the door opened or closed. On the back wall was a shelf of porcelains. She lingered here. The small bowls fit perfectly in her cupped palms, white glaze creamy against her fingers. All the bowls were painted on the inside with stylized flowers in cobalt blue. Four Flowers, Bai Lum had told her, was the name of the pattern. She held it close to her, relishing the small weight in her hands. She thought she could get along quite well with such a bowl. This much and no more, she thought. For soup or tea, or perhaps floating a pink camellia.

As she stood looking into the bowl, a flicker of movement caught her eye. A rough curtain hung over a narrow passage in the back corner, and someone peered out between the slightly parted panels. The person—a girl, Rose thought—pulled away from the curtain and stepped farther back into the alcove.

"Good morning, Rose Allen."

Rose jumped and almost dropped the bowl. Bai Lum reached for it, momentarily cupping his hands around hers. "I'm sorry," he said. "I startled you."

She returned the bowl to the shelf. "I was woolgathering," she said. "I didn't hear you coming."

"Wool?"

"An expression," she said. "Daydreaming. Not paying attention."

"Yes, daydreaming." He nodded. "This is important." He had a strong, square face and to Rose he often seemed on the verge of a smile. "You like the Four Flowers," he said.

Rose ran her fingers over the slippery glazed surface of the bowl's inside. "Yes, they spark the imagination." She glanced back at the curtained alcove, but couldn't see the girl.

"What do you imagine?" As he spoke, he went to the curtain and pulled it completely closed, then gestured toward the front of the store. His queue was thick and splendid, falling past the middle of his back. As Rose followed him, she watched the heavy black braid swing slightly from side to side. She was sometimes amused by a ridiculous stab of envy over the gloss of Bai Lum's hair, as she felt her own to be nearly coarse as hemp.

"Just now I was thinking how beautiful a flower would look floating in the bowl," she said.

"But there are already flowers, painted inside."

"Yes, well. Perhaps all I need is the water." They were back at the long counter. Deep shelves ran floor to ceiling behind it, filled with boxes of miscellaneous goods, half-gallon jars of herbs, teas, shriveled roots and fungi. A few held what appeared to be desiccated insects.

He reached under the counter for a cloth and wiped away a few fingerprints and flecks of tea. "My mother did that," he said. "Every month when the full moon began to disappear, she would leave a bowl of water out all night to capture the moonlight."

Rose had been coming to Bai Lum's store for just over a year now. At first they limited their conversations to what he had for sale and what she was interested in purchasing; gradually they expanded their small conversational forays. He would ask about her tasks at Captain Kendall's house, and she would cajole him to share small stories about the quirks of his customers. There was friendship first, their kind and kindred natures opening to one another by slow degrees. The expectation that they could *not* have friendship—let alone love—offered its own sort of boundless liberty. Slowly, they had closed a distance, first with their eyes, more recently with incidental touches. Then one morning she had woken with a fully formed thought of him, the remnant of a dream. Lying on her side, she reached over to the far edge of her bed, ran her palm over the smooth, empty expanse of white sheet. To love this man. It was an idea untenable, unbearable. Relentless.

Outwardly she fought the desire to visit the mercantile. For some time—she thought of it as months, but it was only three weeks—Rose Allen closed the door on random notions, set aside the thoughts of Bai Lum that constantly swamped her. She congratulated herself for being stoic and levelheaded. Yet all the while during those weeks she concocted elaborate reasons to take her walk down E Street and right onto 4th, the Chinatown block. It came to seem that a great many things were needed that came from only the mercantile. Finally she told herself that going to Bai Lum's was simply a matter of utmost necessity and practicality. The heart tells such stories convincingly; no matter what logic the head may shout, the heart will yawp all the louder.

Now, as he polished his already spotless counter, she studied his face, the perfect curve of his forehead, which was clean-shaven nearly to his crown.

"Why did your mother want to capture the moonlight?"

His hand paused and he looked at her. "To have something to remember, when the moon hid itself. She said that if she looked into the bowl when the moon was dark, she could still see its reflection in the water."

"Did it work? Did you ever see it?"

He tilted his head slightly, smiling. "My mother took care of the moon, so I never worried about it."

Rose imagined him, a sturdy little boy at his mother's elbow, watching, trusting. She was about to reply when two men walked into the mercantile.

She knew one of them: Garland Tupper, the father of a boy she had tutored. He was a big man, coarse and full of himself in a way that certain other men admired and tried to imitate. Bai Lum nodded to the men as he had nodded to Rose when she arrived.

Neither of the men acknowledged him in return. Garland talked loudly about the previous night's storm.

"What can I get for you, Rose Allen?" Bai Lum asked her.

"Tea," she said. "I need some more of the chrysanthemum tea you sold me last month, and some rock sugar."

Behind her, Garland muttered. "She's wanting something sweet." His companion snickered and replied, too low for Rose to hear. She turned and looked them over.

"Something to say, Mr. Tupper?"

He put up both hands in a gesture of surrender. "No ma'am, teacher. I'm good as gold. Wouldn't want a whipping for being naughty, would we Jimmy?" He swayed slightly on his feet.

"Drunk." she said. "At four o'clock in the afternoon?"

He laid his palm on his chest. "I don't normally take anything before sundown, Miz Allen, cross my heart, but it may be that Jimmy and I did visit the tavern today. To ward off the chill, you might say." He elbowed Jimmy, who couldn't look Rose in the eye. "It's been awful damp and cold."

Tupper's son, Byron, had been in Miss Alva Stanley's class, a difficult student. Miss Stanley had asked Rose, who tutored two of her other students after school, to come into the classroom and help with Byron. This was a charity case; Garland Tupper wouldn't contribute so much as a few sticks of split kindling as barter.

As a younger boy Byron—motherless for some time—had been clingy and eager to please, but problems with almost all his schoolwork made him an easy target for bullying. Miss Stanley approached Byron's father about the boy's trouble, but Garland had rebuffed her, telling her that she shouldn't coddle Byron. He was of the opinion that as long as Byron could "write his name and count his pay" he had gotten as much out of school as he needed. By the time he was twelve, Byron had become an awkward, sullen young man; last year, at fifteen, he had dropped out entirely. Rose had seen him in town, sometimes doing odd jobs, but usually skulking in alleys near the waterfront, with idlers like Albert Watts and Billy Kellogg.

Rose kept her back turned to the men and tried to ignore Garland's continued whispering and chuckling. Bai Lum took a jar off the wall and scooped the flower tea onto a sheet of paper. His hand hovered above the little pile as if to ask whether it was enough.

"About twice that much," she said, "and a large piece of sugar."

He measured out the tea and folded the paper around it into a neat envelope. From another jar he took a hefty piece of rock sugar that looked like a chunk of yellow quartz. This, too, he wrapped in brown paper. Garland and Jimmy were now shuffling around the store, Garland trying on a pair of work gloves and Jimmy examining the business end of a rake. Rose could see Bai Lum watching the men from the corner of his eye.

"One more thing for you," he said. "I almost forgot." He brought a small abacus from under the counter, about the size of a child's slate. "To show your pupils." He held it out to her.

The wooden beads were polished and heavy. Months earlier she remarked on how fast he was able to calculate purchases with his own. She had mused that it would be an engaging way to teach younger students arithmetic. "This is so thoughtful," she said, running her fingers over the beads. "The children are going to love it. How much?"

"A gift," he said. "For the children."

Garland Tupper sidled to the counter. "Might just as well teach them kids to count on their fingers and toes," he said, and reached over to flick a bead to its terminus with a bright clack.

Rose tucked the gift under her arm. "An abacus is an elegant means of calculation, Mr. Tupper." To her everlasting consternation, she blushed easily and vividly at the least annoyance, and here was the heat, crawling up her neck. "Maybe I should have tried using it to teach arithmetic to your son," she said. The moment the words were out of her mouth she felt a tired and soggy regret.

His face darkened and he inched closer to Rose. "I think you better not talk about my boy." Despite his rangy brawn, through the face Tupper had a certain effete resemblance to George Armstrong Custer. This close, he reeked of cheap alcohol and insufficient bathing. Beneath the waves of dark blond hair that fell almost to his shoulders, his neck was seamed with grime. He turned his head and spat a stream of tobacco juice onto the clean floorboards.

Disgusted, Rose stepped back. Bai Lum stood silently behind the counter, not taking his eyes off Tupper. Jimmy, meanwhile, had meandered toward the door and glanced furtively out. From where she stood, Rose could see the old man across the street, sweeping the same piece of board walkway he had been sweeping when she arrived. Another man, bent under a yoke from which hung two large baskets of firewood, walked up the center of the street, followed by a little boy carrying a black rooster under his arm. Jimmy shifted from foot to foot. "Come on Garland," he said. "I told you I don't like doing business in a chink store."

"Hold on now, hold your water. Let's get what we came for." He turned to Bai Lum and slapped the counter. "Firecrackers," he said. "Gimme the big ones."

Bai Lum's face was stony. He looked at the brown spittle on the floor, looked at Tupper. "No firecrackers here," he said.

"That's a damn lie."

"All gone. Sold out."

"Let's go, Garland," Jimmy said from the open door. He stood on the threshold, round face pleading.

"Shut up, you jackass," Tupper said, almost in a whisper. Jimmy grunted and stomped out. Tupper glared at Bai Lum, hands opening and closing into fists. "To hell with you," he said finally. "Damn heathen bastard. I'll see you on the street sometime." He passed so close to Rose that she had to stumble slightly to one side, knocked off balance by his hard bicep. "You ever speak about my boy again, and you'll get a lesson yourself," he told her. As he went, he reached out an arm and swept a tall, careful pyramid of cans to the floor. They thundered off the table and rolled everywhere.

Outside, he passed the mercantile's windows in a fury, logger's boots echoing into the street.

Rose looked around the room, a bit stunned, then at Bai Lum, who didn't appear at all surprised. "There are some small minds in this town, Bai Lum," she said. "I'm sorry about that."

"Small minds everywhere. Not only here," he said. He came out from behind the counter and stooped to pick up the mess.

She put her things on the counter and went after several cans that had landed halfway across the floor. When she straightened, hands full, a young Chinese woman stood three feet away, almost near enough to touch. Rose jerked in surprise and dropped everything. The cans hit the floor again and one rolled to a stop at the girl's feet. She retrieved it and held it out to Rose. Her tunic, shorter and fuller at the hem than Bai Lum's, was the faint green of new asparagus, and its diagonal yoke buttoned near one shoulder with elaborate black closures. Her sleeves and trousers were edged in wide bands of black and gold. She wore several bracelets on each wrist, small gold earrings, and was rather plump, with a perfectly round face. She smiled at Rose and nodded vigorously. "Yes," she said softly. "Yes."

"Qū qì." Bai Lum hurried over and snatched the can from the girl's hand. She bent her head, but still looked sideways at Rose as Bai Lum hustled her back through the curtain into the rear of the store. Out of sight, he spoke to her in what was clearly a reprimand, followed by the girl's answering voice, quiet but not sounding at all repentant.

The girl had looked young, surely no older than fifteen. Rose had always assumed Bai Lum lived alone. Was this his daughter? His wife? She felt disoriented, realizing that the most rudimentary circumstances of his life in the rooms above the store were a mystery to her. She stood there, embarrassed to be eavesdropping, and began setting the toppled cans back on the table, listening to the voices rise and fall behind the curtain. She had almost decided to leave without paying for her tea, when Bai Lum reappeared through the curtained doorway.

"I'm sorry, Rose," he said. He approached her, looking even more dismal than he had when dealing with Garland Tupper. "She is my sister." He began deftly moving the cans back into a pyramid shape.

"Oh?" She tried to sound nonchalant, watching as he worked. Their shoulders touched and Rose could feel the heat of his skin through her sleeve.

"Yes. Her name is Shu-Li."

She felt ashamed of her momentary thought that he might be keeping a child bride. "I didn't know," she said. "You've never mentioned her."

Bai Lum made small adjustments to his display and said nothing. She stood uncomfortably in the silence, watching him fiddle with the cans. "I…it's not my business, of course," she said. "She's lucky. To have such a good brother, I mean." Face aflame, she reached to add a can to the stack growing on the table. He took her hand in his and slowly rolled the can out of her grasp.

"No," he said, holding her eyes with his own.

He was so close she could see a small scar on his chin, and she had an unexpected urge to press her fingertip to it. "Just…helping?" she said, the words coming out in a question. Her open palm was still cradled in his. He turned the can so she could see the label: green peas. She looked at the cans he had been stacking: baked beans.

She smiled. "Ah. I almost ruined it." Her voice had picked up a small tremor, and she wondered if he could feel through her skin how fast her heart was beating. He stared into the palm of her hand as if searching for the satisfaction of some boundless curiosity. Then, with one long, work-calloused finger, he slowly traced the long line that transected her palm from wrist to index finger. The small sensation of that touch made her breath catch.

He lifted his attention to her face; when he did, his eyes flicked over her shoulder to the front window, and he immediately dropped her hand. He stepped away and put the can of peas on the table. "Let me get your packages."

A sick sensation flared in the pit of her stomach, and she tried to compose her face into an expression of nonchalance. There was Elsie Dampler, goggling in with an expression of barely-veiled avidity, her mouth open just enough to show a glimmer of pink tongue, like the nose of a small animal. Of all the people who might happen to peep through a window at just the wrong moment, Elsie Dampler was probably the worst. For a moment, Rose stood frozen, filled with a curious blankness about what would be the right thing to do. Smile? Nod? Pretend she hadn't recognized the woman? *It probably doesn't matter now*, she thought wearily. No matter what she did, she was going to hear about this. Oh yes. This evening, no doubt, and in great detail—Elsie was a member of the WCTU.

Rose lifted a hand to wave, a hand that seemed to weigh ten pounds and still bore the sensation of Bai Lum's tracing finger, but Elsie turned and walked away, eyes wide, mouth still open. She moved up the street toward the laundry, throwing a last look over her shoulder as she went.

"The tea," Rose said, wondering wearily what time it was. She had to get back to the Kendalls' and help set up for the meeting. *Where I will probably be crucified*, she thought. She dug in her small drawstring bag. "What do I owe you?"

"Twelve cents."

"That's all? Even for that big piece of rock sugar?"

"Yes, twelve cents." Now he avoided her eyes, and it made Rose want to chase Elsie Dampler and put a boot to the woman's exceptionally wide rear end

"Bai Lum," she said, gesturing at the window, "don't worry about that, really. That woman is such a windbag. No one pays any attention to her blather. Not that she saw anything anyway. Did she? I mean, my back was to the window, so she couldn't actually see that we...that you were—" Rose bit her tongue, not quite able to say *holding my hand.*

"It was a mistake," he said quietly.

"What? No." She shook her head adamantly. "Not to me. It wasn't a mistake at all. It was fine." Fine? she thought. She sounded prim and starched. No, not *fine*. Extraordinary. Something she would like him to do every day, as a matter of fact. For the rest of her life. "I'm not sorry," she said in a fierce stage whisper.

He studied her soberly. "As you said, though, there are small minds, often matched with busy tongues." He handed her the packets of tea and sugar, careful this time that their hands didn't touch. "Twelve cents."

Instead of handing over the money, Rose cocked her head to one side and tapped the coins on the counter as if trying to remember something. "Hm. You know, I think I may need—" She let her eyes roam across the shelves behind him, slowly scanning back and forth, up and down. Then she smacked the counter with one hand. "Firecrackers. Give me the big ones."

His expression was all surprise, and she laughed. A slow smile spread across his face, and he shook his head. "No firecrackers here," he said, and she laughed harder, putting a hand to her mouth to keep from being heard out on the street. Then she tucked the tea and sugar into her bag. "We've had an interesting afternoon, Bai Lum."

"I think it will become less interesting now," he told her. "I hope you'll return soon, Rose Allen."

Rose felt herself flush, traitor skin broadcasting her emotions whether she liked it or not. "Maybe the next time I'll decide about those bowls."

"Four flowers," he said.

"Four flowers." She'd left the abacus on the counter and he held it out. She ran her hands over the wooden beads again. "Are you sure I can't pay you something for this? It looks expensive."

"No, as I said, a gift."

"Then I definitely owe you a favor."

He nodded. "Favor." He looked out the windows at the heavy sky. "Will you see Mrs. Huntington tonight?"

Lucy Huntington was the wife of the Congregational minister, and Rose was sure she'd be at the Kendalls' later. "I should see her, yes. Why?"

"I have some seeds for her," he said. "They came earlier than I expected, and she'll want to pick them up as soon as possible. Will you tell her?"

"Of course. Is that it? Seeds?"

"That is the favor."

"That's an awfully tiny favor," she said. "I'll tell her, though." She shook her head. "I have to get back to Mrs. Kendall's before Aunt comes searching for me." Out she went. Passing the shop window, she smiled and lifted her hand in the smallest wave, knowing he'd be watching. He was.

◻

Bai Lum lifted his hand in return. Rose charged away, head up, square chin thrust forward as if daring the world to interfere with her. It was her earnest face that he loved most dearly, her green eyes so curious and open. He wondered how much the woman at the window had seen, staring in like a dimwitted chicken. Rose was correct, that her back to the window had probably blocked the woman from seeing exactly what was happening, but the woman's expression had made it clear that whatever she had not seen, she had assumed. That he would take such a risk in the middle of the day, holding Rose's hand that way, astonished him. Worse, he had been a breath away from leaning his face into her hair. So stupid.

He had to assume that trouble would come with this, probably sooner rather than later, and Shu-Li couldn't be here if that happened. Now he would not only need to arrange for the girl to leave as soon as possible—if such a thing could be arranged—but he would have to find a way to explain to Rose the disappearance of his "sister." He locked the door to the mercantile, pulled the heavy oilcloth shades and climbed the stairs to his living quarters, hoping that Mrs. Huntington got his message.

◻

After the warm store, the chill outside made Rose pull up the collar of her coat. The sweeping old man was nowhere to be seen, had taken his broom inside, apparently. Many of the doors along the block were still open and she could hear desultory conversations, all in Chinese, mostly men. It sounded like the type of exchange that goes on at the end of any long day, quiet, unhurried, tired.

She wondered what sorts of rumors about her were already circulating. It gave her a crawling sensation of being watched as she marched herself back to the Kendalls'. In less than two hours, a dozen women would be in Prudence Kendall's front parlor, sipping the chrysanthemum tea and shooting little sidelong glances in Rose's direction. She pictured herself standing in front of the group. *You may have heard I was consorting with a Chinese man in broad daylight this afternoon. Yes, it's true: I am in love with Bai Lum.*

Are there any questions?

She could picture the women's faces, how horrified, and thrilled with scandal. At the end of the block, before rounding the corner, she looked out over the bay. Two seagulls stood motionless on the pier as if waiting for sunset.

"Well, Mama," she muttered, "tell the ladies of Paw Paw I've come to ruin after all." This made her smile. When she was much younger, right after her mother's death, Rose had imagined that her mother now possessed a calm and even-handed understanding of the world. This newly-magnanimous mother listened to her daughter's foibles with utmost patience and humor, despite the fact that, in life, Clarissa Allen had been a fussbudgety nitpicker who worried herself silly over the opinion of others. As Rose reached adulthood, though, and grief was tempered by memory, Rose was able to hold her *actual* mother in her heart, to love and miss that person in all her imperfect singularity. She knew that, alive, her mother would have been more scandalized than anyone, would have taken to her bed at the very idea of her daughter with the Chinese shopkeep.

Her mother's death had been sudden, a brain storm, the doctor said. One morning, before twelve-year-old Rose was even out of bed, her father had found Clarissa trying to walk out the back door with a bucket of table scraps for the chickens. But instead of going out, she kept knocking into the left side of the doorway, bumping, backing up, trying again, and looking as placid as milk all the while. Charles had no sooner gotten her settled into a kitchen chair than she had pitched forward onto the floor and curled into a ball, trembling all over. "The last thing she said was 'snap beans,'" Rose's father had told her after the funeral. "Snap beans. I wish I knew what that meant."

She fingered the satiny beads of the abacus with one hand and crossed 5th Street. The sun now rested directly on the horizon, its last, level rays finally lending some color to the end of the day, turning the incoming fog into a veil of pink and gold. Where it hit the unpainted boards of a neighbor's pump house, tendrils of steam rose in lazy curlicues. She passed the Kendalls' steep front porch, rounding instead to the side yard, and let herself into the rear of the house, knocking the mud from her boots first, and hung her coat next to a row of others. The kitchen was warm, the windows filmed with steam, and there was her aunt at the stove, seeming to do six things at once in a blur of supremely competent motion. Rose leaned into the smell of hot coffee, baking cookies, an iron heating on the stove, and something brown and meaty simmering for supper.

"Will wonders never cease!" Hazel said. Her hands didn't stop for an instant, but she fixed Rose in her brilliant blue stare. "I thought perhaps you'd had to actually go to China for that tea." *Tay*, she pronounced it, her brogue at its heaviest when she made a salient point.

"Hm. Not quite that far," Rose said. "I have to tell you something, though."

"Talk while you help. I only have two hands here. Prudence's good tablecloth needs a press. See to that first, will you? It's in the cupboard."

"What about supper?"

"Captain Kendall is taking his meal upstairs—says he plans to hide there until the meeting is finished tonight—and Prudence tells me she doesn't care for anything until later. I told her she should eat, I tried, heaven knows I did, but she insisted she wasn't hungry. The darling is so thin you could read a newspaper through her, but her mind is made up." Hazel spoke the way she worked, in a blur of motion. "You and I will have a bite pretty quick. It's a good stew." She threw another quick glance at Rose. "Lord knows you need it, too. You look cold. Are you? Your fingers are white."

Rose took an apron off the hook behind the door. "I'm fine, Aunt. It's so hot in here I don't know how you stand it."

"Never mind me. Here, now, these irons are plenty hot, get the tablecloth."

Fetching the linen from the dining room sideboard, Rose could see in her mind's eye Elsie Dampler's face, gawking through the mercantile window, goggle-eyed. She thought, too, about the scar on Bai Lum's chin, the warm cup of his palm, and she wondered just what it was she would tell Hazel.

◻

At Salyer's Hotel, Ya Zhen lowered herself into the bath, slowly. She pressed her lips together when the bruised flesh between her legs touched the hot water. She had carried buckets up two flights of stairs from the hotel kitchen, one in each hand, needing to make several trips to half fill the deep galvanized tin tub. She used the steep, inside stairwell, which prevented her from being seen in the parts of the hotel used by guests: the lobby, the dining room, the men's reading lounge.

There were two cookstoves at Salyer's, a large one for preparing food and a mammoth one—constantly in use, it seemed—for heating water: hot water for washing dishes, for guest baths, for laundry, and for the weekly baths of the hotel's full-time inhabitants. The white girl who worked downstairs, Mattie, already had two enormous pots warming when Ya Zhen came with her buckets. No one else lingered around the kitchen—not even the cook, Ivo, who spoke only German and glared at his work as though every task was his mortal enemy.

"Wish I could help you carry these," Mattie whispered. Ya Zhen nodded but didn't stay. Her weekly bath was one of the rare times she was allowed off the third floor, and even though no one else was around the kitchen, she didn't want to risk losing the privilege if she was seen talking to Mattie. She understood, too, that Mattie took a risk, had often done so, in fact, with her many small, secret kindnesses: a piece of sheer yellow fabric to hang in the bedroom window, a trio of violets pressed between tissue paper, illicit bits of food stolen from the kitchen—a biscuit spread with butter and honey or small lard tin filled with freshly-picked blackberries, sprinkled with sugar and a little cream. These gifts only happened on the day Ya Zhen came downstairs—Mattie and all the rest of the hotel's small staff were strictly forbidden from the third floor—and Ya Zhen was meticulous about not doing anything to endanger this strand of connection, however tenuous it might be. Mattie would offer small, conspiratorial smiles or give Ya Zhen's shoulder a little pat, and those moments of simple good will were often the only things that kept her spirit inside her body from week to week. It was a vast grace, and all she could give in return was a nod or a brush of their elbows so brief that not even hawk-eyed Cora Salyer would notice. Ya Zhen hoped it was enough, that Mattie could feel the pressure of Ya Zhen's heart, still alive under her skin.

Back in her room, the tub was long and narrow, coffin-shaped, and barely fit into the bit of open floor space. The edges of the tub were sharply angled, cold under her palms, but already her body was adjusting to the heat. She sank down, gooseflesh jumping up on her neck and scalp. She pulled her arms down to her sides and dropped until her chin and earlobes were submerged. She breathed slowly. In the fading afternoon light she watched her breasts, marred with small bruises, break the surface of her bath, disappear when she exhaled. There would be men tonight, but perhaps not many. Often, when it was this cold, they stayed huddled around their games of chance, or followed the opium down into dreams. She exhaled again and allowed herself to drop completely under the hot water. With her elbows wedged against the sides of the tub, she could lie perfectly still and stare through the wavering bathwater at the patterns on the high, pressed-tin ceiling. When she could hold her breath no longer, she came up for air, tiny beads of water clinging to her eyelashes and glimmering in the dim light like tears.

She reached between her legs, gingerly parted the flesh there, allowing the hot water to enter her. There was still a laceration from the night before, when the man had cursed her for being dry, cursed her mother for bearing a daughter, held her long hair in his fist so that she was unable to raise her head or turn away. Not all the men were this way, so brutal. A few were soft-spoken and tried to be affectionate, and one had tried to smuggle in a kitten.

She hated them all.

When she had arrived two years ago, she'd gathered her nerve and asked the two older women serving the hotel what to do about the pain. They looked at each other and laughed. These were sisters, Wu Lin and Wu Song, indentured to Clarence Salyer for over six years at that point. Wu Lin had opened her mouth to answer, but Wu Song whispered something to her in a nasal lowland dialect that Ya Zhen couldn't quite catch. Wu Lin looked away and began to hum a tune under her breath. There were small sores crusted across her upper lip, and she touched them gingerly while she hummed. Wu Song turned to Ya Zhen, her face placid and her eyes flat and dark, like stones burned in a furnace. "Don't worry, little sister," she said. "You will be old and ugly soon, like Wu Lin. Then it will not hurt so much."

One morning as they worked together over the washtub, Wu Lin had told Ya Zhen about coming to Eureka. The sisters were more than twenty years old when Salyer purchased their servitude from one of the Chinese tongs in San Francisco. He had visited Wu Song and Wu Lin as a paying customer in a tiny curtained alcove right on the street in Chinatown. Terrified of contracting disease, Salyer paid a half-dollar for the two women to stand naked while he handled himself. Childhood malnutrition had contributed to their exceptionally small stature, and once Salyer had gotten the young women to Eureka, he had claimed them to be 13-year-old twins. This double lie had allowed him to charge exorbitant rates to any man wealthy enough to pay for the novelty. Now in their mid-twenties, the sisters were both in poor health from untreated illness and injury. They seldom had to lie on their backs now, but worked out their obligation to Salyer by hard labor, helping Mattie with the hotel laundry, performing the lowest scullery work in the kitchen, occasionally cleaning rooms after the proper guests departed. They usually cooked for themselves as well as Ya Zhen and another bound girl, Li Lau, using whatever wilted vegetables and fatty bits of meat they could glean from Ivo. Just as Ya Zhen had done, they had put their thumbprint to a contract of five years with Salyer. Just like hers, the contract stipulated that one day was added to their time served for every day of illness—which included their monthly cycles. An actual fulfillment of such a contract was a fairy tale; they would be bound to Salyer for as long as he chose to keep them.

Wu Lin had always seemed less antagonistic toward Ya Zhen, but she was cowed by her sister and never displayed any outward sign that might be construed as friendliness. But on the day Ya Zhen asked the question about the men, about the pain, Wu Lin came later to her room. She set in front of the girl an old, cracked teacup covered with a faded scrap of tea towel. Inside was a hardened, yellowy lump of lard. Wu Lin told her she should warm a bit of fat between her fingers and smear it between her legs before the men came to her room. She told Ya Zhen how to use her hand to guide the men, to try and avert some of the physical battery. "You must help him," she said quietly,

Ya Zhen set her jaw. "Help? They take what they want. Do they need my help for this?" She wanted to hurl the china cup at the wall, but she had learned the hard way what happened if she indulged her anger. Salyer employed a tough middle-aged woman, Old Mol, to manage his 'back business,' and with small indulgences she had cultivated the Wu sisters as her extra eyes and ears. A fit of temper could earn Ya Zhen a smack across the face, or worse. When the men lined up at night, Old Mol decided where to send them; if crossed, she chose the worst of them for the girl who had rubbed her the wrong way.

Wu Lin leaned close and shook her head in short, angry jerks. "Not for them, for you. You will do it to help yourself, unless you are *xing zi*. But I don't think you are a fool, are you?"

Ya Zhen had swallowed her rage and taken the cup of lard.

She stood, hating to leave the comfort of the bath. The fire in the tiny grate threw only a little heat. She rubbed her skin briskly with the piece of rough toweling that hung by her washstand and pulled on her daytime clothes. She needed to get rid of the tub and dry her hair in front of the fire before slipping on the dressing gown that was all she wore in the evening.

She opened her door and looked into the dark hallway.

"Old Mol?"

No answer. The tub was supposed to be dragged into Li Lau's room next. Ya Zhen always carried up the pails of bathwater, but they alternated each week who would bathe first. However, they were not to leave their rooms without specific permission and were absolutely not allowed to enter each other's rooms.

"Li Lau," Ya Zhen called. The door next to hers opened and Li Lau peeked out. She was young, fifteen, but looked much younger, arms and legs thin as sticks.

"Help me," Ya Zhen said. "Come out here and help get the bath from my room."

Li Lau said nothing, just stood at her partially opened door watching Ya Zhen.

Deciding she would have to pull the tub out into the hallway by herself, Ya Zhen started to slide it across the bare wood floor. Every few inches she rested before tugging again. When she had the tub half in and half out of the room, Old Mol came up the inside stairway.

"What do you think you're doing out of that room?" the woman bawled.

It seemed obvious to Ya Zhen that her intention was to move the bathtub, but she kept her mouth shut. She had learned to speak English quite well since the steamship had deposited her here. She had learned from the Wu sisters, from Old Mol, from Clarence and Cora Salyer. She had learned from listening to Mattie and she had learned from the men who came to her room. But the better lesson, the one she had learned most stringently, had been when to speak and when to keep quiet.

"You know damned well you aren't supposed to be out here without my say-so." An expression of foul amusement settled on her doughy features. "Guess that's a day for bad behavior."

In the beginning, Ya Zhen had tried to track the extra time as it mounted, calculating the eventual time she would be released. She couldn't remember exactly when it had dawned on her that there would never be a last day.

"Help me pull this out here," Old Mol said. They maneuvered the tub out, and she called to Li Lau to open up. When the tub was in the girl's room, she just stood there looking into the hallway.

"Get stripped," Old Mol said. "What in Christ's name are you waiting for?"

Li Lau closed her door, so slowly and so quietly that Ya Zhen didn't hear the latch catch.

"You clean this mess," Mol said, pointing at a few streaks of bathwater on the floor. "I don't want anyone taking a tumble in their hurry to pay you a visit." She gave Ya Zhen's cheek, a hard pinch, and lumbered back downstairs, humming tunelessly.

Ya Zhen used her own towel to wipe the floor. Her hand itched to slam the door to her room, to feel the reverberation. She had done it before. Old Mol had opened the door and said simply, "Half-price." Nine men had used her in the course of two hours, one of them so drunk he had vomited in her bed.

She built up the fire, slipped out of her clothes, and put on the dressing gown. She pulled the one small chair close to the grate and rubbed her hair with her shirt, not wanting to use the dirty towel. As she combed her hair, she let it fall through her hands in a wide fan, over and over, until it was almost dry and she could hear the first men climbing the rickety stairs behind the hotel.

◻

Byron Tupper was drinking whiskey with Billy Kellogg in the alley behind Kennedy's tavern. They passed a bottle between them and tried to decide where to go to get warm. Old man Kennedy was willing to sell a bottle out the back door, but wouldn't let them drink inside.

"You ever been to the Western?" Billy asked, smirking. He had large ears that stuck out from under his hat. The cold afternoon made his nose run.

"Couple times," Byron said. He took another swig from the brown bottle and wiped his mouth on the back of his hand. It was a lie. He was eighteen and had never been inside the big Western Hotel, let alone upstairs with one of the fancy women.

"Maybe we should go there tonight," Billy said.

"You got money?"

"Not much. How much is it?"

"More'n we got."

Billy picked up a handful of stones and started chucking them at the back of Reilly's livery. Each made a small thud, and the horses inside shifted nervously. "You can get a chink whore at Salyer's for fifty cents, I heard."

"At Salyer's? Where'd you hear that?"

"John Carter's uncle told him. Said they're cheaper 'cause they aren't built like a white woman." He leaned close and spoke in a low voice, blowing whiskey smell. "They got two...you know. Places to put it."

Byron had just taken a mouthful and he choked on it. He started laughing and coughing. "The hell you say." He was getting warm, feeling the alcohol loosen his joints. "Johnny Carter wouldn't know where to put it unless he saw hooves."

"Na, he's been practicing on his old grandma." Billy doubled over laughing at his own joke and fell off the barrel he'd been perched on.

"You're spilling the whiskey, shit bird. Gimme that."

Billy staggered to his feet and brushed off the seat of his pants. "C'mon, Byron. I got enough money, let's go." He threw another rock at the livery and hit the window. The glass shattered and a horse banged into the wall. A man began shouting, and the boys bolted between the buildings toward the street, laughing.

Salyer's Hotel was a sprawling, three-story building near the bay. The boys stepped inside and the heat from the fireplace was stifling. The lobby was ornate, polished wood floors and a plush runner of burgundy carpet in front of the main desk. They stood close to the door, holding their hats.

"What do we do?" Billy asked.

"I don't know how they do it here," Byron muttered. Small beads of sweat formed on his upper lip.

A black-haired man came out of a back room and stepped behind the desk. Byron recognized Clarence Salyer.

"Help you, boys?" he said. He was in shirtsleeves and a brown vest, hair slicked with pomade.

Billy, so anxious to arrive, now hung back running his hat in circles through his hands. He nudged Byron with his elbow. Byron cleared his throat and approached the desk.

"Yes sir, Mr. Salyer, we, uh...we heard—" Everything he thought to ask seemed impossible in this elegant lobby. "That is, we heard that there might be something a fellow could do here, that is, that there are certain rooms—" He trailed off, staring at his feet, blushing fiercely.

"You go around back, take the back stairs," Salyer said, his voice pitched low. "Don't come in here for that. You knock on the door up there and there's a lady who'll see to it."

Byron nodded vigorously and turned to go. His head felt oddly heavy from the whiskey and the heat of the fire. He grabbed Billy's sleeve and pulled him out the door.

The boys hurried around the corner of the building, not looking at each other. They found the back entrance up a steep, splintered staircase that felt like it might give way if they trod too hard. Byron knocked and a bolt was drawn on the inside. A woman who looked nearly as old as his grandmother opened the door. Her face was long and jowled like a bloodhound over the high collar of her dress. She looked them up and down.

"Kinda early. You have money?"

"We do," said Byron. Billy stood behind him again. The wind off the bay buffeted him on the exposed staircase and he held his hat on with one hand.

She stepped back and cocked her head to motion them inside. They stood on a small landing at the head of a dark hallway on the far side of the hotel. When she shut the door, Byron could barely see.

"This way." She led them down the hall. There was a small gas lamp in the center, and doors on either side. She stopped short and turned.

"It'll cost more if you want to go together." Neither boy took her meaning and stood mute. "If you want the same girl at once," she said, sounding tired.

Billy managed to speak up. "No ma'am, we didn't want...we each wanted our own," he said. "How much for that?"

"Dollar apiece."

"We heard that you could get a Chinese for less," Billy mumbled.

The woman snorted. "All we got here is Chinese, and it's a dollar each for twenty minutes. If you got money, let's have it. Otherwise get out. I'd like to have some supper."

The boys stood together and dug in their pockets. Between the two of them they found the two dollars. Byron handed it to the woman, who slipped it into her pocket. She pulled out a ring of keys. "One of you in here," she said, striding ahead. Billy trotted after her. When they passed under the gas lamp, he looked back over his shoulder at Byron, grinning. Without knocking, she let him into a room and closed the door behind him.

She opened the door nearest Byron. "Come on," she said, "the clock's ticking."

Byron stood behind her, running a hand through his hair. His heart thudded against his ribs. His erection poked out the front of his pants and he held his hat low to cover it.

"Twenty minutes," the woman said, and promptly shut him inside.

The bed was narrow, its curving iron headboard flaked with rust. A curtain was pulled aside at the only window, which showed his own awkward reflection. The young woman, dressed in a faded yellow robe, stood next to a small grate where a low fire burned. She stood sideways, not looking at him. He was stunned by the delicate line of her brow and jaw. Her long hair was down, falling in a black sheet past her waist.

"Hello, miss." He shifted his weight from one foot to the other, scarcely breathing. When he made no advance, she stepped toward him, her eyes on the floor. She walked behind and slid his coat from his shoulders. He let her take it, hang it over a chair, then his hat. His pulse roared in his ears. Now standing in front of him, the girl began to unbutton his shirt. He could look at the precise part in her hair. As she opened his shirt, he placed his palm on the back of her head. She stiffened and stood very still. When he did nothing but rest his hand on her, she reached for his belt. He gently took hold of her wrist.

"Wait. What's your name?" He was whispering. She didn't respond. He let go of her arm and put his hands on her two cheeks. He tried to tilt her face up, but she turned her profile to him again. This close he saw that her bottom lip was swollen and a small cut bisected it. Byron tried to kiss her, wanting to taste the salt of that little wound, to feel the swollen lip against his. Gently twisting her head away, the girl stepped backward and untied her robe. He was electrified, yanking his pants down in a rush and pulling her onto the bed. He thrust himself between her legs and she guided him with her hand. This was unexpected, and filled him with the tender sense that she wanted him. It was enough to set him off, and before he was fully inside her his orgasm hit. He collapsed, and she lay underneath him, motionless. He put his face into her neck and breathed deeply, cupped her breast. She lay perfectly still, and he could feel the exquisite sense of love running between them like a taut cord.

When he rolled off, she sat up, pulling her gown closed. He felt ludicrous, vulnerable with his pants around his ankles, his shoes still on. He scooted off the bed and pulled his pants up. The girl held out his shirt. Byron took it and fumbled at the buttons, but when she reached for his coat, he caught her by the shoulders. She tried to step away and he held her.

"Talk to me," he said. "Tell me your name."

"No name." So quiet, he could barely hear her.

"Please," he whispered. "My name is Byron."

She nodded, staring at the floor again.

"Byron," he said again.

She said his name, a soft slur of the *R*.

"Pretty close," he said. "Now tell me yours." He tried to turn her toward him, again wanting to kiss her, but she stood stiffly, holding the dressing gown closed, her hair falling all around her.

Without preamble, the door opened.

"That was quick," the old woman said. "Good. Out you go." Byron could see Billy standing in the hallway behind her.

He picked up his hat and caught a last look at the girl before the door shut. He and Billy passed three men standing in the stairwell, one white and two Chinese. No one made eye contact, and it was too dark to see much anyway.

¤

"Elsie Dampler is a small-minded busybody." Hazel Cleary moved around the large kitchen like a locomotive, washing dishes and putting cookies in the oven for the meeting. "Her type is never happy without a sour word to spread."

"Yes, exactly," said Rose. "The spreading is what worries me." She tested one of the two clothes irons heating on the stove with a wet forefinger, then smoothed it across the snowy expanse of the tablecloth. "It's certainly not Elsie's opinion of me I care for. The woman is a bird brain. I can only imagine what the story will be the next time I hear it. She'll have us *in flagrante delicto*."

Hazel laughed. "I don't know what that means and I don't want to know."

"It was a touch on the hand. That's all." She turned her face away, hoping her aunt wouldn't see any trace of a blush rising. In the retelling, Rose had made the incident at the mercantile sound like a mere accident of timing, that Bai Lum's hand happened to graze hers just as Elsie Dampler put her face to the window.

"It's enough."

Rose banged down the iron in her hand, now cooling, and grabbed up the other.

"Give that to me." Hazel took the iron. "In your state you'll scorch the good linen."

"If they're going to hang me, I should have enjoyed something worth hanging for." This was the actual truth, and now she really did feel her face go red.

"I'm going to pretend I didn't hear that," Hazel said. "I'm sure he's a lovely man, Rose, but you know as well as I do how it is for the Chinese." She worked the iron in long, even strokes. "When I arrived in this country, it was bad for the Irish. When I first got to New York I looked for work as a housekeeper or just anything, you know. I had a lady look me right in the eye and say the Irish were no better than fleas."

"That's despicable."

She waved her free hand like shooing a fly. "It's pure ignorance. That woman wasn't a generation from coming over on the boat herself, from somewhere. But that's the way it is, Rose. A nation of immigrants, every one looking to be better than the next, and the lot of them like a dog biting on its own tail. Here now, help me put this on the parlor table." They carried the warm linen into the front parlor.

"Did you know he has a sister?" Rose said.

"A sister here?"

"She lives with him over the store. She's young—maybe fourteen or fifteen."

"I had no idea. You don't see many women down there, do you?"

"I had no idea, either. All the times I've been in the mercantile, never seen hide nor hair of her. Then today—one moment she wasn't there, and poof! There she was right in front of me." She told Hazel about the girl repeating the word *yes, yes*. "I think it may be all the English she knows. I wonder if Bai Lum would like me to tutor her."

They draped the tablecloth over a large side table that had been pushed to the wall. "You may be playing with fire," Hazel said mildly. "Especially after what happened this afternoon."

Rose felt the old resistance needling around inside her. "I don't care, you know that. Let them talk about me." She twitched one corner of the tablecloth to even it. "It's not like that's anything new, is it?"

Hazel looked at her across the snowy expanse of the empty table. "You can't play ignorant about this. You may say you don't care what other people think, but you should care—a great deal, in fact."

This was so unlike Hazel—who could be counted on to thumb her nose at sanctimony—that the argument was knocked right out of her head. "I'm not going to...I don't—"

"For the sake of your friend, Rosie. He depends on the good graces of the whole town to keep his business, but it's much more than that, and you know it." She touched Rose's hand, the skin of her palm warm and rough. "Only a fool raps a stick against a hornet's nest."

At seven o'clock, a fire blazed in the hearth of the front parlor and reflected in the tall windows opposite. As the women arrived,

Mattie—recruited by Hazel that morning—stood at the door and collected coats and wraps. Rose showed everyone into the parlor, which was filled with folding chairs borrowed from the Congregational Church. Two of the group's members had come a little early to help set up, and both seemed cheerful and unconcerned; Rose assumed they hadn't yet heard the rumors.

Woman after woman pushed into the Kendalls' parlor. Rose felt a little queasy. She had only been to two other WCTU meetings, and neither of them had been anywhere near this packed with people. The folding chairs were soon filled, as were the upholstered wing chairs and six side chairs from the dining room. Two women even sat side-by-side on the chaise longue. By all accounts, it was a full house. At least two whispered conversations abruptly ceased when Rose entered the room, but she just kept smiling and thanking the guests for coming.

Finally, just before the meeting began, Elsie Dampler arrived.

Rose straightened, pulled back her shoulders, and fixed what she hoped was a welcoming expression on her face. It felt to her that every eye in the room was on her now.

"Rose!" Elsie exclaimed, as if she hadn't seen her in years. "I'm *so* glad to be here tonight. The weather is turning nasty, did you see?"

She thought Elsie did look glad, that she looked happier than a pig at the trough. She and Elsie typically had little to say to one another, since Rose had neither the time nor the patience to listen to Elsie's pretentious, behind-the-hand natters. Weather seemed like a safe enough topic, though.

"Is it raining again? I'm going to develop webbed feet if it keeps up this way."

Elsie glanced down at Rose's shoes as if she expected to see the mutation in progress. Then she batted at Rose's shoulder with a coy grin. "Rose Allen, you're a caution." She wiggled her fingers at someone on the far side of the room and began to work her way through the press of bodies.

Rose kept the little smile plastered to her face like armor, and stayed near the door.

Once the room was full to bursting, the Congregational minister's wife, Lucy Huntington—acting president of the WCTU—addressed them. She was a tiny person, not even five feet tall, and she stood on a small footstool to be more easily seen.

"Thank you all for coming this evening. Thanks also to Hazel Cleary and Rose Allen, and to Prudence Kendall, of course, for hosting us this month." The group smiled and nodded, and there was a polite smattering of applause. "Before we begin, are there any announcements?"

Annabella Briggs, wife of a wealthy timberman, stood and faced everyone, impeccably dressed in clothing purchased in San Francisco. She and her husband Daniel lived next door to the Kendalls, and Rose had tutored their daughter Juliet in upper mathematics. "I'm sure you all remember," Annabella said now, "that the temperance recital is a week from tomorrow at the school. How many of you are recitation leaders?" Four or five hands went up. "Wonderful," she said. "Be sure you tell the children they must be at the school at least a quarter-hour before the program begins." She sat again, smoothing her hands over her lap.

"Thank you, Mrs. Briggs," Lucy said. "Now ladies, I open the floor for ongoing business."

Mary Reilly, a slight woman with buck teeth, stood. Her husband owned the livery behind Kennedy's tavern and he was known to be a prodigious drinker. "Madam Chairwoman, I'd like to address the issue of suffrage," she said. "As you may recall, we did not have time last month to open a discussion regarding votes for women, and the matter was tabled." She sat again, and a quiet rustle ran through the room.

"Yes," said Lucy, "the chair recognizes the issue of women's suffrage, to be adopted as a tenet of our chapter, open for membership discussion."

Prudence Kendall raised her hand. Captain David Kendall's wife was a soft-spoken woman with a mass of faded brown hair.

"When I opened this matter for discussion last month," she said, "I suggested that our local WCTU might adopt suffrage. Several chapters have done so recently, and I applaud their progressive thinking."

"I have concerns about taking that direction," said another woman. "It seems to me that temperance is the more pressing issue. What woman has the time to worry about politics if her home has been sundered by drink?" A few women nodded vigorously.

"I agree," said a plump woman at the rear of the room. "It is our job, we women, to keep the home fires safe. That is plenty for me. Why should I exert myself into the political realm? Should I also wear britches and smoke cigars?" There was ripple of laughter at this.

Prudence Kendall answered again, standing now. Her eyes were large and tender-looking, and always made Rose feel a little protective. "I agree that our primary influence is in our homes," she said, gesturing at the room in a proprietary way, "but the wider world of politics has a direct impact on our homes. Why shouldn't we have a voice in the larger arena?"

"Is this to keep your husband in office?" piped a voice near the door. There was more laughter, and heads turned to see who had spoken. Prudence smiled tightly. "Yes," she said, "I would most certainly vote for David. I believe he is a fine city councilman." She crossed her arms, uncrossed them. "I'd like to have that opportunity. Any of you who disagree with my husband would be free to cast your ballot otherwise. If you were able." She took her seat, and the woman sitting to her left leaned over and patted her shoulder.

Rose angled herself toward the front of the room with her hand raised. "Women in Wyoming have had the vote for sixteen years." Several women looked at her encouragingly, but a few put their heads together and whispered. She made a point of catching every eye. *May as well give them a good look*, she thought. *Jezebel speaks!*

That was when Elsie Dampler took the floor. She got to her feet with a great deal of fuss and throat-clearing and self-conscious adjusting of her clothes. A spray of tiny silk violets nestled atop her hat, and one that had come loose from its fellows bobbed back and forth. "I have to wonder where it ends," Elsie said. She gazed around the room, clearly pleased to be in the center of things, and the stray violet nodded jauntily. "Not all people *should* vote, should they?" She folded her plump, dimpled hands demurely in front of her. "I mean, what's next? Giving the vote to the Indians? To the Chinese?"

Heads immediately swiveled in Rose's direction. She swallowed a lump in her throat and forced an amused expression. "Elsie, for heaven's sake. We're talking about matters concerning women, within the scope of one small chapter of the WCTU." She shook her head. "This was never intended to be a discussion of universal suffrage." She looked around the room again. "We're all citizens of the United States. Why shouldn't we be allowed to vote for our leaders?"

Elsie cocked her head, staring back at Rose. "Perhaps you have a somewhat different viewpoint, Miss Allen, being the only maiden woman here."

Hazel jumped to her feet. "Oh, what nonsense. My Jimmy died eight years ago, God rest him. I don't have a husband to tend anymore. Does that nullify my opinion?" Her blue eyes bore down on Elsie Dampler, who shuffled her feet but remained standing. "I'll tell you one thing," Hazel continued. "If he was still alive, he would be foursquare in favor of votes for women. He placed stock in my opinion."

Elsie put her hands on her hips. "Well my husband *is* still alive, and he says the whole thing is about—" She paused and lifted her chin. "Free love!"

Everyone gaped, and the room was silent. A log broke into embers in the fireplace. Then Rose began to laugh. She tried to control herself, to hold it in, but that only forced her to snort loudly. In seconds, most of the women in the room were also laughing, red-faced and teary-eyed. Even Lucy Huntington, normally imperturbable as a stone boat, hid a smile behind her hand. Elsie Dampler glared, first at Rose and then around the room. Just when the laughter started to ebb, Mattie opened the door and looked in, her expression all perplexity. This got the women going all over again, and Elsie had had enough. She blundered out of the press of seats, pushed past Mattie and out the front door, not even bothering to retrieve her coat.

The women got themselves under control by fits and starts, until finally Mrs. Huntington was able to call the meeting back to order. It was decided, in the interest of group harmony, to table the discussion of women's suffrage for yet another month. They briefly discussed other minor items of business, decided who would host the next meeting, and broke early for refreshments.

Rose stood behind the table she and Hazel had laid out at the side of the room. She passed out molasses cookies and shortbread, and Lucy Huntington volunteered to pour the tea. When the group was served and chatting in small groups, she poured a cup for Rose and herself.

"I wonder if Elsie will be back," said Rose. "I feel sort of awful for laughing."

Annabella Briggs sidled up and held out her cup for a second helping of tea. "Believe me, Rose," she said, leaning close, "she'll be back. Martyrdom suits her. I imagine she went home tonight feeling like Carrie Nation." She arched one delicate eyebrow and turned back into the midst of the group.

Rose looked at Lucy Huntington, who simply nodded, never losing her expression of calm propriety. A fist of tension in Rose's middle relaxed. "I suppose you've heard a story about me today," Rose said.

Lucy was quiet for a moment, looking at the women in their small knots of conversation. "I have, yes," she said finally. "I imagine Mrs. Dampler told what she did in the utmost confidence, though." Another little pause and the harmless smile. "To everyone. As Benjamin Franklin said, three may keep a secret if two are dead."

Rose blew air over her bottom lip. "And the story is that I was throwing myself at Bai Lum in the mercantile?"

"Something like that." Lucy shrugged, a little what-can-you-do shrug. "Why do you think our WCTU has such an excellent turnout on a damp night in February?"

Rose leaned close and whispered. "They wanted a firsthand look at Whore of Babylon."

"Perhaps it's not quite that extreme," Lucy said. She smoothed her palms over her temples. "Or maybe it is. You're old enough to know how people are, Rose. They are just like chickens.

"Chickens?"

"Mm-hm. Chickens. If a chick is hatched with an unusual mark on its little feathers, all the other chicks and even the hen that hatched it will peck at that difference until the chick is bloodied and broken."

Rose looked at the women, standing in their twos and threes. "I'm the chick in this story?"

"You go your own way, Rose. I admire that." She laid her hand on Rose's arm. "I wouldn't ever suggest you change. But this is a small town and the situation for our Chinese neighbors—" Lucy shook her head. "I don't have to tell you about that."

No, Rose thought she knew it as well as anyone. The anti-Chinese rhetoric that had been raging across the country for years, especially on the West Coast, had been slow to take root in Eureka. Perhaps that lull was due to the town's relatively small Chinese population—it was hard to think of the single block of 4th Street as anything like a "Chinatown," although they did call it that. Or perhaps the competition for jobs had not seemed so severe, until economic hard times had brought great numbers of unemployed men to the timber region. Whatever the reason, the hysterical scapegoating had finally taken hold even in small coastal outposts, and in Eureka smoldering resentments had recently broken out into flames of blatant hatred. Rose nodded. "I understand." She didn't want to promise she would stay out of the mercantile, couldn't promise that, but remembering the look on Bai Lum's face when he realized they were being watched helped. "I know it's a bad time," she told Lucy. Then she remembered the favor she said she'd do. "I almost forgot," she said. "Bai Lum asked me to tell you that your seeds have arrived."

Lucy looked down at the table and arranged the remaining cookies into neat little stacks. "Did he?" she said quietly. "Then I'd best go see him. I wasn't expecting those seeds to arrive so soon."

"He said you'd want to know." Lucy suddenly wouldn't meet her eye, and Rose thought she seemed oddly prickled about some flower seeds. Then something else occurred to her and she glanced around to see if anyone was within earshot. "Are you uncomfortable going to the mercantile? Would you like me to get the seeds for you?" she whispered. "I don't mind, honestly. Even if Elsie Dampler decides to trail me with bloodhounds." She gathered used teacups and saucers. "If the town wants to hang me for it, or...or peck me for it, I guess, let them. I'm almost twenty-seven years old and, as Elsie made quite clear to all, a poor, benighted maiden woman. What other excitement do I have?"

Lucy laughed, but underneath her face was watchful. "Not necessary," she said. "I'm fine taking care of this myself, and you need to let things smooth out a bit. Probably Elsie's tattling will blow right over. She's hard to take seriously. But for Bai Lum's sake, let things smooth out, yes?"

"Lucy, did you know Bai Lum has a sister?"

The older woman's gray eyes widened. Finally there was a shift in her tranquil expression, and she spoke to Rose *sotto voce*. "A sister."

Something about Lucy's changed demeanor brought back Rose's earlier sense of unease, and she tried to change the subject. "Your new seeds—what kind of flowers are they?"

"Clematis," Lucy said. Her eyes fixed on Rose. "A beautiful white variety that blooms in the shape of a star. Rose, how is it that you—"

Then, to Rose's great relief, Hazel—who had been scurrying between the kitchen and the parlor ever since the meeting broke for refreshments—interrupted. "I do believe," she said, "that we've just survived hosting the WCTU." Sure enough, women were gathering their things to leave. Rose hurried over to help Mattie return the ladies' coats as they left, sliding out from under Lucy Huntington's suddenly steely attention. A fine, drizzling rain had started, and several women lamented their lack of umbrellas as they filed out into the wet weather. Many gave Rose a little dry kiss on the cheek as they passed. *Just like chickens*, she thought, smiling. A few busied themselves with their hats and wraps, saying goodnight to Mattie while pointedly ignoring Rose.

Annabella Briggs trailed the group and gave both of the young women hearty hugs before she left. "A lovely evening, Rosie. Stimulating." She pinched Rose lightly on one cheek with her gloved hand. "Fiddlesticks to Elsie Dampler. She's in a pucker, but she'll get over it." Then she leaned close to Rose's ear. "I'm proud of you," she whispered. "Forget the tongue-waggers. Soldier on."

Rose wasn't certain just what it was that Annabella was proud of, but nonetheless she felt tears prick the backs of her eyes, and she could only nod, for fear she might cry in earnest if she tried to answer. Annabella raised her umbrella and hurried down the porch steps and across the lawn to her own home.

Last to leave was Lucy. She was bundled into her coat and hat, and wore a pair of buttery-looking kid gloves. She was back to her pleasant, neutral expression, but Rose's heart thumped hard anyway.

"Rose, thank you so much for offering to go to the mercantile for me. I'm going, in the morning, and on second thought I'd love to have your company. I reckon it would be a judicious move for both of us, don't you think so?"

It actually sounded like the very best way Rose could imagine being able to see Bai Lum again so soon, without risking her own reputation—which didn't concern her overly much—or risking his, which concerned her a great deal. "I suppose it would be better," she told Lucy, "but I'll need to check with Aunt Hazel about what time. We're going to do all the inside windows tomorrow."

Lucy waved dismissively. "Never mind the windows. I spoke to your aunt about it while you were seeing your guests out. She said she'll give you a list of things to pick up when we go. Ten o'clock."

Rose blinked. "I'll meet you there at ten."

"No," Lucy said, "I'll fetch you in the buggy, right here."

"It's so close. I don't mind—"

Lucy drew her out onto the covered porch. "I'm going to carry you there in the buggy. That way we can have a little visit before we get to the store." This was clearly an order. "And listen to me," she said, making certain she had her full attention. "It's really better that you not mention Bai Lum's sister to anyone else." Her eyes roamed Rose's pink face, and she smiled wanly. "Who have you told?"

"I told Hazel, when I got back this afternoon. Only her."

"Did anyone else hear? Mrs. Kendall or Mattie, perhaps?"

Rose was mystified by Lucy's intensity, remembering the angry words she'd heard between Bai Lum and the girl. "No one heard. But why does it matter?"

"For now, just keep it mum and we'll talk tomorrow."

Rose watched the little woman climb into her small carriage. It was a delicate-looking cart that fitted Lucy's stature, but looked almost like a child's wagon hitched behind Buster, the Huntington's astoundingly large draft horse. Lucy touched Buster with the shaft end of a whip, so softly it couldn't have seemed like much more that the flick of a moth's wing on his enormous haunch, and off they went. Rose went inside and leaned her back to the closed door.

"Thank God," she said. "Matilda, I never want to do that again."

"But it sounded like you were all having a grand time." Mattie used a hand broom to whisk dropped bits of cookie from the parlor floor.

"Hm. I suppose some of us had a grand time. I imagine there were several, in fact, who were absolutely thrilled to watch the old maid and sometimes schoolmarm make a jesting-stock of the town gossip."

Mattie removed the pins from the bodice of her apron. "Gracious, I believe I might have enjoyed that myself." She sighed. "But then, I don't get out much."

Rose laughed and put her arm around Mattie's shoulders. "Let's go help with the dishes. Do you think there's any pie left from dinner?"

Clean teacups were stacked on the drainboard and the windows were steamy from the hot dishwater. Prudence Kendall and Hazel moved around the room together, putting things to rights for the night. Prudence went to the table and pulled out chairs. "You two were so much help tonight," she said. Sit down here now before you go, and have a last cup of tea."

"I'd love some, Mrs. Prudence," said Mattie. She glanced around the tidy kitchen. "Did you ladies do *everything* in here? You should have let us help." She hung her apron on the hook behind the door and dropped into a chair.

"Never mind," Prudence said. "You all worked so hard to make it a lovely evening, especially you, Mattie, after working all day at the hotel. Sit. Rose, tea for you?"

"I suppose I could do with one more cup, but you'd better make it chamomile."

"We'll all have chamomile and turn in early," Hazel said. She poured from the old pot that stayed in the kitchen, serviceable despite some nicks and cracks. "Prudence," she said, "you're to be congratulated. I thought it went quite well this evening."

Rose coughed over her cup, and Mattie patted her companionably between the shoulder blades. "I'm sorry about the upset with Elsie Dampler." She put her head in her hand. "I offended a woman who already has me halfway to hung for something that is all in her imagination." That wasn't entirely true, of course, and she stared into her teacup least they see the fib on her face.

"You weren't the only one who laughed at Elsie," Prudence said. "That remark she made to you. 'Maiden woman' for heaven's sake."

Mattie frowned. Waves of dark hair framed her delicate features. "She called you a maiden woman? You're twenty-six years old." She looked at Hazel. "I'm twenty-four, by the Jesus. What does that make me?"

"Eligible," said Hazel. She poured herself some tea and sat down. "Or a free spirit, perhaps."

"Not that," said Rose with mock horror. "Doesn't a free spirit lead to free love?"

"I can't be that free," Mattie said. "I believe it's a mortal sin."

Rose raised her teacup. "To maidenhood."

They touched their cups to Rose's. "Maidenhood," said Prudence Kendall, laughing. "In whatever guise it takes," added Hazel, and they all drank.

Even though Hazel Cleary's house was only a short walk, David Kendall—who had sequestered himself in his upstairs library during the WCTU meeting—insisted on carrying Hazel, Mattie, and Rose home in his carriage. The night had gone from drizzle to outright rain, and they were all tired and grateful for a quick, dry trip, and for Captain Kendall's gentle humor. Having heard about the "maiden woman" remark, he claimed that it put him in mind of a headstone he had seen in his youth.

"Mr. Kendall, you're having us on," said Mattie.

"Not at all, dear," he said, a little smile playing at the corners of his mouth. "This was an old churchyard I passed through in Maryland." He lifted a finger, as if running it under a text. "It stated quite clearly: 'Here lies Ann Mann, who lived an old maid but died an old Mann.' I remember like it was yesterday." He winked at Hazel, who flapped a hand at him and smirked for the rest of the ride home.

Once inside, they all trooped off to bed, Hazel to her big room downstairs. Rose and Mattie went upstairs together and paused at the doors to their own rooms, which were directly across the hall from each other.

"Good night," Mattie said, and blew a little kiss.

"Excuse me, Matilda," Rose said before closing her door, "but please call me Ann Mann." Even after she had gotten into her nightgown and climbed between the sheets, Rose could hear Mattie laughing.

¤

The boy was the first one tonight, a boy close to Ya Zhen's own age. Instead of closing his face afterward, he made eyes, trying to kiss her and have conversation. He wanted her name, had insisted she speak his, but it had no place in her mouth. While he stood there, staring with a stupid sheep's face, she longed to squat over her bucket and rinse herself and was relieved when Old Mol burst in early to make the boy leave. Salyer tipped the old woman for keeping the customers coming through, and nervous young boys rarely got a full twenty minutes. Never did she offer a knock or shouted warning to the newly initiated. Old Mol's thinking was this: if they thought she would walk in, they'd keep it short.

If another man was waiting, Ya Zhen was allowed a few minutes to ready herself. She was expected to have washed, combed her hair, tied her gown and straightened the bed as each man came in. On nights when there were a lot of men, she rarely had time to do all of this, and washing was always her first concern. If Old Mol brought someone in and the bed was unmade, she reported it to Mrs. Salyer, who kept strict accounts for the four indentured women. Each infraction was jotted in a ledger, and if a half-dozen incidences were recorded, the woman had an extra day added to her contract of servitude.

"Mr. Salyer isn't running some cheap peep-and-grab crib like they got in the city," Old Mol had told her when she first arrived. "You girls are damned lucky. This is a quality place. You got your own room in off the street and meals besides. Best situation you could have fallen into, all things considered."

After the boy, only two men came that night. The first was a gray-headed man from town. His clothes and body were dirty and he had still been holding her tightly from behind, his skin greasy with effort when Old Mol called time.

"I'll pay extra," he shouted. He held Ya Zhen's face into the pillow, and she had to bend her neck painfully in order to catch a breath. "Two minutes," Old Mol called back. Redoubling his effort, he twisted one of Ya Zhen's breasts until she cried out. This was enough, finally.

Afterward, she quickly sponged her arms and back and belly, trying to purge some of the man's sour stench, while he argued out in the hallway about having to pay another dollar for such a little time. Her neck ached and her nipple was crusted with a bit of blood. She dabbed at it, wincing.

It was almost half an hour before another man arrived. She used a small hand broom to sweep the dirt tracked in earlier, and shook out the bedclothes. There were gray smudges on the ground sheet where the man's knees and elbows had been, so she tore the sheet off the mattress and turned it over. She could still see a ghost of the stains, but they were easier to ignore. She sat on the narrow, ladder-back chair and, as she did every night, combed her hair with the wooden comb her mother had packed during the last night with her family. After two years, she thought of them, her parents, as dead, and counted herself an orphan. Even Hong-Tai was a ghost to her now, although she often visited him in her dreams. In spring, when the wind blew in hard from the north and drove the usual low clouds off the coast, Ya Zhen thought of her little brother in his fine blue clothes, purchased with her life. *Yù fēng dì di*—her little brother, flying on the wind.

¤

Rose woke in the night at some uncertain hour. She lay still and waited, hearing only the steady *tock, tock* of the pendulum in

Hazel's big clock downstairs. Despite the deep quiet that enveloped the house, an echo of something had followed her up into wakefulness, a sound she couldn't place. Then it came again, a quiet moan from somewhere in the house. Worried that her aunt might be ill, Rose kicked back the covers and went to the head of the stairs, not bothering to put on a wrap. There it was again, the moan, coming from the back of the house. Tiptoeing through the parlor, she heard the sound, low and stifled, inside the narrow pantry that appended the kitchen. The windowless room stood open and Rose could barely see a slender figure sitting just inside the door.

"Mattie?"

There was a startled but somehow slow shuffle of feet and clothing, and when Mattie turned, Rose could see her face in the ambient light from the kitchen. "Oh, hello Rose," she said, her voice coarse, as if she'd been asleep.

"What...Mattie, what are you doing in here? Are you ill?"

"Is it late?"

There was a strange odor in the confined space of the pantry, something sweet and burned, definitely coming from Mattie. "Yes, very late." A cold vein seemed to open under Rose's skin, smelling that smell, hearing the disorientation in her friend, who was normally so clever and razor-witted.

"I mought need to sleep a little, then." The girl shifted as if to make herself more comfortable, seated as she was on Hazel's molasses barrel. Her speech was so muzzy that Rose barely understood her.

"Why don't you come upstairs with me now?"

A long pause, then she finally stirred. "I suppose I could catch a few winks before dawn." She managed to stand, though it took two tries, and Rose had to snug her arm around Mattie's waist.

The smell was in her hair and clothing. "Mattie," Rose whispered as they walked to the stairs, "did you go out tonight? After the meeting? I thought you were going to bed."

Mattie didn't say anything, just walked docilely beside Rose. When they made it upstairs, she went straight to her room. Rose followed her in this time, wanting to be sure Mattie got between the sheets. But instead of going to the bed, Mattie went to the window and touched her forehead to the glass, where her warm skin left a cloudy halo. She was crying.

"Matilda, sweetheart, what is it?

"God, Rose, I miss home. I miss it like I'm missing a limb off my body itself." She closed her eyes. "Don't you miss your home? And your da? I've been missing my people for years."

What could Rose say? She missed her father, yes, like having a little splinter in the heart. Sometimes, when the summer was a low, gray ceiling of coastal overcast, she thought she might give up her whole life in California for five minutes of fireflies, and prairie grass tossing its baked smell into the night. But this was her life, here in this isolated place where the damp made mildew flourish on the inside walls of the house and made redwood trees grow so large that, when one was felled, a dozen or more people could stand on the stump and never once rub shoulders. Now love, unexpected and impossible, to tie her heart to this place. Her Latin was serviceable. Eureka: *I have found it.*

"Let's get you to bed," she told Mattie. "The wee hours are the worst time to think about hard things." It sounded like the worst sort of cliché, but with Mattie so impaired it would have to do.

"Bed." Mattie heaved a sigh that condensed on the glass. The smell—Rose couldn't bring herself to actually think the word *opium*—was so strong that she expected to see a fine film stuck there. Mattie shuffled the few feet to her narrow single bed and sat on the coverlet fully dressed, leaning over slowly until she dropped to her side on the pillow. Rose squatted and unlaced the girl's boots. She seemed asleep already, her breathing deep and steady. Rose lifted her legs onto the bed and pulled the comforter over her, not bothering to take off Mattie's outer garments. Let her sleep. Rose, chilled in just her winter chemise, turned to leave.

"Don't tell Hazel."

It almost sounded like sleep-talk, and Rose hesitated, not wanting to rouse Mattie with an answer. "Shh," she whispered faintly. "Don't worry."

She ran across the hall on tiptoe and burrowed back into the warmth of her bed, shivering, smelling of Mattie's clothing. She had rinsed her hands at the washbowl, but must have gotten the smell on her chemise. Surely tonight was the first time Mattie had done such a thing—how could she have hidden it, otherwise? She pulled the quilt snug around her shoulders, right under her nose, where she could breathe in its clean, familiar scent. The clock downstairs chimed the hour: three o'clock. She yawned mightily, hearing the tendons in her jaw creak. There was no sound from Mattie's room, so she must be asleep now.

Don't tell.

All this time they'd lived under the same roof, and Rose had never suspected that Matilda was anything but content—no, more than content. Mattie seemed genuinely happy, lighthearted, even. She wouldn't say anything to Hazel, not yet. But she'd have to talk to Mattie tomorrow, sometime. *Don't tell. Don't tell.* Now she was keeping two secrets—this, and the fact of Bai Lum's sister—and she didn't understand either of them.

She was warm now, and her mind ambled. Her own pilgrimage had not been so far as Mattie's, to be sure, but Eureka had seemed like a world away from Paw Paw.

Hazel had put the idea in Rose's head to begin with, in her letters. It was obvious that her aunt loved her life here. *It's one of the wild places left in the country*, she had written, *but I wouldn't wonder if it becomes another San Francisco one day.*

Rose had read that particular letter more times than she could count, and managed to wait three weeks—just so she could claim to have thought it over—before she announced to her father her intention to move to the Pacific coast. Charles Allen had looked at his daughter long and hard, convincing her that he would put his foot down. She needn't have worried. "If I was a younger man," he'd finally said, "I'd pack a bag and jump on the train with you." That settled it. Rose's rail ticket was purchased, and Charles saw her off in Chicago. He stood on the platform long after everyone else had gone. Rose put her head out the window as they pulled from the station, and watched as the train gathered speed, watched until he was a tiny lone figure waving the caboose farewell.

The overland trip from Chicago to San Francisco was hot and dirty, and Rose had loved it. Seatmates on the train were carefully arranged by the conductor and Rose ended up sitting with a young woman from Finland. Her name was Sophia and she spoke no English. Sophia had a note pinned to her coat with her destination written on it for the conductor's sake—Cozad, Nebraska—and a name: Hiram Belknap. Rose could not imagine being left to such circumstances, a refugee entrusting herself so utterly to the scruples of strangers. The two women took turns sitting by the window and managed to communicate by gesture and facial expression. When she wasn't looking out the window, Sophia spent a lot of time gazing at a tintype photo set in a little gilt frame. It was a woman, an older version of Sophia, with her hair pulled back severely from her face.

"Your mother?" Rose asked. "Mother?" She pointed at Sophia and then mimed rocking a baby in her arms. Sophia smiled and nodded. "Äitini." She brushed absently at a tear. Rose made a circular gesture around Sophia's face and tapped the photo. "You look like her," she said. She wished she had a photograph of her own mother, something to show Sophia in return, then tuck away for safekeeping.

The train made hurried stops in places that looked so scruffy and slapped-together Rose wondered that they could even be considered towns. At a place in Eastern Nebraska, passengers rushed into a makeshift restaurant, which consisted of a large, dirty tent with a false front built around the door. The only food served was a small boiled potato and a gristly piece of steak topped with an egg. As all the passengers packed into the tent, the chaos reached a crescendo, people calling for food and coffee, several small children crying or running between the jostling adults. The floor was wretched with spilled food and dirt from the street. In one corner a big girl sat watching the crowd, mouth open, holding a ragged valise on her lap from which the damaged head of a doll protruded, its painted eyes chipped and blind. No boarding call was issued at any of the scores of stops made, so the passengers bolted their food, keeping one eye on the train lest it start without them.

Back on board, the conductor showed the passengers who needed his help how to pull their seats forward and lay the backs down, creating a small sleeping platform. Rose and Sophia spread out their shawls and coats to create rough bedding. The sound of the train's wheels on the tracks vibrated through the wooden bench, but Rose was exhausted and fell asleep in minutes, despite the continuous noise of the other passengers trying to settle for the night. All night long the train stopped, for water, for passengers embarking and disembarking. At some point, the conductor woke Sophia to tell her that her stop was coming. Rose wanted to sit up and say goodbye, but she could hardly open her eyes. By the time she managed to rouse herself, Sophia was gone. The window was fogged over. She wiped it with her sleeve, but could only see two men pushing a trunk across the platform. Sophia was nowhere in sight. Rose lay back, feeling the engine building steam. Once they were underway again, she settled into the sounds of her fellow passengers coughing, snoring, moaning in their sleep. Sparks flew past the window from the massive diamond-shaped stack, each one like a meteor tearing through the flat Nebraska night.

Right after the chiming of the quarter-hour, Rose fell back to sleep in her clean, plain room. As she went, she could almost feel the sensation of that train moving under her, bearing her into the unknown future.

¤

Byron Tupper and Billy Kellogg hunched into their coats, collars turned up against the wet. Several blocks from the hotel, Billy stopped. He stood in the fine drench, morosely shaking his head. They were among neighborhood houses now, and a gnarled apple tree crouched in the yard beside them, naked branches black in the rain. A number of moldering windfalls poked out of the grass at the base of the tree. Billy grabbed one and hurled it at the street, where it exploded into pulp. He stared dully at the mash, looking miserable.

"What's wrong with you?" Byron asked, although he didn't care what Billy's problem was right now. He was cold and just wanted to get in out of the wet. When he lifted his hands to his mouth to try and warm them, he could smell the girl, an odor like warm grass. He thrust them deep into his pockets, wanting not to wash that smell away in the rain.

"It was the whiskey," Billy said. He kept his eyes on the street. "I had to use her chamber pot before we did it, and then I...I couldn't." When Byron said nothing, Billy finally looked at him. "What about you?"

Byron shrugged. He found he didn't want to tell Billy anything about the girl, so he kept his mouth shut. Billy took a long look at his face, and a black expression settled over his face.

"Damnation!" he yelled. He took up another apple and this time hurled it at the house. This apple was not as badly rotted and made a resonant thud when it smashed next to the front door. As if someone had been standing inside waiting for the noise, the door opened and uncertain yellow light fell onto the porch. Billy took off at a dead run, leaving Byron standing there, stupidly staring, with a thin stream of rain running off the brim of his hat. It was a girl he knew, Frances Jane Beebe, wearing heavy nightclothes, holding a guttering candle in one hand and a huge orange cat under her other arm.

"Byron Tupper, did you throw that apple?" she asked. She was thin, thin as a March wind, his grandmother would say, and Frances Jane had been bossy even when he stood next to her in Miss Stanley's classroom trying to recite some poem about an old woman who hung out a flag during the war.

"No. Sorry."

"I suffer from insomnia," she said, as if he'd asked why she was awake so late. "I find that warm milk can be soothing."

Billy said nothing.

Frances Jane glared at him. "Are you just going to stand there dripping?"

"No." But he didn't move.

"So? What are you waiting for?" She clamped her skinny arm tighter around the cat, who tried to worm out of her grasp.

Byron smiled. He had a beautiful, guileless smile. It changed him utterly, though he would have been surprised to know it. "*On that pleasant morn of the early fall when Lee marched over the mountain wall*," he said in a singsong. It was the only part of the long recitation he had ever been able to remember.

Frances Jane's scowl softened and she smiled a little, too. "*Over the mountains winding down, horse and foot, into Frederick town*." She stepped inside. "Byron Tupper, you're a wet fool," she said, and closed the door.

¤

A knock brought Ya Zhen out of deep sleep, a bright jolt of confusion lighting her mind. Was it the door? Another man? She lay still, sensing the late quiet of the hotel and gathering back her racing heart. Then the knock again. It was Li Lau rapping on the wall, a signal that she needed help. The girls were not supposed to leave their rooms at night and visiting each other was strictly forbidden, but Ya Zhen threw off her blanket and tiptoed out anyway. The girl was curled on her bed, biting her pillow to stifle a moan.

"Bad fish," she said. "I'm sick with it."

"Have you vomited?"

"No, just the pain in my belly," she said, her face pinched and drawn. She sweated profusely. Another cramp hit and Li Lau writhed on the bed.

Ya Zhen rubbed the girl's back, then slipped one hand over her lower belly. It was firm as a melon and rigid.

"Li Lau," she whispered when the contraction had passed. "When did your blood stop?"

"Right after I came here," she said. "*Jiŭ yuè*, before the full moon."

Ya Zhen counted on her fingers—almost four months.

It took most of the night. For two hours, Ya Zhen did what she could to make the girl comfortable, but finally the contractions wrenched screams from Li Lau and Ya Zhen had to go downstairs for Old Mol.

The big woman rolled Li Lau onto her back. "Hold her," she said to Ya Zhen. "I have to see how far gone she is." She pushed up the sleeve of her flannel robe and thrust three fingers deep inside Li Lau, who bucked under Ya Zhen's grip and made a guttural sound. "She's opening," Old Mol said, and crossed to the washstand. "I think she's further along than she says, though. Maybe five months."

While Ya Zhen wiped a wet towel on Li Lau's forehead, Old Mol went to the kitchen for hot water and rags. When she came back, she and Ya Zhen spread the rags under the girl's bottom and Old Mol put a compress on Li Lau's belly. Then she poured tea.

"Got something stronger, too," she said. She pulled a dark, corked bottle from her pocket and filled one of the teacups. "Help me lift her head a little." Ya Zhen got behind Li Lau and propped her up. She struggled and tried to turn her face away. Old Mol grabbed her chin, hard, and gave her face a shake. "You take a big swallow of this, or I'll tie you down," she said. Ya Zhen whispered in her ear, begging the girl to drink. Li Lau did. After two cups full to the brim, Li Lau laid back, her eyes open but glassy, her legs thrown apart. When the next contraction came she moaned and lifted her head off the bed but did not scream. Old Mol nodded and took a nip from the bottle herself. "Only a wee sip for me," she said, "or I'll be on the floor."

Ya Zhen stayed, wiping Li Lau's face and arms and legs, as the granny woman had done for her. She wished she had some of the elderflower water the old woman had used. For three more hours, while Old Mol alternately dozed upright and peered between the girl's legs, Li Lau labored, twice vomiting into the bucket. Finally, the fetus slid into the world. Old Mol tugged on the umbilicus and the afterbirth came free. She wrapped baby and placenta in a rag and put it in a basin.

"This gets burned," she said. "See to it while I get her clean."

Ya Zhen left the room with the bowl, not looking, feeling her way down the dark inside stairs. In the hotel kitchen, she pulled a chair to the biggest stove, which was still warm from the banked fire inside. Even before she drew the rag back, she knew the child was alive. It was a tiny boy, no bigger than a squab. He grimaced, one translucent fist pressed at the side of his face. She put her hand under him, shocked at the delicate weight on her palm, his skin warm and thin, mottled with Li Lau's blood.

She sat there in the dim kitchen with her back to the outside wall and held him in her hands. He moved more slowly as the hour slid away, the little chest rising and falling sporadically, until finally he lay still. Ya Zhen thought about a world filled with people, all of them beginning just like this fragile thing, no more harmful than a moth newly out of its cocoon. She wrapped him in the rag again. "Better for you," she whispered. She opened the stove, stirred the coals, and poured on some kerosene. When it blazed up and lit the room, she lowered the little bundle, light as a held breath, into the flames.

CHAPTER FOUR

I T WAS 6:40 IN THE MORNING, and Mattie wouldn't look Rose in the eye.

Hazel had left a note that she had made coffee and was going to the Kendalls' at the very crack of dawn. When Rose came downstairs, Mattie was already in the kitchen. Her dark hair was disheveled, but she had changed into night clothes at some point and wore a soft flannel wrapper. She leaned against the counter, holding her cup in two hands and gazing out the window. The sun was out, like a small miracle after the deluge of recent wet weather. Three African violets perched on the sill, and the sun lit the little hairs on the broad, furry leaves.

"Good morning, Mattie."

She startled slightly, and pulled her robe tighter around her, tilting her head so that her hair fell in a little curtain across the side of her face. "Morning, Rose."

"So, we have some sun today."

"Indeed."

Rose poured herself some coffee and sat at the table, giving Mattie a wide berth. After a few wonderfully hot and bitter sips, she cleared her throat. "Feeling well?"

"Me? Grand, Rose. Are you working today? Hazel's gone off without you already." She went to the dishpan and rinsed her cup, keeping her thin back to Rose.

"I'm going in a little while." *And as long as we're talking about me,* she thought, *the less likely we are to talk about why you were moaning in the pantry last night.* "Listen, Mattie," she said, moving her finger through a few grains of sugar spilled on the tablecloth. "I'm keeping a big secret and it's about to make me crazy."

That did the trick. Mattie's face was guarded and wan, but she met Rose's eye. "A secret?"

Rose nodded. "May I confide in you?"

Mattie pulled out the chair opposite and raked the hair away from her face. "Of course. You can tell me anything."

Rose currently harbored a multitude of secrets, it seemed—one for Mattie, one for Lucy Huntington—but this one was hers. Not quite believing she was doing it, she spilled the truth. "I'm in love, Mattie. I didn't *want* to be in love. Part of me wishes I wasn't. It's a mess, really."

Mattie's eyes went wide. "Rose, no. It's wonderful that you're in love. That is, I know you're an independent sort of person, but—"

Rose shook her head. "No. It's not that, exactly. It's…well, it's complicated."

"Doesn't he love you back?" Mattie spoke in low, confidential tones and her freckled skin had pinked up. The idea of star-crossed love apparently agreed with her. "You aren't unrequited, are you? That can't be."

In for a penny, Rose thought. "I believe my feelings are returned, yes. We haven't spoken about it, but I think that he…I have a sense that he does feel the same. For me." Rose's face had now turned a much darker shade of pink than Mattie's.

Mattie frowned at Rose, clearly confused. "Why is it a mess, then?"

"It would be a…a social impossibility. He's—"

Mattie's hand flew to her lips. "God, Rose," she whispered. "You've gone and fallen in love with a married man."

"Married?" Rose shook her head, a little stunned.

"What's so impossible, then?"

"It's Bai Lum. From the mercantile." She couldn't seem to say it fast enough. "I'm terribly and completely in love with Bai Lum. Elsie Dampler saw us yesterday, just my hand on his arm, or…him holding my hand, maybe, I don't know. It was nothing, not really, and I don't think she could even see. But I know she'll be telling everyone that she *caught* us—"

Mattie's face softened all at once and a host of emotions swam there: distress, anger, love. "To hell with Elsie Dampler," Mattie said. "It's grand that you're in love. Really, it's pure wonderful."

Rose couldn't help it—she stared. "Really?" she asked, dumbfounded. "You think it's wonderful?" She needn't have asked though, it was clear by her expression that Mattie meant it, right to the soles of her feet.

"Of course I do!" She pulled her chair so close to Rose that their knees touched, and leaned in, resting her elbows on her thighs, as if too tired to sit up straight. "Rose, listen. I have a secret, too. Nothing good about it."

She told everything. How much she missed Ireland and wished she could go back. How she had longed for her father's love all her life and had never seemed good or sweet or clever enough to keep his attention. How afraid she was of hurting Hazel's feelings, who had been better to her than her own mother. And how she had gone to the opium room one night, a few nights after Christmas when she felt so lonely it was like a bottomless pit in her heart.

"Mattie, you can't. You have to promise me. Last night you were so *gone*, like a ghost of yourself." She squeezed Mattie's cold fingers. "I can't stand to think of you like that, out there somewhere like you were. Something terrible could happen."

Mattie brought Rose's hand to her lips and kissed it. She cried and promised. Last night had only been the second time, she said. Never again. Never.

"If you swear to me that's done, I'll believe you. We'll keep each other's secrets."

"On my oath, my lips are sealed," Mattie said, wiping her face on the sleeve of her robe. "But what will you do? About your dilemma?"

Rose stood and pulled Mattie to her feet. "I haven't the slightest idea," she said. "Not today, anyway." She hugged her. "Come on, then, we both have work to do. Mrs. Kendall is a softie, but Aunt will scorch me if I'm late. I hate to even imagine what that nasty Cora Salyer would say if you were tardy."

Maddie nodded. "I can imagine it. Quite clearly. That woman has a curdled disposition."

A few minutes later, as she washed and dressed, Rose felt an amazing liberty just for having told Mattie about Bai Lum, for saying it straight out loud. It didn't change a thing, not really, but being able to say it—*I love*—was astonishing. She believed Mattie would keep it in confidence, too—believed, actually, that Mattie was more likely to keep Rose's secret than she was to keep her own promise about going out at night. She wished she didn't think that, but there it was. Just thinking the word was too bizarre to make sense of. Rose whispered it to herself once, then twice: opium. Opium. It started to sound odd, the way a word does if it's repeated over and over. It was a word out of a cautionary tale, some story not fit for the eyes of the average person, written for salacious periodicals sold on shadowy corners in big cities.

¤

After Ya Zhen took care of Li Lau's baby, she came upstairs to find that Old Mol had cleaned the girl, and the room as well, having rolled all the bloodied bedding into a pile by the door. Li Lau was tucked in, the blanket pulled to her chin, her round face still and ashen. "Never mind," Old Mol said, "she'll be fine in a few days. I'm afraid you're going to be awful busy, though." She made a toad-like sound that Ya Zhen took for a laugh. "See that these things get into the wash today. That's good timing." The hotel laundry was always done on Thursday, as opposed to the usual *wash on Monday, iron on Tuesday* rhythm of home life. Everything was done in a single day—wash, iron, and mend. This allowed a full complement of clean bedding for the rooms and clean table linens for the restaurant, all before the weekend trade got into full swing. Week in and week out, Wu Song and Wu Lin helped wash everything and had it hung out by half-past twelve to allow time for drying on the hotel roof.

Exhausted from the long and nearly sleepless night, Ya Zhen went to the window and pushed it open a few inches. The sky was just lightening in the east, clear and colorless, without a single cloud. She breathed in the cold air and watched as a raven, its features indistinguishable as a shadow's, settled on the roof across the road and shook itself. Her palms echoed with the sensation of Li Lau's son, the delicate beads of his curved spine as he tried to wake into this world, tried to breathe the air of the hotel. She pressed her hands together, tight as she could, to force the feeling away. The raven made a ratcheting sound, like the creak of a tree limb. She closed the window and stripped the bed, rolling Li Lau's bloody linens inside her own dirty sheets. She had just changed into her daytime clothes—rough-woven trousers and tunic, baggy and faded with long wear—when there was a peremptory knock at the door. Cora Salyer opened and stood on the threshold. Her hair, a rusty dark color from the henna she used, was tied in rag curls that stuck out in wild confusion on her head. Dressed in a brown morning wrapper, she greatly resembled a scrawny and misshapen tree.

"You're going to help with the laundry today," Cora said. Her eyes traveled around the room as she spoke, from washstand to narrow window to the bare mattress on its iron bedstead. There were stains in several places, some old, brown; others were newer, still dark red. She grimaced and looked away. She rarely entered the girls' rooms and carefully avoided this side of the hotel, although her husband made regular visits.

"You'll work with the kitchen girl all day, the Irish girl. Once the wash is finished, you should have time to assist with some other cleaning. Do you understand? Plenty of time, before you have to...to be back here." She clutched the neck of her wrapper so tightly Ya Zhen was surprised the woman could breathe. "No sloth. I absolutely won't tolerate it." She shook her head for emphasis and the rag curls bounced and bobbled. "Those older ones," she said, meaning the Wu sisters, "will be out doing other errands, and Molly seems to think I can trust you. I'd use that other girl too, her in the next room, but I'm told she's indisposed." Ya Zhen knew Li Lau would not be doing any sort of work that day, would be lucky if she could squat on the bucket without help. "The kitchen girl will be here soon. Bring all of this." She tipped her chin at the bundle of sheets, lips so thinned they were nearly invisible. "Molly will get you started. Hurry, so she doesn't have to come up here after you. She does enough complaining as it is." Cora Salyer walked out, not touching so much as the edges of the door. Ya Zhen waited until she had disappeared down the hall toward the main staircase. She gathered the pile of bedding and went the inside way, back down to the kitchen, back to the stove.

¤

"I don't disagree with your impulse. I'm concerned, though." Standing at his oak commode, the reverend Charles Huntington wiped away the last bit of shaving soap from his neck. Age had softened the skin at his throat into a wattle, but the boxy line of his jaw remained firm, giving him a deceptively pugnacious profile. "There's a danger that she could mistakenly unravel the whole effort with some innocent remark to the wrong person."

"That's what had me tossing all night," Lucy said. "It seems we're in a corner, though, don't you think?" Standing in the open door of their bedroom, her eyes followed him as he finished dressing—spotless white shirt, stiff collar, dark tie and black vest. "There's no question she's gotten emotionally attached to Bai Lum." She sighed. "Which is a different kettle of fish entirely, but I can't even think about that right now. After what happened yesterday, the girl actually coming into the store while Rose was there—well, now it's just a matter of time before Rose realizes something unusual is going on."

Charles bent and kissed the top of his wife's head. He was quite tall, well over six feet, and towered over her. "If you think we can trust her, then we'll have to," he said. They had been married over forty years and he gave great credence to her instincts. He slipped into his day coat while they walked to the kitchen. Sun poured through the amber sidelights flanking the wide front door, painting bars of light across the entry hall. "Isn't this weather a blessing," he said.

"It is. Coffee or tea?"

"Coffee. Paper here?"

"Full of bad news," Lucy said, and handed it to him. "Ranting and raving. No jobs, so let's find a scapegoat."

"As ever."

Lucy nodded and looked out at the backyard, where every wet branch and blade threw off a coruscating reflection. The economic panic of the late '70s had brought a steady stream of men to Humboldt County, some with families, many on their own, all looking for whatever work they could find: lumber, fish, gold. There was virtually none of the latter and a great lot of the former, but even the largest timber operations could afford to hire only so many.

"Not all the shouters are the rough-and-ready crowd, anyway," said Charles. "It's coming from every quarter these days. Idiots like that fool in San Francisco—what's his name, the big shouter?"

"Denis Kearney."

"Yes, Kearney. Hate-mongering loudmouths, and the next thing you know they're running for public office. Elected by the sheep. *Baaa!*"

Lucy laughed. "Are you going to eat something?"

"Just this." He blew on his coffee and sipped it. "Now, I know I don't need to tell you, but after what happened with Elsie Dampler yesterday, you'll have to be extra careful at the mercantile. Bai Lum should keep the store open and you should all make yourself as conspicuous as possible. I wish I could come with you, but I told Mrs. Farley I'd visit this morning. Her husband's so ill—there's no putting it off."

"Of course not. It's better anyway. If we all showed up at the mercantile together it would only raise more attention. I'll make sure Bai Lum understands that you're putting the wheels in motion."

"Good. I don't know how quickly I can move the girl, but if we have to, if things get too complicated, we'll bring her here."

"I should probably start getting a room ready, just in case."

He stood and took her hands. Such a small person, but always steady, his temperamental match in every way. "I have no doubt the Lord will provide recourse," he said. "I'll put Buster on the carriage for you."

¤

When Byron Tupper opened his eyes, the sun shone in around the edges of the drawn shades. Thin slats of light crossed the dark room and shone on the opposite wall where the old wallpaper curled at the edges, showing dirty bare plaster underneath. He lay still for a little while, watching dust motes rise and fall in the sun.

He felt good. He felt—exalted. It was not a word he used, was not a word he even would have considered part of his own vocabulary. But he understood it to be a true word. "Pearl," he whispered into the stale air. He had decided that this would be what he called her. Even when he knew her real name, he could use Pearl as a special term of endearment. He thought about how smooth the top of her head looked when she unbuttoned his shirt, how the back of her head fit into his cupped palm. For a few minutes Byron tried to resist the nagging impulse, tried to hold Pearl in a purer place, but each thought of her placed him back in the moment when she had taken him in her hand. He had almost been inside her, had felt the head of his penis graze her body, when he lost control. Now he groaned and grasped himself, imagining over and over that he was plunging into that perfect place with her name on his lips.

Afterward, it was a relief to think about her more clearly. Her chin was a perfect point, her forehead a broad, gentle curve. Her skin was flawless, the color of new beeswax, and her voice—so soft he could hardly hear her. He closed his eyes and remembered her small room, spare and clean. How many men went into that room every day? What did they do with her?

He threw back the sheet and put his feet on the floor. The first thing he needed to do was earn some money. There was no way that old cow at Salyer's would let him in unless he paid. But if he paid his way in again he could explain to Pearl that he wanted to help her out of that place. Once she knew how he felt, they could make a plan to get her away.

His pants were crumpled on the floor next to his bed. The room was a dingy mess—dirty clothes dropped around, his muddy boots crusted by the door, his rifle standing in the corner where he left it after duck hunting four days ago. He hadn't even cleaned the gun, and if his father knew it he would clout Byron upside the head. If he was going to bring Pearl here, to marry her and make a home, he would have to make some changes.

First he raised the shades, something he hadn't done for months. The paint around the window casement was buckled and filthy. Byron grabbed an old shirt and rubbed away the mildew and grime. There was also a scrim of mildew along the baseboard under the windows. This was the north side of the house and in the cool damp climate mold was tough to beat back. He managed to wrestle one of the windows partway open, but the sash weight was broken so he had to prop it open. The nearest thing at hand was a childhood picture book, a story about a duck preparing to throw a garden party for her animal friends. His mother had read it to him over and over before she died. All he could remember now was that the duck had gathered bayberries to make bayberry candles for the party. His mother passed away with the scarlet fever when Byron was six. He had opened the book only once after that. The ensuing struggle to read had convinced him that he would only ruin the story by trying and he had closed the cover for good. He wondered if Pearl could read. When they had children she could read the book to them.

Out in the overgrown yard, droplets from the previous night's rain depended from the mass of blackberry brambles covering the fence, throwing tiny prisms of color. A hugely rambling morning glory engulfed the leaning tool shed; it had opened a few purple-blue blossoms to the sun.

With the window open, Byron went through the room, picking up, throwing the bed together. He'd have to wash the sheets and blanket, but he would wait until his father was out in the woods. It had been three days since he'd seen the old man, although there was evidence that he'd been around, clothes slung into different corners, an empty bottle on the porch floor. Byron wasn't sure how he would work his way around Garland, but if Pearl could cook and see to the house for them, he thought that would go a long way toward convincing him.

He began to sing under his breath, *shall we gather at the river, the beautiful, the beautiful river.*

¤

Rose Allen stood at the bottom step of the Kendalls' front porch, fingering the small shopping list of things her aunt had given her. It seemed silly to stand and wait for a ride when Bai Lum's was such a short walk, but when she had said so, Hazel had given her such a thunderous look Rose raised her hands in surrender.

"Have you already forgotten what happened yesterday?"

"Of course not, but—"

"Don't you dare give me a *but*, girl. You'll put yourself out on that walk and not make the least move in the direction of the Chinese block without Mrs. Huntington. Isn't that right."

It wasn't a question.

The morning was a buttercup, so yellow in the sun that even the muddy, horse-beshitted streets seemed glazed with a rumor of spring. Rose unbuttoned her coat and relished the fine air. It was a good thing she had a list in her pocket, because even though it was short, she couldn't keep it in her mind. She couldn't even keep her thoughts still long enough to wonder why Lucy wanted to take her to the store. The only thing she could fix on was Bai Lum, his angular face, the line of his hair falling down the middle of his back, the way his fingers had felt yesterday, making a small, warm track in her palm. That moment played again and again in her mind's eye, and each time it did, a stab of heat spiraled from her belly, up to her face and down through the center of her. She pulled out the list and read it again: *butcher's twine, 5 lbs. lard, 2 pkts each beet and carrot seed, washing soda.* Then Lucy's carriage rounded the corner, Buster looking just as pleased to be out in the sun as Rose was.

"Good morning," Lucy said when Rose climbed in. "Isn't it a beauty?" She twitched the reins with the slightest motion of her wrist and the horse was moving again, giving his massive head a little toss. "Even Buster feels like a youngster today, don't you, old man?"

Not knowing what Lucy wanted with her made her feel skittish and awkward. As they ambled along, Lucy keeping Buster at a slow walk, Rose stayed quiet, looking around and smiling as though she'd just stepped off a steamship and for a first visit. She had a harder time keeping her hands quiet, though, and they kept moving in her lap, fingers twisting around each other, then stretching, until she clasped them tightly enough to make her knuckles pop. Lucy, who waved to everyone she saw on the street, reached over finally and placed a hand over Rose's.

"Not to worry," she said. Her face was still and serious, but her palm was warm.

"I'd worry less if I knew why we were on this errand."

Lucy took the measure of Rose's face, scrutinizing her so carefully that Rose felt a bit like a prize shoat up for auction. "It's a great deal more than an errand, Rose. There are some things you need to know about Bai Lum and his—" Lucy hesitated ever-so-slightly here. "His sister."

Rose's stomach dropped a little. Her initial reaction in the mercantile yesterday when she had seen the girl, thinking for a queasy moment that Bai Lum had a child bride, returned. Suddenly she wished she had never agreed to come along with Reverend Huntington's wife, who sat so stiffly erect and proper-looking in the carriage next to her. Could she not just turn back the clock a mere twenty-four hours? She would go to the mercantile early, buy the rock sugar, buy the chrysanthemum tea, hope for the touch of Bai Lum's hand long before Elsie Dampler and Garland Tupper were out creating complications. She opened her mouth to say something, anything, but could only nod, looking straight ahead.

Lucy went on, soft and implacable. "I'm going to take you into my confidence," she said. "Not just mine, either. There are reputations at stake. Reputations and *lives*, including Bai Lum's."

Rose looked at her, the upright form and calm face, and a little worm of fear coiled in her chest. "Lives."

"Lives."

They pulled up to the mercantile. Buster planted his enormous hooves at the walk and loosed a great stream of piss onto the street, loud and long. Lucy laughed. "God's creatures put the world into perspective," she said, tucking at the edges of her hat, even though not a single silver hair was loose. She stood in the buggy and gave Rose's earlobe a little tug. "Come on, then. Let's go in, and I'll tell you the whole story."

¤

Mattie had built a roaring fire in the elephantine secondary stove, where a few hours prior Ya Zhen had burned the body of Li Lau's baby. The stove roiled with heat and a large tub of water sat atop, nearly at a boil, when Ya Zhen came, holding her bundle of wash.

Old Mol sat at the rough work table, shoveling up a great greasy plate of eggs and bacon. "There you are," she said, chewing noisily while she spoke. She pointed at the ceiling with her fork. "Her majesty wants you to help with things around here today, so make yourself useful." She scooped the last of her food with a biscuit and left her plate sitting on the table. "This one," she said, cocking a thumb at Mattie, "will show you the ropes. Start with laundry. But hear me. Don't you dare let the guests clap eyes on you. Stay out of the dining room, stay off the front stairs, and if you should see anyone who *might* be a guest, you'd better make yourself disappear. That's the main worry of Mrs. Salyer, and if I catch any hell for you showing yourself, I'm going to make sure you pay for it later." She heaved herself to her feet. "Now, as you know," she said, "I was awake wiping tails all night. I'm going back to bed. One of you see to my dishes." She went out, sucking at her teeth.

"Mullingar heifer," Mattie muttered when Old Mol was out of earshot. She smiled at Ya Zhen. "So we're on the wash together today. Lucky you." She tilted her chin at Ya Zhen's armful of sheets. "Bring all that out here and I'll show you how we do it."

The back kitchen door opened onto a low covered porch and small fenced yard that consisted mostly of dirt and a few bedraggled weeds. Two metal barrels stood against the wall next to the tin tub Ya Zhen used for bathing, along with an odd contraption that sported wooden rollers bigger around than a man's arm, with a spoked iron wheel on one side. Mattie saw Ya Zhen looking at it and laughed. "The mangle," she said. "Terrible name, isn't it? We'll feed the wet stuff through there before we haul it up to hang out. See?" She loosened a knobbed handle at the top of the machine and spun the iron wheel. Gears moved and the rollers thudded around. "You don't ever want to get your fingers too close in there. When it's tightened down, you'll break a bone for sure." She gestured to the metal barrels, which were actually tall washtubs. "Let's pull these out where we can get at them,"

Ya Zhen heaped her sheets on a pile of dirty laundry sitting in one corner of the porch, heart beating hard, knowing that she and Mattie would soon unroll the bloody mess tucked into the center of the pile. It was good that someone should see it. Let Mattie make of it whatever she might. They dragged the wash barrels out side-by-side, leaving plenty of room to move around each one. "Once the water's boiling in there, we'll put it in this first tub with the soap, add a pile of wash and bash it about for a bit with this." She held up a wooden implement that looked like a four-legged stool attached to a long, T-shaped handle. "Then we'll rinse in the second bucket, and run it all through the mangle." Ivo was in the kitchen now, banging pots and pans around, getting his day under way. Mattie stepped down into the weedy patch of yard. Hands on her bony hips, she looked around at the clear sky. "A perfect day for us," she said. "We'll get this done and out on the lines and it'll be ready for the iron before afternoon." She bounded back onto the porch and took Ya Zhen's arm. "Who knows what sort of mischief we could get into with so much time to waste," she whispered. She drew Ya Zhen over to the piles of dirty laundry. "Now the fun begins. All this here needs a quick sorting out. We'll start with the least dirty stuff and finish with the worst of it. You start the sort and I'll get the old grouch in the kitchen to help me pull the wash water off the stove." On her way inside, she told Ya Zhen she'd best roll her long sleeves as high as she could. "You'll soon be past your elbows in it," she said.

Ya Zhen hurriedly rolled her sleeves almost to her shoulders and began pulling apart the small mountain of things to be washed. First she untangled the sheets she had brought down, then sorted through tablecloths, towels, napkins, heaps of hotel sheets, and a relatively small amount of clothing, most of it belonging to the Salyers and Old Mol. Some of the table linen was filthy with spilled food; this she shook out over the edge of the porch and piled on top of Li Lau's fouled bedding. By the time Ivo and Mattie struggled out with the huge kettle of boiling water, Ya Zhen had three big piles sorted. Together, they set the edge of the kettle on the lip of the tub and poured. Ivo was ropy with muscle, but he wasn't a young man, and the tendons stood out in his leathery neck.

When the tub was full, he took the kettle with him. "*Das alte Schwein war in meiner Küche,*" he said. His voice was gravelly, as if not much used.

"*Ja,* always eating," Mattie said. She smiled at Ya Zhen. "He'll clean up after that sow. He's almighty particular about keeping the kitchen tidy. Now then, we'll need this." She dipped into a crock of soft brown soap and added that to the wash water. Clouds of steam wafted into the cool morning, along with the astringent smell of lye. "Let's see what we have here," Mattie said. She picked through each pile that Ya Zhen had made, nodding, pulling a few darkly-colored things aside, but leaving everything else as it was. At the final pile, she looked the soiled tablecloths and wrinkled her nose. "This lot will need a bit of extra attention," she said. "People spill so much, sometimes it looks as though they didn't use plates at all. I'll take care of these while you get started at the tub. Take that whole pile, there, and we'll put as much in as will fit." They loaded handkerchiefs and shirts, towels and underdrawers into the steaming tub. Mattie grabbed the wooden stick and dunked the pegged end into the tub, plunging and twisting everything in the pallid murk. "This is your dolly stick," she said. "Hold these handles and pound it around, just like that." When she handed the stick to Ya Zhen, she put her hand on Ya Zhen's arm. "You know," she said quietly, "the old bitch didn't even introduce us. I'm Matilda Gillen, but I'm called Mattie—you know that."

"Yes, I know."

"And what should I call you?"

Ya Zhen thought of the boy who had been with her last night, asking the same question. Since she had been sold and brought here, she had guarded her name. Certainly there were people who knew she had a name, but those who might remember it did not use it. To Clarence Salyer and his wife, to Old Mol, to the Wu sisters and to Li Lau, she was no one who needed a name. To the men who came, men who gave names even to the scabrous dogs that lived under their porches, she was nothing at all. Upstairs, under the mattress, she hid the small bundle of things her mother had sent with her into this terrible life; in the same manner, she had put her name away into the center of her heart, hiding it there. But she looked into Mattie's kind and open face, and she chose.

"Ya Zhen."

"Ya Zhen," Mattie said. "Lovely. Well, Ya Zhen, let's get the wash done."

Back at the wash tub, Ya Zhen began to pound and twist as Mattie had shown her, wincing as small splashes of the scalding water leapt onto her arms and hands. Through the cloud of steam, she kept one eye on Mattie, who was now sorting through the dirty tablecloths to the sheets at the bottom.

¤

By mid-day, Byron Tupper had done a fair job of mucking out the house. He washed dishes and put them on the open shelf over the sideboard. More windows were pried and propped open. He swept the uneven floorboards, then went at the worst of the dried mud and spilled food with an old piece of wet sacking. He heaped a great pile of rubbish behind the shed and soaked it with kerosene. While he tended the fire with a broken rake, Garland came home.

Byron could tell by the way he walked that he had been ill-used by his excesses the night before, but this was his usual posture, unless he was in the middle of a drunk. He moved in a tender, stiff-legged gait so as not to jar his head, with his hat pulled low over his eyes. Byron could only make out his father's face from the nostrils down, his mouth a grizzled line slashed in his face, stubble glinting.

"What the hell is all this?" Garland said, his voice a dry husk. He stood on the far side of the burn pile and his form wavered in the lines of heat rising into the day.

"Thought I'd clean some," Byron said.

"Watch you don't set the shed on fire." Garland turned and made his careful way across the yard toward the house. "I'll kick your ass if you burn that shed." When he got to the pump, he took off his hat; his long hair stuck to his head. He jerked the pump handle and put his face directly under the stream, letting it pour over his head and neck and drinking in great slurping drafts. Then he shook his wet hair out of his face, put his hat back on, and climbed to the porch, one slow step at a time.

Byron stood by the fire, raking the refuse in, turning it, knocking back charred bits that wanted to float off. Garland cursed loudly and the windows banged shut one after the other, rattling in their loose frames. Byron tamped the burning trash, pushing it into a smaller, smoldering heap. Setting the rake aside, he loped over to the house. Sometimes a serious rage could be dampered by catching his father before he got fully wound up. This morning Byron wanted to catch Garland before he denned in his room to sleep.

Garland's boots were under the table and the powerful stink of unwashed feet filled the kitchen. He stood in the door between the kitchen and his bedroom, one blockish hand propped on the lintel, his head hanging. He squinted up when Byron came in.

"Make me some coffee," he said. "And close the damned door. What kind of fool are you, leaving this all open? Are you soft in the head? You'll have every yellow-jacket and horsefly for miles in here."

Byron had made himself coffee that morning; he lit the stove and moved the enameled pot over the heat. "You want food?" he asked Garland.

"No. Coffee."

"It's almost ready. Why don't you sit?"

"Why don't you mind your business?" Garland grunted, but he pushed himself off the doorway and slumped into a chair. The worn rush seat creaked under him. He rested his forehead in one hand and rubbed his eyes with the other.

Byron put a cup and saucer in front of his father and poured him coffee. "That's hot," he said.

"Good." He slopped some coffee into the shallow saucer and blew on it, then sipped. He had taught Byron to drink coffee this way when he was eight years old. Byron watched, remembering how patiently Garland had demonstrated cooling the brew before trying to sip it. After a few swallows, Garland sat back in the chair and fixed Byron with a smirk. "I hear you had quite a night last night."

Heat rose into Byron's face. He said nothing.

Garland laughed, a phlegmy wheeze that ended in a fit of coughing. "Whoo. Gonna have to lay low on the pipe for a while," he said, still chuckling, the veins in his nose and cheeks standing out purple. "So my boy laid the old rod to some little Mongolian sweetheart." He sucked up some more coffee and leaned forward, grinning at Byron. "Hope you didn't think Billy Kellogg would keep that a secret. Make her howl, did you?" His tone had become softer, conspiratorial.

Byron felt himself gathered into his father's regard. "Yeah," he said. "She liked it." He didn't like to talk about Pearl this way, but he felt it was true, the way she had taken him into her hand, so gentle. Here, perhaps, was a door he could move through, a way to convince Garland of his plan to bring Pearl out of Salyer's. "You know anybody hiring? I've got to earn some money."

Garland snorted. "You and every other man jack around here. Timber's bad right now for cutters and haulers—woods are too wet. The only ones making money are the big bugs, Carson and that crew." His face clouded over with a sullen pall. "Bastards in their big houses. That place he's building up 2nd Street? Damnation. No matter where you are in town, you look around and there it is. That lot wouldn't give the sweat off their asses for the men pulling the trees down, so long as they can dress their wives in fine clothes to show off on a Sunday morning." He pushed his coffee cup toward Byron. "More."

Byron poured. He needed to get Garland off this track before he got himself into a full rage. "I thought maybe something in town. I'll ask around."

"You do that," said Garland. "Watch out, though. That little bit over to Salyer's will get to be a pricey habit." He drank again, belched. Despite the coffee, his eyelids were getting heavy. Byron knew he would soon lie down for a few hours of sleep before going out again. "You better watch your pecker, boy. That type will give you the pox."

"She's not like that." Byron kept his face calm, but his voice had an edge. "I'm not going to let that happen."

"How do you plan to prevent it?" Garland shook his head and got to his feet. "You know how many men get on the inside of that?

Pretty soon laying with her will be like putting it to an old heifer. She'll lose her grip." Garland clenched his fist shut in Byron's face, grinning.

"I'm getting her out of there," Byron said in a rush. He stood, toppling his chair. "That's why I need a job, Pa. I want to marry her. I'm going to marry Pearl."

"Pearl?" Garland gawped at his son, blinking stupidly. "Marry?"

"She's not like those other women, she's pretty and—" The look on his father's face made his heart bang hard against his ribs. His voice rose as if to shout down that look. "You'll see, it'll be nice. She'll help take care of this place, of us."

The only sound was some small thing scratching around under the front step. Garland squinted at him with a look like trying to add sums in his head, and he scratched at the back of his neck. "Are you wit-scoured boy? You think you're gonna marry a Chinese whore and bring her into your mama's house?"

Byron trembled, could feel the long muscles of his back quiver. "Don't call her that," he said. His hands rolled into fists.

Garland's entire body went still. "What did you say to me?"

"I said don't call Pearl a whore."

Garland was around the table with Byron's shirt front bunched in his fist with a speed Byron could barely credit. He was two inches taller and at least forty pounds heavier, his meaty frame only just beginning to soften with age and too much whiskey. His bloodshot blue eyes bore in on Byron's brown ones. "You listen to me, sonny boy. That girl has one purpose in this life, and that's to lie still when she's told. Just like she did for you, she does for any swinging pecker who ponies up the six bits, or whatever her boss gets for her. You got that?" He emphasized his words with a hard shake of Byron's shirt. "Now you get a job if you can and you go ride that little Chinese pony all you want, but don't you ever—" another shake, "—*ever* speak to me about bringing her into this house." He shoved Byron backward and released him. The boy stumbled and flailed his arms, but kept his feet. "A white man doesn't marry an animal, got it? A white man doesn't marry a sheep, a she-panther, or a Chinese." He went to the door of his room, his shoulders bunched.

Byron stared at his father's back, fury pouring through him like a bad wind. Every cell in his body strained toward some violent release and he could feel Garland's whiskered neck under his palms, the tendons taut, his Adam's apple bulging. The desire to fling himself across the room crested like an actual pain in his muscles just as Garland looked over his shoulder at him. His face was like cold stone, waiting for the least move, ready. When Byron just stood there shaking, Garland smiled, went into his bedroom and closed the door.

He fled the house, tripping down the front stairs and falling to his knees, jumping up again. Behind the tool shed, the refuse pile had smoldered to a stinking black heap, barely smoking, a charred scar on the ground. He stood next to it, his muscles twitching wildly. The sun was warm but a rash of gooseflesh raced across his scalp. He threw one look back at the house; his bedroom window was still propped open with the storybook, the gray rag of a curtain luffing out in the mild breeze. He grabbed the rake and pulled the burn pile apart, raising ash and smoke. A tongue of flame leapt from the uncovered embers. He thrust the rake handle into the fire. When it caught, he went to the shed and used the makeshift torch to start small blazes all around the old building. He tossed the rake aside and ran, not looking back until he was a quarter-mile away. Black smoke billowed into the blue sky and when a window shattered, Byron ran harder.

¤

It was the expression on Bai Lum's face that wound Rose's insides like a corkscrew: his confusion, concern, and genuine happiness to see her already, mixed with his obvious relief at seeing Lucy Huntington.

"Rose tells me my seeds have come in unexpectedly soon," Lucy said, her voice loud and cheerful.

"There is no one else here," said Bai Lum. His eyes rested momentarily on Rose again, and back to Lucy.

Lucy nodded. "Good. We need to talk about Shu-Li, and I have reason to believe that Rose here may just as well be in on the discussion. First of all," she said, "I understand Shu-Li and Rose met yesterday?"

"She came downstairs while Rose was here, yes."

"I wouldn't exactly say we met," Rose said. Whatever peculiarity was going on here, she found herself wanting to hover near the door for a quick escape. "We weren't introduced."

"Close enough," said Lucy. "Bai Lum, do you think anyone else has seen her?"

"Why is your sister such a secret?" Rose interrupted. "I don't understand. Why does it matter if she's been seen?" She waved one hand to emphasize her point and managed to clip the broom leaning near her. It fell to the floorboards with a declamatory slap and she stood it upright, cheeks flaring.

Lucy stared until Rose fidgeted to a stop. "Perhaps a little patience," she said. "Bai Lum, we're going to explain everything to Rose, and I'm going to speak plainly to you both." She pointed at the ceiling. "That little girl's life could depend on it, I think." She went to the counter and rested one elbow, so that she faced the windows and door. "While we talk, perhaps you could put some things here for me to look at. Some spices, and some actual seeds? I believe Rose needs some things, too. We may as well make this look like business as usual."

Rose pulled the now-rumpled list from her pocket, still utterly confused. Lucy smiled at her daft expression. "It's called an alibi. In case anyone comes in. At any rate, Mrs. Cleary does actually expect you to bring something home, I think."

Chastened, Rose stood by Lucy and watched Bai Lum move around the market. He set things on the counter, one by one. When she glanced down, she had to bite the inside of her cheek to keep from smiling; on top of the five-pound lard bucket was a short string of firecrackers.

"Now, the first thing for you to know," Lucy said, "is that Shu-Li is not Bai Lum's sister." She looked at Bai Lum, gray eyes shining. "She is actually Bai Lum's guest. Because of his kindness, she's here as a favor to Reverend Huntington and myself."

Rose looked at him. "Your guest?"

"She is," he said.

"In a manner of speaking," said Lucy. The girl is a runaway and we're helping her find a safe place. All of us are working together to get her to safety."

"Safe from *what?*"

"From—" Lucy frowned looked toward the windows again. When she answered, her voice was almost too quiet for Rose to hear. "From a hell." She ran her fingers back and forth over the smooth grain of the countertop. "Reverend Huntington has associates, friends in San Francisco with whom he stays in close contact. These friends found Shu-Li there, on the street, held in conditions more appalling than I can tell. Our friends got her out."

Rose looked from Bai Lum to Lucy. "What do you mean, held?" The look on both their faces was so grim that Rose almost covered her ears, suddenly not wanting to hear.

"Rose Allen," Bai Lum said softly, "Shu-Li was the property of Bing On tong. She was purchased by them, to be used by men. For money."

She pictured Shu-Li as she looked yesterday, so young, her face curious and open, holding out the can of peas. Her throat constricted. "My God."

"My husband's associates managed to smuggle her away," Lucy said. "He arranged to meet them in the city, and he brought her here."

"But now that she's here, in Eureka, why are you hiding her? Won't everyone assume she's Bai Lum's sister?" She looked at Bai Lum. "That's what you told me yesterday, and I believed you." There was a hint of accusation in her words, but she didn't care.

"There is still a danger here," Bai Lum said.

"What you read in the papers about their turf wars and shoot-outs is only the tip of the iceberg," Lucy said. "When it comes to these girls, the tongs are vicious. Vicious and relentless. For the Bing On, Taking Shu-Li was just like robbing from their persons, and they simply don't give up. A tong will send out members whose only job is to chase down a girl like Shu-Li."

"The tongs are in Eureka, too," Bai Lum said. "If Bing On came here, they would offer a reward for the girl."

Rose felt nauseated. "Girls," she said, looking at Lucy. "You said 'when it comes to these girls.'"

"In the city there are more than you would ever want to imagine, Rose. So far, Bai Lum has helped us with four others, before Shu-Li."

The door of the mercantile opened and the three of them stiffened. Lucy and Rose looked in that direction, but Bai Lum had already turned to the shelves behind him, as if shuffling through the jars and containers.

Old Chen Ma stood there holding his own broom, which was worn into a short, curved brush, his shadow laid down on a trapezoid of sunlight across the painted floorboards. His thin hair was pulled tightly back, and he looked around the high-ceilinged room, eyes moving over the bright kites as if mesmerized. He caught sight of Bai Lum and broke into a wide grin, showing his few teeth. He hailed Bai Lum, greeting him like a lost friend. Bai Lum lifted his hand in return. "I'll take him out." He put a hand on the old man's elbow, chatting in an amiable way, and led him across the street.

Rose closed her eyes and tried to catch her breath. "I almost jumped sideways when that door opened," she said, "like I was going to see Jacob Marley's ghost."

"Everything's fine," Lucy said softly, although Rose could see that the older woman's face had blanched.

"Lucy, if Shu-Li isn't safe in Eureka, then I don't understand why she's here, at the store. Chinatown seems dangerous for her."

"Yes and no," Lucy said. "Although the mercantile's right in the middle of everything down here, we're hiding her in plain sight. Think about it, Rose. If Charles and I had Shu-Li at our house, if anyone saw her there at the rectory, how in the world would we explain it? We've always taken every precaution to keep the young women out of sight, but our thinking is that, if they *are* seen here, it's at least a little bit less noticeable. If Elsie Dampler, say, took a notion to ogle through the front window."

Bai Lum returned and closed the door behind him, looking bemused. "Even with his son standing right next to him, saying 'Father, come inside now,' he was calling me by the son's name."

"A good enough reminder that we need to finish up," Lucy said. "Do you see now, Rose, why I asked you last night how many people you'd told about Bai Lum's 'sister'? The more people who know she's here, the greater the risk."

"I only told Hazel."

Lucy thought for a moment. "Is she likely to talk about it, do you think?"

Rose shook her head. "Not if I tell her that it needs to be a secret. She'll probably stare daggers, but she won't ask. And she wouldn't tell a secret if you hung her by the thumbs."

"I'm sure. As soon as you can, then, ask her to keep your confidence—and be *certain* you're alone." She lifted her chin and looked hard at Rose. "We have an even more immediate problem now, though," she said, "and I don't have time to be anything but blunt about it." She glanced at Bai Lum when she said this. "This trouble with Elsie Dampler."

Heat flooded back into Rose's face. "I don't care what that stupid—"

"Stop," Lucy said, her voice quiet and stiff. "Keep your mouth shut and listen to me. It doesn't matter if the entire town sees Elsie as a gossip with her mouth hung in the middle and running at both ends. The problem isn't that she's telling the world she saw Rose Allen acting inappropriately. It's that she's telling the world that the man was Bai Lum." She let that sink in for a moment, then continued. "If the wrong person hears that news and decides to act rashly, it's not your reputation I'm concerned for. In such a situation, not only is Bai Lum in danger, real and immediate danger, but so is that little girl upstairs, and she hasn't done a thing to bring any of this misery onto herself."

Rose put an unsteady hand to her mouth and said nothing.

"I understand that you two have feelings for each other," Lucy continued, and she spoke in a low voice. "My goodness, in a perfect world, you'd be taking strolls by the bay and going out for evening carriage rides. If I'm speaking to you like children, I'm sorry— that's not at all my intention, and the last thing you need is a lecture. But under the present circumstances, I'm asking you to be as discreet and careful as possible, especially until we're able to move Shu-Li."

Rose stole a look at Bai Lum, just a quick flick of the eyes, and was startled to see him studying her face. The expression there, though grave, was filled with tender affection. It nearly unraveled her, that look. "Of course," he said to Lucy, keeping his eyes on Rose. "Shu-Li is the most important thing right now." He was clearly not denying the feelings between them, only reassuring Lucy that they would not repeat the mistake that they had made the day before, and Rose got the message loud and clear. Holding his eyes, she closed her fingers around the firecrackers and slid them into her coat pocket.

"Good," Lucy said, and reached to put an arm around Rose's shoulder in a brief hug. "As for little Shu-Li, what's your sense about the situation right now, Bai Lum?"

He shook his head. "She finds it difficult to stay upstairs alone when I'm down here. So many times I've warned her not to come down, to stay away from the windows in the daytime, but she says she wants to see the sky, and other people."

"Bless her, of course she does," Lucy laughed. "Frustrating as that may be, Bai Lum, that stubborn streak will do her a world of good. She has a lot to put behind her and plenty of tough challenges in her future. But if she's determined to show herself, you're going to have an impossible task keeping her hidden while you're trying to do business."

"How long does she need to stay here?" Rose asked."

"There is a place for her," Lucy said, now almost in a whisper. "Up in Portland."

"So far?"

"Yes, it's a long trip," Lucy agreed, "and most of it by water. But the farther from San Francisco, the better. Charles doesn't take her all that way himself. There are several people, all along the way, who will be sure she gets there safely."

"An underground railroad," Rose said, stunned.

"In a manner of speaking, that's just what we're trying to do. Once she's in Portland, there's a wonderful safe place for her, the home of an older Chinese couple, Mr. and Mrs. Yeung. They have a large home that they operate like a boarding house. She'll live there with a few other young women, and they'll train her to work in one of their businesses as soon as she's ready. But first we have to get her there. Bai Lum," she said, leaning toward him, "I think you're right that we need to move Shu-Li out of the mercantile, but I need a day to get a room made for her in the rectory. I'll send Charles to pick her up tomorrow. In the meantime, do your best to keep her occupied."

Rose thought he looked tremendously relieved at that. "Yes," he said. "I'll make sure she's ready to leave when your husband arrives. What time?"

"I think mid-day is best. People will be busy with the concerns of the day or eating their dinners. Have her all set to go by noon."

"How can I help?" Rose asked. "I could come over this evening and help you get the room prepared."

Lucy shook her head. "Best if you bide your time now. Coming here together was risky enough. I need a chance to talk to Reverend Huntington about all this. If you hear anything worrisome, come see me at home. Otherwise, we'll take care of it."

Rose felt a little deflated, but she agreed.

"Good. Let's go enjoy this lovely day, shall we?"

Bai Lum helped them carry their purchases to the carriage. On the street, Buster dozed in the sun. Lucy affectionately tugged on his forelock, her small hand like a child's next to his brawny head. When they drove away, Rose looked back; Bai Lum had already gone inside. So many questions rattled through her mind, she felt dazed, not sure if she should ask any of them. The image, though, that kept spooling around, was of crowds of girls and young women, all of them miserable, all of them desperate.

"How many are there?" she blurted.

Lucy looked at her equably. "How many?"

"The girls. You said there are more than I can imagine. All from San Francisco?"

"A lot of them, but no, not all. Not by any means." Buster's hooves *clop-clopped* his familiar slow and steady gait, and the sun pulled up a strong smell of salt, drying mud, and green, growing things. Lucy shifted the reins and the carriage took an unexpected right turn. Now they faced the bay, and could see a steep bank of fog, like an ethereal gray range of hills hovering over the ocean.

"Where are we going?"

Lucy clucked her tongue and the horse picked up his pace a bit. "I want to show you something. A little detour."

Two blocks north and a block west, they stopped in front of Salyer's Hotel, three stories at the front and two in the back, the main entrance resplendent with heavy brass door handles. An elegant octagonal cupola room, each side with a window looking out, towered over all. The building dominated most of the block. Lucy, stopped in the middle of the street, craned her head to look up at the hotel. "There are four Chinese women being kept right here."

At first Rose was confused, thinking that the Huntingtons and Bai Lum were hiding more runaways at the hotel. But Lucy's face told her a different story. "Salyer's?" she said. "But Mattie works here. She's never mentioned anything like that going on."

"Clarence Salyer is keeping four women as prostitutes at the hotel, and I've heard that two of them are young, one maybe as young as Shu-Li. Kept against their will, right in the city limits."

"Can't you tell the sheriff?"

"The girls sign a contract, offering themselves as prostitutes. Not that they can read what's put in front of them, but Salyer can fall back on a legally binding document." Lucy chucked the reins and they began to move again. "Whether it's legal or not isn't really the question, is it? Legal or illegal, it's reprehensible.

Rose looked back at Salyer's, its ornate Victorian construction bulking over the street, flawlessly whitewashed, every window clean and reflecting the bright sky back into the day. "So, you're hiding a girl from San Francisco when there are girls right here who need help." She shook her head, incredulous. "That doesn't make sense. Why? Why not hide *these* girls?"

Lucy drove on, looking for all the world like an elderly lady with few earthly concerns. "One of the reasons our enterprise has worked as well as it has, is precisely because the girls come from somewhere else. No one thinks about a runaway girl landing in such a small, remote town." She held up a hand peremptorily when Rose started to object. "Now listen. Being small and remote is also the very reason it would be a serious risk to get one of Salyer's girls away. First of all, and you know this all too well, in a small town there are a great many people ready to mind everyone else's business. Second, we know virtually nothing about them—whether they are in good enough health to run, whether they have the stamina to hide and end up in completely unfamiliar circumstances. These are questions we don't have to ask about the girls who come to us from out of the area; the friends who get them to us ensure that the girls we help are ready."

"How could any of them not be ready?" Rose nearly shouted. "I would think they'd do anything, go anywhere to get away from…from a life like that."

"It's hard to comprehend because you and I have never lived with circumstances so dire. For some of these women, though, it's a matter of 'better the devil you know than the devil you don't.' They're in a country they don't know, have no family or friends to help, and many of them speak very little English. It isn't entirely illogical that in such a state one might come to believe that, bad as life is, it can always become worse."

They rode the last two blocks without speaking, although Rose's silence was a deep, angry frustration. She picked and picked at this information about Salyer's. How many people knew? How could anyone ignore it?

When they stopped in front of the Kendalls', Lucy put her hand on Rose's arm. "Listen for a minute, before you charge off," she said. "It's a terrible thing to find out. Terrible. It isn't something Reverend Huntington and I take lightly. On the contrary—there have been several nights when we've hashed out the possibilities until almost sunrise. Do you believe that?"

"Yes," Rose said. The anger diffused a little, leaving tears in its wake. She looked into Lucy's beautiful calm face, and the kindness there was unmistakable. "It's just so awful."

"Yes it is. It is awful beyond comprehension. So we do what we can to beat back the dark with a little love. A little hope. We help a girl here and there, and when we can find a way to help *all* of them, we will, yes?"

Rose nodded and, not having a handkerchief handy, blotted her eyes on her sleeve.

"Good." She patted Rose briskly on the back. "Now take your aunt's groceries in, have a glass of water, and be sure Hazel knows not to mention Shu-Li to anyone else."

"Simple as that?" Rose said. "Step back into the day like everything is normal as can be."

"That's all you need to do for now."

Rose jumped down from the carriage, already thinking about getting Mattie alone later to find out what she knew about the nasty secret at Salyer's Hotel. She gathered the can of lard and the other things she'd bought. The string of firecrackers was already tucked deep in her coat pocket, a small secret explosion.

□

"Mother of Christ."

Mattie stood straight up from a squat, dropping the bloody sheet as if it was on fire. Ya Zhen stopped churning the laundry. The sheet lay on top of the mound, the stain spread like a map, a dark continent ringed by browning archipelagos. Part of a footprint was clearly visible at one edge. Li Lau had lost a great deal of blood after the birth, it seemed.

Mattie looked from the sheet to Ya Zhen. Her mouth moved as if to speak, but not so much as a whisper crossed her lips. "*Wasser jetzt?*" Ivo yelled hoarsely from the kitchen, making both women startle.

"Not yet," Mattie shouted back. "In a minute." She plucked the sheet up, grimacing, and pushed it back underneath the rest of the pile. She hurried over to the wash tub and dipped her fingertips in and out of the steaming wash water with a little hiss of pain, and wiped them on the bottom hem of her apron. Her eyes searched Ya Zhen's face. "Is that yours?" she whispered.

Ya Zhen shook her head. "Another girl."

Mattie stared. "Is she…is she all right?"

She made no reply, only looked at Mattie's distressed face. Mattie let out a shaky breath and nodded. "We'll need cold water. Lots"

Together, they carried the bathtub off the porch and laid it next to the back wall of the hotel, out of sight. Mattie had Ivo bring out the hot rinse water for the second washtub, and while Ya Zhen used a long paddle to lift the scalding laundry from the soapy tub into the rinse, Mattie dropped the fouled sheet into the bathtub and covered it with cold water. They fetched more water from the kitchen pump. When they came back to the soaking sheet, an opaque veil of red drifted from the fabric. Mattie pursed her lips and reached in, grasping the sheet at two corners and dunking it repeatedly, until the water was completely clouded with blood. When they tilted the tub, it soaked into the bare ground, leaving the dirt faintly stained.

"What is going on out here?" Cora Slayer yelled from the porch. "Is this wash being done or not?"

"Stay here a minute," Mattie murmured. "We're here, missus," she called, stepping out from behind the corner of the building. Then she lowered her voice, in a confidential way. "Just taking care of some stains. Of a certain nature, if you take my meaning, Mrs. Salyer. A monthly nature, you might say, from your girls upstairs."

"*My* girls? I don't...oh shut up," Cora snapped. "I don't need to hear about any of that. Get this damned eyesore finished out here. Do you think we have all day to get the laundry done?" She stomped back into the hotel and slammed the door behind her.

Mattie came back to find Ya Zhen bending over the bathtub, working the sheet hard, scrubbing the fabric together, rinsing, scrubbing again. Mattie took the sheet from her. "That's enough now," she said. "It looks a sight better than it did—not as shocking, anyway. We'll give it some more clean water and let it soak while we do up the rest."

They finished washing and rinsing everything. They ran the wet clothes and wet table linens and wet sheets through the tightened rollers of the mangle. They made three trips and carried everything up to a section of roof on the second story of the hotel that was flat and hidden from view of the street, and they hung everything out on the lines strung there.

"Ya Zhen," Mattie said, not looking directly at her. She held a chemise, probably Cora Salyer's, to the line and plucked clothespins from the big patch pocket of her apron. "What happened to her? The girl."

Ya Zhen had no idea how to answer. The baby happened, but the hotel and the men happened. Clarence Salyer happened, and whatever had come before that. It was Li Lau's life, and it was her own life. "A bad thing," she said finally.

Mattie waited, and Ya Zhen told everything. She told how she was taken away from her home, about the weeping of her little brother Hong Tai, about the long voyage and the girls standing in a line like sheep for sale. She told Mattie about the men who came to the hotel at night, so many she had stopped counting. She told her about Li Lau crying out in the night, and about Old Mol giving the girl whiskey. Finally, she told Mattie about the tiny baby, alive in her hands until he wasn't, and about putting him into the fire. She said it all while she worked, even after Mattie stopped working and stared. She told her story with the voice of one carrying bad news from a great distance, and she kept working because the sun was shining, and on the roof an intermittent breeze flapped the clean wash, making a useful sound, the towels and shirts and clothespins felt real and substantial against her palms, and in the distance the ocean was a blue expanse under a limitless sky.

¤

Byron was most of the way to Billy Kellogg's house when the fire truck pounded down G Street in the direction he had come from, horses at a gallop and the foot-powered bell clanging away. He felt mildly surprised that the town would bother. He and his father had no near neighbors and he doubted there were many who cared a fig whether Garland Tupper's whole house went up in flames, and Garland right along with it. But he knew his father would make the most of the situation, allowing the usual crowd of laid-off loggers and miners in from the outlying hills to buy him a round of drinks at Kennedy's, or one of the even seedier drinking holes near the waterfront. And as soon as he could lay hold of his son, Garland would thrash him, probably try to kill him.

He figured he'd hide out awhile with Billy. He'd lain up at the Kellogg place before when Garland was in a black temper, out in the Kelloggs' back shed. The ramshackle outbuilding warehoused a variety of broken tools and furniture and several flea-ridden hunting dogs. A gaping hole sagged in the far north side of the roof and it was damned hard to get warm at night when the damp came in off the water, which was probably why Byron had had to push one or another hound off his legs whenever he slept there. The Kellogg place was in worse repair than the Tupper house and was overrun with people as well—due, according to Billy, to his parent's devotion to the Popish religion. There were seventeen Kellogg children of various ages, some grown with burgeoning families of their own, but all tending to remain around the home place. Even old Mrs. Kellogg lived there, who was Billy's grandmother and mostly sat in a chair by the stove. She had a great many missing teeth and tended to stare a great deal at anyone who got close. Once Byron had opened the door to the privy and there was old Mrs. Kellogg, perched on the board seat and dozing over her own bare thighs.

This afternoon none of the Kelloggs seemed to know where Billy was, although it was rare that anyone ever knew for sure unless he was in the same room when the question was asked. Byron wandered the place for a few minutes, decided Billy wasn't there, and headed downtown.

The sun was just west of noon and the day felt like deep spring rather than the rump end of winter. Byron circled through a warren of connecting alleys and unfenced yards, keeping his eye out for Billy. Behind the livery, Joe Reilly was nailing a couple of boards over his broken window. Three big nails were clamped between his lips and he struggled to hold a board in place while he hammered.

"Need a hand, Mr. Reilly?"

He looked around, squinting at Byron. He wore a tweed cap and faded brown vest and his dirty shirtsleeves were rolled to the elbow. "Yuh," he grunted around his mouthful of nails. "Hold this here for me while I give it a blow, eh?"

The man obviously had no idea Byron had taken part in the window's breaking. Byron held the board in place and Reilly pounded the nails. The man's hands were creased with dirt and he threw a powerful smell of horse and whiskey. "Too bad about your window," Byron ventured.

"Hoodlums," Reilly grunted. "Miserable little bastards running loose what should be tied to their mama's apron strings."

"Maybe you need a little extra help around here. I could give you a hand with whatever you need, and keep an eye out for trouble, too."

The man scratched one whiskered cheek. His back had a permanent stoop that forced him to look up at the world. "I might could use some help. Have to be a day at a time, though, muck out stalls and such. Are y'afraid of shit, boy?"

"I've shoveled it."

"Ha! Out your mouth like as not, being a Tupper." He hobbled off toward to the side door. "Well, Tupper, come in and show me what kind of help you are."

"How much?"

"Money? More than you started with, which is nothing much, by the look of you. I see you put your back to it, I'll give you two dollars for the afternoon."

Byron thought that sounded fine.

¤

"There you are, Rose. Thank goodness you're back." Prudence Kendall, arranging something in a pitcher, motioned Rose over. "Give me a hand with this, will you? I was telling Mrs. Cleary not three minutes ago that you had the finest way with arrangements. I never seem to be able to get things...I don't know, balanced. I always end up with a bald spot somewhere."

"Ah," said Rose, looking at the clumped mass of plant life in the pitcher and strewn across the table, "it's, um—" There was a heap of woody stems from the backyard camellia bush, studded with a few scruffy pink blooms, many leathery leaves, and not much else.

Prudence laughed. "I know, I know. Just fix it, if you can. There wasn't a lot in the yard to work with. It's not *all* my fault— it's February!"

Rose started pulling the camellia branches apart, trying not to bruise the flowers. Most of them already sported brown spots from rough handling. "I'll go out and find some more to put in here," she told Prudence. She knew there was a little patch of narcissus in the side yard, and figured that the pussy willows down at the back fence had probably sprouted their fuzzy catkins. "Where do you want it when I'm done?"

"The sideboard in the dining room, if you would. Phoebe's coming for dinner tomorrow night." Phoebe was the Kendalls' daughter, who had been married for almost a year to a fresh-faced law clerk named Will, but she still took frequent evening meals without him, at her parents' house. Although Rose thought the world of Prudence and David Kendall, she disliked their daughter and had to work hard to maintain an air of pleasant neutrality when she was around. In Rose's estimation, Phoebe still acted like an indulged child, and her parents seemed besotted by behaviors that Rose found nearly intolerable—simpering chatter about clothing, for instance, had always made Rose want to beat her own head against a wall.

"I was afraid if I waited until tomorrow to cut the flowers," Prudence was saying, "I'd be out doing it in the rain. She might sleep the night, too, so I asked Mrs. Cleary to spruce up her room." It cost Rose some effort not to roll her eyes. *Yes*, she thought, *this will put Hazel in a lovely temper*. Since the wedding, her aunt had several times (in private) shaken her head with a *tsk* and told Rose and Mattie that she found Phoebe's clinginess with her parents "a wee bit peculiar. She's leaving that young husband to his own devices all the time." Rose's opinion was that Phoebe's young husband must find his evenings alone delightfully restful.

"I'll leave you to work your magic, then," Prudence said. "I'm going out for a while." She touched Rose's shoulder. "Thanks for the rescue."

After Mrs. Kendall left, Rose went out to the yard, large shears in hand, and hurriedly collected what she could to finish the arrangement. She usually enjoyed this particular task, but after being with Lucy and Bai Lum, it seemed pointlessly stupid to her, standing at a table fussing over a bunch of cut flowers that would probably be halfway to dead by dinnertime tomorrow. She shoved stems and branches into the pitcher, and in the end had a knobbed and twiggy mass interspersed ludicrously with delicate narcissus cuttings. It was good enough; she knew that as long as it was overly full, Prudence would be satisfied. She carried it to the dining room sideboard before running upstairs to find her aunt.

"Hazel, are you up here?" she called at the top of the stairs.

"Right here," Hazel answered. "Come give me a hand if you're free." She was putting fresh sheets on Phoebe's old bed. "I'm forever changing the linens in here. As if she slept in the bed every night of the week," Hazel grumbled, "when she has a home of her own, a bed of her own, and a man to sleep in the bed with her." She gave the edge of the ground sheet an almighty tug, snapping out any trace of a wrinkle or crease. "So, what have you to say for yourself?"

Rose tried to tread lightly when Hazel took a perturbed mood. "Say for myself?"

"You've been off to the mercantile. Again. I hope you didn't have trouble *today*."

"I went with Lucy Huntington. You know that."

"Mm-hm."

"I got the things on your list." Her voice sounded small and defensive, and that made her mad. As they pulled the comforter up, Rose jerked her side hard enough to pull it out of Hazel's grasp. Hazel grabbed it back, her eyes snapping blue fire.

Rose huffed exasperatedly. "Don't be mad at *me*," she said in a rough whisper. "I just had to make a centerpiece out of sticks and weeds."

Hazel glared, but then she pursed her lips, trying not to smile. "Let's finish this before we brawl," she said.

Rose plumped a pillow, her face hot. "Aunt, something did happen this morning—no, now, don't get in a huff again."

"Does it involve Elsie Dampler?" Hazel asked, in a *please, not again* tone of voice.

"Remember yesterday I told you that Bai Lum has a sister?"

"I do."

"Yes, well, she's the reason Lucy asked me to come with her this morning to the mercantile." Her heart sped up as she reasoned out just how much to tell. "The sister, Shu-Li is her name, she's...she's a secret."

Hazel looked hard at her. She didn't suffer fools lightly, and Rose knew she wasn't going to tolerate a lot of equivocation. "What is it you're really trying to tell me, girl? Better to heave it off your chest and be done."

Rose plunged in. "Shu-Li isn't really Bai Lum's sister. He told me yesterday that she was, but it wasn't true. She's a girl that the Huntingtons are helping, and Bai Lum is helping by letting her stay with him." The words tumbled out in a rush. "After I saw Shu-Li in the store, Lucy thought they might just as well tell me the truth, and Bai Lum was worried, too, because of what happened yesterday, and since you were the only one I told about Shu-Li, Lucy hoped I could ask you to keep the secret." Rose sat down on the blanket chest at the foot of the bed, feeling deflated, but relieved.

Hazel sat beside her. "What happened yesterday—so you *are* talking about Elsie Dampler."

They sat there for a few moments, saying nothing. Somewhere, blocks away, the fire truck bell sounded, growing fainter as it raced to its destination. Hazel shook her head. "Troubles, troubles," she said. "I can see by the look on your face that there's more to it, but I'm not going to ask why they're hiding her. You can stop worrying—I won't breathe a word. But maybe I can help."

"No need," Rose told her. "Reverend Huntington and Lucy are going to make a place for Shu-Li to stay with them until they can take her out of town."

Hazel shook her head again and stood. "Come on. Let's us make a quick supper for the Kendalls and stow it in the warmer. I think we need an early day. I'm feeling my age this afternoon."

An hour later, while her aunt penned a note for Prudence, Rose waited on the stoop of the wide front porch, sweaty from mopping up. She swung her legs, letting the heels of her boots bump gently against the bricks. Hazel seemed satisfied that the Huntingtons were taking care of their problem, and that was good. She wanted to see for herself, if she could, what was going on at Salyer's Hotel. With her aunt's guard down, getting out of the house tonight would be much easier.

¤

By the time Charles Huntington came upstairs at the end of the afternoon, Lucy was hard at work in a small storage room at the end of the second-floor hallway in the rectory. "I know you must be up here somewhere," he called, picking his way through the detritus she had pulled out into the hall: a wooden box of mismatched, cracked, and chipped china; moldering bedding that had been too stained or threadbare to use for quilts or rags; the rusted hulk of a dressmaker's form that looked like a large birdcage with bosoms.

"You found me." She was wearing an old dress, hair swathed in a rag, attacking cobwebs in the upper corners with a broom. The floor was bare, except for a moth-eaten daybed, a battered end table, and a wicker rocking chair with a hole the size of a tea saucer in the caned seat. "These can stay," she said, rubbing the end of her nose with the back of one hand. "I can cover them well enough to use."

Charles stepped over a box and into the room. Two arched windows at the top of the far wall let in a little light, and the ceiling sloped at an angle, forcing him to duck slightly. "This should be fine," he said. "She won't need it long."

"I told Bai Lum you'd come for her tomorrow at noon."

He nodded. "Good. I've decided to take her north first thing Monday morning."

"Four days? Will they be ready for her?"

"I wish the telegraph was working, but wishing never gets the cows milked. No matter, though. They'll do what has to be done."

Lucy looked around. "Little Shu-Li is a bit of a wanderer, apparently. That's how Rose caught sight of her—she went right into the store during the day," she said. "I hope I can convince her not to wander downstairs while we're in church Sunday."

"No one in the rectory this Sunday, then, not even in the kitchen." Charles fingered the wide hole in the wicker chair. "Why did anyone keep this?"

"All for the best," she said. "I'll put a cushion on that chair and make up the daybed with quilts. Can you bring that small lamp from the parlor, though? It's already getting dark in here."

They gathered the rubbish that had come out of the storage room and carried it out to the stable in three loads. Charles made a humorous apology to the dressmaker's dummy before wresting it down the narrow stairs. After making the accommodations as comfortable as she could, the last thing Lucy did was poke around the rectory library for anything that had pictures. She found some old copies of *Godey's Lady's Book*, a children's reading primer, and an illustrated volume of *Black Beauty*. Upstairs, she placed the books on the table next to the lamp, and stood back for one last look at the room—she thought it would serve for just the few days of Shu-Li's stay. Satisfied, she closed the door behind her and went down to start supper and to tell Charles about her talk with Rose and Bai Lum. She had not the slightest inkling that Shu-Li would never lay eyes on the little upstairs room.

¤

Old man Reilly made Byron earn every last cent of his pay, not only shoveling stalls but hefting bales of hay and sacks of grain. He climbed into the loft with a broom and knocked down generations of spiders while several barn cats eyed him from different corners of the upper space. One was a young tom, all black, with a long sleek body. Pearl's hair was just that color. Throughout the long afternoon, he thought about her exquisite face, how pleased she would be when he told her that he wanted to marry her. He'd have to find a place for them as soon as he could. Remembering the line of men waiting in the hallway outside her door made Byron feel ill. He picked up a broken chunk of an old bridle and hurled it at the cat, which fled the loft with a yowling spit. A cloud of chaff floated in banded motes where narrow sheaves of sun fell through the unchinked board walls. Perhaps he could bring Pearl here, show her how beautiful it was. He'd lay out a pile of fresh hay for them and she would open herself to him. In her arms, her legs, deep inside the heat of her, Byron knew he would find himself home, finally.

At the end of it, Joe Reilly spent a half-hour nit-picking Byron's work and several minutes scuffling around in his dingy side room while Byron waited, shifting impatiently from one foot to the other. Finally, Reilly reappeared, wiping his nose on a voluminous and none-too-fresh bandanna. "Listen," he said, "I can give you your two for today, but if you let me hold onto it, you can come back tomorrow and earn another two, with four bits thrown in extra. It's a good offer," he said, and wiped his nose again.

Byron took off his cap and slapped at his soiled and chaff-studded britches. "If I want my wages now?"

"Got it right here." The old man tapped his breast pocket. "Thing is, though, if you need it pronto, I guess I won't need any help tomorrow."

Throughout the long day, he'd worked a regular stint at the livery into his fantasies, and didn't relish going around, cap in hand, just to feed himself. "Yeah, that'll do. What time do you want me?"

"Not too early. Make it nine o'clock."

"I'll be here." He'd be here long before that. He had already decided to loiter around town and then sneak back into the livery to sleep tonight. It would be a suitable place to bring Pearl for a while, too—not that he would ask Mr. Reilly about that. Byron would hide her in the loft during the day and have every night with her there, until he found them more secure accommodations.

¤

The bloody sheet would not come all the way clean, but the stain had paled to pink and yellow marks, like a fading bruise. It was the last thing to come off the line, the final bit to be pressed and folded and put away. Mattie performed all these tasks mechanically, moving as if her bones had turned to glass. Her head pounded with a terrible headache that had started as a small throb at the base of her skull and spread up and around so that now even her eyes and teeth hurt, and she felt bathed in a murky sweat.

It was so odd. The more awful things Ya Zhen had told her, the lighter and brighter the girl seemed to get, while every word landed on Mattie like a chunk of granite. Before they finished pegging out the laundry, Ya Zhen was smiling, her hands flying through the damp baskets, briskly snapping out a shirt here, a chemise there. She purposely alternated a long row of handkerchiefs and tea towels so that they resembled a line of festive white flags, and laughed when showing Mattie how they flapped in a wave when the breezed flirted through. Meanwhile, Mattie moved more and more slowly, feet dragging as if she were fording a shallow creek.

Matilda, you're an idiot, she thought now, folding the sheet and slipping it into a pile of the Chinese women's things, stuff that Old Mol would take upstairs herself. Had she not known the Chinese women lived in the hotel? Of course she had—she'd been doing scullery work and laundry with the Wu sisters since the day she'd started. And Ya Zhen, slipping into the kitchen each week to fetch bath water, so quiet and still she seemed almost transparent. Mattie had given her little gifts in the hopes she might cheer Ya Zhen, to perhaps build a bridge of friendship and trust. She had simply assumed that Ya Zhen and the other young girl—Mattie couldn't recall her name, and it made her head pound fiercely when she tried—did some other menial labor in the hotel, perhaps in exchange for their room and board. *They do*, she thought. *My God, they do.* She refolded the sheet so that the worst part of the remaining stain was clearly visible, and placed it squarely on top of everything.

The broad plank they used for ironing, laid across the backs of two sturdy chairs, had been put away. The last thing to do before leaving was return the three flat irons to a shelf in the kitchen, and put on a final kettle of water to heat; Ivo—now gone on his own early dinner break—would use it later for a final washing of pots and pans. She filled the pot at the kitchen pump and hoisted it to the cooling stovetop, trying to hold her pounding head steady.

The fire in the big stove had burned low. Hands shaking, she opened the top lid of the firebox. Instead of putting in fresh kindling, she picked up Ivo's big meat fork and gently spread the remaining coals apart. There was very little ash, since most of it fell through into the pan below as it burned, but there were several inches of white and yellow embers, perking to a fresh burn as the oxygen hit them. The skin on her fingers and the back of her hand seemed to shrink in the heat, and she shook enough now that the tines of the fork clittered a tattoo against the cast iron.

There, toward the back. A cup of bone not much bigger than an eggshell, but thicker, blackened and jagged at the edges, smooth as a china cup on the inside. The trembling fork slipped through her fingers and clattered into the firebox, sending up a tiny shower of white sparks. Not thinking, she grabbed after it. Radiant pain lit her hand and seemed to fire off nerve endings throughout her whole body. Without a sound, she plunged her burned hand, fork and all, into the cool pot of water.

When Ivo returned several minutes later, the big stove blazed, so heavily stoked that he felt the heat of it before he even got into the kitchen. The kettle of dishwater boiled madly, throwing gouts onto the stove top in steaming confusion. He threw open the back door, as well as the window over the sink, then reached into the pulsing heat to push the stove damper almost closed. In a minute, smoke began to trickle from around the burner lids and the firebox. He fanned the kitchen with a towel, flapping it in tremendous arcs, swearing fluently in German. Sweat poured from his face and dripped off his blunt chin. When the pot of water had dropped back to a reasonable simmer and Ivo could no longer hear the roar of burning wood, he opened the oven door to cool the stove even faster. Using the heavy towel to protect his hands, he hurried the kettle over to the sink and poured it into the outsized dishpan. His big meat fork landed in the metal pan with a splash and a bang, making him flinch. One side of its slender wooden handle was scorched completely black.

CHAPTER FIVE

OLD MOL MIGHT THREATEN, but if the men did not come, there was nothing she could do about it. Hard rain, their holidays—these things sometimes made a difference, though not always. Other times business got quiet for no discernible reason. Always, it was a gift, and tonight, especially so.

Ya Zhen had been forced upstairs not long after she and Mattie finished hanging the wash. They had just returned to the back porch to set up a board for ironing when Clarence Salyer appeared from the kitchen.

"Hm," he said. "Ain't this tender? You girls sure do work hard. Can't tell you how much I appreciate it." He crossed his arms on top of his meager pot belly and slouched with one shoulder against the door jamb. "I guess you're showing my girl here a thing or two, eh Irish?"

Mattie stiffened. She'd gone almost silent on the roof—the happier Ya Zhen got, the more Mattie seemed to pull into herself. Now she looked almost rigid. "I'm glad for the help," she said through her teeth.

Clarence smiled. "My pleasure. Don't let me interrupt. You go ahead with it, now. I'll just watch awhile."

Ya Zhen was already ironing a pillowcase. She didn't think Salyer would approach her here, where others could see, but she wasn't sure. Her hand bore down on the handle of the iron, relishing the heat and heaviness. Mattie came alongside, putting herself between Ya Zhen and Salyer, and began to furiously press handkerchiefs, needing only a few seconds to iron and fold each one. Ya Zhen didn't look at Salyer, but she could see him leaning there, and could smell the sweet grease he put in his hair.

He glanced over his shoulder to where Ivo was at work in the kitchen, then back at Mattie. "I expect she could teach you some things, too," he muttered.

Mattie slammed the iron on the board and folded the handkerchief with a couple of deft strokes. "Maybe," she said, her voice careless on top and steel underneath. "Mrs. Salyer was here a little while ago. Probably she'll be checking on us again. I'll be sure to mention your idea to her." She slapped the handkerchief down with the others and grabbed up a new one. "I'm sure she'll be glad to know that you were here, praising us. Keeping us company."

Salyer straightened out of his slouch. He said nothing, but his breath sounded as though he'd done some hard running. "Looks like you can handle the rest of this on your own," he snapped. "You," he said to Ya Zhen, cocking his head inside. "Upstairs. We have some things to talk over."

"We aren't near done!" Mattie said. "Mrs. Salyer wants—"

Clarence Salyer took two large steps and put his face next to Mattie's, so that their foreheads nearly touched. "Mrs. Salyer wants the laundry done, Irish. That's *her* concern. This one, though," he said, taking Ya Zhen by the bicep, "has other work. That's *my* concern." With his free hand, he grasped Ya Zhen's chin and sniffed at her like a dog would, all around her neck and hairline. His breath was thick with whiskey and onion. Ya Zhen closed her eyes. She heard Mattie's sharp intake of breath, and her own free hand clutched the iron tighter, tighter, so that her whole arm began to shake. Salyer clamped his hand over hers. "Now, now," he said into her ear. "We wouldn't want you to have an accident with this." She could barely open her fingers, and he pried them apart until the iron thudded onto the board. "Best pick that up," he crooned to Mattie, "if you like your job. My dear wife would be so upset if you scorched something." He pushed Ya Zhen ahead of him and into the hotel. She risked a single look back; Mattie's face was chalky white and furious. As they climbed the stairs, his breath, rank and warm, played across her neck.

He stayed in her room a very long time.

Now it was almost full dark. After Salyer went out, she had washed herself all over, imagining the deep washtub, filled to the brim with boiling water and brown soap, imagined lowering herself into that scalding barrel and turning, turning, until her skin loosened from her muscles, and she could step out into the morning, something different, something terrible and clean.

Naked, she built a fire in the grate with a small split of kindling, then slipped into her dressing gown and pushed the window open as far as she could. It had begun to rain lightly, and the smell, after a day of warm sun, was sweet. A few voices and a bit of horse traffic were audible down in the street, but they had a sparse, muffled quality. She turned the chair so that it faced away from the bed, and removed two or three hairpins that Clarence Slayer hadn't torn free; she slowly worked out knots and snarls.

Three years ago, when he had brought her to Eureka on the ship, he had hurried her straight from the dock to the hotel and into the room she had haunted ever since. Her only view was the small section of street visible from her window, and the scraggly yard outside the kitchen. But on the roof today, she had been able to turn in a complete circle and see everything—not just the water and the sky, but almost the entire town. Whitewashed houses and church spires, a grid of dirt roads hemmed by wooden sidewalks, wrought iron fences and ornate storefronts with hand-lettered signs that she could not read. She saw piles of logs—stripped of bark and incredibly long—some heaped on land, others floating in clustered confusion at the water's edge. Smoke rose from at least a half-dozen timber mills along the coast. To the north, just visible, was another town, and to the east, forested hills that reminded her, achingly, of the mountains around her village. Combing, remembering the sun on her arms and face, and the salt smell of the ocean, she didn't feel the places that hurt, couldn't smell the stink of Salyer. Didn't feel Li Lau's baby in the palms of her hands.

It was so quiet. No voices in the hallway. No sounds from the next room, and none of the usual muttered conversation between Wu Song and Wu Lin across the hall. Not even Old Mol's heavy tread around the stairs or her voice barking at the men as they came and went, came and went. After almost fifteen minutes alone, Ya Zhen stole a look into the hall—no one there. Scanning the corridor in both directions, she slipped the comb into her pocket, gave the sash of her robe a tight pull, and tiptoed out. She rested her hand on Li Lau's doorknob and put her ear close. No sound. Slowly, ready to bolt back if she needed to, she cracked open the door and peeked in.

The lamp was not lit and no fire built, but the last hint of lingering twilight from the window showed her Li Lau's small self, huddled beneath the blankets. Ya Zhen went to her. "Are you asleep?" she whispered. The girl was on her back, so still, and Ya Zhen's breathing seemed loud in the silent room. She leaned down and put her hand on Li Lau's face. It was soft and warm. She sighed and curled over, tucking her hands under her cheek like a child; a wave of relief fell over Ya Zhen. The room was cool, so she built a little fire. By the light of the flames, she could see a plate on the washstand—buttered bread and some sort of meat. She hadn't eaten since breakfast and her stomach reacted loudly to the sight of the food. Wrapping the meat in the bread, she ate it all in a few quick bites. She went to Li Lau and listened to her regular breathing, looked around the room, pushed Li Lau's bucket closer to the bed. There was nothing else to do.

Back in her own room, she wiped grease from her fingers, put another stick of wood on the fire, and felt able to put the bed in order. She sat in the chair again, pulling her feet onto the seat, folding herself in half so that she could rest her head on her knees. No one came. Cool air from the window and the warmth of the fire created a pleasurable round of sensation, and she watched the shifting flames, holding her comb in one hand, running her thumb over the smooth points of its teeth. No one came. The distant sounds of people and horses in the street had stopped entirely, and the only sound was the rain.

No one came.

¤

"Get her a glass of water, Rose." Hazel Cleary's wooden medicine box was on the kitchen table, and she took out a rolled bandage. Mattie's blistered palm was shiny with ointment Hazel made from honey, beeswax, and calendula flowers. She winced a little as Hazel began to gently wind the clean strip of rag around her hand. Rose handed her the water, and Mattie sipped at it.

"Tell me how you did this?" Hazel said.

"Again?"

"Again." Hazel used small scissors to carefully cut the end of the rag into twin tails. These she tied together to secure the bandage at the wrist.

Mattie took another long swallow of water. "I took hold of a skillet handle that had just come out of the oven. It was a stupid mistake—I was in a hurry."

"This will do for now," Hazel said. "I'll check it again in the morning and see if those blisters have gotten any bigger." She tucked everything back into the chest and clicked the latch in place. "What I don't understand," she said, "is how you burned the skin on the top of your hand, too—by grabbing a hot skillet." She tilted her head, obviously waiting for an answer.

"It's laundry day," Mattie said. Her voice was threadbare with fatigue.

Hazel and Rose exchanged a glance over Mattie's head and Hazel patted Mattie on the back. "You'll not be able to work tomorrow, at any rate," Hazel said. "Not at anything Cora Salyer would set you to do."

"Oh ho," Mattie said. "Cora Salyer would love to fire me. I have to go and just make the best of it." She drank the last of her water and got to her feet. "Thanks for this," she said, waving her bandaged hand.

"We'll see about that in the morning," Hazel said emphatically. "Now, I'm going to make some beef broth. You need the protein to heal. Rose, get this one tucked in—she'll need some help tonight, and don't you dare argue, Matilda Gillen."

Mattie raised both hands as if in surrender. "I have a beastly headache, too. I must be coming down with something."

Hazel's brow furrowed and she looked Mattie over. She laid the back of her hand on the young woman's forehead, which looked clammy. "Yes, you're sick," Hazel said quietly. "You get into bed, darling."

Rose followed her upstairs. This morning Mattie had been a bit ragged, smudges under the eyes, but tonight her cheeks were gray. There were large patches of perspiration on her dress and Rose had seen her unbandaged hand shaking when she held her water glass. She looked worse right now than she had last night while muzzy and disoriented in Hazel's pantry.

In her room, Mattie dropped onto the bed in a slump. With an elbow propped on her knees, she cradled her head in her unburned hand and began to cry, dry wracking sobs that put a knot in Rose's stomach. After the trouble last night, it seemed that Mattie—who was always so tough and cheerful to Rose, a kindred soul—was deconstructing before her eyes. Part of her wished she could help Mattie into her nightgown, then run across the hall and slide into her own bed with *Great Expectations*. Instead, she sat next to Mattie. "Tell me."

Mattie tilted her head back, eyes streaming and nose running. "She put a baby in the stove," she moaned. "They made her do it, Rose. Merciful Jesus, she burned a little baby." She lifted her skirt and sobbed into it.

Horror nailed Rose in place. The words *baby in the stove* seemed to echo around the room. She wanted to touch Mattie, but her hands wouldn't move, wanted to say something calming, but her breath died in her throat. Was this some sort of weird hallucination? Had she smoked opium again? There was none of the garbled lethargy or bad smell that had been there last night, but Rose had to admit she didn't have the vaguest idea what to look for. Finally, she stood, her movements spastic as a marionette's. "Mattie," she whispered. Mattie kept crying. "Mattie!" she said, trying to get Matilda's attention without rousing Hazel.

She jerked one of Mattie's shoulders sharply. "Stop it, now," she hissed.

Mattie looked up at Rose then, and the eye contact seemed to bring her back. Her shoulders hitched as she worked to stop the tears. Rose went to the bureau and got a handkerchief; Mattie wiped her face, then balled the hanky in her good hand and rocked back and forth, catching her breath.

"I'm feeling very sick, Rose."

"So you said. Coming down with something."

"Aye. Everything hurts."

"I'm going to help you to bed. But first you're going to tell me just what the hell you mean. A baby—" She swallowed hard. "A baby in the *stove*, Matilda? What in God's name are you talking about?"

Mattie nodded, as if giving herself permission to speak. "There are girls who live at the hotel. Chinese girls."

Rose's mouth opened, a small O of surprise. "Yes," she said, the word a little whistle of sound in the room.

Mattie's gray face was now blotched red, and she stared at Rose. "You knew?"

"No, I didn't...I just found out this morning. Mrs. Huntington told me about them when we—" Here she stammered, realizing she had very nearly told Mattie about Shu-Li.

"They're like captives, Rose," Mattie said. She stood shakily and began wandering a slow circuit of the room, touching the furniture for balance as she went. "I should say they *are* captives. All this time, I thought they were just...I don't know. Servants. I thought they were hired help for Mrs. Salyer." She sagged against the washstand, causing the ewer to joggle noisily in its bowl.

Rose took her by the arm. "Come back over here and sit. I'll get your buttons." She opened Mattie's dress at the collar, and Mattie lifted her chin like an obedient child being undressed at bath time. Rose hesitated, her heart thudding. "Mattie, listen. I want you to tell me now, what you meant about a baby. Shh...not like that. Slow down and just tell me." Mattie held the wadded hanky to her mouth, as if to stifle whatever awful thing wanted to pass her lips. Suddenly she stood and rushed to the washbowl and vomited, a terrible grinding retch that brought up nothing but the water she'd just drunk. Two times, three times she heaved, then hovered over the bowl, bracing herself on both hands, even the burned palm, and shuddered violently. She moaned.

"Come on," Rose murmured. She managed to slide Mattie's sweat-stained dress off her shoulders and slip her soiled chemise off as well. It was shocking to see how thin she was—her visible ribcage appeared more prominent than her tiny breasts, and her hips were almost as straight as a boy's. Didn't she ever eat? "Lift your arms. Good girl." She pulled the clean nightgown on over Mattie's head. Then she held her friend's elbow, not trusting her to walk under her own power, shaking as she was. She turned down the bed and Mattie climbed obediently in. Rose dampened a second hanky in the pitcher and wiped Mattie's face, her mouth, her neck. "You are sick," she said. "You need to rest now."

"The opium," Mattie said, her voice such a croaky whisper Rose had to bend close to hear. "Stopping. Was never this bad before." Her teeth started to chatter.

Rose pulled the blankets in around her and, despite everything, felt a wash of relief—Mattie was keeping her promise. "You'll be okay," she told her. "Aunt will think you have the grippe. Try to rest."

Mattie turned on her side. Tears dripped across the bridge of her nose and make a dark spot on the pillowcase. "Rose," she muttered, "her name is Ya Zhen."

"Ya Zhen?"

"She told me today. It's not her fault." Mattie moaned and curled into a fetal position.

"Never mind," Rose said, although she wished she could sit Mattie up and demand some answers. "Don't think about it now. Try to sleep, if you can."

She gathered the soiled clothes and the washbowl and hurried downstairs. Hazel was stirring the broth when Rose came through the kitchen. "She's sick," Rose said. "She'll need a bucket by the bed." She went directly into the backyard. It was very nearly raining again, and goose bumps rose on her arms. She dropped Mattie's clothes on the back porch and worked the pump handle. Rinsing the fouled washbowl, she tried not to gag at the sour smell of vomit; it was probably a blessing that Mattie hadn't eaten much today. Finally, she washed her own hands and face and carried the clean bowl inside.

Hazel had a bucket in one hand and her medicine box under the other arm. She pointed to the pot of broth. "I'll go check on her. Put some of that in a bowl and bring it up. You should probably have some too." Marching up the stairs, she called back, "We can't have everyone getting sick around here."

"I think we'll be fine," Rose said, and—horribly—laughed. She clapped a hand to her mouth. No response from Hazel—thank God, she must be upstairs already. From the cupboard she fetched a bowl, and the china vibrated a little rhythm, one dish against another. She set the bowl down and gave her hands a brisk shake, as if she could knock the tremble out of them. Ladling the broth, Mattie's words spun through her like a top, coming around again and again: *merciful Jesus, she burned a little baby.* The first part of her plan for the evening, concocted while she sat on the Kendalls' stoop, had been to get Mattie alone after Hazel retired, and find out what she might know about the Chinese girls. There'd be no more talking with her tonight, but perhaps that was fine because now Rose had more than Lucy's information: she had a name. *Her name is Ya Zhen*, Mattie had said. *It's not her fault.*

After taking the tray of broth upstairs, she crossed the hall to her own room. Even with the doors closed she heard more retching, and Hazel's soothing voice. Rose's book was on the bedside table. She dropped into the upholstered chair by the window and opened to the place she had left off reading, but couldn't anchor her thoughts on the troubles of Pip and Miss Havisham; her eyes grazed the page like sliding over a frozen pond. Earlier in the day, she decided she'd convince Mattie to get her into the hotel somehow so she could see the women for herself. Staring down at the book, Rose realized her jaw was clenched so hard her teeth felt in danger of breaking. She tossed the book onto the bed and leaned on the window sill. It faced south, and other than the few houses nearby, it showed nothing but dark and more dark. Her breath made a hazy little cloud on the glass. Even now, she imagined storming into the hotel all on her own, could feel her entire body kindling to the idea of making a terrible scene until—in shame—the Salyers brought the girl to her (she was *Ya Zhen* now, not "the girl," and oh, whatever was happening to her seemed so much worse because of that).

Her fantasy reached no further than her expression of righteous indignation. The Huntingtons would take the next step. Thinking of Bai Lum and Lucy—of the things they had done already, all their care and risk—slowed her barreling train of thought. Better Harriet Tubman than Joan of Arc. Stealth, not just discretion, might prove to be the better part of valor. She couldn't go to the hotel.

But she knew who could.

She grabbed her heavy wool cape from the wardrobe and stepped into the hall, closing the bedroom door behind her as silently as she could. Pausing to listen at Mattie's room, she heard nothing. Hazel might still be in there, but she may also have slipped out without Rose hearing her go. She crept downstairs, holding her breath and listening. At the foot of the stairs she still heard nothing. She threw the cape around her shoulders and slipped out the front door, wincing when the latch clicked shut. On the wet street, she pulled up the broad hood so that no part of her face showed, and hurried, once again, to the mercantile.

¤

Byron Tupper was afraid to bed down in the livery too early, figuring that Mr. Reilly would be less likely to come around later at night. He wasn't sure what to do with himself, though. It had started to rain again, and he was famished. At some of the

waterfront saloons he could get food; Kennedy's would serve a plate
of potatoes and a chop, but he didn't want to risk running into his
father. He was certain Garland was looking for him, so he moved
through town sticking to back alleys. It seemed as though everyone
must be cooking supper—the smells were everywhere. Finally,
after more than an hour of spooking around, he got lucky. Down
one alley, a group of small, ramshackle houses had been slapped
together almost on top of each other; several of these had neither
rear yards nor fences. Slipping past one place, Bryon realized he
was looking through a steamy window straight into a kitchen. The
door stood ajar, perhaps to let some heat out, and an old woman
bent over a stove on the far side of the room. On the table behind
her stood a steaming bowl of stewed cabbage and a pan of biscuits.
Acting quickly before he could lose his nerve, Byron stepped right
into the room, grabbed three biscuits with one hand and the entire
serving bowl of cabbage. He expected to hear the woman shout
after him, but she didn't seem to hear a thing. Still, in case she
raised an alarm over the pilfered grub, he trotted several blocks
away before tucking himself under a dripping eave and dipping
into the bowl. The biscuits were tough, but the cabbage, which he
had to scoop with his fingers, was cooked in bacon fat and onions,
and was hot and good. He ate until he was almost bursting, and
after a mighty belch left the bowl sitting atop a fencepost.

It was still too soon to sneak into the livery, but he was
warmed and energized by the food. He decided he'd make his way
over to Salyer's. He couldn't spend any money there tonight—not
with a wife in his near future—but he wanted just to look at the
building, knowing Pearl was there. Perhaps, if he waited in the
street below, she would look out her window at him. Maybe she
would even wave. His gut burned thinking that other men might be
there with her, and he hoped she would tell them to leave her
alone. The two of them had shared something so good last night. In
his memory she had openly welcomed him, had been tender and
demure. The love he felt was so obviously reciprocated—surely she
would refuse anyone else. When he reached 2nd Street, he first

went around to the rear of the hotel and was greatly cheered when he saw that no men waited around the back stairs—maybe the wet weather was keeping them away. He retreated to the side of the building and positioned himself across the street in a dry doorway alcove that lent him a clear view of Pearl's window. Nothing in the room was visible except the ceiling, but he saw low lamplight flicker on the sheer yellow curtain. The other windows nearest hers were dark.

Pulling back as far as he could, he kept an eye on that yellow window, imagined how delighted she would be to know he was here, keeping watch. So intent was he on catching the least glimpse of her face, Byron failed entirely to notice Garland standing a half-block over, even though his father made little effort to stay out of sight.

¤

The street running through Chinatown was deserted, except for the skinny shadow of a cat that crept along the muddy gutter, probably hunting. When Rose got near, it pelted away, disappearing between two buildings. Her nerves were frayed, but she told herself the anxiety was due to the terrible thing Mattie had said—and not that she was out alone, in the dark, taking yet another trip to the mercantile. Still, it was a relief that the only other people she saw on her walk over were in carriages. No one seemed to be out on foot except her, but she kept her face well-submerged in the hood of her cloak.

At the mercantile, she couldn't think of any way to get Bai Lum's attention, other than knocking at the door of the storefront. She hated to make that much noise, but she'd certainly attract even more attention if she shouted up from the street. For one ridiculous moment she imagined tossing a handful of pebbles at his upstairs windows, as the White Rabbit had done when Alice was stuck in his house, and Rose had to stifle a gust of nervous laughter; with her typical grace, she'd undoubtedly end up hurling a rock through the glass. The shades had been drawn on all the windows that fronted the street, and the store itself was dark. She rapped at the door, a tentative knock, but the noise seemed unconscionably loud in the quiet evening. She shrank even deeper into her cape and waited, counting slowly under her breath. When she got to twenty-five, she tried again, five heavy knocks. A bit of reflected light moved on the sidewalk. She pushed back her hood and looked up. There was the round face of Shu-Li looking down at her. Rose waved and pointed at the door. "Tell Bai Lum," she whispered, hoping the girl would read her lips or understand her pantomime. Shu-Li smiled and waved again. Before Rose could respond, the glow of a lamp showed through the oilcloth shades, and Bai Lum opened the door.

"Rose." He cracked the door only a few inches. "What is it?" His face was grave, his usual welcoming smile nowhere evident.

"I have to...I'm hoping you might—" she stammered, nonplussed by his reticence. She glanced into the street, abruptly certain that someone would see her here, at night and alone. "Please, Bai Lum, may I come in? I need your help," she whispered.

He hesitated just long enough to make her think that he was going to turn her away, close the door in her face. Instead, he nodded and stepped aside. When she was in, he glanced out at the street, much as she had, then closed and locked the door.

Her stomach churned, trying to decide how to explain why she'd come. "I'm so sorry to disturb you this way, and I'm wet, too," she said. "I probably shouldn't have come, but Mattie is sick and I don't think I can do it myself, because—"

"Come with me," he said, and started for the rear of the store.

"Come where?"

"Upstairs."

"Upstairs?" All the admonitions drummed into her since childhood, the dire social strictures regarding unmarried men and women being alone together, clamored for her attention. She looked at the paper kites, swaying in their shadowy world near the ceiling, and took a breath. "Of course."

He held the kerosene lamp so that they could both see, and led her back into the store and through the plum-colored curtain.

The small alcove where Rose had seen Shu-Li peeping at her yesterday opened into a larger storage area. It was filled with marked bags of oats and rice, barrels that bled salt from the cured meat inside. Two garden spades leaned against the wall next to a large coil of hemp rope. On the far right side, a narrow stairway. Bai Lum led the way, his steps quiet, Rose's boots louder on the wood risers. Near the top was a ninety-degree landing. A tall window looked out on E Street and probably out to the bay, though there was only dark now. Rose paused there, gathering courage. When Bai Lum realized she had stopped, he turned.

"Well," she said. "Well—"

He simply stood, looking at her. His face had lost the guarded expression, and now seemed curious, but patient. *I can wait*, that expression seemed to say. *Whenever you're ready.* They were almost of equal height, and Rose saw that his eyes, in the light of the lamp, were a clear brown that was almost amber. After a moment, he leaned forward so that his cheek rested wholly against hers. No other part of their bodies touched; only his face, skin smooth over a hard jaw, placed by hers. His lips were near her ear and when he put his nose into her hair and breathed deeply, she closed her eyes. Then he straightened.

Rose nodded. "Fine, then," she said, a little breathlessly.

He led her the rest of the way up.

When they entered his rooms, Rose immediately had the feeling of being in a place apart. Ivory curtains covered the tall double-hung windows, which she knew must let in a great deal of afternoon light. Over the small fireplace, red satin draped the mantel. An altar was there—a bowl of rice, some apples, several sticks of incense standing in a dish of sand. A black vase held a single spray of pale cherry blossoms—*oh yes*, she thought, *these bloom in February, too*, picturing the awful arrangement she had mashed together for Prudence Kendall. Although the board walls were roughly milled, Bai Lum had softened their appearance with more fabric, hung like paneled curtains. Parchments with long lines of intricate characters painted in calligraphy were above the altar. A fringed carpet covered the floor. The room smelled of the incense, a rich woody odor Rose could almost taste.

"Bai Lum. Your home is—it's beautiful."

He finally smiled. "Welcome."

Shu-Li looked in from the other room. Her eyes widened and she looked back and forth between the two of them.

"Shu-Li, *jìn lái,*" he said, motioning to her. The girl stepped forward and stood next to him.

Rose held out her hand. "Hello, Shu-Li." She put her other hand on her chest. "My name is Rose Allen." Shu-Li smiled and touched Rose's hand tentatively.

"I'm very glad to meet you," Rose said, and Bai Lum translated.

"Yes," Shu-Li said. *Yes, yes,* just as she had said in the mercantile yesterday. "English," she said carefully.

Rose smiled. "Yes, English."

"Yes. English." Shu-Li beamed, obviously proud of herself. Bai Lum spoke a few words; the girl nodded and left the room, still smiling.

"She's a quick learner," Rose said.

"She's been getting ready to go to the Huntingtons' tomorrow," he said. "Will you sit?" He led her to a low divan under the windows and sat next to her. One window was open a few inches and the curtain rippled softly.

"Tomorrow. Right. That's what I want to talk to you about." He only waited for her to continue, and she took a deep breath, wanting to somehow inhale the sense of deliberate stillness he seemed to carry with him always. "After Mrs. Huntington and I left here this morning, she drove me past Salyer's Hotel."

There was the smallest flicker across his face. "I know the hotel," he said. "There are two sisters there who sometimes buy things at my store."

Rose sat straight. "What else do you know?" she asked. Then she rushed on. "Did you know that they keep women there—girls, really—that they keep them for—" The flush lit her throat and cheeks, but she forced herself to say it. "Clarence Salyer makes the girls live as prostitutes. The same as Shu-Li in San Francisco."

"Have you noticed, Rose, all the men here in Chinatown? How many times have you seen a woman?" He looked at her steadily. "A Chinese woman, I mean. White women are often here."

Despite her racing heart, she couldn't help smiling a little.

"Your United States government has put a terrible burden on the men who came here from my country. For three years now it is almost impossible for a woman to come here legally, even if her husband arrived long before her."

"Wait." She stared. "Why are you telling me this? Are you defending Salyer, what he's doing with those girls?"

"No," he said. "What he is doing is very bad. You asked me if I knew about the Chinese women at Salyer's Hotel. What I want to say is that, because there are no wives, no women for the young men to marry, all the men in Chinatown know about the hotel. I think many other men know, too—white men."

"It's horrible," she said, her voice low but angry.

"Other places here also have prostitutes," he said mildly.

"I know that," she said, trying to rein in her frustration. It was no secret that several brothels operated openly down among the saloons; more than once, when she had passed by on her walks to the bay, she'd seen the women who occupied the upstairs rooms sitting in windowsills and on rickety balconies, chatting in dressing gowns or chemises. Often, they waved, and she waved back. "It's different, though. Those other women can leave, if they want to. What happens to them—" she paused, thinking. "Maybe they do it because they don't know what else to do, or have nothing else, nowhere to go. But if they wanted to pack up and leave, they could. It's not like that at Salyer's. He *bought* them. Went to San Francisco and paid money for them, just like what happened to Shu-Li."

He looked away and nodded.

"Let me tell you what Mattie found out today," she hurried on. "A girl, very young, like Shu-Li, had a baby last night, in the middle of the night. One of the men who, as you say, knows about the hotel, one of those men is the father of that girl's baby, and do you know what happened?" She paused, breathing heavily. Bai Lum waited. "They made another girl—her name is Ya Zhen—they made her take that tiny thing down to a stove in the kitchen and burn it!" Hot tears filled her eyes and she took both of his hands in hers. "Bai Lum," she whispered, "Ya Zhen told Mattie about it today, told her the most terrible things about how she came here." She swiped angrily at her tears. "Her life is so—" She closed her eyes and took a shaky breath. "It's a nightmare."

"Yes, it is," he said. He crossed the room to the altar, picked up one of the apples and rubbed his thumb over the smooth skin. "I was once married," he said. "Before I left China. My wife, Jun-li Yan, and my mother both died during the famine that started in the North." He put the apple back in the bowl and lit two sticks of incense. Twin tendrils of smoke curled upward.

She was dumbfounded. "Died," she whispered, trying to reconcile him with that other life, with a wife, a family far from here. "I'm so sorry, Bai Lum."

"Jun-li was expecting our first child. She was already so thin when the child began, and she hid it for a long time. The child withered inside her and Jun-li was poisoned with it."

She put a hand to her mouth and closed her eyes again. He continued, his voice a dark river through the room.

"I had been so worried about my wife that I blinded myself to what was happening to my mother. She had been giving her ration of rice to my sister and to Jun-li. Deliberately starving herself. Two days after my wife died, my mother also died.

"This was when I decided to come to America. It was seven years ago, before the exclusion. Other men from our village and the villages all around were traveling to the southern provinces, to Guangdong, getting on ships. There were stories about great wealth everywhere, about becoming rich. My father told me it was my duty, that I would be able to save the family by going away, sending money home." He crossed to the windows and pulled the pale curtain aside. Rose sat very still and watched him. The light from a nearby lamp flickered on his face and the strain of remembering showed in the set of his mouth.

"I wanted to bring my sister," he said. "But she was very young then, only seven. It was dangerous to take her on the ship. I couldn't bring her with me, but I was afraid to leave her with our father. There were people, bad men, roaming all over the countryside, buying girls, some even younger than my little sister, five, six years old. Some were sold as concubines to rich men. Little children like that. Others—" He did not continue.

"You thought your father—"

"I had seen the girls weeping, the mothers weeping while strangers led their daughters away like cattle. He swore to me that he wouldn't sell her. I had to believe him." He watched the smoke from the incense float toward the ceiling. "I sent money right away, but it didn't matter. He was hungry, and they promised to take good care of her."

Listening to him, seeing the old pain on his face, she felt a terrible regret at her earlier impulse to anger. "And this is why you help the Huntingtons. Why you keep the girls here."

He didn't reply. Another bit of cool breeze luffed the curtains; the haze of incense smoke swirled into competing eddies. There were small sounds of Shu-Li humming in another room. "She is very happy," he said, "to go to a new place—tired of being here with no one but an old man."

She thought of her father, of all the years Robert Allen had raised her alone, his patience and perplexity when she struggled against the conventions expected of her, her bedrock understanding that, under everything, he was her ally. "It would be hard to stay so secluded," she said.

"It is the custom for many Chinese women," he said. "There are a few living here, Rose, but you'll never see them. They are proud—it's a sign of prosperity if the woman can stay inside, at leisure. For Shu-Li, and the other girls who have stayed, my thinking was that a pleasant home would bring a feeling of shelter. Safety." He shook his head. "This girl does not feel safe. She feels...*bì yín dài le lóng zi*." He locked his hand around the opposite wrist. "Caught in a trap."

"You care for her," Rose said. "I can see that you've been trying to protect her." She went to where he stood by the mantle, feeling the pressure of passing time. "After Mattie told me about Ya Zhen, all I could think was that I needed to see you. I came here tonight to ask you to do something. It's something big. It might be...I don't know. I may not be thinking clearly about it," she said. "But maybe there's a way we can help Ya Zhen." He looked at her cautiously and she hurried on. "I know you've been very careful about which girls come here. Lucy explained that part to me. Trying to smuggle one of them away right under Salyer's nose is more dangerous—I see that, too. But what's happening to her right now—to Ya Zhen, I mean—is so terrible." She paused for a breath and pitched forward with her idea. "Reverend Huntington will be taking Shu-Li out of Eureka, sooner than he had planned; maybe he could take Ya Zhen at the same time. It's a risk, I know, and I haven't even asked Lucy about it, but Bai Lum, you could go to the hotel. If other Chinese men go, Salyer won't notice, will he? You could pay to...to meet her." The hateful blush returned. "See if she's strong enough to go, right away."

He rubbed his jaw with the palm of one hand, seeming to consider. "Tonight," he said.

"Yes, tonight."

"Shu-Li—"

"It's fine," she said hurriedly. "I'll stay here with her while you go. My aunt will roast me when I get home anyway, and I may as well be hung for a sheep as for a lamb." She smiled at the puzzled look on his face. "Another expression," she said.

"Like gathering the wool."

This made her laugh. "I guess I know a lot of expressions about sheep." She felt a great sense of relief, now that she had made her proposal. "Will you go? Please say that you will."

He cupped her face in his two hands. "I will. And you understand that this does not mean we can help her. There is no way to know now if we can do anything. You shouldn't put all your hope into the idea."

"But we don't know at all unless you go."

He smiled, a rueful quirk of the lips. "I'm going. Shu-Li can make tea while you wait."

¤

Byron wedged his hands under his armpits. He was taking a chill, even tucked into the doorway. Nothing had changed at Salyer's; the light still flickered in Pearl's room, and all the other windows near hers stayed dark. Just as he decided it would be safe for him to go back to the livery, a man hurried across the street and around to the rear entrance. The cut of his clothes made it clear to Byron—it was a Chinaman, headed upstairs. A ghastly dread ballooned in his gut. He clenched his fists until his nails threatened to break the skin of his palms, and he stared at the lit window above. At first, there was nothing, and then, clearly, shadows moving across the visible bit of ceiling: a door opening, closing. A person moving, then two. The seething in his belly exploded through him, and he voiced an inarticulate growl as he moved out of the doorway. There was no thought behind his trajectory, no plan, just the imperative of rage, the heat driving him. And then he was on the ground.

Before he reached the corner of the hotel, a juggernaut flew out of the night, a solid weight of force that hit Byron's left side, driving him down so that his right shoulder and the side of his face slammed into the wet dirt. His breath was knocked loose with the impact, and he gasped, getting nothing but a painful thimbleful of air. Before he even realized he was down, he was straddled, someone on his chest, making it even harder to breathe. "Off!" he wheezed, no voice, just a thin whistle of sound. He tried desperately to jackknife his assailant off, bucking his legs, but his arms were pinned and he was going nowhere.

"You're goin nowhere, sonny boy." Garland Tupper tittered and clutched his legs even tighter around Byron's arms. "You got much bigger problems than your darlin upstairs, there. Much, much bigger." He punctuated each *much* with a ringing slap to the face, first one cheek and then the other.

"*Hngh!*" Byron grunted and dug his heels frantically into the ground. He managed to lift his buttocks several inches, but his father rode him like a rodeo steer, laughing. Finally Byron, barely able to breathe, sagged and gave up the fight. Garland was forty pounds heavier, all of it hard muscle, and Garland was not bested. Not by Byron. It was a fact of life as dependable as gravity waiting to meet you at the bottom of a tall gorge.

His father planted his hands on either side of Byron's head and leaned down into his face. The smell of whiskey was almost eyewatering. "You burned my property," he crooned. "Burned that shed right to the ground. You know your mama's trunk was in that shed? Hm? Oh yes, it was," he said, as if Byron had tried to contradict him. "It had the clothes she brought with her from Missouri, where I met her. Had the little straw bonnet she used to put on when she worked in the garden. Awful vain about her pretty white skin, was your mama." His voice trailed off, almost to a whisper, as if he'd forgotten where he was, sitting on top of his son in the cold wet of the road. Then he reared back and punched Byron in the face.

There was a white starburst in his left eye, and he felt the skin between his cheekbone and Garland's fist split open. The second blow connected with his nose, and the pain in his head was a fiery explosion of agony. Hot blood immediately poured over his lips.

Garland lurched to his feet then, flexing his hand. "I hear you got a job mucking out horse shit for Joe Reilly," he said, as if finishing some mundane bit of business. He bent and brushed loose mud from the wet knees of his pants, in a fussy, self-important gesture. "That's good, boy. You got a lot of paying back to do."

Byron curled into a ball, holding his head between his hands. The pain was so exquisite he couldn't even moan. He lay there trying to breathe through his mouth, gagging on the taste of blood.

Garland walked toward the corner, still flexing his hand. "Be sure you work real hard," he said.

¤

Shu-Li came in with tea on a tray. She had twisted her hair into a bun at the back of her neck and wore small silver earrings. Rose was touched by this little change; the girl had so obviously decided to make herself look more formal, a hostess taking care of a luncheon guest. The tea soothed, was hot and good, and even the first swallow seemed to melt off a fraction of Rose's tension. She had been concerned that Shu-Li would feel awkward with her, but she should have known better. The girl sat back, relaxed, and sipped from her own cup. She seemed so self-contained. Rose couldn't imagine what sorts of things she had lived through, yet here she was, looking perfectly content with a perfect stranger.

"Thank you," Rose said, and lifted her cup. "The tea is very good."

Shu-Li smiled and took another sip. "Yes."

Rose stood and wandered over to the small altar, carrying her cup. The fireplace was a dark mouth sitting in shadows. She touched the apples as Bai Lum had done, ran her fingertips over the red satin on the mantle. The incense had burned into tiny piles of ash. A box of matches was at hand; Rose struck one and held the yellow flame to a new stick. It started with a bright blaze, then tapered down until just the tip glowed, a tiny spark winking in the room.

¤

The sound of rain and the crackle of the fire had caused Ya Zhen to drowse off, so when the door opened suddenly, she scrambled to her feet, heart pounding, still holding the comb. Old

Mol led a man into the room. He was taller than many of the Chinese men who came to her, and wore an impeccable black tunic and coat. She didn't remember having had him in this room before.

Old Mol arched her eyebrows at the man, a question. He nodded slightly. "This man's paid for the hour. Whatever he wants," she muttered, heading for the door. "That's a damned long time. She better be in one piece when you're done here, or the boss will see you hanging by that long pretty hair." She winked at Ya Zhen and closed the door.

The man's face was pleasant, but he seemed greatly on edge, not willing to look her in the eye. No one had ever paid for such a length of time. Old Mol's 'whatever he wants' hung in the air between them and she waited, confused as to what, exactly, he expected. When he said nothing, she pulled at the sash on her gown.

"No," he said.

She was stung with recognition when he spoke in a mountain dialect similar to her own. She pulled her robe shut and stood still.

"Sit here," he said, gesturing to the chair, "near the fire." As if he was her host, she did, and he sat on the edge of the bed. He took the brimless hat from his head and smoothed it over one leg. "You understand my words, yes?"

"Yes," she said, feeling dazed to hear her own language spoken so clearly.

"Then you are from the north," he said, smiling. "When I saw your face, your long fingers, I knew."

She sat silently.

"You're very young," he said. Now he looked at her directly, his face grave. "How long have you been away from your home?"

Li Lau made a soft sleep sound in the next room, and from outside came the noise of a scuffle between men, familiar as some rough birdsong.

"I have no home."

He shifted his hat from one knee to the other. "How long ago did you leave China?"

"A very long time," she told him. "Two years. Almost three."

"I have been here seven years," he said softly.

Ya Zhen turned to him, sitting on the bed in his fine clothes, his hands and fingernails clean, looking at her solicitously, and she felt fire leap in her belly. How was this man different than the man who brought her the kitten, or the men who left behind little things to ease their sorry consciences—pennies, peppermints. "Why did you come here?" she asked. "Two years, seven years—you are interested in time passing, so we should probably take off our clothes before this long hour has flown away." She stood and untied the sash at her waist, allowing the robe to fall open. "Would you like me to wash you first? Do you want to put your fingers in my mouth and count my teeth? Shall I crawl on the floor and lick your feet like a dog?" The anger flowed from some dark and bottomless place inside her, her voice growing louder and louder. Being able to say the words to someone who understood them made her feel reckless. She yanked up the sleeve of her gown, revealing three round, purple scars. "Do you want to burn me with a cigar or bite my flesh as if I am a roasted pig? Do you want to tie my mouth shut, or shall I beg you to stop, stop, while you use me, whispering your sister's name into my ear?" She was right next to him now, and began to straddle him.

He pushed her away and stumbled to his feet, looking ill. "No," he said, holding her by the shoulders. He dropped his arms to his sides and shook his head. "No, Ya Zhen. I don't want any of those things."

She stood there, breathing hard and shaking, her gown open. Hearing her name this way, in the soft lilt of her own village, her own place in the world, made the anger fall out of her so suddenly her knees buckled. He caught and steadied her. When she seemed able to stand, he pulled her robe together and gently tied the sash closed. "Please, lie down here."

She curled on her side. The soiled sheets stank of Clarence Salyer and made her stomach turn, but she felt a terrible exhaustion, so profound she couldn't even turn her head from the smell. The storekeeper moved to the bed and pulled the coverlet over her, tucking the edge in under her chin. He stirred the fire and put on another piece of wood, then leaned toward the flames, warming his hands. "My name is Bai Lum," he said. "I have a market in Chinatown."

"Wu Song told me about the store. I don't go out." She said. Her throat was dry from the shouting and it made her voice small and scratchy. "Do you have a wife?"

He shook his head. "My wife died before I was able to bring her here."

"So you came tonight because you are lonely." Ya Zhen closed her eyes. "I don't feel sorry for you."

Bai Lum was silent, and when she finally looked at him, he was gazing into the fire. "I have friends who want to help you." He turned and looked her in the eye. "I want to help you."

A bitter little smile, not much more than a grimace, flitted across her face. "How can you help? Will you shoot Old Mol?"

He studied her face for some time, and seemed finally to decide something. "They can take you away from here, my friends. It's north. A long way."

She stared. What if he was lying? If she agreed, perhaps he would run to Salyer. Her heart made a little gallop. What if he was telling the truth?

"Ya Zhen," he said. "Do you wonder how I know your name?" When she said nothing, he went on. "Your friend Mattie told us. She told us everything."

She lay perfectly still and felt tears rising. She did not let others see her cry, rarely allowed herself tears at all, though sometimes they came against her will in the hidden hours of the night. But Mattie was the only person to speak to her in genuine kindness since the old ēn mā, almost three years ago. So she let the tears come and her weeping was deep and hoarse. It didn't matter how loud she was; in this place, no one paid attention to the sounds in her room, as long as the money had been paid. At first her cries were inarticulate sobs, but then, like the girls on the ship from

Guangdong, she called for her mother until the word *mā* drew itself out into a long, faltering wail, the innate plea of all wounded souls desperate for respite and rescue.

There was a long silence then. Ya Zhen was at first aware only of her own breathing catching up with itself. Then she could hear the small sounds of the fire as it drew down, and finally the sound of rain outside, dripping steadily on her windowsill, just as it had been before he arrived.

"This place," Bai Lum said quietly, continuing as though her storm of tears had not interrupted a thing. "It's a hard journey. There will be a lot of people helping, but they'll be strangers to you. You must understand, Ya Zhen—there is some danger. If you're caught trying to leave, especially."

Holding his eyes with hers, she lifted her arm and exposed the purple burn scars again.

He nodded. "I don't know yet when it will be. Soon."

She couldn't seem to move or speak.

"I'll go."

"Wait." She pulled her knees to her chest, huddled there trying to quell the shaking in her arms and legs. "Can you...can you stay here for a while? You can sit on the chair." She gestured with her chin. "Old Mol won't give you back the money. Can you stay and just talk to me?"

Bai Lum pulled the chair over to the bed, its wooden legs squalling across the board floor. He sat and rested his hands in his lap. "What would you like to talk about?"

"Tell me about the mountains," she whispered. "Tell me what you did when you were a little boy."

He looked at the ceiling. "That was a very long time ago." He thought for a moment, then smiled. "When I was very small, I was master of the chickens. This is what my mother told me, though I was a scrawny child and I think the chickens were the masters of me."

In a soft voice, he began to tell her about searching for eggs, how one black hen would hide her nest in a new place every day to fool him. Slowly, she felt herself sliding into sleep. Sometime later she woke when Bai Lum touched her hand. She turned her face up to him.

"You can sleep," he said. "No one else will come tonight."

"Take me with you," she whispered, asking again for the impossible. She didn't think he would reply, but he squatted next to the bed so that their faces were close.

"I cannot take you," he said. "But I will come back, Ya Zhen." His strong face looked immensely tired. "For now, that is what I can do. I can be your friend." His eyes searched hers for some sign that she understood him, so she nodded. He stood and put a little more wood on the fire, then put on his hat and left the room.

After he was gone, she lay still and watched the light from the fire reflected in the pressed-tin ceiling. She searched her heart for a sign of hope, but such a large thing as hope was impossible to grasp. It was easier to indulge a more familiar fantasy: that she was the only person alive on the earth; that she was rich with the great gift of loneliness. Then a man's boot thudded against the wall and a there was a low curse as he made his unsteady way down the dark hallway and past her door. Old Mol let him into the Wu sisters' room. As Bai Lum had promised, no one else came to Ya Zhen's room that night.

Home again, Bai Lum took a cup of tea from Shu-Li. He had been gone for nearly three-quarters of an hour. "*Xie xie, mèi mèi,*" he said, thanking her. A slight frown creased the girl's brow and she blew air through her pursed lips. He shook his head. "She doesn't like me to call her this," he told Rose. "It means little sister."

"No young lady wants to be thought of as a little girl," said Rose. Bai Lum translated to Shu-Li, who replied so adamantly as she left the room that Rose had to stifle a smile. "No need to tell me what she said. I think I got the gist of it." Bai Lum took a long drink of the tea, and Rose watched his mouth on the rim of the cup, his throat moving as he swallowed. Despite how apprehensive she was to know what had happened at the hotel, the desire to touch the skin on his throat was an incredible distraction, like an ache in her fingers. "You were gone so long," she finally said. "Did you...did you see her?"

He nodded. "I told her we would help."

Rose put a hand on her chest and gusted an enormous sigh. "Thank you for doing this."

"Right now, it is only an idea," he cautioned. "Not our decision." He took another drink of tea. "I don't know if she really believed me," he said. "She is—" He sat for a moment, watching the curtains ripple. "Her life is very bad."

"But she wants to try? To get out?"

"I think she would have come with me tonight, if I had asked her to."

"Good," she said. "That's good. Now we need to tell Lucy." She stood. "I have to go home. Hazel will be worried. And furious." She pulled her wrap around her again. "I'll go to the Huntingtons first thing tomorrow, early. I'll tell them everything, tell them you met with Ya Zhen."

Descending the stairs, he once more held the lamp high, and placed his free hand on the small of her back. It rested there, a warm and certain weight that she could feel all the way through her cloak, her dress and chemise. The sensation ran the length of her body like a fever. They came out into the storeroom and passed through the curtained alcove. He stopped her at the mercantile door.

"Your heart is very kind, Rose Allen."

The sound of his voice was a phenomenon. The myriad small parts of her—pores on the backs of her hands, the tops of her ears, the two dimples at the base of her spine—every molecule from eyelashes to toenails came to attention and sang hallelujah just to hear him say her name. His eyes moved over her face. He set the lamp on the counter and took her left hand as he had done the day before. She could feel her own pulse under his fingertips. He looked down and once more traced over the heel of her hand, across her palm to the tip of her middle finger. The blood raced under the surface of her skin, making all the fine hairs on her arms and legs stand up. She had an image then of Hazel's African violets, their fuzzy leaves prickling in the sun that morning, and she laughed. He looked up quizzically.

"Sorry," she said, a little breathless, feeling stupidly awkward. "I was just surprised."

He smiled. "I was afraid you saw a face in the window."

"No." She laid her palm on his. He curled his fingers around her hand, and leaned down to kiss her.

It *is* like falling, she thought later. Like falling and like landing in a safe place. When he pulled away, she was almost afraid to open her eyes, because the whole world had just shifted—what would she see? But he said her name again, and when she looked, it was Bai Lum, the heavy braid of black hair hanging over his shoulder, his eyes quiet on her face, as they always were, and she knew, as she had when she chose to leave Illinois: she would go whichever way this wind wanted to blow her.

She didn't even try to come in quietly—she knew Hazel would have found her missing some time ago, so no use sneaking. What she didn't expect was to find Hazel sitting in the front parlor, rocking. The lamp was turned so low that the room was thick with shadows.

"She's resting now," Hazel said. The rocker ticked back and forth in a slow arc. She glanced at Rose, who stood in the doorway. "You're wet."

Rose took off her wrap and hung it over the back of a chair. She sat on the loveseat opposite Hazel. "I'm sorry, Aunt—"

Hazel held up a palm. "Don't say it. I'm too tired."

She waited. Hazel rocked. "Is it the grippe?" Rose asked finally, not able to stand this weirdly silent version of Hazel's normally frenetic self.

"No, not the grippe. Better by far if it was."

Stopping, Mattie had said. *Never this bad before.*

"It's soul-sickness, Rose. Absolute melancholy, like her father."

"She told me this morning how much she misses him. Wishes she could see him."

"I'm sure she does. But we're not allowed that, are we? No one puts her head beyond the veil for a last look or one more word of comfort."

Rose was mystified. "Beyond the veil?"

Hazel stopped rocking. "Mattie's father hung himself when she was eight years old."

Rose sat back in the love seat as if pushed by an invisible hand. "Dead."

"Dead as Caesar for years," Hazel said, her voice tender. "Like your mother. Such a lovely man—Mattie's ma was never the same, after. Certainly no good to her children." She started rocking again, and her faint shadow, large on the wall behind her, rocked too. "It's grief that brought Matilda to the opium."

Rose was flummoxed. "You knew."

Hazel made a derisive little huff. "I'd have to be blind." She turned her head, and even in the low light, Rose could see the blue eyes boring in. "There's no end to the things I know."

Rose's mind made a reeling return to the feel of Bai Lum's kiss, the sensation of his lips moving on hers, and felt as if her face might actually catch fire. Wildly grateful for the dim light of the parlor, she decided that there might be some things about which Hazel could only speculate—at least Rose hoped so. "How long will she be sick?"

Hazel looked away again and shrugged. "She's already much improved, if you mean the shakes and the puking. I gave her a little laudanum."

"But laudanum has opium in it."

"Indeed it does. Just what Mattie needed to settle her." She nodded, as if confirming the decision. "Only a few drops diluted with water, to keep her from shaking her senses loose." Back and forth she rocked, back and forth the shadow kept pace. "We've been down this road before."

Rose dropped her face into her hands and massaged her eyes, which burned with fatigue. "I give up. I've stepped through the looking glass," she said, remembering her earlier thought about the White Rabbit. "Curiouser and curiouser."

Hazel laughed, a low chuckle. "Yes, Horatio. More things in heaven and earth, etcetera. You'd best get off to bed. We'll hope morning puts a different shine on things."

"And you?"

"Not just yet. I'm too tired to sleep. Peek in on her when you go—in case she needs something."

"I will." Rose put her hand on Hazel's shoulder as she passed. "I love you, Aunt. I'm sorry if I worried you."

"Sorry won't fill the pipe," she said. "Neither will worry, but I wish I had a teaspoon of something to make *you* settle." She patted Rose's fingers. "No cure yet for your ailment."

A candle burned on top of Mattie's bureau, and a faint smell of vomit hung in the air. She huddled in bed, facing away. Rose left the door open and tiptoed in. "Mattie?"

"Hi," she said, and pulled herself slowly into a sitting position, leaning back on the headboard. "I'm awake."

"Water?"

She nodded, and drank deeply from the glass Rose handed her. "Thanks."

"Hazel said you're feeling a little better. How's the hand?"

She held up the bandaged palm, and cocked her head, as if she hadn't noticed it until just now. "Feels pretty hot," she said. "Like it's still burning." Her voice was a little dreamy-sounding, but nothing like the ugly disorientation of last night. "Not so bad," she said.

"Aunt gave you laudanum."

"Just a little taste." She met Rose's eyes. "I always think it won't be so bad."

"Oh Mattie. You could have told me."

She shook her head. "Hazel has been so good to me. Every time, I promise and I promise—like I did to you this morning." She closed her eyes. "I always mean it, too. With all my heart." Her voice petered out.

Rose sat on the foot of the bed. "Listen to me. The girl at the hotel—the one you told me about, remember?" Rose glanced at the bedroom door, and lowered her voice. "We're going to help her."

"Ya Zhen," Mattie said.

"That's right."

"I saw that baby's skull." She cupped her uninjured hand. "Part of it, anyway. Like part of a duck's egg." She stared into her hand as if the burned portion of bone was sitting there. There was no more of the broken weeping from earlier, but her eyes were wet.

She took Mattie's hand. "I'm so sorry you had to see that, but I want you to listen to me now."

Mattie nodded.

"Bai Lum went to see her tonight. He visited Ya Zhen and he told her we're going to help."

"Help? How can we?"

As simply and carefully as she could, she explained what Bai Lum and the Huntingtons had done for other girls, and what they planned for Shu-Li. The more she said, the more carefully Mattie seemed to be listening. "We haven't talked to them yet, about Ya Zhen. I'm going to go over in the morning, early. Since they're going to take Shu-Li north soon anyway, maybe they can take Ya Zhen, too."

Mattie chewed her lip, brow furrowed. "They watch her like hawks, though. She's hardly ever downstairs. Yesterday was the first time I ever saw her for more than a couple of minutes, and it seems like that fat bitch is always looking right over her shoulder."

"Who's that?"

"They call her Old Mol. She's like—" Mattie shook her head. "Like their keeper, at least for Ya Zhen and the other young one. I don't think Ya Zhen ever leaves the hotel. How can anyone sneak her out?"

"I don't know. Maybe in the middle of the night."

"Who, though? If they got caught...truth, Rose? I think Clarence Salyer would shoot someone and then claim he was being robbed. Awful poxy bastard." The candlelight exaggerated the dark circles under her eyes, giving her thin face an almost skull-like appearance.

"What if she got herself out? Ran out before dawn. We could wait, and then hide her."

"If they caught her—" Mattie tilted her head back and shook her head in slow negation. "Dear God, I hate to think."

Rose passed a weary hand over her face. "You're right. It's not going to do any good trying to figure this out right now. You should get some sleep. We both should. Lay back."

Mattie slid down until her head was back on the pillow. "I want to go with you in the morning."

Rose considered. She'd have to admit to the Huntingtons that she'd told Mattie about Shu-Li and the other girls. But Mattie knew more about the hotel—and about Ya Zhen—than any of them. "Let's see how you feel in the morning."

"I'll be better," Mattie mumbled, half asleep. Rose wasn't sure if it was a prediction or another promise.

¤

Getting back into the livery was harder than Byron expected. Old man Reilly had locked things up tight; even the windows were shuttered and bolted. After what seemed like forever, he finally managed to create enough space at the bottom corner of the big front door to push inside, squatting and duck-walking through. The long hasp popped like a gunshot, the nails pulling partway out of the rough wood, and just as he got all but his right leg inside, the edge of the door scraped a gouge across his lower back and buttock. He hardly felt it, so miserable was the throbbing hell of his face. His nose had stopped bleeding, but only because it had swollen to such gross proportions, inside and out; there was a steady, nauseating drip of blood at the back of his throat, making him spit repeatedly. The flesh under his right eye puffed so that he could see it slowly impeding on the vision in that eye.

There were only two horses stabled, and neither paid him any attention as he stumbled over to the ladder and climbed into the loft. On hands and knees, he pulled loose hay together, yanking a few handfuls from a loose bale. He wished he could smell the crisp, old-grass smell, an aroma like the last gasp of summer, but his swollen nose was out of commission for God knew how long. He settled into the straw, but sat up again in less than a minute when his entire head began to throb to the rhythm of his heartbeat, lighting his face with exquisite pain. Whimpering a little, he pushed some bales around so that he could sit on two and lean back on a third. He pulled loose straw over him to serve as a blanket and tucked his hands in his armpits.

Huddled there in the hay loft, trying to ignore his pain and shifting restlessly to avoid the surprisingly sharp ends of straw, he didn't think about his father. There was some relief, actually, to being accosted by Garland—Byron had known there would be a retribution, and he was mildly surprised he'd been left able to walk away. Instead of his father, Byron's thoughts turned on the man who had cast his shadow on Pearl's ceiling. A deep core of rage weltered in his gut. He couldn't picture his Pearl now, couldn't conjure her sliding out of her robe without imagining someone there with her, putting his hands on her, forcing her. He shook his head, viciously, relishing the bolt of pain that followed. He had to stay clear. Tomorrow he would earn his wages and he would take Pearl out—after he found the man, and killed him.

CHAPTER SIX

R OSE, WAKE UP."

Mattie's voice. There was so little light at the windows, Rose thought at first that it must still be night, a candle on Mattie's bureau. She propped herself on an elbow and squinted through her hair, which was a bright cloud of frizz. "Are you sick?"

"I'm dandy, see? Good as new. But you need to get up."

Rose dropped back onto her pillow. "Why?" She was still tired, which always caused her bed to exert a weightless, downy pull on her. "Go back to sleep. It's the middle of the night."

"It's half-six. Up. Come on! We have to get over to Reverend Huntington's house. Look here."

Rose cracked an eye. Mattie sat on the bed, waving a cup in front of her face.

"Good and strong, as you like it. Coffee, Rose."

She groaned a little and sat up. Mattie lifted Rose's hand and wrapped Rose's fingers around the cup.

"Ow!"

"Careful," Mattie said. "That's hot." She jumped off the bed and threw open the doors of Rose's wardrobe.

"Thanks for the warning," she mumbled, and took a tentative taste. It was not only hot, but incredibly strong, and Rose winced. "Oh, this is...I can almost chew this, Mattie." Even with a single sip, she could already feel the caffeine zinging into her brain. The windows had gone from charcoal to pewter, and Mattie rummaged through drawers, finding clean underclothes. The bandage on her burned hand was still wrapped snugly and she was dressed, combed, and bustling around as though she'd been awake for hours—a completely different person than the fragile woman, weeping and shaking on the bed last night. "How can you be so awake? Rose asked.

"Three cups, sugar and milk." She laid all the clothes on the quilt and turned to Rose with a hairbrush in her good hand.

Rose took it from her before she could start brushing. "Stop," she said. She put the now half-full cup on the bedside table and threw back the covers. "I'm not in the market for a lady-in-waiting. I'm up, you see?" She pulled her nightgown off over her head and washed her face at the commode, then slipped into the fresh underclothes and the blue striped dress Mattie had chosen. "Uck, this thing," she said. "It looks like pillow ticking."

"Prickly. You've never seemed terrible particular about wardrobe before."

Rose, now pulling the hairbrush through her rowdy curls, stared at Mattie's reflection in the mirror. "What—"

Mattie's chin was cocked, a smug smile all over her narrow face. "Look who's awake." She batted her eyelashes theatrically.

Rose managed a smile and brandished the hairbrush at her. "You're incorrigible."

"So they say."

"You're also right. We need to go." She wrangled her hair into a knot and anchored it in place, using so many hairpins she didn't think a tornado could tear it loose. She turned then and gave Mattie a long look. "Really—are you sure you want to do this? You don't have to. I can go myself."

"There isn't a thing you could do, short of tying me to the table leg, that would keep me from it." Mattie was all business now, and Rose could see that her frantic and cheerful hurry was painted over a great, determined weariness. There were still dark circles on the skin beneath her eyes and her pupils were small pinpricks, but her expression was dogged. "I'll do anything to help that girl."

They bundled up to go out into the bone-chilly dawn and hurried along in the waning dark toward the Congregational church. At first they were quiet, the wet grit of their footsteps quick and rhythmic. Then Mattie tilted her head back and inhaled deeply. "God, I love that," she said. "Smell the ocean?"

"I do."

"Rose?"

"Hm."

"Thank you."

Rose hooked her arm through Mattie's and they walked on, dodging puddles.

Charles Huntington opened the door of the rectory and peered out, hooking his glasses over his ears. It wasn't yet seven o'clock and still nearly dark. "What's happened?" he said. Lucy appeared at his side, wiping her hands on her apron. "Come in you two, it's cold." She hustled Rose and Mattie inside. "Get in the kitchen where it's warmer. I'll get coffee."

Rose and Mattie looked at each other and Mattie smiled wickedly. Rose gave her a small pinch on the arm, which made her blink. Rose was almost shaking, and she couldn't tell if it was the brisk morning or her own nerves.

"We need to talk to you both," Rose said. "It's about one of the girls at the hotel. Salyer's."

Lucy, reaching for the big enameled coffee pot, paused. "Is there trouble?"

"Here, ladies, sit down." Reverend Huntington, still in shirtsleeves and suspenders, took a seat at the table and gestured for Mattie and Rose to do the same. He struck a match and lit his Meerschaum, the sweet smell of tobacco filling the room. "Tell us."

Rose took a deep breath. "Lucy, you remember I told you yesterday that Mattie works at Salyer's."

Lucy lowered herself into a chair. "I do."

"She worked yesterday with one of them that Clarence Salyer...one of the girls he keeps." She looked at Mattie, who nodded for her to go on. "Her name is Ya Zhen," she said. "We have to help her."

Then they both explained, Mattie's voice strained but resolute as she recounted the bloody sheet, the story Ya Zhen had told her on the roof. She told what Clarence Salyer had done in the afternoon. Finally, with Rose's encouragement, she told about the bones in the stove, the tiny skull. Midway through this atrocious litany, Charles reached over for wife's hand, closing her small fingers within his large ones.

"Last night, I asked Bai Lum to go to the hotel and meet Ya Zhen," Rose said. "He did. He paid to see her. He told her he would help. That *we* would." She realized that she was squeezing her hands together under the table so hard that she'd lost feeling in her fingers. "You're going to take Shu-Li north soon—what if Ya Zhen went, too?"

The four of them sat in the slowly brightening kitchen, the only sound the simmering hiss of the abandoned coffee pot.

"Lucy," Rose said finally, "yesterday you told me that if you could find a way to help all of them, you would."

"I did."

"Maybe there's a way. Maybe we can find one."

Reverend Huntington clamped his pipe between his teeth and tipped back in the chair so that its two front legs were off the floor. "Getting her out of the hotel will be the first problem."

¤

"You look like hell, Tupper." Joe Reilly shook his head with a low whistle. "Guess your old man found you. You'oughta mash that nose back onto the middle of your face before it settles off to the side there."

Byron said nothing. His entire head was a throbbing woe, and he wished the old whore's son would tell him what he wanted done first so Byron could get to it. He'd had nothing but scratch sleep all night; when he wasn't choking on the dribble down the back of his throat, he tried to find a way to rest so the spines of hay weren't jabbing him. Sometime in the deepest reaches he had finally dozed off, only to be brought bolt upright by some brazen critter running crosswise over his legs; he had thrashed out with a roar, thinking *rat,* and only got himself settled again by clinging to the idea that it was only the barn cat on his nightly rounds.

The horses had alerted him to Reilly's arrival, a soft whinny and thud as they moved in their stalls, anticipating a feed. Byron scuttered behind a stack of bales. After the big livery doors were pulled open, he waited until Reilly went into the small side office and then scrambled down the ladder. In the alley, he picked as much chaff off himself as he could, and gingerly washed his outraged face in a rain barrel. As the surface of the water settled, he got his first look at what Garland had done with his fists. The thought occurred to him again that it was a smaller price to pay than he had feared; retribution was done and he was still standing.

"A'right then," Joe Reilly said. "You can start by feeding the beasties, then muck 'em. Food and shit, food and shit. That's a horse. Joe Kenton will be after that bay mare before noon, so after she's fed, put the curry comb to her. I'll take care of her hooves, though—all you need is a little kick to the face to knock that nose the rest of the way off your gob." He handed Byron a bucket of grooming tools. "That one's the curry comb, he said, pointing. "Go easy around her belly—she's ticklish." Hobbling away, he said, "Next time you want to doss down in the loft, let me know. I'll throw you a blanket."

Byron stared stupidly after him, thinking how a blanket last night might have guarded him from stiff bedding and small, night-roaming animals. Perhaps he'd ask for a few more nights—and a blanket—before he finished work. He set aside the bucket with the curry comb and brush, and slit open a sack of oats that slumped in one corner. One thing was sure: no matter what kind of deals old man Reilly tried to foist on him today, he would insist on the wages due him this afternoon. He planned on buying a decent meal, and when it was dark he would go to Salyer's and get Pearl out of there. There was also the matter of the Chinaman who'd gone to her last night. There were a couple hundred of them around town, and he didn't know which one it was. But the coolie bastard had not only interfered with Pearl—who was very nearly Byron's wife—but he'd gotten Byron a beating in the bargain. He was going to by-God find out who it was (one way or the other, Pearl would have to tell) and he was going to make him a very dead Chinaman.

¤

It was Lucy who landed on an idea, finally.

They had talked the possibilities around and around, rejecting one scheme after another until it started to seem as if they'd have to scrap the whole plan entirely. Then Lucy slapped the table in front of her. "Your birthday," she said to her husband.

They all stared confusedly at this apparent non sequitur.

"What about it?" he said.

"A party!"

"Don't care for them." A perplexed line showed between Reverend Huntington's bushy white eyebrows.

"You do now," she said, giving his shoulder a hearty pat. "We're going to be throwing you a dinner party next week, and I'll need help getting ready. I'm going to hire that girl from Cora Salyer this afternoon."

Mattie looked skeptical. "The sisters are the ones that get sent around on errands, mostly—the two older ones. Ya Zhen told me she's never allowed out."

"What if Salyer's wife tries to send one of the others, instead?" Rose asked.

Lucy looked out the window, considering. "I'll be very specific that I want one of the young girls, a hard worker, otherwise I'm not interested."

"She can't send the youngest one, at least, I don't think so. She's too frail, because of—" Mattie faltered, looking at her bandaged hand.

"Because of her infirmity," Charles said quietly. "I think you're right, Mattie."

Rose shook her head. She couldn't see how the plan was workable. "What good will it do, even if they send Ya Zhen?" she asked. "If the Salyers know she came here, they'll just come after her—you won't be able to hide her, or Shu-Li, either. Even if you raced them both out of town today, there'd by hell to pay. They'll know you were behind it."

"Not if there are witnesses who see her leaving the rectory on her own," said Lucy. "They can take this house apart board by board—the church, too. It won't do them any good, because Ya Zhen won't be here, and they won't have any idea where to find her. Don't look so confounded, you three—it's simple. Rose, you know all too well how tongues wag around here. Today we *want* them to wag. I know exactly how we can do it, if Bai Lum is willing to help."

She told them her idea then, step by step, and as she talked, Rose began to feel a glimmer of real hope. It would take every one of them to pull it off and it was definitely risky, but helping Ya Zhen suddenly seemed entirely possible.

"Let's hope Cora Salyer lets the girl come," Charles said. "That could be a fly in the ointment that foils us right at the start."

"I don't think that will be a problem, Reverend," Mattie said.

"Why so confident?"

"The almighty dollar," she said, and rubbed her thumb against her first two fingertips. "There's a woman whose blood runs green. She'll do it."

"Splendid," Lucy said, smiling broadly. "I'll be renting a prostitute for the afternoon."

Charles Huntington looked at her with those bushy eyebrows raised and began to laugh, laughed until he had to wipe his eyes on his sleeve. He stood and wrapped his arms around Lucy. "Let's try to keep ourselves out of the papers, shall we?"

"Go get your coat, Reverend," Lucy said, "and take these two back into town. We all have jobs to do."

¤

When Ya Zhen opened her eyes, she was surprised to see the sun at her window, not yet fully risen, but lighting the sky behind the hills and transforming the few visible wisps of cloud to tailings of polished brass. It was a rare day that she didn't wake long before morning, only to lay in the dark and begin the arduous process of not thinking—not remembering her life in Hunan, not hearing or seeing or smelling the men in her room, and not considering what the coming day and evening would bring. There was a tremendous, glassy boredom in her days—a boredom that hid, at its heart, a misery so black it could not be contemplated. Last night, when the man, Bai Lum, was gone, even as she drifted off, she had been sure that the glimmer of hope he had incited—*it's north, a long way*—would give her a wakeful night. Instead, she had dropped into sleep so consuming that she seemed to have lain motionless all night.

She hurried into her clothes, tying her hair behind her, and once more slipped into Li Lau's room after scanning the hall. She was curled under her blanket much as she had been when Ya Zhen saw her the day before, but this time she turned over and sat up, wincing just a little when she got into a sitting position. She rubbed her eyes with the heel of her hand. Ya Zhen saw that the empty plate—empty because Ya Zhen had eaten everything on it—still sat on the washstand. "Are you hungry?"

"Yes, very hungry." Li Lau had the slightly dazed look of a child wandering out of a long nap.

"I'll get breakfast."

"Old Mol—"

"She's not awake yet. If I hurry, she won't know. Ivo will find me something, and he hates her, too. He won't tell."

Li Lau pushed back the blanket and eased herself out of bed. She lifted her night dress and pulled away a thick padding of rags—easily three times the number they wore when they bled during the month. The rags were heavily stained, but not shockingly so; Old Mol must have been up to help Li Lau more than once. Ya Zhen was relieved to see that Li Lau's bed was unmarked with even a small spot of blood. She helped her squat over the bucket. When her water came, she uttered a small gasp and pinched her eyes shut.

"I'll be right back," Ya Zhen said, helping her back into bed and refolding the rags between the girl's legs as well as she could.

"Listen," she said. "When Old Mol comes, don't sit up unless she forces you. You need to act very weak, very tired and stupid. Make her think you have pain and no appetite."

Li Lau nodded and didn't ask why. She knew.

Not bothering with shoes, Ya Zhen slipped quickly down the inside staircase, listening for Old Mol before coming out into the kitchen. As she had suspected, Ivo was already deeply into the preparation of the Friday dinner. This time of year, Salyer's dining room served crab every Friday; the meal attracted so many diners that Ivo and Mattie were kept running all day, and the strong and lingering smell of seafood wafted all the way upstairs. Vivid orange heaps of cooked Dungeness crabs steamed on the table next to a bowl already filling with the picked meat. Ivo glanced up, looking mildly surprised to see her, but not terribly interested. "She'll make a row if she catches you," he said, his inflected English hard for her to penetrate.

"I need food for Li Lau," she said. "She didn't eat yesterday."

He turned from the crabs, wiping his hands on the apron he wore every day and somehow kept shockingly white. "Salyer," he muttered. "*Hund Ficker.*" He took a cracked serving bowl from a corner of the top shelf and from pans inside the warming oven he spooned a mound of potatoes, one of cooked apples, and another of scrambled eggs. He reached around and plucked up two spoons, stabbed them into the food. "Go eat. Hide the bowl."

Ya Zhen's stomach came loudly awake. Most days, breakfast was little more than thinly-buttered toast and the occasional plate of beans. She looked at Ivo, who had turned his perpetually sour face back to his crab butchery, and just as she was about to thank him, Mattie rushed in through the rear entrance.

I have friends who want to help you.

She looked tired, her face drawn to the point of being haggard. Dark smudges nested under her eyes and her left hand was heavily bandaged. Despite her flagging appearance, though, there were twin spots of color high on her cheekbones, and when she laid eyes on Ya Zhen, she broke into a broad grin, which she immediately hid by coughing into her arm.

"Morning, Ivo," she said to the cook's hunched back. He made no response. She hurried across the room, gesturing for Ya Zhen to follow. Up the inner stairs they went, Ya Zhen trying to keep pace. "I have to talk to you before any of the bad lot are awake and roaming around."

At the top of the stairs, Mattie, having never been in this part of the hotel, hesitated; Ya Zhen pointed to her room. "In there," she told Mattie. She took the food to Li Lau. "Eat some," she told the girl. "I'll come back for the rest." Li Lau dug into the potatoes, and it made Ya Zhen's mouth water to watch. "I'll come back," she said again, hoping Li Lau wouldn't eat everything. "Put the bowl under the bed if Old Mol comes."

In Ya Zhen's room, Mattie stood by the cold fireplace, seeming almost to vibrate with nervous energy. "We're going to do our level best to take you out of here," she said. "Today."

Ya Zhen stared. *Who?* she wanted to ask. *How?* A hundred questions jostled for attention, but she couldn't seem to ask any of them.

Mattie laughed and hugged her. "Do you understand?"

She stiffened in the close embrace, making herself bear it. "Today?"

"I'm going right now to find Mrs. Salyer and tell her that Lucy Huntington wants your help today." She laughed again and flapped a hand at Ya Zhen's blank look. "It doesn't matter," she said. "You don't know her, but she's going to—"

From the head of the stairs, Old Mol announced herself with a guttural belch.

Ya Zhen's eyes grew large. Mattie put her finger to her lips and crossed to the threshold in what seemed a single enormous step. Hand on the doorknob, she positioned herself to look as though she wasn't quite inside the room. "...so be sure you do a good job. Mrs. Huntington is a lovely person and I don't want to hear that you—"

"What in holy hell do you think you're doing?" Old Mol barked, marching down the hallway hard enough to make the floorboards jump. She shoved the door open; it slammed into the wall and bounced back. "You got no business up here," she said, her jowly face ticking from Mattie to Ya Zhen and back to Mattie. "What are you telling her?"

Mattie looked unperturbed, almost disdainful of the outburst. She lifted her chin self-importantly. "Mrs. Lucy Huntington— *Reverend* Huntington's wife—sent me to speak to Mrs. Salyer about a matter of some urgency."

Old Mol gaped, then pointed at Ya Zhen. "Does that look like Cora Salyer to you?"

"Of course not," Mattie said, managing to sound both bored and impatient. "I just wanted to be sure that this girl understood what was expected of her." She tilted her head toward Old Mol in a conspiratorial way. "There were a few problems with the laundry yesterday, if you know what I mean."

"Hang your goddamn laundry troubles. I don't want to hear another word." She gave Mattie a small shove out of Ya Zhen's doorway. "Get your skinny shanks downstairs. We'll find her highness and sort out this load of tripe. You—" she said to Ya Zhen, pointing one large, blunt finger, "you know better." She stood that way for a moment, glaring, and slammed the door shut behind her.

Ya Zhen stared at the closed door, her breathing quick and shallow. When Old Mol had thrown the door open, the inside knob put a deep divot in the wall, scattering broken bits of plaster onto the floor. Turning a slow circle, Ya Zhen looked at the unpainted walls, the single rickety chair, the tall window with its scrap of yellow curtain, the piss bucket, the thin blanket still rumpled on the bed. Normally she would clean the mess of plaster; normally by this time of day she had straightened everything and put the bucket out for Wu Song to dump in the outside privy. Her heart beat high and hard under her ribs, making the place on her shoulder where Clarence Salyer had bitten her yesterday throb in time. Just before Old Mol pushed her out, Mattie had dropped Ya Zhen a wink.

First, she slipped into her shoes. Then, in the center of the room where a small bar of sunlight hit the floor, she bent at the waist and spat. The thin line of spittle clung to her bottom lip and glimmered orange and yellow the instant before it hit the scratched floorboards. Not bothering to peek out first, Ya Zhen opened the door and went to get her breakfast from Li Lau. She had gone from hungry to ravenous.

¤

"It's best if I speak to Bai Lum myself now." Reverend Huntington said. After Mattie had climbed out of the big wagon a couple of blocks from the hotel, he had parked the rig in the alley behind the mercantile, next to the sliding door of the storeroom. When Rose began to object—she told herself she simply wanted to see Bai Lum's face when they told him about helping Ya Zhen— Charles held up one large hand. "Hear me. We're going to need you later, when it's time for the girl to go off on foot. Best if we stick to the plan and keep our visibility to a minimum."

She wanted desperately to protest but knew he was right—the less any of them was seen together, the better. "I'll be back to the rectory by four," she said.

He smiled down at her. "You were absolutely right to tell us about this, Rose. Absolutely right."

Her throat closed around an ache of tears, and she could only nod. Now that the wheels were in motion, the reality of what they planned to do made her feel a bit like Pandora with her hand on the lid of the box.

He raised a fist and knocked hard. "We'll need your help—Ya Zhen will. Four o'clock."

Rose was out of the alley and around the corner when she heard the storeroom door rumble sideways along its track, when her heart tried to turn her feet around. *Just a look, the smallest*

wave. She put her head down and made a beeline for the Kendalls'
house, boots like thunder on the boards.

¤

Old Mol deposited Mattie in a downstairs hallway, ordering
her not to budge an inch. It was more than fifteen minutes before
Cora Salyer finally appeared, a pillow crease across one cheek and
the corners of her mouth pulled down so far she resembled an
English bulldog. Now she eyed Mattie as if inspecting a plate of
gone-over fish. Old Mol hulked nearby, arms crossed over her
prodigious bosom.

"Why doesn't she want *you* to help her?" Cora said. "Why
would the pastor's wife want one of those back room girls?"

"I wish I *could* help her," Mattie said, throwing a load of regret
into her voice. "I'd surely love to have the four dollars she offered,
but I've had an accident, missus. A nasty burn, I'm afraid, and the
Reverend's wife, she needs some things done that will take two
good hands. She didn't even know those girls stayed here until I
told her." She gave a pouty little sniff. "I thought you'd be pleased."

"Four dollars, you say?" Cora's downtrodden expression
became   alarmingly   bright.   "My   my.   Apparently   the
Congregationalists are doing well for themselves."

Easy enough, you old spider, thought Mattie. "Yes, Mrs.
Salyer, that's what she said. Said she needs a younger girl,
someone she can work hard, since the Reverend's party is only next
week."

"Clarence won't think much of that idea," Old Mol said. "He
doesn't let the young ones out."

"Don't meddle in," Cora snapped. "During the day I can work
them as I please—that's the bargain he struck with me to have
them here at all." She gave Old Mol a look that Mattie thought
would suit Queen Victoria herself. "Go up and get the new one. If
the pastor's wife wants young, we'll give her the youngest."

The new one. Mattie opened her mouth and closed it again.
She wanted to blurt something, anything that might redirect Cora's

attention to Ya Zhen. *What about that girl who helped me with laundry yesterday?* The words hovered on the tip of her tongue, and she waited, waited, waited.

Old Mol uncrossed her arms and shifted uneasily. "I, uh...that one is not feeling well. Still indisposed."

Cora rolled her eyes. "That's what you told me yesterday. Indisposed how? A little dyspepsia? Her free meals have disagreed with her delicate constitution?"

"Certain female troubles."

"Like I mentioned when we did wash," Mattie jumped in, heart racing. "That particular laundry problem with the bloody—"

"All right, all right," Cora interrupted, "don't start in with that again. Just send the other one. I'd rather have her gone for an afternoon anyway."

Mattie was flooded with relief, but did her best to look blandly indifferent to the decision. "Mrs. Huntington said she would pick the girl up in front of the hotel at eleven o'clock. Sharp."

"How am I to be paid?"

"She said that she'd pay you herself when she returns the girl this afternoon at supper time," Mattie told her, hoping like hell that the arrangement wouldn't make Cora balk.

Indeed, Cora didn't look thrilled with the terms. "Seems like I ought to be compensated first," she said, looking Mattie over, as if it was Mattie's decision to make. Finally, she turned to Old Mol. "Be sure she's outside on time. You," she said to Mattie. She scowled at the bandaged hand. "Of all the times to be careless, Friday is certainly the worst. You're not going to be any use in the kitchen or waiting tables, and I'm going to let *you* tell that madman in the kitchen. You can lay out the dining room, though. Get the tables set first. Then upstairs—can you manage turning a guest room?"

"Yes ma'am," she said. "Getting the rooms clean won't be any problem." She intended to stay all afternoon, as usual. As Lucy had stressed as they sat around her kitchen table, the more typical Mattie's day appeared to everyone around the hotel, the less likely that a suspicious eye would turn on her when Ya Zhen failed to return. Up before dawn, she'd corked some of Hazel's laudanum into an old cologne bottle, admiring the ruby-red color a little before she slipped it into her pocket. The little bit she'd taken with her first cup of coffee had helped the pain, and she had more for later, just in case.

"There are eight rooms to see to," Cora said. "Ask Mr. Salyer which ones." She started to walk away, but stopped and looked at both of them. "You don't need to mention any of this to my husband," she said. "If he has questions about where that whore got herself off to, tell him he'll have to speak to me."

Just before eleven o'clock, Old Mol let Ya Zhen out the back stairs entrance.

"Go out front and wait," she said. "The reverend's wife will pick you up on the corner." Her voice was unaccountably soft. "Listen to me, little sister. Here's the reason I'm not going to wait down there with you: there's nowhere for a girl like you to hide, understand? You got the woods on one side and the ocean on the other, so if you get out there by yourself and decide to run off, better think again." She put her head out the door and glanced around the outside stairs before adding a final warning. "You'd miss us plenty if the Chinese Six Company grabbed you," she said. "They'd drag you back to Frisco and have you working the street cribs. Two bits a feelie." She reached out as if to caress Ya Zhen's face. When the girl flinched away from her, Old Mol smiled thinly, showing a glimpse of her horsey teeth. "Well enough—you don't have to love me, but you best mind me. Get out there and wait now."

Ya Zhen picked her way down the rickety staircase, trying not to catch her clothes on the rough banister. Many of the stair risers were bowed and the banister wobbled, a far cry from the ornate front entrance, which was lovingly maintained and less exposed to the weather and the depredations of salt air. Rounding the side of the building, she realized she was out on the street she had seen hundreds of times from her window. She looked up, and yes, there was the yellow curtain. The window looked so small from here. She was seized by the awful idea that her own face would appear there. All the hotel windows stacked above her felt like eyes, and Ya Zhen wondered if Old Mol or Mrs. Salyer was watching her right now, or one of the Wu sisters, put on guard to see if she would try to run.

At the corner, there was no one waiting for her, so she stood close to the building, several feet away from the big double doors. The relative freedom of the open street wanted to amplify her strangely claustrophobic fear, causing her heart to beat thickly in her ears.

She leaned against the warm side of the hotel and lifted her face to the sun, working to slow her breathing. The late morning traffic was heavy, but no one seemed to notice her standing there; everyone looked happy to be out in a second day of mild weather. An onshore breeze carried the salty tang of high tide. For the first time in years, she thought about her mother's small vegetable garden. In spring, little moles would sometimes burrow out of the earth with their long toenails, eyes almost invisible. The face of Li Lau's baby had looked that way, his eyes tightly closed against a world for which he was still unformed.

She looked out at the bay, then turned and let her eyes roam the hills at the opposite edge of town. Again she was struck by how different her perspective was, here on the street, than it had been yesterday up on the hotel roof. The forest looked so much larger, easily accessible. Couldn't she live there? It was said that people lived in the trees, far back in the woods. Couldn't she find a place to hide, eat berries and fungus, trap birds, find a stream for fish?

Two couples came around the corner, strolling toward the hotel, the first of many who would tuck into the mountain of crab Ivo would be hustling out of the kitchen all day long. She backed against the wall to let the couples pass, keeping her eyes on her feet.

"What's she doing here?" said one of the women. She wore an elaborate hat that towered over her head with a swath of purple netting and peacock feathers. "Aren't they supposed to stay with their own kind?" The group stopped in front of the entrance.

The man walking next to the peacock woman leaned close to Ya Zhen's face. "Are you lost, Ching Chang Janie? Or are you just stupid?" He grinned at the others, showing a large gap between his front teeth.

The peacock woman batted at his arm, laughing. "Teddy, you're terrible."

The other couple—a fat woman and a man with a bushy mustache—said nothing. The mustached man had been to her room several times, and he stood with his hat pulled low. The fat woman clutched his arm with both hands.

"Go on now, girl," said the one called Teddy. "You don't belong on this side of town. Move on." He stamped his foot and pointed up the street. Ya Zhen moved away from them, not sure whether she should try to go around back or move off in the direction the man had pointed.

"There you are!" A white-haired woman, quite a bit shorter than Ya Zhen and with a military bearing, stepped out of a carriage right at the corner. "Hello there, everyone," she said to the two couples. "Elsie Dampler, it's so nice to see you again." She lowered her voice a bit. "I hope we didn't hurt your feelings the other night."

The fat woman smiled stiffly. "Heavens, no," she said. Her ears turned bright pink. "I'd already forgotten about it, Mrs. Huntington."

"Well, that's grand." She held out her hand to Elsie's husband. "Charlie Dampler, how are you? Isn't it a lovely day? I told Reverend Huntington that we'd have sunshine again and goodness if I wasn't right."

Charlie took off his hat and shook her hand. "I'm fine, ma'am," he mumbled. His eyes slid toward Ya Zhen and then away.

"Heavens, where are my manners?" the small woman said. "My dear, I'm Lucy Huntington." She took Ya Zhen's hand and shook it; her grip was strong, and the fierceness under her sweet expression made some wild thing break out inside Ya Zhen. It wanted to roar, that wild thing, wanted to turn on the four people standing at the hotel door with tooth and claw. It was all she could do to smile calmly in return. "Elsie, Charlie," Lucy continued, "this young lady is Ya Zhen. She's been good enough to agree to help me get ready for Reverend Huntington's birthday dinner next week."

Elsie's mouth opened as if to speak, then closed again. Charlie kept busy, inspecting his fingernails with tremendous concentration.

"Now listen, you four," said Lucy. "I want you to tell me you can be there. I know, I know you're Methodists, but we certainly expect an inter-denominational guest list." She chuckled, a surprisingly deep and throaty sound.

The man called Teddy snorted. "I'm not interested in being introduced to a Chinese whore. Come on folks, we're going to be late for lunch." He pulled open the hotel door and ushered the peacock woman inside.

"Enjoy your crab," Lucy called. Charlie made as if to follow them, then looked back at his wife, who was still on the sidewalk.

Elsie hesitated, and lowered her voice to a confidential tone. "Mrs. Huntington, it does seem as though you ought to have picked her up over in Chinatown." She nodded toward Ya Zhen. "It doesn't look good, a...a person like her standing on a street corner in the middle of town."

Lucy had taken Ya Zhen's elbow and helped her into the carriage. "Nonsense. That wouldn't have been convenient for either of us," she said. "After all, Ya Zhen lives here at Salyer's." She climbed up next to Ya Zhen and took the reins. "Anyway," she called, "it's a free country, isn't it? Can't a person stand outside on a weekday afternoon enjoying the weather? Certainly that can't be a crime. Come on, Buster." She touched the end of her whip to Buster's flank and waved to Elsie and Charlie as the horse pulled away.

Ya Zhen turned in her seat and looked back. Charlie held the door for his wife, but was watching the carriage. Ya Zhen, face solemn, waved. Charlie Dampler hurried behind Elsie, white-faced and cringing, looking as though someone had just given him a nasty scare.

Lucy, thinking that Ya Zhen was looking over her shoulder at the hotel, gave Buster an extra flick of the reins, picking up his speed. "You won't go back," she said. "Not if I can help it." Even as the words left her mouth, she wished she could retrieve the boast, her head suddenly filled with Burns's lament to the mouse:

> But Och! I backward cast my e'e,
> On prospects drear!
> An' forward, tho' I canna see,
> I guess an' fear!

We cannot see, Lucy thought. Better not to guess at all.

¤

Even as busy as they were—October chipmunks, Hazel said— it was the longest day that Rose could remember. The minute she walked into the Kendalls' house, she found Hazel elbow deep in preparations. Phoebe Kendall had arrived at her parents' house sometime shortly after dawn, with big ideas. Not content just to have dinner as planned, she instead told her mother that she longed to have "a proper British tea." Prudence, of course, told Phoebe it was a wonderful idea.

"Where does that girl get these things into her head?" Hazel said. "She wouldn't know a British tea if it jumped down her throat. Look at all this." The entire surface of the kitchen table was covered with food in the midst of preparation, as was the long counter near the sink—jars of candied ginger, chow-chow, and dilly beans to be put in serving dishes; eggs to be hard-boiled and deviled; quarts of blackberry jam and cherry preserves to be put into china saucers along with dainty silver spoons.

"She also wants finger sandwiches—chicken salad, no crusts— cream scones, and *petit fours*. Petit fours, if you don't mind. I didn't even know what they were. Prudence had to tell me—little cakes. Tiny little frosted cakes. 'Now Hazel,' she tells me, 'I know this is above-and-beyond. Just do what you're able.' You know what that means, though, don't you?"

Rose still gawked at the preparations that covered every available inch of flat surface. Her mind was swamped with the details of Lucy Huntington's plan, and she wasn't entirely sure what her aunt had just asked. "I...what does *what* mean?"

Hazel cleared her throat for emphasis and spoke in an exaggerated imitation of sweet, cultured voice of Prudence. "It actually means, 'I'd like you to do it all, Hazel, just as asked, without so much as a wrinkle in the plans or a substitution in the menu. Make it look simple, dear. Make it look easy, so that I can always ask you to do it again sometime.' That's what it means. Thank heavens you got here a little early," she said, beating butter into creamy submission in a large bowl. Her sleeves were rolled high, and her mixing arm looked strong as a young man's, bicep bulging and tendons standing out. "*Rose*," she said loudly, seeing her looking around in stunned confusion. "Jump in somewhere, girl—we have a beastly day bearing down on us. You can pick that bird, to start with, and chop it up fine for the salad."

The boiled chicken rested in a pan, under a tea towel. Rose sat at the crowded table and began the greasy job of getting the meat off the bones. "How long do we have?"

Hazel laughed, a not-very-amused snort. "The princess has asked for a tea," Hazel said, "and a tea it is. They've invited five others; we'll serve the eight of them at four o'clock."

Rose's hands, glazed with fat and amber bits of jellied broth, froze over the diminishing chicken carcass. "Four? Aunt...I can't—"

Hazel stopped whipping the butter, and she glared at Rose. "Don't—you—dare," she said. Her voice was low, almost a whisper, and she punctuated each word by stabbing her mixing spoon in Rose's direction. Tiny flecks of butter flew off and speckled the floor between them. "I've had enough, Rose Allen. Enough of you rambling off to Chinatown and not coming back until long after you're needed. Enough disappearing without a word—last night was bad, but then this morning—you and Mattie both rushing out before first light. Oh, yes," she said, "I heard you go. I was born at night, but I wasn't born *last* night, by Christ." Rose was alarmed to see tears in Hazel's eyes. "She's a sick girl, Rose. Mattie is ill. More than you know."

Rose kept her eyes on her work. "I know about the opium."

"You *think* you know." Hazel snapped. "She got into the laudanum, did you know that? Poured some right out of the bottle. I don't know if it was last night or this morning, but there's quite a bit gone. That's something she's never done before—broken trust with me." She measured sugar into her bowl and began beating again. "She's broken trust with herself, time and again. This is the first time she's broken trust with me, though. It hurts, I admit it, but will hurt her more." She looked around the chaotic kitchen then, as if just remembering where she was. "Do you know what to put in the salad after you've minced that chicken?"

Rose looked stupidly at the bird and went back to pulling the last shreds of meat free. "Yes," she said. "I remember." A ball of regret and hurt and worry swelled inside her, a hydra-headed mass of concerns that made it hard to breathe. Her hands shook as she set the pile of picked-over bones aside and grabbed the butcher's knife to dice celery and pickles. She wanted to go find Mattie and see that she was safe—or slap her. She longed to be back at the mercantile with Bai Lum, and little Shu-Li. And a part of her—a rather distressingly large part, she thought—wanted to stay right where she was, helping Hazel with this mountain of tasks, and then simply go home and climb into her own warm bed with a cup of cocoa and her books. Most desperate of all, though, grinding around inside her like a mill wheel, was the knowledge that the Huntingtons were counting on her help.

"Don't forget a dab of horseradish. Gives it a little kick. Captain Kendall likes that."

"I won't forget."

A long silence spun out between them, filled only with the sound of Hazel's bowl and spoon, then the flour sifter and more stirring. A peal of female laughter came from the front parlor, Phoebe saying, "But it's *true,* Mama!"

Hazel made a long, weary sound, like taking up a dirge.

¤

"I'll give you a task to do," Lucy Huntington said. "Something to keep you looking busy. That's the story we're concocting, and we want everyone to believe it."

The carriage ride had taken three times as long as it needed to. Lucy's most immediate concern when she collected Ya Zhen at Salyer's was to stay visible and be sure that as many people as possible saw her bringing her to the rectory. Every time the carriage passed someone on the street, she waved, called—*Good morning! How are you! Wonderful day, isn't it?*—even when it meant leaning halfway out of the buggy to be seen. Not wanting to risk distressing the girl, Lucy explained only a little of what they had planned, promising that she would tell her everything later. She expected confusion, perhaps fear, but Ya Zhen seemed utterly content, looking around at everything as Buster clip-clopped up one street and down another, happily taking a route home that seemed to cover nearly every road in town.

Now she sat at the long dining room table, surrounded by every bit of silver in the house, and even some of the candlesticks from the church. Lucy showed her how to coat each item with a dab of polish, to work her way into the crevices and concavities, and then rub with a clean cloth to get a shine. "Slowly," she whispered, "and don't be too careful. Let's see if we can make this job last. If you get through everything, just pick up a fork and start over, yes? It's all for show." Ya Zhen nodded, starting right off with a squat little cream pitcher.

She's all in, Lucy thought, relieved by Ya Zhen's apparent composure. She took a seat nearby and spread a voluminous tablecloth over her lap, one which she'd been embroidering for weeks with a wide ramble of violets and English ivy around the hem. "I'm going to stay right here and keep you company, if you don't mind. We'll have visitors soon enough." She'd already poured tea for each of them, and sipped from her cup before threading her needle. She was, in fact, counting on the usual parade of parishioners, a few of whom couldn't survive Sunday-to-Sunday without an invariable load of snipes and petty jealousies for Lucy's or Charles's listening ears. "You just sit there, Ya Zhen, and pretend you don't understand a blessed thing. Most of it is blather that isn't worth a spit in the ocean anyway." Ya Zhen surprised her by looking up and laughing, and Lucy smiled back, two co-conspirators.

Almost as if on cue, not six minutes passed before Louise Biddle, a tall scarecrow of a woman who seemed to spend more time at the rectory than she did in her own home, sat primly next to Lucy, her thin brown hair stuffed haphazardly under a tiny hat that sported a stuffed bird so large and badly attached that it wobbled back and forth as if looking for its chance to fly off. Lucy worked her needle and nodded while Louise told an occasionally tearful story about the bad behavior of her husband. Every few minutes she threw a sidelong glance at Ya Zhen.

"Now, Mrs. Huntington, are you sure she can't understand English?" the woman finally whispered. "I can't help feeling peculiar telling you all of this with that girl sitting right there."

Lucy didn't lie outright. "She won't understand you in the least." *Isn't that the truth?* she thought. *I don't understand you, either.* She smiled benignly. "Not to worry, Louise. I assure you, you can speak freely. Of course," she added in a quiet voice, "it's best that I stay nearby while she polishes the silver. More tea?" Ya Zhen continued with the ornate ladle in her hands, seeming to pay no more attention to their conversation than she would have to two ravens calling each other from opposing tree branches.

Louise Biddle nodded sagely at Lucy, took the tea, and recollected how her Joe never failed to fall asleep before she even had a chance to wash the supper dishes. A world of woe.

Didn't it always come down to some damned woman? Garland Tupper's wife—God rest her—had forever mealy-mouthed him. Couldn't say boo to a goose. Wouldn't cuss a rat if it ran over her boot. His own mother—also long dead—had known the way to cope with life, and with a man. Many the time was that Garland's father had taken after his wife with whatever was at hand—stove length, bridle, razor strop—and though she might come through it black-and-blue, his mother gave as good as she got, leaving her stripe on the man she married, and many a dark mark on the men she bore. Garland Tupper's wife had had no such starch in her spine. He'd married her for her sweetness, but it soon chafed him. His wife had been a creeper, a coddler, a timid trifle of a person. Once the vows were said, once he got under the crinolines and got her kindled with their boy, she'd wanted to turn Byron into a wilting willy, filling his head with fairy stories and flower picking and the naming of animals meant for the table. Garland thought that Byron losing his mother early would thicken the boy's skin, shave some of the dreamy edges off him, but here he was so soft-headed over a Chinese whore that he'd burned up the goddamned tool shed.

It was all much on his mind when he woke on Friday, conscious even before he opened his eyes of the powerful stink of wet char hanging about the yard. His fist was stiff, too, from giving that boy his licks, and he flexed it a few times, sitting on the edge of his bed.

Catching Byron mooning around Salyer's last night had been a lucky thing, especially grabbing him before he'd gotten upstairs with that little painted cat again. This was always the way with his son, some remnant of his mother's soft-headedness, a bad seed that had sent down roots and couldn't be grubbed out. Byron grabbed like a starfish onto things that tripped his fancy, always had. And, like a starfish, getting him to turn loose usually meant nearly ripping a limb from the boy's body. Much as Garland hoped the lesson he'd given last night would break this new fascination, deep down he knew it wasn't so. Letting the air out of his son's half-cocked notion was, he reckoned, going to require getting into Salyer's and—one way or another—spoiling the fantasy.

He shuffled to the cold stove and poured some of the coffee Byron had made yesterday—gone bitter as bile, to be sure, but dressed up tolerable by a fat first knock of Thistle Dew.

ᛘ

The day passed in a sprint. By two o'clock, Rose and Hazel had baked and simmered and sliced and polished and set out a dozen china bowls and saucers. At half past three, Prudence put the hideous flower arrangement in the center of the table, and Phoebe made a face and took it away. By three forty-five, Rose had arranged chairs, answered the bell, taken coats, and looked at the clock more times than she could count.

Captain Kendall arrived home just as the last guest arrived; they could hear him in the parlor, charming everyone. Desultory murmurs became animated conversation. In a moment, he poked his head in at the kitchen door. When he saw that Hazel's back was turned, he winked at Rose and put a finger to his lips. He darted into the room and grabbed Hazel into a quick polka, dancing her around the room. She swatted at his shoulder, trying to bluster, not able to keep a straight face. The floor was still greasy where Hazel had earlier flicked butter when lecturing Rose, and as David Kendall spun Hazel around, his right foot flew out, landing him squarely on his prat with a thud.

"Serves you, doesn't it," cried Hazel, out of breath and trying not to laugh, the color high in her cheeks.

"Nothing damaged but my terrible pride," he panted, "and that's not a mortal wound." He got to his feet and brushed at his trousers. "Thanks, both of you, for all of this. Phoebe's delighted."

"Then I suppose all's right with the world," Hazel said in her sweetest voice. Rose could hear the peeve underneath, but Kendall pretended not to notice.

"Thanks for the dance, too, Hazel," he said, and ducked out quick.

"Good Lord," she said, shaking her head. "Gammy man."

Rose didn't reply. She frantically scraped dishes into the swill bucket and stacked them next to the deep soapstone sink. It was almost four-thirty, and her desperation to leave was nearly strangling her. The platter she held banged against the edge of the counter and broke. Pieces fell to the floor at her feet. "Damn!"

"Careful," Hazel said. She bustled over and took the remaining wedge of broken china. "Here," she said, handing her a towel. "Wipe your hands." Rose did, and couldn't help another quick glance at the time.

"Listen to me," Hazel said. "I'm an awfully impatient person. I don't mean to be, but I was born with it. So were you, Rosie." Rose nodded, feeling tears burning at the back of her eyes. "I used to tell my mother it was like an itch I couldn't scratch," Hazel continued, "wanting things to happen right away, getting mad when they didn't. My ma told me over and over that the only cure for what ailed me was to stay on the lookout for the next right choice, and to do it, whatever it was." She smiled wearily. "You're not a child. I told your father that you'd do well here, and I intend to keep my word. So you tell me you'll stay on the lookout, too, for that next right choice, and I'll believe you."

"I promise."

Hazel kissed her cheek. "Go on, then. Do what you have to do."

¤

"Hired out? The hell you say. I didn't okay that. Son of a bitch!" Clarence Salyer pitched a fit when he discovered Ya Zhen gone—sounded like a bear with his pizzle snagged in the underscrub, in fact—but it was Old Mol he jabbered at, and perhaps Cora. Mattie only heard him from a distance, and his tantrum put a little shine on the day for her. Ivo was every bit as pissy as Clarence, and she *had* been forced to listen to him (though she only understood about every fourth word). No sweat off her brow. She got the dining tables fully set while he muttered and growled and slammed things around in the kitchen, then she disappeared upstairs.

Before she was half done turning guest rooms, the burning in her injured palm told her she'd almost certainly broken the blisters. She tipped the perfume bottle of laudanum repeatedly— only tiny sips, just enough to keep herself going—and still the fire under that bandage made her entire arm an agony.

By late afternoon, she got so muddled about what she had done and what she hadn't yet finished, she had to sit every few minutes, hoping the dizzy spin in her head would lift a little. When the last room was as orderly as she seemed able to make it, she gathered an armload of soiled linens and made her way downstairs. The hotel hummed with guests now, all happily eating their crab dinners in the dining room. Everything seemed in fine order; it was clear that no one—not Clarence or Cora or even Old Mol— suspected in the least that a bamboozlement had been pulled, and Mattie didn't intend to be anywhere around when it dawned on someone that Ya Zhen wasn't ever coming back. She dumped the linens in the back-porch baskets, grabbed her coat, and scatted.

It was still light out, a little bit of sun fading into the approaching murk. Her intention all day had been to go from work to the mercantile, to see if there was anything she could do to help Ya Zhen settle in there. But she couldn't face all that just now. She was done in. She still hurt, and she *needed*—that terrible feeling of emptiness, as though her very bones were hollow as a bird's. Even when she saw Rose, just two streets over and hurrying away, she couldn't call out. Instead, she crouched out of sight behind a myrtle hedge and counted to twenty.

When she crept out, the street was empty. With her arms crossed tightly over her bosom against the shakes that threatened, Mattie faced toward Chinatown. Blinked. Pivoted toward home. She stood that way for several minutes, counting her breaths, first in, then out. Finally she turned in the opposite direction and started for the waterfront.

¤

"We can't wait," Reverend Huntington said. He was the tallest man Ya Zhen had ever seen. When he first came home, she was astounded; his explosion of white hair looked to her like clouds that hover around a mountain summit. Lucy—for perhaps the tenth time in the past half-hour—wandered to the front windows of her parlor, as if wishing for Rose Allen would make the woman appear. She held a little pile of women's clothing, and she smoothed her hand over the folded fabric again and again.

"Lucy?"

When they had talked over their plan that morning, Reverend Huntington told her, it was decided that at four o'clock Rose would come as far as the corner, a half-block from the rectory, and wait. When Ya Zhen left the rectory on foot, she would simply follow Rose—from a distance—until they got to a stretch of road about a quarter mile away that dipped into a swale. Here the road was bordered by a hilly stretch of woods along one side and an overgrown snarl of berry briars on the other. There were no houses with a clear sight line to this spot; Rose would wait there for Ya Zhen to catch up, and Reverend Huntington would pick them both up in the back of his wagon. Then to the mercantile.

But now, no Rose.

"Yes," Lucy said, "you're right. We'll have to go ahead without her."

Reverend Huntington nodded. "Then let's make sure we all know what to do." He went to a small oak secretary and came back with paper and pencil. While Ya Zhen watched, he sketched a little map, drawing in tiny houses and trees and fences. "Now here," he said, marking one of the little houses with a cross, "is where we are—the church. Where you're going to walk, Ya Zhen, is here. No houses—that's how you'll know it's the place." He counted out the number of streets between the rectory and the meeting place— right turn, left turn, right again—then had her repeat it back, without looking at the map. As she recited the route exactly, he nodded. "Just so."

In the next room, an enormous clock marked time. Ever since Lucy had picked her up that morning, Ya Zhen felt at giddy loose ends—simultaneously thrilled to be away, and utterly convinced that at any minute someone would come through the door to drag her back to the hotel. Now she was about to step outside, all on her own for the first time in nearly three years, and instead of feeling free, there was fear, like a live thing set loose under her skin.

"When you see the place with no houses, wait there," Lucy told her. "Reverend Huntington will be right along for you." She looked at her husband, apprehension showing in wavy lines across her forehead.

"That's right," he said. "I'll drive the wagon around a bit, but I'll be close by."

"They will look for me," Ya Zhen said. "Clarence Salyer. Old Mol. They'll come to find me."

"Not until you're safe with Bai Lum at the mercantile," Lucy said. "I'll send a note to Mrs. Salyer thanking her for sending you, and telling her you had to walk home because the carriage wheel broke. But you'll be tucked upstairs with little Shu-Li before they even think of searching. You'll stay put for two days, get some rest, and off to your new home in Oregon."

Charles Huntington took Ya Zhen's hand in one of his. His big palms and long fingers were warm and helped slow her racing heart a little. "When you get right there," he said, and tapped the spot on the map, "if you don't see me coming, step a little way into the trees. Not too far, and don't come out until I call." He bent his knees to be sure Ya Zhen was looking at him. "I'll come."

She nodded. All she could do now was try.

Reverend Huntington put on his coat and hat. Lucy handed him the folded clothes she clutched. "Get back just as quick as you can," she told him. "I don't dare send a note to Cora Salyer until you do."

Out the back door he went, and two minutes later he drove past in the wagon, a heavy canvas tarpaulin tied across the bed. Lucy put her hands on Ya Zhen's shoulders. "Ready?"

"Yes." She was shivering a little. Lucy grabbed a shawl from the coat tree and wrapped it around Ya Zhen's shoulders. "Here we go. Wait here on the front steps while I go next door. As soon as you hear me chatting up Mrs. Holtz, off you go, confident as can be."

It only took a few seconds. When she heard Lucy laughing and talking, she pulled the shawl tight and started walking. As she passed the neighbor's front gate, Lucy called out in a coolly imperious voice: "Girl, you go straight home, and quick. Cora Salyer wants you back by supper time." Ya Zhen looked around at Lucy, standing at the open door of her neighbor. Her expression matched that of the other woman—neutral and careless, as though Ya Zhen was no more or less to them than a cloud passing over the sun.

And then she was at the corner, and out of sight.

¤

Reilly didn't try to negotiate Byron's pay, just handed it over. Late in the day, when Byron had climbed into the loft to shove down a bale, he found an old horse blanket folded neatly near where he had bedded last night. "There's a ladder up to the hay mow from outside," Reilly told him as he left, "and that hatch door don't hardly ever get bolted from the inside. See you tomorrow."

The day narrowed toward sunset, and an incipient fog bank hovering over the ocean inched its nebulous face toward landfall. Byron fingered the money in his pocket, rubbing the coins together as he walked. He felt good, tired from his day of work. The swelling in his nose had gone down some, and over the course of the day the pain had faded, as long as he didn't bend over for too long. He wanted to go straight to Salyer's and fetch Pearl, lay with her, explain his plans for them, find out who it was that had come to her last night, but he should wait until dark, and he felt ready to eat something. No stolen cabbage tonight.

In Chinatown, three narrow storefront rooms sold chow, a fragrant hot mix of vegetables, noodles, and bits of meat. Even with his injured snoot, Byron could smell the hot oil odor of the chow shops from two blocks away, and his mouth watered. He stepped into the nearest small eatery. The room was dim. Rough stools stood by tiny plank tables. Off to one side, two Chinese men chopped and stirred mounds of food in large cast-iron bowls, throwing a tremendous sizzle when they dropped the sliced vegetables into the heated oil. Byron held up one finger and the cook nodded. He scooped a plateful of chow out of the wok and handed it over. Byron put a half-dollar on the table and the man fished change out of a box behind him. Several men ate late lunches, early suppers, two or three white men and the rest Chinese. The Chinese men ate from bowls with chopsticks, a nimble manipulation that Bryon found baffling. Pearl could teach him how, maybe, and he would teach her to use a fork, like regular people.

The food was delicious, hot with ginger and some kind of red pepper. Byron bolted it, wiping his chin on his coat sleeve while he ate. He was nearly finished when none other than Billy Kellogg walk past the shop door. "Billy," he yelled, his mouth full. A noodle slithered off his bottom lip and onto his lap, and he laughed. *I feel good*, he thought again, satisfied in the belly. Billy stuck his head in the shop door, squinting around the dark interior. Byron lifted a hand before shoveling in the last bit of his dinner.

"Hells bells, Tupper, there you are. What are you doing in here, eatin rats?" He honked laughter at his own joke, but sobered when several Chinese men looked over at him. Every one of them was bigger than all five-feet-two of Billy Kellogg, who had the build of a much younger boy.

Byron joined him on the sidewalk, still chewing. Billy got a look at his face and whistled low and long. "I heard you burned your daddy's house down," he said, and grinned. His front teeth were uneven, broken during a fight with one of his nine older brothers.

"It was the tool shed. You seen my old man?"

"I ain't seen him anywhere. Just got the story from Eustace Kilgore. I don't know where he got it. Maybe your daddy told it to him. You sure it was just the shed?"

"Was when I left."

"So you must be hiding out a while, I guess. Garland was asking around for you. Guess he musta found you."

"I'm done with that bastard. Got a job."

"The hell you say. Where at?"

"Livery. I helped old man Reilly fix his broken window and he gave me a job."

Billy laughed so hard at this, spittle flew from his lips and his face turned pink. "Shit, Tupper, you ought to celebrate. What do you say? Let's have some entertainment, then head back to my place."

Byron hesitated. He didn't want to spend too much money. He had to save back at least enough to get him into Salyer's again. "I don't want to get too drunk," he said, remembering Billy's lament from the night before.

"I got a better idea than drunk. Let's go downstreet. Let's do the palace."

"Palace?"

"The poppy palace. Opium," Billy said in a stage whisper. He winked at Byron. "Better than a woman." When Byron just looked at him, Billy's color rose again and he studied the toe of his boot. "You didn't tell anybody about last night did you, about what I told you?"

"I don't want to talk about that."

"Me either.

"I'm not paying for you."

"Yeah, so? I have some. I stole some of the egg money from my ma. Come on, Tupper, do I have to talk you into everything?"

Byron looked toward the bay, in the direction of the hotel. The sun wasn't even set yet. He could kill some time, get off the street in case the old man was hunting him again. He nodded at Billy, who looked at him like a dog waiting for a scrap of food. If he had a tail, it would be wagging, Byron thought, and smiled a little.

Billy broke into his own snaggled grin and pulled Byron by the sleeve until Byron yanked loose of his grip. "Over there, across the street," he said, giggling. "You're gonna love this."

"How long you been doing it?"

"I've been there a time or two." He shot a sideways glance at Byron. "Garland knows the place pretty well. I hear." Byron ignored him.

About halfway down the block, Billy knocked on a door. There were no windows, and when the door opened, the room inside was dark as the bottom of a well. The smell was strong, like burned coffee beans, but sweeter. The person who had opened now closed the door behind them, and Byron felt a momentary sense of claustrophobia at being shut into the dark room. Then a match flared, and he could make out the dim outlines of furniture and people. Several men, Chinese and white, reclined on bunks built onto one wall, or sat across a single bench that ran the width of another. A Chinese man lit a thin taper and held it to the bowl of a long pipe. The smoker inhaled, a deep draw. He lay back on his bunk, eyes open and unfocused in the thin light of the little candle. The man with the light gestured to the bench. Byron followed Billy, picking his way through the dark room, hoping no one was stretched out on the floor. He had been hearing about the opium den for years, how the smoke corrupted the mind and was part of the Chinese plot to destroy democracy. Most of the stories had come from Garland. As far as Byron could see, at least so far, the men leaning about inside this place didn't seem any more or less impaired than the ones puking or shooting out gaslights in the alleys behind every tavern in Eureka.

The candle man stood waiting, and Byron realized he wanted money. He left his one dollar piece in his pocket and held out the rest of his day's wages. The man swept it off his palm and said something in Chinese. Another man appeared, holding one of the long pipes. He handed it to Byron. The bowl was set in the center of the stem, which was nearly as long as his arm. The candle man lowered the taper and gestured to Byron to lift the pipe to his mouth. Billy watched it all, his pupils large in the dark and his broken teeth glinting in the glow of the flame. Byron inhaled deeply as he had seen the other man do, and held the burned, sweet smoke in his lungs. Immediately he felt a warm and powerful contentment slide over him, as if some large, benign creature, an angel or a butterfly, was folding its wings around his body. He groaned softly, barely a sigh, and rested his shoulders and head on the rough wall behind him, a wall that felt as soft as a spring hillock. Somewhere next to him Billy took the opium, but Byron felt cocooned in the sensation of pure contentment, separate. He remembered a certain consciousness from young childhood, before his mother died, when he would waver between sleep and waking, and this was like that, but far stronger. He did not close his eyes, but rode on the sensations like floating in warm water, the sound of his own breathing very much like the in-out rhythm of the ocean.

¤

Which way? Rose's feet were moving—running a little, then walking, running again—but every half-block she faltered, her mind pulling her in opposing directions. What if Ya Zhen had already set out? Maybe Reverend Huntington had picked her up at the spot by the gulch and was taking her to the mercantile even now—*should I go there instead?* But no—surely they'd have waited for a little while, wouldn't they, before sending her out on foot? Mattie was probably home by now—maybe she should stop there first and ask her to check at the mercantile for Ya Zhen, to tell them Rose would be there as soon as she checked at the Huntingtons'. Thinking about Mattie scared her, too, after what Hazel had said about the missing laudanum. The fathomless pressure of the afternoon was about to crash into her like a rogue wave.

Think, Rose. She stopped dead in the middle of the sidewalk, breathing hard.

There was no time for a detour—a last wispy remnant of February sun hung on, but foggy twilight was already creeping in. If Ya Zhen had already made it to Bai Lum's, she was safe, but if she was out on the street, Rose might still be able to help. As for Mattie—well, that was a worry that had to wait. She pushed every other thought out of her head and made a beeline to the meeting spot, clipping along as fast as she could without breaking back into her previous unnerved gallop.

Just a block from the dip in the road, she saw the Huntingtons' wagon stopped in the street, and a second wagon drawn alongside. Reverend Huntington sat up front holding the reins, and the other man leaned forward with his arms on his knees, talking. Heart hammering, Rose slowed to a normal pace and approached them.

"But I told him I didn't care how many apples that pig had got into, that was my pig. I showed him the notch in its ear, and he had the nerve to tell me—"

"Good evening, Reverend Huntington," Rose called. Both men turned to look at her, the man with the pig looking none too pleased to have his story interrupted.

"Hello, Rose Allen!" The look on the reverend's face was sheer relief. "Mr. Potts and I are having a natter about the fine points of animal property rights."

"Nothing fine-pointed about it," said Potts, sitting up out of his slouch and shaking a finger at the reverend. "By point of law that barrow—"

"You're absolutely right, Potts," Charles Huntington interrupted. "Say, Rose, I can't let you get away before I tell you that Mrs. Huntington went back to the spot you told her about and found those early fiddleheads, right where you said they'd be—do you know the place I mean?" He stared fixedly at her, ignoring the other man, who now squirmed in his seat as though stricken with poison oak, so anxious was he to state his case.

She swallowed hard and nodded. "I...I do know it."

"If you know where to look, you're bound to find more. That's according to my wife, anyway." He tipped her a little salute. "See you soon."

"Good night," Rose said, and strolled away, pretending she had all the time in the world, as the fog rolled ashore in earnest.

¤

"Jesus. Oh Jesus." Billy's voice sounded muffled, close but soft. It might be a prayer. Byron hoped he would not talk anymore. For a time—perhaps it was a very long time, or not, Byron wasn't sure—Billy was quiet. Then he was whispering. Byron could hear the whispering, but at first it wasn't words, just sound. He liked the sound, quiet and smooth.

"...and he's going to see that girl...kept asking me...wanted to know which one."

Byron rested, floated in the dark. The taper flared again, across the room.

"Was she good?" Billy's voice hovered somewhere over Byron's shoulder. "Like this?"

Pearl's long hair, a black river falling down her back. The slope of her breast when the robe opened and the smell of her neck as he climaxed. Lying in a bar of dusty sunlight, clean hay in the livery loft. Floating again, safe, everything just as it should be. Byron dozed.

"I'll try her next time."

"What?" It was like pulling up from deep sleep. The door was ajar. Byron could see gray, late afternoon light falling over the jamb. The cooler air helped him think a little. His limbs felt heavy. He sat slightly forward. His head bobbed, straightened. He looked at Billy, still slumped against the wall, but eyes wide open, like always.

"The other girl...I didn't like her much. Her face was sort of...flat." He giggled. "She kept on yanking me—"

"Shut up, Billy." It came out in a whisper.

"I'm just saying, is all. I want to try." In the long pause, someone stretched out on a bunk coughed from deep in his chest. "Try the pretty one."

Byron turned his head, as if it weighed fifty pounds on his shoulders. There was something he needed to say here, but his thoughts stood at the back of his mind, just beyond reach. "Going out." He leaned forward and tried to rock to his feet. When he landed heavily on his ass again, he laughed. Billy laughed, too. The men around them lolled, some seemed to sleep. In the far corner of the room, someone started to sing. *Blessed assurance. Jesus is mine.* Byron recalled singing a hymn when he woke that morning. Was that this morning? He tried to pin it down, how long it was since he sang and cleaned the house. This morning. Yes. He rocked himself forward again and this time managed to gain his feet. For a moment the room tilted and Bryon stumbled, but then he steadied and walked to the open door. The last bit of daylight, a lambent streak shooting beneath the roiling fog bank and across the surface of Humboldt Bay, dazzled Byron so that he had to raise a hand to shield his eyes. He squinted out at the water and was surprised to see two steamships at harbor, the *Humboldt* and the *City of Chester*. It was rare to see two ships at once; they must be expecting rough seas tonight. A lone hand stood on the *Chester's* deck, running a mop back and forth. Two little girls, dressed in the way of sisters, with matching yellow pinafores, stood at the foot of the pier, throwing rocks into the water. Their voices drifted back to Byron: "Mine went farther." "No it did not. I'm stronger than you." "Watch this, smarty britches," said the smaller girl. "I'm going to hit the sun with my rock." The child put so much effort into her throw she nearly threw herself into the bay. "Missed," said the bigger girl.

Billy Kellogg came staggering into the street. His eyes were bleary and he had lost his hat. "Damn. Bright out here."

Byron nodded.

"So, what do you think?"

"About what?"

"The Chinese poppy palace. Isn't that a place to go?"

Byron nodded again. Little by little he felt his head clearing.

"Let's get some whiskey before we go to my place," Billy said.

"I don't want any. I have to do some things for a while."

Billy gave him a blank look. "What?"

"I'll be there later."

"Why later? I'll come with you."

"No."

Billy frowned, looking more than ever, Byron thought, like a not-too-bright dog. Then he laughed. "You're going back to Salyer's, aren't you. Not without me, brother." He draped a skinny arm around Byron's shoulders.

Byron shrugged him off. "Christ, Billy, do you have to follow me around like an old bird dog? Go home."

The crooked smile faltered then dropped away. "Home? I guess I can go upstairs at Salyer's if I want, same as you."

"Shut up, Billy."

"Shut up yourself! When did you get up on a high horse? One night with a Chinese whore and you're royalty, giving orders?" Billy strutted back and forth while he talked, stiff-legged. "You don't own me, and you don't own Salyer's, now do you?"

Byron started away. Billy fell in behind him.

"I'm talking to you, your majesty. I can spend my money on that girl just as fast as you can, Byron. You think you're better than me 'cause you had her first?"

Byron grabbed Billy by the shirtfront. When he yanked him forward, there was a small tearing sound. "I told you to shut up, Billy. She's not like that. I'm getting her out of there." They were both breathing hard, and Byron could smell the odor of opium on Billy's skin. He twisted Billy's shirt hard in his fist and shoved him backward. The shirt tore under both arms and Billy fell, landing hard on his tailbone. The tears in the other boy's eyes made Byron look away, battling the urge to hit him, to kick him in the ribs while he sat on his butt in the dirt.

"Big man," Billy called after him. "You know your daddy's in line before you tonight, don't you?"

Byron stopped. He turned, and it seemed to take forever, turning, turning, turning toward Billy Kellogg. He could still feel the opium in his head, making him slow. "Liar."

Billy was on his feet. There was a small smear of blood on his lower lip, so he must have bitten his tongue when he fell. He tried to smile at Byron, but there the fear in his face made it an ugly grimace. "He told Eustace he was going to show her what a real man was made of."

"Piss ant liar!" Byron roared, raising his fist.

"Go see for yourself if you don't believe me."

Byron could see it was the truth and that somewhere, underneath, it hurt Billy to tell him. That shred of sympathy was terrible and he wanted to kill the boy, to throw him to the ground again and beat him senseless. He dropped his hands. The fog had finally closed around the setting sun. The late afternoon was now uniformly gray and chilly. Gooseflesh rippled up Byron's neck as he stalked off.

"Don't come looking for a place to sleep tonight, Tupper," Billy yelled after him. "I'll tell my brother Albie to shoot you in the ass if you come around."

But Byron was long gone.

□

Ya Zhen was able to find the meeting place easily because of Reverend Huntington's map, but she couldn't wait by the road, not even for a minute. From the moment she'd gotten out of Lucy's sight, she'd been gripped by a terrible barbed awareness, trying to see in every direction at once. She wanted to listen for the wagon, but everything she *did* hear—someone splitting wood behind a house, a dog barking monotonously—scraped at her nerves. When she recognized the way the street dipped and then rose again as it continued toward the middle of town, she hurried to the base of the hill and stepped into the woods. In here, it was almost fully dark, even though she had only stumbled some eight or ten paces from the road. The trees were like something from a grandfather story, a boasting jest told to a gullible child; they rose so high above the forest floor that Ya Zhen felt vertigo when she looked up to judge how much light was still in the sky. As she picked her way through huckleberry bushes and scrubby alder saplings, she found in the base of one massive redwood tree an opening the size of a small cave. It appeared to have been made by fire, and was so blackened it was impossible to see how far back the declivity went. She held her breath and listened, afraid she'd hear some animal denned for the night, but there was only silence. She screwed up her courage and ducked just inside. The ground was springy and damp, and she huddled there, hugging her arms around her under the shawl. The day had been long and disorienting; she was hungry and needed badly to urinate. Had she really imagined, standing in front of the hotel this morning, that she might be able to disappear into the forest and survive, all on her own? *"Xing zi,"* she whispered. *Fool.* For one terrible moment Ya Zhen wished she were back at Salyer's, in her room, a small fire snapping in the grate. Immediately she was swept with revulsion, horrified that the hotel might seem like any sort of asylum.

I have no home, she thought. She tried to see the road through the underbrush, in case the wagon came. *There is no place in the world that is mine, no refuge for me.* In her mind's eye she saw a bird, flying, flying over the dark sea she had crossed to come here, a bird that would beat her wings looking for a place to rest until finally her heart gave out and she hurtled into the cold water like a stone. Ya Zhen began to tremble, first her hands, then her chin, until her whole body seemed to vibrate. She clung to the edges of the shawl. Her teeth chattered and she remembered her fever on the night the men had taken her from home. Gray blots spread across her field of vision. As she lost consciousness and fell onto her side, a slow and easy sensation, someone cried out. It is Hong-Tai, she thought, calling for the cuckoo.

¤

"Ya Zhen!" Rose called, then listened. Nothing. "Ya Zhen, where are you?" Again, no response. She stood at the edge of the trees, peering in, seeing nothing but shadows. If she was here, she must be hiding. She didn't know Rose, had never laid eyes on her—why would she answer? "Please, Ya Zhen, come out now, it's Rose Allen. I'm a friend." She nearly shouted that she was helping Lucy, but then looked up and down the street, worried that someone would hear. She eased her way into the woods, not wanting to appear a threat. "Are you here?" she said. Some small animal, bird or squirrel, scattered through the underbrush, making her jump. The staccato rattle of a woodpecker echoed from some distance, nothing else. The panic rat was nibbling around the edges of her thoughts again—if Ya Zhen wasn't with Reverend Huntington, and wasn't here, then where? Had she taken a wrong turn in her short walk from the rectory? The idea that Clarence Salyer had come looking for her or that—perhaps worse—someone else had accosted her, kept edging in on Rose's thinking.

Then she realized two things: the woodpecker's hollow thrum had resolved into the steady clop of hooves and creak of wheels—the reverend had arrived at last. And, several yards deeper into the woods, a young woman seemed to materialize from the side of a redwood tree.

CHAPTER SEVEN

ROSE PICKED REDWOOD NEEDLES and bits of duff out of Ya Zhen's hair and off her clothes as they helped her out of the woods and over to the wagon. She seemed disoriented, as if she'd been asleep, and was trembling.

"Jump up in there and give her a hand," Reverend Huntington said, "before someone sees us. She'll get warm under the tarpaulin."

Rose rested a boot on the high edge of the wagon bed and boosted herself up, then reached down to help Ya Zhen climb in beside her. The wagon had been lined with old quilts, and the waxed canvas of the tarpaulin not only kept out the damp, but it did, indeed, make the space much warmer than the outside. There wasn't enough head room to sit up, so both of them lay on their backs. The quilts smelled of hay and horses. Reverend Huntington tied the covering neatly in place and climbed onto the seat, making the wagon rock to one side and back again.

"The clothes are in there with you, Rose. Ready?"

"Ready."

He made a double click with his tongue, and with a single rocking lurch, they were on their way. "Keep it quiet, now, or someone will think I've gone over mad, talking to myself."

Rose laughed. She couldn't help herself. She turned on her side and propped her head on her elbow. "Are you all right?" she whispered.

Ya Zhen nodded and rolled over too, so they were face-to-face. "I'm feeling much better now."

"Why did you hide? Did someone see you?"

Ya Zhen shook her head. "No one saw."

Rose smiled. "Good." She reached for the small pile of clothes. "Lucy sent these for you," she said. "A little costuming, in case anyone sees us going into the mercantile." She was about to hand everything to over, but stopped short. "I'm Rose Allen, by the way. Very, *very* pleased to make your acquaintance."

"Mattie is your friend."

"Mattie is my dear friend, and she will be so happy when she knows you're safe."

"Will she be at the store?"

"I don't know," she said, and plucked another bit of dead foliage off the front of Ya Zhen's shawl. "I hope so. Here," she whispered. "Let me help you get these things on over your clothes." There was a blue shirtwaist, faded almost gray with a great deal of washing, and a capacious apron. By much wrestling around, they managed to get these twisted in place, buttoned and tied. Last was an old-style working bonnet. Seeing it gave Rose a pang of homesickness for the ladies around Paw Paw, out laboring in their kitchen gardens all summer, protecting themselves from the prairie sun. The bonnet had a brim so deep and wide that it hid Ya Zhen's face entirely. Rose helped wind her hair so that it was completely captured inside.

Twice along the way, someone hailed Reverend Huntington and he called back a happy remark in return. The calm sound of his voice helped Ya Zhen feel tethered to her body. Rose Allen reached over and squeezed her hand, hard. "Almost there," she said. Ya Zhen squeezed back.

Finally they rolled to a stop. Reverend Huntington climbed down, and then he was behind the cart, untying the cover and letting it hang loose.

"Rose?"

"I'm here."

"When I tell you, I want you to come out of the wagon. When you do, go straight into the store and find Bai Lum. I'll bring Ya Zhen in when one of you tells me the store is clear."

"Here we go," said Rose. She turned to whisper in Ya Zhen's ear. "Be ready."

"Yes, I will." Ya Zhen said. Her heartbeat made her voice shake, but she wasn't afraid now, only excited that they had nearly made it, and in two days she would be gone from Salyer forever.

"Only a minute," Rose said, and scooted out the back of the wagon.

When she stepped into the mercantile, Bai Lum was transacting a purchase with Muriel Pinchbeck, probably the oldest person in Eureka. He had lit the overhead gas lamps against the early dusk. Even in her apprehension, Rose had a moment of amused incredulity that Mrs. Pinchbeck, thin as a stripped reed and hunched at the neck, shopped in Chinatown. At the moment, she was bent over a tiny coin purse, counting out pennies onto the counter. Bai Lum looked up, and Rose nodded once. Then she walked directly to the counter.

"Hello, Mrs. Pinchbeck. Hello, Bai Lum." Mrs. Pinchbeck didn't even glance at her, so intent was she on paying for a small tin of mackerel. "Bai Lum, I've come to look again at the bowls you showed me the other day. Do you recall the ones I mean?"

"Four Flower design," he said. "This way." He came from behind the counter and started for the rear of the store.

"We'll only be a moment, Mrs. Pinchbeck," Rose said.

The old woman stared into the palm of her hand at several coins, counting in a whisper. She craned around to look at Rose, her filmy eyes blinking behind heavy spectacles. "Of course," she said in a tiny voice that was hardly more than a coarse whisper. "Go ahead, young man, and see to this lady," she said, not seeming to realize that Bai Lum was no longer standing near her. "I can wait." She bent back to her task.

Rose hurried after Bai Lum. When they were standing next to the porcelains, Rose took one of the bowls and cupped it in her palm. "Ya Zhen is right outside with Reverend Huntington."

"Will she be seen?"

"No, no. We have her hidden in the back of the wagon. Can we get her upstairs?"

Bai Lum glanced over his shoulder. Mrs. Pinchbeck had finished counting her money and stood with one hand on the counter. A Chinese man Rose recognized, who sold vegetables from a prolific truck garden he cultivated in town, was also waiting to speak to Bai Lum.

"Yes," he said, "I'll take care of it."

Rose stayed where she was, making a pretense of looking at the dishes. Bai Lum crossed the store in a few quick strides and collected Mrs. Pinchbeck's change. He thanked her for her purchase. She began to fidget her coin purse back into her drawstring handbag.

"That's fine, then," she said, her voice tremulous and breathy. "You're a good boy. Very clean." She spoke without looking up. "I don't care what the busybodies say. I've never minded a whistle for gossip."

Bai Lum looked over at Rose, worry stiffening his features. She crossed the store with the bowl still in her hand. With a small tilt of her head, she gestured Bai Lum toward the waiting man. "Are you out alone tonight, Mrs. Pinchbeck?"

The old woman lifted her chin slightly. "Of course I am," she said. When her attention was on Rose, Bai Lum went to the man and they began to chat amiably.

"Even on a foggy evening like this?" Rose asked her. "Are you sure you can get home?"

"I've lived alone in this town twenty-three years," she said, "and in twenty-three years I've done for myself." Her quavering voice took on a firm edge. "I was ninety-two on my last birthday, you know."

"Ninety-two? You certainly look well," said Rose. She tried to see Reverend Huntington out the front window, but the evening had gotten so dark, she could only see a reflection of the inside of the store. She took a small step toward the door, hoping Mrs. Pinchbeck would follow, but she stayed planted near the counter.

"I was just telling that young man, I like a clean place. A clean place and a clean person." Rose watched Bai Lum from the corner of her eye. She recalled the other man's name now, Wei Chang. Around town he was called Charley Wei. Bai Lum laughed at something he said. Wei Chang bowed slightly and went out.

"All that rubbish they write in the paper. They're clean people. I told my granddaughter, Eliza, that our Celestials are probably the cleanest foreigners in California. All they need is a bit of Christian charity." She retrieved the tin of mackerel with her knobby right hand. Fat veins stood out prominently over and around her knuckles, deep blue under the mercantile's gas lamps.

It seemed to take forever.

The mercantile door opened and closed. Reverend Huntington greeted someone. "Hello, Mr. Wei. How's business?"

"Very slow now, sir. Cold winter."

"Yes, we've had some storms, haven't we? You know, the telegraph lines have been down between here and the city."

"Oh, yes. Very bad. Too cold for vegetable."

"Warmer today, though. Spring will be here soon. Mrs. Huntington will be by to see you for cuttings."

"I have some, maybe two weeks. Good evening."

"Good evening, Mr. Wei."

Footsteps receded down the boardwalk.

"It should only be another moment," Reverend Huntington said quietly. The mercantile door opened once again.

"All clear." Reverend Huntington said. "Hurry."

Bai Lum and Rose looked at each other over Mrs. Pinchbeck's bowed head while she spoke. When Rose gave him another single nod, he stepped to the door and motioned to Reverend Huntington.

"It's a very clean store," Rose said. "Have you seen the Four Flowers dishes?" She held the little bowl under Mrs. Pinchbeck's nose.

"Dishes? No, I don't need dishes. I have a houseful. If I broke a plate every day until the day I die, I'd still have plenty left to eat off of."

Ya Zhen came into the store with Reverend Huntington right behind her, walking as if she wanted to run, her face completely hidden inside Lucy's old bonnet. Bai Lum stood so that he blocked Mrs. Pinchbeck's line of sight, but Rose doubted the woman's rheumy old eyes would know who she was looking at, even from such a short distance.

"Hello, Mrs. Pinchbeck. What a pleasure to see you here this evening." Reverend Huntington stepped neatly around Ya Zhen and held out his hand to the old woman.

Her withered face lit up. "Pastor! Gracious, what are you doing here?"

"No rest for the weary, I'm afraid. Mrs. Huntington has sent me after supplies. Are you here alone?" His eyes never left her face, but, holding her hand, he turned her ever so slightly toward the front of the store. Rose hurried Ya Zhen through the curtained partition in back, and there was Shu-Li. She took Ya Zhen's arm and up the stairs they went. Rose slipped back into the store, her knees wobbling precariously. Bai Lum approached her, holding the delicate white bowl with its dark painted flowers.

"Have you decided then?" he said loudly. Where they stood, between two tall shelves, they couldn't be seen from the front of the store.

"Done," she whispered, and leaned her face into his shoulder, shaking slightly.

Reverend Huntington was still caught in his chat with the old woman. "I have to get home and have my supper," she said, "although I can't eat much anymore. When I was a girl, my mother used to tell me I ate like a field hand." She laughed, a whispery little chuckle in the back of her throat. "But I could work then, from dark to dark, and then more if it was a full moon."

He rested a gentle hand on her back. "Can I give you a ride home, Mrs. Pinchbeck? I have the wagon just outside."

"No, no, I like the fresh air. I have to get out, like anyone else. Walking helps my appetite." She started for the door with the slightly tottering gait of a pigeon. "Pastor, you can get the door for me." She said this as if bestowing a favor.

He walked her to the door and held it open. "I'll see you on Sunday, Muriel."

"Goodbye Mrs. Pinchbeck," Rose called.

She was gone, picking her careful way past the window. Bai Lum pulled all the shades and threw the bolt on the door.

¤

The room swayed, back and forth, back and forth, and Mattie knew this was what it had been like in the cradle, rocking under her mother's hand. She had no such actual memory of her mother, who had shrunken in on herself after Mattie's father died, dried up and turned inward like the husk of some long-neglected melon. There was precious little memory of Da, either, just a vague blur of brown hair and soft voice.

She lay on her side, eyes not quite closed in the dark room. It had taken her several visits here to adjust to the sweet, burned smell of opium, but now the odor alone started the work of pulling her outside herself, even before she took the pipe. It was better than the laudanum, which she had first used for headaches when she was fourteen. The pipe was smoother and deeper. Her burned hand had stopped pulsing. She loved the smoke and she loved the dark room. She loved all the others laying in the dark with her, as if they were all in a womb together, but a womb without boundaries, room for everyone, infinite. A womb. A room. Mattie laughed. Mostly it was men here, and that had been difficult at first, but now she was perfectly at ease. They were all there to ride the same wave together. It was fine. People sometimes laughed and sometimes they wept quietly. Sometimes someone would begin to talk and Mattie would travel along on the surface of their words. It was fine, a fine ride. The door opened and feeble evening light fell flat on the threshold. A brawny man entered and Mattie tried to remember something about him. She couldn't recall his name, but something she knew about him flirted at the edge of her memory.

How strange! He sat on the long bench by the wall. Mattie was glad she got one of the reclining spaces. The man's eyes roamed across her hip and wandered away again as he waited for his turn. The flame briefly illuminated his face and the hand he used to steady the pipe. A dark stain marred his sleeve, nearly to the elbow, red as blood. *Tupper*, she thought. *Rose told me something about him.* His Christian name was a flower, too, like Rose, wasn't it? She sailed for a while, and it floated past—Garland, that was it. Rose's Garland, garland of roses, the one who was rude in the store. Yes. But he was quiet here in the room, and everyone rode on the wave of smoke. Here it was not so bad. Here it was fine.

¤

6 Feb 5:20 pm
Dear Mrs. Salyer,
I send this note ahead to thank you for so graciously allowing me to hire your young lady today, and hereby remit the agreed-upon amount of $4. Due to a problem with my carriage, I have had to set her home on foot—with the strictest instructions to go immediately to the hotel and nowhere else, of course. No doubt she will arrive shortly after your receipt of this note. She was a great help, and I hope that I might retain her again sometime in the future.
Yours very truly
Mrs. Charles Huntington

¤

Four men milled around the back stairs of the hotel. There was little conversation among them. Mostly they stood hunched against the growing chill coming in off the bay, waiting as if for a streetcar. Byron slowed as he approached them.

A burly man standing at the foot of the stairs folded his arms and gave Byron a hard face. "The line starts back there, Tupper."

"I have to see someone," Byron said. "It's an emergency."

"I'm having an emergency myself," another man said, and grabbed his crotch. Rough laughter at this.

Byron looked from face to face and knew that he would be given no quarter here, no matter what he said. He made as if to stand away from the group, then turned and sprinted up the stairs. What the men possessed in numbers, Byron more than made up for in youth. He hit the top of the stairs and found the door unlocked. Despite threats shouted from below, no one made the effort to follow him.

It was dark in the inner hallway, even darker than he remembered it, and he didn't realize the old woman was there until she was in his face. At the same moment a girl cried out, a wrenching scream that rose in pitch before trailing back into sobs. Every nerve in his body stood at attention.

"What in the holy hell do you think you're doing?" the old woman shouted. "You can't bust in here like that!"

"Did he hurt her? Let me in there, I have to see her!"

The old woman was as tall as Byron, and she blocked the narrow passage with her beefy carriage. "Like hell you will. She'll be good for nothing, even if she lives through the night. The doctor's in there trying to tie the pieces together and there's so much blood it looks like breakfast in Hades." Another horrible wail split the air, this time rising until the vocal cords behind it failed.

Byron shrank back. He tore the cap from his head, turned and punched the wall with all his strength. The skin on his knuckles split open and cold pain shot up his forearm to the elbow. "What did he do?" he yelled. "God damn him to hell, what did he do to her?"

She stared at Byron. "You know him?"

"Tell me what he did," Byron roared, spittle flying from his lips.

"I told him no, but he said he only wanted a feel." Under her bullish exterior, Byron could hear a note of panic, someone about to deny responsibility for a mighty backwash of vexation. "I told him the girl couldn't manage the other thing, not tonight, and he swore on his mama's name he'd only grab a feel. He tore her open every which way, though—after gagging her to hide the screams." She glanced over her shoulder at the partially open door. "Christ almighty, I wish they'd gag her now."

Byron straightened, his left hand bleeding but feeling senseless and frozen. Without warning, he backhanded Old Mol across the face, knocking her backward. She stumbled and went on her ass with a grunt. Her nose poured blood and she clapped a hand to her face.

"Clarence!" she bawled, her voice choked and nasal. "God damn it, Clarence, get out here!"

Byron was already out the door and pelting down the back steps. Before the men below could react, another awful scream went out into the foggy evening, and every man there took a step away from the stairs.

¤

Hazel Cleary hummed a ballad their father had often sung of the fair Mailí Bhán, lost when her lover mistakes her for a swan. The Kendall's guests were gone and the family was having coffee, lingering at the table with Phoebe. The spectacular mess in the kitchen was ridded up, dishes done, and Hazel couldn't wait to put paid to this day of work and worry. She prayed that Mattie and Rose would be there when she got home.

She had just thrown the dishwater out the back door, when David Kendall came in with the coffee things. The painted tray looked like a child's tea set in his big hands.

"That was a fine feed," he said. "I'd walk a mile in foul weather for your scalloped potatoes, Hazel. Wish I had room for another helping."

She took the tray, and the cups rattled lightly in their saucers. "I'm glad to hear it," she said, "since you'll be facing the leftovers in your dinner tomorrow." Music started in the other room, Phoebe at the piano, playing Bach. "Listen to that girl," Hazel said. "What I wouldn't give to play a piano like that."

"You ought to take a lesson. She could teach you."

Hazel smiled and wiggled her fingers. "These hands have already learned their tricks. I'd hate to hear what kind of noise that would be." She draped the dishtowel over the end of the counter to dry. "Do you want some more pie?"

He laid a hand on his belly and groaned. "Woman, do not tempt me."

"Perhaps some vigorous dancing would refresh your appetite."

"Walking will be enough of a challenge, thank you."

"Good," she said. "But I'll leave the pie on the sideboard, in case you change your mind in the middle of the night."

"I'm going back to the office for a while. May I see you home on my way?"

She glanced outside, and even in the dark could see the fog that had settled in at sunset. "You're out again in this mess?" She rinsed the coffee cups and set them back in the tray for the next morning, upside-down on their saucers. "It's cold as clay out there."

"No doubt it is, but there are papers to be shuffled and numbers to tot." He held the dining room door for her.

"In that case, you'd better go on. I want to visit with your ladies a few minutes before I leave."

Prudence held his overcoat, picking at a spot on one sleeve. "You're a mess, Captain Kendall," she said. "This coat needs a good brush. What did you run your sleeve into?"

"Let's see that," he said, taking the coat from her. He scratched at the crusty patch. "Paste, maybe." Then he sniffed it. "Yes, definitely the paste pot."

She rolled her eyes and helped him into the heavy coat. "Don't be too late, will you?"

"Home before ten." He leaned in and kissed her on the temple.

"Don't forget me," Phoebe called from the piano.

Prudence pushed him gently. "You're awfully popular."

Kendall planted a kiss on Phoebe's cheek, which she proffered with a tilted head, not missing a note. "You may be asleep when I get back," he said. "See you in the morning." She nodded without looking away from the music.

"Very well," he said, "time and tide, *tempus fugit*, and so forth." In the foyer, he took his hat from the hall tree and tipped it. "My dears. You too, Hazel."

In the dim light near the front door, his grin made the years drop away. Prudence thought he looked hardly older than the day they met. Before the door had closed behind him, she was talking to Mrs. Cleary about laundry. Later, she could not forget that she had missed a last glimpse of his departure because she was discussing the unkempt state of his overcoat.

¤

"Well done, everyone," Reverend Huntington said. "Now I have to get home quick so Lucy will know we're in the clear and she can send her thank-you note to Cora Salyer. Bai Lum," he said, grasping the younger man's hand and giving it a firm shake, "I'll leave it to you now. I'll be here before dawn on Monday to take the young ladies north."

Bai Lum nodded. "We will be ready."

"Rose, can I drop you at Mrs. Cleary's on my way?"

"No," she said, and looked at Bai Lum. "I'm going to see how the girls are faring before I go."

"Splendid. You'd do well to bolt the door behind me, I think. Goodnight, you two"

"Wait," Rose said. She wrapped her arms around him and hugged him tightly.

He smiled and patted Rose's back. "We're in this together, now, aren't we."

She looked up into his face. As always, his wiry white hair stood out in a nimbus around his head. "We are."

When the bolt was once more in place, Bai Lum put out the lights. He took Rose's hand, leading her through the darkened storefront and through the curtained alcove. "I want to check the doors and windows back here, too, but it's dark," he said. "You go up." He kissed her, a sweet, lingering kiss, and stepped into the dark storage area. In his black clothing, he was little more than a silhouette.

Rose climbed the narrow staircase and stood at the top, listening. There was no sound from the small apartment. "Hello?" she called quietly.

"Rose Allen," came the answer. It was Shu-Li. The soft light of a candle illuminated a room across the hall from the kitchen. She sat next to Ya Zhen on a thick mattress. Her hair was loose over her shoulders and shone like spilled ink in the low light. Ya Zhen had stripped off Lucy's old clothes; everything was folded neatly on the floor next to the bed. The same fabric panels were draped over her walls and windows as hung in the sitting room, and a heavy yellow coverlet was spread across the mattress. The room was a small, warm haven. Shu-Li scooted to her left and gestured for Rose to join them.

She sat on the edge of the bed. "We did it, Ya Zhen. You're really here."

"I am," she said, her face solemn. "Before, when I was in the tree, I thought it might be a dream."

"You must be exhausted."

"I'm very tired," she said, and immediately translated for Shu-Li. Shu-Li nodded "Yes," she said and sighed.

Rose smiled. "Me too."

Shu-Li had a lacquer box on her lap, and began to show Ya Zhen what she kept in it. The two of them talked quietly, and when Rose heard Bai Lum on the stairs, she realized she had been nodding toward sleep. She thought she should get up and meet him, but was tired and suddenly self-conscious at the audacity of inviting herself to stay. She waited.

He came to the door and looked at all of them sitting on the bed, and Rose tried to read his expression.

"Shu-Li," he said, "*Mào shòu xiāng ba?*" Shu-Li nodded. She launched into a breathless explanation of some kind, but he put his fingertips to his lips and she quieted. "Ya Zhen," he said softly. He spoke English, and Rose knew it was for her sake. "I'm honored to have you as a guest, if you would like to stay. You can share this room with Shu-Li."

There was no viable alternative, of course, but in the invitation, Rose felt him returning to Ya Zhen a small measure of agency—a gift: to stay or go as she chose. And Ya Zhen knew. The hope on her face was so fierce that Rose couldn't stand to look at it. She turned away the way she would, in reverence, from a birth or the consummation of love. All three women looked at Bai Lum standing there in the doorway, his face quiet in the candlelight, and Rose's heart broke open with the knowledge that they all loved him, and that she would remember this moment with gratitude as long as she lived.

"Are you hungry?" he asked.

No one said anything.

He nodded. "I'll make tea."

"Let me help," Rose said. She followed him into the small kitchen.

He squatted before a one-burner cast iron stove and took a bit of kindling from a box under the window. The room was dark, and when the fire caught, it cast a quick yellow light on, his face. He shut the firebox with a clang and put the kettle on. Rose lit a candle that sat in the center of the table. Celadon dishes lined a short shelf nailed to the wall, their watery green surfaces glimmering in the uneven light. Bai Lum took down four cups and measured tea into the pot. Through all this preparation, they were quiet; the only sound was the muffled crackle of the fire in the stove and occasional quiet conversation between Shu-Li and Ya Zhen.

"Rose."

She looked, but he didn't say anything, seemed to weigh his words. He was silent for so long she felt sure he was about to ask her to leave.

"You were right. It was good to bring her here. Ya Zhen."

Rose felt the weight of the day drop into her then, all her limbs like wood. "Thank you," she said. She lifted both hands and rubbed her eyes. "That's what Reverend Huntington told me this morning."

Then his hand was on the small of her back. "Come and sit," he said. "I'll bring your tea." She let him guide her into the small sitting room. The windows had gone deep blue behind the white curtains. "Did Reverend Huntington explain what he plans to do?" she said. "To take them north together?"

He brought the candle along and tipped it to light incense, as he had the night before. "It is a very good idea."

Rose sank onto the divan and watched the smoke curl into the light of the candle. "You are so kind." She closed her eyes.

"You are so tired." There was a small sound of dripping water on the outside sills as heavy condensation began to puddle and drip off the eaves.

"Yes."

"Rose."

She opened her eyes. The candle was behind him, making his face hard to see in the last light from the window.

"Lie down here and rest."

She fought a losing battle to keep her eyes open, and had a sensation of floating. "I should leave. I should go home now."

"Stay."

"I'm tired."

The last light faded from the room.

"I never want to move from this spot," she said.

He worked open the laces of her shoes. She managed to open her eyes one last time and he was sitting next to her, holding both her feet in his hands. "Stay, Rose."

She lay over on her side with a deep sigh. "I don't want tea."

As she fell asleep, he went into the kitchen and it was the last thing she knew until she woke to the sound of someone outside, screaming.

¤

Byron ran until he couldn't breathe, had a deep stitch cramping his side, and even then he limped forward in a shambling jog. It took him ten minutes to get home. He could smell the acrid odor of the burned shed long before he could see it, black boards jutting from the old foundation like rotten teeth. In the fog, the charred bulk of it looked like something materializing out of a bad dream. The morning glory that had covered it lay in burned ropes all around and a black, trampled circle was pressed into the grass on every side. He ran right past it to the house, which was dark. Maybe the old man was inside, waiting for him. Maybe he had his hunting rifle aimed at Byron's chest right now, just waiting for a clear shot. But Byron didn't think so.

He stumbled up the front steps and into the unlit kitchen, now almost completely dark. He went directly into his father's room, shoved the sour-smelling bed away from the wall and pried open the floorboard closest to the wall. Underneath was a metal box, which Byron lifted out. Inside, wrapped in a greasy rag, was Garland Tupper's Colt revolver, a .44 caliber sidearm that he had brought home from the war. Byron had taken it out and handled it many times when Garland was off on a drunk, always careful to wipe away smudges from the grip and barrel before replacing it. As long as Byron could remember, his father had been hauling the Colt out to clean it, snap the cylinder open and closed. He'd let Byron sight down the barrel while he told the boy grisly stories about the battles he had been in, skirmishes which inevitably ended with Garland standing over some sniveling Johnny Reb who pissed himself in fear. As far as Garland knew, Byron had no idea where he hid the gun, but it hadn't been hard to find. Garland would stagger into his room and bash around, usually leaving his bedroom door wide open while he replaced the gun. Byron had known where it was since he was eight years old.

He loaded the cylinder, six shots in all, and dropped several more cartridges in his jacket pocket. In the woods beyond the bedroom window a bird called, the ascending trill of a Swainson's thrush. He closed his eyes for a moment, waiting for the next run of climbing notes. It was early in the year and late in the day for this bird's song, and it seemed like a proper omen. When he opened his eyes, tears tracked his stubbled cheek, feeling hot against his cool skin. He wiped his ruined nose on his sleeve and went out with the big revolver and extra cartridges weighing down his jacket pocket. In the kitchen, he opened a cupboard and broke a piece of stale cornbread off a pone he had baked over a week ago and stored in the Dutch oven. A little bit of mold dusted one edge and Byron crumbled it away. Chewing, he looked around the dark kitchen, looked into his own room, where the window was still propped open with his old storybook. He yanked the book out; the glass came down with a bang that shattered the lower pane and threw long shards onto the floorboards. Byron pressed the little book, which had swollen in the damp air, flattened it between his palms and tucked it under his belt at the small of his back. He walked out of the house, chewing his cornbread, feeling the Colt swing back and forth against his thigh while he walked. It was almost entirely dark now, and as he walked away from the house, Byron could see the bated glow of gas lamps, already lit in town, reflecting a faint yellow against the cloud cover.

Once he got to the waterfront, it took him less than a quarter-hour to track Garland back to the poppy palace. He found a spot in the alley, a dozen long paces from the door, and he crouched with the Colt in his hands to wait behind a stack of crates.

It was nearly an hour. From time to time he set the gun between his feet and stood to slap the circulation back into his legs with his uninjured right hand. He was cold and wanted more supper. The book tucked into his belt felt like a board against his back. But for all his discomfort, he seemed to be floating outside of time. The lights were on in the Episcopal Church a block over, and the stained glass picture of Jesus holding a lamb on his shoulders threw a red and yellow glare into the fog. He could hear people singing inside. He had a strange sense of floating on the sound.

Finally, the door he was watching opened. Smoke curled out into the low light. Two men appeared, moving slowly, talking.

Garland. Suddenly, Byron was not cold or hungry. He lifted the gun and aimed, wanting him to come closer. The sound of his heart rushed through his head. The point of the gun barrel trembled minutely in time to his pulse, and he breathed through his mouth, knowing the plume of his breath was invisible in the fog.

Then there was a moment. *Bastard*, he thought, and fired. The sound of the revolver was enormous. Before he could fire again, a muzzle flash lit the fog. A corner shattered off the top crate, showering splinters into his hair and swollen left eye. He jerked, clapped a hand to his face. His head roared and he could barely see, but he fired again.

Someone was right there, had stepped into the street from nowhere, someone who dropped to his knees and fell face down in the wet dirt of the road.

Byron leapt up and ran through the alley, away from the street and into the dark, away from the man he had shot and the voices coming from the church. More shots were fired behind him and a boy began to scream.

¤

When the worst things happen, most of us scarcely know it. The world does not hold its breath—not for the joys, nor for the terrors.

Beyond the narrow inlet of Humboldt Bay, past the breakwater, in the deep meters of cold ocean along the continental shelf, a sperm whale hunted. She had been moving through the lightless fathoms, more than a thousand feet down and sightless in these depths, feeding on giant squid that lived near the ocean floor. At twenty years, she was in the prime of her life, a mother for the third time. All over her massive head, circular tentacle scars overlapped in rings, evidence of her proficiency as a hunter. So far down, she used sound, rhythmic clicking that bounced through the water, to navigate and to find her prey.

It had been almost an hour and she began to move up, ready to breathe, to rest with her family. Near the surface, her calf floated with a pod of other females and juveniles. The water warmed as she surfaced. There was dim light now, and she could see again. With her huge fluke, she gave a massive heave and propelled herself, arching her broad back through the evening air, taking it in, sliding back under and gliding toward her infant daughter, unique and particular among all the others. One of her sisters trumpeted mildly, a greeting, and the calf moved under her belly to nurse. The night came down and a half moon broke through, rippling light over the surface of the water. This was her life. This was joy.

☐

It was always so quiet after supper, when the Illinois winter had dropped its late loads of snow and it was too cold to work in the shop, too cold even to step out for a look at the hard night sky. Rose's father, Robert Allen, missed his wife. Each of them had always had strange dichotomies in their basic natures; he was quiet with a love of adventure, Clarissa gregarious and bound to the home place. But they complemented each other and her death had left him feeling as though some vital element, some indispensable constituent was missing in his heart. The hearth log broke into embers, startling Homer, who had been dozing on top of the kindling box. Now the cat stared around the room, eyes wide.

"Take your rest old man," Robert said, and wondered if he was speaking to the cat or to himself. His pipe had gone cold in his hand and he set it aside. He stood, stretched, felt the chill working on his joints, a sour, muttering pain like a faint toothache in his knees and shoulders. Homer stood too, arched into a stretch, then hopped off the kindling box and into the warm seat Robert had just vacated. Robert scratched him behind the ears and under the chin. The cat's purr was rickety and uncertain in his old age.

He put out the lamp and took the stairs by the light of the half-moon reflecting off the snow and in through the windows. It was bright as a lantern. When he reached the landing, he looked out at the stand of naked walnut trees behind the house. Their black branches spread in a delicate lacework high above the place where their trunks divided, and they grew close enough that it was impossible to see where one set of branches ended and another began. Their shadows, thin and indistinct in the moonlight, laid a net on the snowy ground. Closer to the house was a lone maple, old and spreading. When Rose was little, Robert had hung a swing in its branches. Over the course of years, the tree had grown bark around the stout hemp lashing, like skin growing over a wound. The swing was gone now, but in the moonlight Robert could make out the gnarled place where the tree had healed itself, two short tails of hemp still protruding from the stout, lumpy branch. His breath fogged a circle on the glass; he wished he could see all of this with someone else, to explain about the swing and the tree.

He climbed the remaining stairs and went into his cold bedroom, undressed and slid under the woolen quilts. Made from old coats and blankets that had gone to seed, they were heavy things in dark colors, black and brown and ocher. Clarissa's work. The faint, chilly smell of mothballs wafted out as he settled himself, a smell he had liked since childhood, when it meant sledding with his brothers, popped corn after supper, delicata squashes piled in the root cellar. As the bed warmed, Robert Allen's thoughts traveled out to Rosie, out across the broad expanse of snow-bound prairies and cold barren desert, over the Rocky Mountains and up the Pacific coast to his girl, probably eating supper now. He sent the same small tiding each night as he journeyed into the dream world, a push against an unfathomable universe, a delicate shield of hope for himself and his beloveds: all is well.

¤

On the outskirts of Eureka's Chinatown, Wei Chang filled his watering can a final time, a tin bucket pierced with small holes. He made sure the soil around all the pea plants was uniformly damp.

It had been a beautiful day, so much sun, and it seemed to him that the pale yellow blossoms of the peas had popped out on the vines in a single afternoon. Despite the recent storms, his garden was producing well. Radishes and broccoli were up, looking sturdy, and the kale, purple and gray-green, was already heavy and ruffled. He had made a burlap frame to protect the young plants from hail or hard rain, and it had worked well. The new year, just nine days away, should be a successful one. It would be the rooster year, and Wei Chang knew this was an auspicious year for farmers.

His real concern was that there would be no full moon this month. This had happened two other times in his life, always around the time of the new year: once it had been when he was a boy of eighteen, and again when he was grown into full manhood. Now the dark month had come around again, and he had taken extra pains to prepare. In the northeast corner of his garden, Wei Chang had constructed a moon gate, bending thin saplings of green alder and weaving them into a circular arch. The lattice was braced by heavy redwood posts, wood that was nearly impervious to rot or insects. He had worked on his gate during the wet winter and finished it just last month. Already he was raising wisteria cuttings, sweetened with potash from his woodstove. These he would plant all along the moon gate, and in the course of time the garden entrance would become a flowering circle in the spring, a sturdy net of bare branches in the winter. The next time the full moon was lost at the new year, Wei Chang would be a very old man of eighty-five. But his moon gate would come back around over and over, young with purple flowers each time the earth tilted toward the sun.

¤

Old Mol kept sneezing, making her nose bleed again. After five years sitting in the attic crawlspace next to her room, her two threadbare carpetbags were covered with dust and cobwebs. Another small spider made a run for it across the bedclothes, and she mashed it with her thumb. She looked at the crushed thing on the gray blanket, still waving a single leg around from the middle of its broken guts. Could just as well have let it ramble, she thought. Old Molly Blevins wasn't going to sleep in this bed tonight anyway, nor ever again.

The whole mess had gone over bad, and she was going cross-lots tonight before somebody brought in the sheriff. That little girl was just about dead in there, and she knew Clarence Salyer well enough to know that he'd point blame in her direction as soon as he opened his mouth. Right now Clarence was behind the hotel front desk and overseeing the kitchen while Cora, that stick of kindling he was married to, hid out in her room with an account book to keep herself company. One of the Wu sisters—the one with whore blossoms around her mouth, Molly could never keep their names straight—was sitting death watch on Li Lau. The other one was helping the German with dinner. Men had been showing up at the back door, business as usual, but Molly told them to come back after six o'clock, when the other girl got brought back from the preacher's house. It was now six now, and they milled around at the foot of the stairs outside. Those fellows would be Clarence's to deal with, though, because Molly was leaving.

Over these five years, she had managed to hold back quite a plush little bankroll. Just over four hundred dollars was tucked into an old wool stocking in one of her bags. If Clarence knew, he would give her a bloody lip to go with her bloody nose. If Cora knew, she would probably shoot her. It was plenty to get started on somewhere else. She was taking the old Wu sisters with her. They weren't much use for whoring anymore, but they knew how to work, and when she promised them a piece of the profit wherever she landed, they ran off to pack their things and wait for her signal.

One of her regulars, Jack Ball—so quickly done with his business that she called him jack rabbit balls—had come around earlier in the afternoon. He'd been half in love with Wu Song since her first days at Salyer's. After explaining to him the situation upstairs, Molly had slipped Jack five dollars to meet her on the

next block with his buggy shortly before six o'clock. He had an old
sister, half blind, up the road in Arcata where they could stay for a
couple of days and make arrangements to head north and east, up
into Trinity County, maybe Weaverville. The mining operations
were not what they once were, but with the money she'd saved,
Molly knew she could start a little business, a tavern with rooms to
rent by the half-hour. After the row upstairs with Li Lau, she had
waited until Clarence went downstairs, then she sent the Wu
sisters out the back, telling them to wait with Jack Ball until she
got there.

Old Mol clapped her bags shut and went out without a second
glance. She took the side passage that opened onto the second-floor
landing and walked right down the wide front staircase, and out
the front doors of Salyer's Hotel.

¤

It didn't hurt anymore. Now Li Lau felt weightless, like the
downy silk from an open milkweed pod, ready to lift off. She could
feel her spirit pulling away from her body, and it made her heart
light. She knew that once her spirit broke loose from her flesh, all
the suffering of this life would be less than a memory. Even now,
the leaden agonies of the past two days were passing, as if she had
dreamed them.

When her little baby had come through her, she felt that her
heart could not bear anything more. But she had been wrong. She
had tempted fate by believing she had already faced the greatest
suffering. Then the laughing man, the worst of all the men who had
used her badly, had come and shown her that suffering had no
outer boundaries. Pain could always grow, like counting numbers,
always there could be more. She tried to stop him, to tell him she
was torn already from the birth, but he wrapped her shirt around
her mouth, grinding her lips against her teeth. He was a strong
man, a large man. The last thing she remembered was his fist
drawn back.

She knew something happened after that. Who found her, she did not know. All she remembered was a room filled with people, all talking at once, someone pressing rags between her legs, probing the wounds, sewing something, washing her breast with a foul brown liquid that burned. And she remembered hearing herself scream again and again, but it was like hearing someone else screaming, something her body needed to do while her consciousness stood in a far corner of the room, waiting for them to finish.

Finally they left, not bothering to clean her or pull the blankets up. Wu Lin sat on a chair next to the bed, looking out the window and humming. From time to time she looked at Li Lau and smiled, then continued her small song. Li Lau asked her for water, and Wu Lin gave it to her, slowly. She had made a small fire in the grate, too. Li Lau watched a fly bump the glass, making a little tap and buzz. She felt safe now. No one would hurt her again. Perhaps, then, it was not such a bad thing. To die.

◻

Cora Salyer locked herself into room 36 on the third floor, as far from Clarence's mess as she could get. A few minutes ago he had burst into their parlor where she sat reading the paper, blood on his shirtsleeves, and hair hanging in a greasy clump on his forehead. In their bedroom he fetched his pistol, all the while babbling about the women. His whores. One of them was dead, he said, Garland Tupper did it, walked in off the street and tore her up, and that other girl, the one Cora had hired out to the ministers wife, still wasn't back. His favorite whore. Cora stared at him, her thin smile frozen in place. She knew what he did with them in those rooms, especially the two young ones.

Cora Salyer, the one-time Cora Hutchins, had been woefully uninformed about the trials of married life, her wedding night a terrifying blur of Clarence's smothering weight and the bruising, burning pain of the marriage act. It was no wonder her mother had never enlightened her! Then, to add insult to injury, he had

brought the sisters here. After countless nights when he would
come back to her bed whistling and smelling of his own spent seed,
she had put her foot down, told him he wouldn't lay in their bed
until the nasty women were gone. He'd laughed at her, laughed
right in her face. That very night he moved a bed into the room he
used as an office and seemed not to miss her company at all. For
her part, Cora had been wonderfully relieved to be rid of him, done
finally with the intermittent nights when he would grab her in her
sleep and pull up her nightgown.

Right now she didn't care. She had the four dollars from Mrs.
Huntington, and it was fine with her if that girl had put rocks in
her pocket and walked straight off the pier. Down to the bottom of
the bay with her. Cora would prefer it, actually—just to see the
look on Clarence's face.

¤

Thy Word commands our flesh to dust,
'Return, ye sons of men':
All nations rose from earth at first,
And turn to earth again.

Thomas Walsh was a man certain of his place in the larger
scheme of creation. He was a tenor in the choir at Christ Episcopal
Church, and mayor of Eureka. Friday was rehearsal night for the
choir, and in Thomas's estimation, the group was in fine voice.
Even Bethellen Stanhope, a lovely girl, a soprano who tended to
warble up out of key with vigor, was blending with the other
women. Their voices were reedy and robust, and Mayor Walsh felt
his heart swell with emotion at the powerful sentiments of the
hymn.

Fifteen magnificent stained glass windows hung along both
walls and over the altar. Thomas was particularly moved by the
large central depiction of Christ, barefoot in the fields among His
sheep, carrying a lamb across His shoulders, the shepherd's crook
in His arms. During his growing-up years, Thomas Walsh's mother
had instilled in him a deep love of the Twenty-third Psalm. On

childhood nights he frequently woke from unpleasant dreams; his mother would sit by his bedside, repeating the old words over and over with him, *He maketh me to lie down*, and *my cup runneth over*, until young Thomas was finally able to fall back to sleep. The altar window embodied his most intimate feelings about the Savior, that He held Thomas in His tenderest regard, much as He did the lamb on His shoulders. From time to time, Mayor Walsh marveled at how personally he felt the care of Jesus, how gentle and how human the Good Shepherd seemed to him. He could not embrace a wrathful deity and secretly disdained much of the Old Testament.

Thomas had as much reason—more, if truth were told—to feel a measure of earthly pride for this fine church. He had been the driving force behind its construction. Longing to worship in the tradition of his Anglican upbringing, he had pledged a thousand dollars toward construction. He made a trip home, back to Ireland, and successfully raised enough capital to allow building to commence. He modestly believed that he had been a faithful servant to Christ, and that God had thus seen fit to entrust the souls of this town to his oversight. It was a good place, Thomas thought. Rough around the edges, yes, but hadn't San Francisco once been a rough-and-ready boomtown? Thomas Walsh firmly believed that with unflinching, yet caring leadership—the type of leadership any circumspect shepherd lavished on a beloved flock— a cosmopolitan city could be carved out of the redwood wilderness. Eventually, this coarse portion of the Pacific coast would be subdued in the manner prescribed by scripture. When it was, intemperate and profane loggers, miners, and fishermen would be replaced by the better classes, as seemed to be the natural order of things.

If thoughts about the increasing hostilities between white citizens and the Chinese trembled at the periphery of Thomas Walsh's consciousness on this evening, in this consecrated place he was able to keep them at bay. Thomas Walsh believed in the supremacy of noble intentions.

¤

The other men were gone for their evening meal. Dong Li Ha kept working at the largest washtub. He had taken in more laundry this week than any other he could remember. The recent rain had turned the streets sloppy; the hems of the women's long dresses and men's trouser cuffs smelled strongly of mud and horse offal. Tonight he would work far into the night to finish as much as he could before morning. He still took in some laundry from his neighbors, Chinese men living without wives, mostly. But the shirts and sheets and undergarments of the white people he would wash first. They enjoyed wearing their clean clothes on Sunday, would pay extra to pick everything up on Saturday. For six years, he had done the work. He started this place with next to nothing. His strong back and powerful arms, his ability to labor on very little sleep and not much food, had enabled him to build a reputation in the town. One of his first employees had recently started his own laundry at the opposite end of the street, but Dong Li Ha was unconcerned. Let him wear his hands away over the filthy clothes of laboring men who had no woman to wash for them. Dong Li Ha would wash the fine shirts and collars, petticoats, chemises and little girls' pinafores. No white person, it seemed, wanted to confront the soil of the body, not if they could pay someone else to do it. So he continued to prosper, to help support his parents and younger brother in Shanghai, and the wife he had not seen for almost a decade.

In China, laundry was work for women. But after he had arrived in San Francisco, it became clear that doing the work no white man would touch guaranteed not only survival, but also success. He cultivated an open mind and a blank expression. Over the years he had learned that laundry hid many secrets. Tablecloths, aprons, and boys' shirtfronts told what meals had been shared. Trouser knees revealed carefully tended gardens. Perfumed handkerchiefs advertised how well a husband's business was prospering. Pockets were filled with scribbled notes that Dong Li Ha could not read, seashells, eggshells, and pencil stubs. And blood. There was apparently no article of clothing or item of household use that did not meet with blood. Blood on shirts, coats, sheets and underdrawers, blood on hand towels, rags, and antimacassars. If he saw the blood he tried to clean it, but usually it was hidden. By the time it hit the hot water and soda crystals, it was already too late. Blood resisted him, and he did not fight it.

He moved the lamps closer as the light drained from the evening. When the men returned from their meal, Dong Li Ha was already pounding out a second tub of steaming shirts.

▢

When Bai Lum took tea to Shu-Li and Ya Zhen, they were under the blankets, sitting close, whispering together. In her straightforward way, Shu-Li was all smiles, obviously delighted to have a companion. Ya Zhen looked done in, her face lined and eyes ringed with fatigue, but greatly changed from the person he had encountered last night. There was, underneath her mask of exhaustion and almost childlike posture in the bed with Shu-Li, something fiercely present, some essential thing that was rising and running.

He poured their tea, appalled again by what he had seen at Salyer's, the abysmal old woman, the grim little room, Ya Zhen's blank endurance. The most wretched thing, though, was his near-complicity.

His wife had been dead for ten years, carrying their son away with her, still in the womb. Although he worked every day until he dropped, bone-weary, into his bed, although he had surrendered to this life as a widowed man, his heart had grown restive and hungry. When Rose had first arrived at the mercantile, dripping rain, it had gotten much worse.

Her angular face had a wide-open quality as she gazed around his store, looking at the kites, asking questions about the herbs and medicines behind the counter. Time after time he chastised himself as the worst sort of fool when his heart leapt at her approach, but it did no good. Impossible, but month-by-month he allowed love to take root. Every time she came into his store, he reveled in her straightforward manner and the utterly certain timbre of her voice. The more often she visited, the closer he dared to stand, so that he knew the particular line where her neck curved into her jaw, knew the place near her temple where a curly wisp of hair always worked loose, a delicate ginger corkscrew. When she left, he felt worse than ever, ragged and worn thin. He was lonely, tired of taking himself in his own hand when his desire for a woman, this *wrong* woman, woke him in the night.

So he had considered, over and over, walking to Salyer's Hotel in the dark, his money in hand. He would soothe his conscience with a high-minded story about companionship. Last night, even after Rose had told him what was happening at Salyer's, had begged him to help Ya Zhen; even when he saw how brutally the girl was living: when she had started to undress, that dark hunger had flared.

And she had seen right through him.

He had sheltered Shu-Li and the ones before her, hiding them so that they would be relieved from exactly that life, or worse. But he had also been willing to cause suffering—perhaps to Ya Zhen herself. He would have been another heavy body pressing her down.

With a final goodnight, he closed the door to Shu-Li's room. It was a dark thing, to know such things about oneself.

He returned to the sitting room where Rose, like a found treasure, slept under his roof. He stood near the window, first watching the fog twining around the street lamps, then looking down at her, half in silhouette, half lit by the moving reflection of the candle across the room.

He sat on the floor next to the divan and watched her sleep. Her eyelashes cast spiked shadows on her cheeks, and her mouth, relaxed, was partly open. He reached out a finger and, not quite touching her, traced all the angles of her handsome face—nose, eyelids, ear. Without warning, she opened her eyes. His hand hovered above her face like a bird caught on an updraft. She drew his palm to her cheek and pressed it there, kissed the cup of his palm, her face solemn and her breath warm.

A series of loud pops like firecrackers made them both jump, and out in the street a young boy began to scream for help.

By the time they had rushed downstairs, a gabble of voices came from the end of the block, shouting and upset.

Then, over everything else, a woman's voice keened, a wordless wail that made Bai Lum's skin bunch into hard gooseflesh.

¤

One block from his home, between Christ Episcopal Church and a back alley, something slammed David Kendall hard under his right shoulder blade. His face hit the street. The iron taste of mud filled his mouth and gritted between his teeth. More shots were fired and he flinched hard, tried to curl into a ball. Men shouting, in Chinese he thought, then footsteps echoing away in every direction.

"Mama, help me." It was a boy, somewhere across the street. "I'm hurt bad." His cries fell against the fog and sounded flat in Kendall's ears.

He tried to raise himself but could not. He felt as if a lance of ice was driven through him, and when he moved the blade turned to fire, radiating a nauseous, greasy pain through his belly. He vomited, and could smell the dinner he had recently eaten, and blood, and the living odor of the bay.

The boy still screamed and wept, and now other voices approached. A warm pool seeped under Kendall. It's my blood, he thought, but it seemed distant to him, a problem he couldn't hold in his mind.

"David?" Prudence, running toward him. She knelt and tried to roll him over. The pain glanced through his center again and he groaned.

"Help me," she screamed. "My husband, someone!" More running footsteps and a confusion of voices.

"Holy Christ, it's Dave Kendall."

"We got another one shot over here, the Baldschmidt kid."

"Easy Dave, easy does it. Watch his head."

Many hands were on him, turning him face up. A blanket came from somewhere and they wrapped it around him. Each time they moved him, another pain radiated through his gut, but it was less intense now, seemed farther away. His hands and feet had no feeling. His wife moaned high in her throat when they lifted him, and he knew that she could see the black stain of his blood on the street. He tried to speak, to tell her not to worry, but he couldn't form the words. Strong hands bore him up the street to his home, there were dozens of voices now, and he could no longer make out what they said, it was like the sound of birds, melded into background noise. He looked up at the streetlights, diffuse in the fog. They were beautiful.

PART III

CONVERGENCE

Just as we were going to press last night a serious riot broke out in the Chinese quarters just opposite our office. Some ten or twelve shots were fired, and noise enough made to shake the bones of Confucius. We do not know the extent of damage, but saw one Chinaman laid out with a bullet through his lung. Dr. Davis took the ball out of his back. He is a gone Chinaman.

Daily Humboldt Times
February 1, 1885

If ever such an event does occur—if ever an unoffending white man is thus offered up on the altar of paganism, we fear it will be goodbye to Chinatown.

Editorial: WIPE OUT THE PLAGUE SPOTS
Daily Humboldt Times
February 5, 1885

Before you embark on a journey of revenge, dig two graves.

—*Confucius*

CHAPTER EIGHT

A T LEAST A DOZEN PEOPLE milled at the corner, everyone agitated and talking at once. Several knelt around a crying boy, tending some wound, his leg or foot by the look of it. His cap was off, his face streaked with dirt and tears. The doors of the Episcopal Church stood open, throwing light on a ghastly puddle of blood and vomit in the street. Rose started to shudder and realized she had come outside without her coat. People appeared from all directions, everyone shouting, asking what had happened. At the far end of the street another group, big men, carried a body, rushing away. Hazel followed with her arm around Prudence Kendall. Rose hurried after them.

Before she could catch up, they were inside the Kendall house. The injured man was David Kendall. Dark blood, smeared by many feet, preceded her up the steps and across the parlor floor, and she tried to avoid it, horrified. They were laying him on the dining room table when Rose caught her aunt by the sleeve. "What's happened?" she whispered. Her chin trembled, and it was hard to talk.

Hazel looked at Rose and her face seemed slapped clean of expression. She backed against the parlor wall and closed her eyes.

"Aunt Hazel, what is it? What happened to him?"

"He's shot," she breathed. "God help us, he's been shot by the Chinese."

Rose stared at the doctor and Prudence, who hunched over the table, the doctor's hands at work, Prudence looking into her husband's face. Mayor Tom Walsh was there, too, and two or three others. All she could see of David Kendall were his boots and the cuffs of his trousers. Phoebe stood wide-eyed at the end of the table, her face blotched with crying. She clutched a hank of her own hair to her lips, sobbing into it. Two women stood at her elbows, murmuring to her, averting their eyes from the wounded man. She reached out and grasped the toe of her father's boot, then crumpled into the arms of those around her. Rose looked away, looked at her aunt, whose lips moved silently.

"They caught someone?"

"I don't know." Hazel crossed herself and kissed her fingertips.

"But you said it was the Chinese."

"They've been shooting each other to pieces down there. Now this."

The front door stood open and a crowd formed around the porch. As more people came, the volume of the voices swelled into an unintelligible backwash of sound. The men who had carried Kendall in from the street filled the room, hats in hand, craning to see. She looked at their faces, most of whom she recognized, now rigid with the terrible thing happening on the dining room table.

Rose drew her aunt into an empty corner.

"There are two young girls," she said. She looked at David Kendall's feet again, thought about his boisterous dance with Hazel and his tumble to the greasy floor, and him smiling all the while. The room began to smell rank, of blood and sweat. "It's the girl Bai Lum and the Huntingtons are helping, and another, from Salyer's. They're at the mercantile right now, with Bai Lum, but it's not safe. I want to take them home." She searched Hazel's face. "To your house," she whispered. "If they stay in Chinatown—"

Hazel said nothing, watched the table where a crowd of lamps was held high for the doctor. Then she looked hard at Rose, who stood shaking, her teeth chattering. She took her niece by one arm and pushed through the people now packed in the entry. At the hall tree she took a heavy woolen scarf, one of Mr. Kendall's, and twined it around Rose, pulling it over her head and around her shoulders.

"Do it," she said. "Hurry."

As Rose threaded her way into the street, a single voice rose from inside the house, a thin arching crescendo that ended in a howl. The crowd fell silent for a moment, then a wave of voices pushed out into the damp night like some terrible dark birth.

¤

Byron Tupper lingered on the edge of the crowd, moving back and back as people arrived to gawk and mill in front of Captain Kendall's house. The man's name passed from person to person as the town emptied itself into the cold evening. Somewhere he had lost his hat; the tips of his ears felt numb. He had hurled the gun into the bay and doubled back through a warren of alleys, staying away from street lamps. When the story came his direction—the Chinese had shot a white man, finally went and killed a white man—he couldn't make sense of what he heard. He stood frowning, trying to piece it together. Then it dawned on him, and he was flooded with cool relief: he hadn't shot anyone after all. He had been so certain, the way the man fell in the street. But he got things confused sometimes, he knew that. He shook his head and allowed himself a small smile. He was probably lucky not to have been shot himself, getting so close to the fight as he had. Someone inside the Kendall house all of a sudden pitched a fit, let out a bawl that sounded like a snared animal. A surge of sound and movement rattled through those in the street and Byron took several instinctive steps backward. In the center of this storm, there was no eye of peace. All choices were dropping away.

¤

Bai Lum held open the door of the mercantile when Rose got back. He closed and bolted it behind her. Before she could say anything, he wrapped his arms around her.

"It's awful." She spoke into the crook of his neck and her lips were warmed by his skin. For a solitary moment, she breathed in the smell of him and let herself be held, feeling the hard joint of his shoulder under her cheek. He took hold of her at arm's length.

"Tell me."

"David Kendall was shot, and a boy...I'm almost sure David's dead. Oh God, the way Mrs. Kendall screamed." She pulled the scarf off her head and balled it between her fists. "It's bad, Bai Lum. There was blood everywhere, all over the steps, and they're blaming the Chinese.

"The tongs?"

"Maybe. I don't know." She took one of his hands in both of hers. "We have to go somewhere safe. My aunt's house is close."

"Shu-Li and Ya Zhen are sleeping, they've slept through everything." He went to the window and looked into the street. "We can't take them out again. Not into this." The sound of voices was closer, and now they could hear running along the sidewalks.

"We can't stay here." Outside, another loud report, a rifle from the sound, and the shatter of breaking glass on the next block. Rose felt dumb fear seeping into her limbs. "Please. You know I'm right."

He posted himself at the door again, now holding a makeshift cudgel, the broken end of a shovel handle. "Go get them."

She flew up the stairs and into the room where the girls slept. They lay back to back, curled into commas, making a butterfly shape under the blankets. The crowd below was loud, perhaps closer, perhaps not. Rose couldn't tell at first which girl was which. She shook a shoulder, and it was Ya Zhen.

She came awake immediately. "What's wrong?" The commotion outside hit a pinnacle and she scrambled to her feet. "They're here," she said, stumbling two steps backward.

"No," Rose said. "It's not about you, Ya Zhen. No one knows you're here." Shu-Li sat up looking dazed, her hair bushed wildly around her face and shoulders. "But there's trouble. I don't have time to explain right now." She grabbed the dress Ya Zhen had worn over in the back of the wagon. "Put this on, and the bonnet. We'll put the apron and this scarf on Shu-Li. Hurry."

Shu-Li pulled the apron over her clothes without question. Ya Zhen did the same, once more yanking the bonnet low over her face. *Let us help*, Rose thought, a prayer sent out into the universe like a small stone dropped down a well, *one more time*. She swaddled Shu-Li's upper body in David Kendall's wool scarf, and then they were rushing downstairs.

Bai Lum hurried from his post at the front door and guided them into the dark storeroom. He had pulled on a padded coat, the shovel handle tucked most of the way up his sleeve. "We must leave by the back," he said. "There are already people coming into the street." He bent close to Shu-Li and Ya Zhen. "Stay close to me." He slid the back door open on its track a few inches and peered out, then opened it just enough to slip into the dark alley. Shu-Li followed, and Rose motioned for Ya Zhen to go. As she did, she reached back and took Rose's hand, bringing Rose with her.

The four of them huddled together behind the building, listening. Bai Lum nodded at Rose.

"Here we go," she said. "Only three streets over. Stay close."

They crept to the end of the alley and paused again. People were everywhere on the next block, packed into the street, on the sidewalks, huddled in front yards. Everyone talked, shouted. Women wept into handkerchiefs. One woman, dry-eyed and stone-faced, stood on the periphery with a little boy who idly knocked a twig back-and-forth against a fence. Someone's dog began to bay, a deep monotonous howl immediately answered by other dogs in the neighborhood. Even with the numbers of people milling about, attention was so fractured and chaotic Rose felt as if her little group was invisible. It seemed to her that, if they were lucky, the pandemonium would work to their advantage.

"Which way?" said Bai Lum, close and almost conversational. Ya Zhen seemed preternaturally calm, but Shu-Li looked terrible. Even under the bundle of scarf, Rose could see that her lips were white, as though she might pass out. Rose put an arm around her shoulders. "We can do this," she said. "We'll be fine." They stepped from the alley, staying back in the shadows as much as they were able.

Before they had taken three steps, someone stepped out of nowhere and grabbed Ya Zhen.

People hovered everywhere. The metallic odor of blood and something darker, more foul, was strong in the dining room. At the Kendall's house, the men had gone off, except the doctor, and Prudence Kendall didn't know what he could still be doing. Already it seemed the intention was to separate her from David as quickly as possible, never mind that there was no way they could get farther apart. She would stay with him for now, as long as she could, fill her eyes with the physicality of him. She refused to be led away, be comforted out of his presence. Women twittered and hushed in all the corners of the house, and Prudence waited. She kept herself straight and held back the weight of anguish pressing up.

She stroked her thumb over the long bones of his hand, over the prominent knob at his wrist, smoothing the few dark hairs there. There was dirt on his cuff and some under his nails. She thought about the paste on his coat sleeve. He was always clean about his person. He would hate this.

Doctor Gross had rushed in with everyone when they carried David off the street. Neighbors urged Prudence to move away while the doctor looked at the wound, standing around her in a protective bunch, but she had pushed them away and stayed with him. The doctor had taken a cursory look at the wound and then taken off his own jacket, spread it over David. His somber face told Prudence everything. Her husband had been able to speak a few words, something about the streetlights, a gargled whisper that made no sense to her. In the space between words, his face went blank. Here, and then not here. Now Prudence held his hand under the doctor's jacket, which was pulled over his wound and his face.

Mrs. Cleary came into the dining room from the kitchen. The smell of coffee wafted in and Prudence had the sense for a moment that it was early morning, that she was patting David's hand to wake him. It had been her small ritual to bring him a cup of coffee before he rose. He would lean against the oak headboard and sip his coffee, she would sit facing him, and they would start the day this way in quiet conversation.

"Pru, dear heart," Hazel said. She put her hand on Prudence's shoulder and spoke quietly near her ear. "Won't you come with me for a bit of rest? We'll take care of Captain Kendall for a little while. Phoebe needs you, too."

Prudence could hear her daughter crying, had been hearing her for some time she realized, but it seemed somehow disconnected from everything else.

"Where is she?"

"Doctor Gross has her upstairs. He'll give her something to calm her, poor little thing, and Will should be here soon. Someone went to fetch him." She patted Prudence's shoulder. "Come up, dear, and lie down awhile. The doctor will give you something, too."

Prudence looked at Hazel Cleary's soft, wrinkled face, at the white hair wound in a heavy braid, and she wanted to abandon herself to the old woman's ministrations. She imagined she might collapse and allow herself to be taken up and rocked like a child. But she looked down at David's hand resting in hers and shook her head.

"Not now," she said. She cleared her throat. "I need a basin and some wash rags, Mrs. Cleary—can you get them for me?"

Hazel looked from Prudence to Mr. Kendall's body, and it took several seconds before she understood what was wanted. "Prudence, you can't mean to do this yourself." She drew up a chair and looked hard into Prudence's eyes. "Mr. Kendall has a terrible injury. Let the other women do this for you."

"I need some soap, too." Prudence stood and laid David's hand beside him on the table. "Not the soap in the kitchen. The good lavender soap from upstairs. Please."

Hazel sat for a moment, pinching the bridge of her nose between thumb and forefinger. Then she got to her feet again. "I'll get everything for you, darling, right away." She paused. "May I help you, Pru?"

Prudence shook her head.

"I'll go upstairs to see about Phoebe, then, and if you need anything else, you'll call me, won't you, if you need anything at all. I'll be right here."

"Yes, there is something, Mrs. Cleary," Prudence said. She made her request, and in the space of two minutes all the other women—perhaps a dozen or more—were herded out of the house. The doctor went too, leaving his jacket behind.

¤

It happened in seconds. All day she had feared this moment, had imagined and dreaded being accosted, yet at the moment the boy caught her by the arm, Ya Zhen felt only a short, resistant surprise. Here he was again, Byron, staring. Something bad had happened to his face; his nose was smashed to one side, blacking both eyes, and along one cheekbone was a terrible, crusted gash. But he smiled rapturously.

"You're here," he said, pulling her into him. He buried his face against her neck. His breath was humid on her skin and he began to weep. "Thank God, I thought you were dead, I thought he killed you." He whispered on and on, a rush of words into her hair.

Revulsion surged through her. She pushed against his chest and wrenched backward, stumbling out of his embrace.

"Pearl, it's me." Before she had a chance to get beyond his reach, he clutched her sleeve again. "You're safe now. I can marry you." Tears welled in his eyes, but he looked euphoric. He laughed and tried to pull her toward him again.

She slapped him, hit him so hard she felt the concussion fly up her arm and into her shoulder. His head rocked back. Tall and muscular as he was, he staggered and nearly lost his feet. A thin line of blood trickled from the cut on his cheek, and his hair was in his eyes. She leaned forward into his face, panting, feeling a wild urge to reach out and tear handfuls of hair from his head.

"No," she said through clenched teeth, a guttural rasp that seemed to rise straight up from the ground under her feet. "Don't touch me again."

Before Byron could stand straight, Bai Lum stepped between them. He put one arm out behind him and pressed Ya Zhen backward toward the alley, where Shu-Li had already retreated. In his other hand, held almost behind his back, he held some sort of weapon.

Rose was already at Byron's shoulder, speaking his name in a low voice. Ya Zhen drew close to Shu-Li. All the feeling had run out of her limbs except the palm of her right hand, which tingled wildly from the shock of the slap. Shu-Li put her arm around Ya Zhen's waist and pulled her against the side of the building. They stood so close that Ya Zhen couldn't tell which of them was shaking. She could no longer see the throng around the corner, but she could hear them, men's voices mostly, roiling into the amorphous night sky in a furious, unarticulated bellow.

Byron flipped the hair out of his eyes and lifted his fingers to his bleeding face. The smear of blood looked black in the dim light and he stared at it.

"Byron?" Rose put her hand on the boy's arm. "It's not safe out here." He looked up from his bloody fingers. "Byron," she said again, "you're hurt. You should go home."

He did not respond, but turned his head and peered toward the alley. Ya Zhen flattened herself against the wall, although she could tell by his expression he didn't see her clearly. Then he looked at Bai Lum, seemed to notice him for the first time. Shu-Li's fingers tightened, and Ya Zhen's whole body went rigid at the expression that hardened on the boy's face.

He shook Rose's hand off his arm and fell back a step, wiping a hand across his mouth.

"Was it you?" he said to Bai Lum.

"Byron," Rose said.

He took another backward step, almost in the middle of the street now, not taking his eyes off Bai Lum. "It was you, wasn't it. You were with her last night. You shot the man." He nodded to himself. "You did it."

Rose reached for him again. Each time Rose got close to Byron, Shu-Li flinched. "No, Byron," Rose said, "It wasn't—"

"Shut up!" he screamed at her. "Do you know everything? Were you there? I didn't see you there!" He closed his mouth and stood panting, his breath sending white feathers into the chilly night air. He was crying now and even in the faint light, Ya Zhen saw tears track through the smear of blood on his cheek.

Around the corner, a man's voice rose over the din. "Go to the hall. They're meeting at Centennial Hall." A bell began to clang and the voices rose. Byron glanced in that direction as if just noticing the noise, looked at Bai Lum, and disappeared around the corner and into the fog.

¤

It was strange to wash her husband's body this way, the way she had washed her daughter when Phoebe was a child. Prudence pulled back the quilted throw, steeling herself against the sight of the bullet wound. At first she felt she might lose consciousness, not so much because of the blood or even the injury, like a ragged mouth. It was the sense of overwhelming intrusion— that her husband's body, as familiar as her own, had been rendered foreign.

She took several deep breaths, not taking her eyes off him, and found she could bear it. First she undressed him, struggling to wrench the bloodstained things out from under his body. She folded each piece of clothing and laid it on the chair beside her. Taking a chunk of the fragrant soap, she began to wash away the blood and clean the wound. She expected it would bleed, but it didn't, and this kept surprising her. She swabbed directly into the torn flesh, wiped up purple fragments that looked to her like bits of a calf's liver. She rinsed the rag repeatedly, and there was little in her mind but the knowledge that she must finish this, like leaping into deep water and holding her breath until she came up again. Outside she could hear shouting and someone ringing a bell, but it came from the other end of town. Three times she went to the kitchen, poured off the bloody water and refilled the basin.

David was not an exceptionally large man, but he was strongly built. Prudence had to use force to roll him onto his side. In his back, the wound was small and looked almost harmless, a minor accident in the flesh. As she balanced him, his right arm fell behind, the knuckles banging against the mahogany table, so she bent the arm at the elbow and rested it on his waist. She wiped blood from table and quickly washed her husband's back and buttocks, then eased him prone again. Sweat trickled between her breasts and her hair stuck to her forehead. Once the blood was completely washed away, Prudence tore a clean rag in half and laid a folded square over the wound. The smell in the room was still organic, even under the fragrance of the soap, but not so declamatory. She remembered her bedroom smelling like this after Phoebe's birth—things washed up but with a faint scent of blood recently spilled. She went for another basin of water.

Coming back from the kitchen, she could hear Mrs. Cleary upstairs with Phoebe. Her voice was quiet and rhythmic, and Prudence realized she was reciting the rosary. She wondered if Phoebe had ever heard the rosary before. It seemed to be helping, that and the sedative; the girl's sobbing had quieted. Perhaps she would fall asleep soon.

Each time Prudence returned to the dining room, the remarkable stillness met her again. David lay just as she had left him, of course he did, but this absence of agency, the utter loss of volition stunned her. She could expect him to move no more than she could expect the chairs to rearrange themselves. Where can he be? she wondered. Where is it he's gone to?

She washed the rest of him, beginning with his face. Mud from the street was in his nose, clung to the surface of his eyes and tongue. When the basin was fouled, she freshened it. Every part of him came under her hand. A childhood scar on his shoulder, the shape of his toes, the way the hair on his belly trailed in a thin line to his pubis—all of him utterly particular and beloved. Although she used warm water, his flesh became cool and inert. Only his hair, which had stayed thick and silky into his middle years, felt the same, cool and soft in her fingers. Often, while they made love, she would comb her fingers into his hair and hold his head that way, looking into his face while he rocked above her. With closed eyes, he would whisper her name.

Finally, there was nothing else she could do. She went to the linen closet and got the quilt her mother had made them as a wedding gift, a Baltimore Album quilt appliqued with birds and fruit and flowers. After David was covered to the chin, Prudence climbed onto the table and stretched out beside him. She turned on her side and rested her hand on his chest, the way she had slept every night for twenty-six years. His chest did not rise under her palm. She turned her face into his shoulder and fell into grief like off a precipice.

¤

As Lucy Huntington finished washing the supper dishes, she realized she could hear voices out in the street. Someone began to pound the front door. The plate she was drying slipped from her fingers and shattered on the floor, splinters in all directions. Parishioners often arrived at odd hours, but this thudding was relentless, and now she heard men shouting. *It is because of the girl*, she thought, *because we have hidden the girl.*

She picked her way through the shards of china and hurried into the front hallway. Through the sidelights, she could see people on the porch and a crowd in the street. She stood still with the tea towel in her hand, not wanting to answer. Charles came to the door of his study holding a page of the sermon he was working on. The lamp behind him lit his hair in a wiry silver penumbra.

"It sounds like half the town is out there," he said. Now there were shouts for the reverend to open up, to come out.

"Have they found out, do you think? What should we tell them?"

"I can't imagine this many people would care," he said. "Let's see what this is about."

Lucy touched his sleeve as he passed her, wanting to hold him from whatever black message stood behind all those voices. But she smoothed the front of her dress and pressed forward to stand next to her husband. When he opened, several men crowded the doorway and tried to tell the news all at once.

"Dave Kendall is dead—shot down in the street," yelled one, "but he lived a little bit, until we got him home."

"It's the Chinese. We're gonna hang them all." A wave of male voices erupted through the open door. Lucy could see a shifting throng of people moving beyond the edge of the yard, heading toward town. Several of their neighbors came outside and fell in with the crowd.

"You men listen to me," Charles shouted from the porch. "Stop here and think about what you're doing." He lifted his hands over his head, trying to draw their attention. A few glanced up, but most ignored him. Then she spotted Jacob Weimer, a deacon in the church, and Charles's close confidant. He shouldered his way onto the porch and shouted to be heard above the hundreds of men moving around them.

"Charles, you have to come with us," Jacob said. "They're going to Centennial Hall. Someone has to try and stop this." His normally boyish face was haggard. "The mayor just came from Captain Kendall's. He's trying to get to Centennial Hall ahead of them."

Cold filled the entryway and Lucy hugged herself. Charles was already taking his coat from the rack. She wanted to put herself in front of the door, find some compelling way to keep him, but the expression on his face made clear his intention to go.

He shrugged into his coat. "I have to try." His eyes were steady on hers. "Don't open the door," he said. "I'm sure you'll be fine, but—" He tugged one of her earlobes, an old gesture between them.

When he was gone, she returned to the kitchen and swept the pieces of dropped plate. The house seemed cavernous and the sounds of the broken china too loud. Outside, whoever carried the bell was relentless, all of them shouting bloody murder. She tipped shards into the dustbin and her mind vaulted in every direction—

her husband, Ya Zhen and Shu-Li, Mattie and Rose. Standing in the doorway had chilled her and she sat near the stove, which still radiated a little heat from cooking supper. She wrapped her hands in her apron and thought about Prudence Kendall, whose husband had gone out tonight, too, and come home mortally wounded.

She tried to pray but found she could not adequately articulate her concerns. How does one begin to ask for relief from death, even on behalf of another? Lucy's parents had died from cholera within a day of each other when Lucy was eleven years old. She learned at a young age that death interjects itself and refuses all entreaties to the contrary, no matter how earnest. Instead of praying, she simply held Prudence Kendall in her mind, in the same sacred space that she was holding Charles.

There were still voices in the street and then a gunshot. Lucy shivered and leaned a little closer to the stove, then caught sight of her reflection in the kitchen windows—a feeble old woman hunched into a chair. She stood so fast the chair fell over backward and hit the floor. "Enough of this," she said into the empty room. "Enough."

She strode to the kindling box and broke several pieces over her knee, then stoked the stove again for tea. *No*, she thought, *let's have some coffee*. When the pot was on, she went upstairs for a sweater and her small fowling rifle.

¤

"You can't go out there, Bai Lum. Please. Didn't you hear those people?" Rose couldn't believe what he suggested.

"That boy knows where we are. We need a way out. Huntington could take us somewhere to wait until this passes."

"Where can he take us tonight? We can't keep running from hiding place to hiding place." She didn't say what she was thinking, that this was not going to pass. A man was dead and it would not pass. It seemed as if something inside was beginning to unravel and her hands shook. She pressed the heels of her palms together to steady herself.

They had not lit a lamp and Bai Lum was a shadow, weaving between tables and shelves with the makeshift club at hand. Ya Zhen had taken Shu-Li back upstairs. "Those girls can't take much more of this."

"I know. You stay here with them. I can go faster alone." He crossed the room and stood close enough that she could see the outlines of his face. "I'll bring help."

"You know where the Congregational Church is? The Huntingtons live in the house behind."

"I know where it is."

"Stay in the alley," she said. "You can take it all the way over there and cut across into their side yard."

"Yes." He cracked open the mercantile door. The street seemed oddly quiet now. "Take this." He pressed the shovel handle into her hand.

"No," she said. "You could meet trouble—"

He held her hands firmly against the weapon. "Keep it here, in case the boy returns."

"Hurry."

He touched his lips to her forehead and went out, disappearing around the side of the building.

She listened at the door. The only sound was a dog barking somewhere nearby. "Hurry," she said again.

¤

Centennial Hall stood open and hundreds of men were shoulder-to-shoulder, trying to get in. The shouts outside were overmatched by the roar inside. Charles Huntington and Jacob Weimer stopped on the far side of the lawn, looking at the mass of men.

"This is bedlam," Jacob shouted. "We'll never get inside."

"I have to," said Huntington. "Look at them." These were men who worked crosscut saws and rigged massive redwood logs to steam donkeys to be hauled out of the deep woods. Work was slow in the winter, the woods boggy and mucked. The saloon trade was as profitable as lumber in the down time, and a great number of this crowd had arrived from the bars that ran up and down the waterfront. Every face, clean-cut or unshaven, bore a dark expression that looked akin to rapture.

"I want you to wait for me," said Charles.

"You can't go in there alone." Jacob grasped his elbow. "I have an idea," he said. "Back here." He pulled Charles off to one side and around the corner of the building.

"They'll be at the back doors, too, Jacob."

"Not the back. I know another way."

They moved along the far side of the building, feet squelching in the mud of a flowerbed. It was quieter on this side, but Charles could feel the vibration of the crowd inside rising through the soles of his shoes.

"It's right there." Jacob pointed to a narrow staircase, tucked behind an alcove.

"Where does it come out?"

"On the third floor, the storage room. Once we're in, we can take the back stairs through the kitchen."

The storage room was long and narrow, not much more than a crawlspace; the two men picked their way in the dark around brooms and pails and a stack of old newspapers. Jacob led him to the door on the far side and then they were hurrying through the back of the building, into the massive kitchen. The voices out in the main hall were a single bellow that made the room pulsate. When Jacob stopped short, Charles grasped his shoulder.

"It's enough, Jacob. Go home."

Jacob's face hardened and he shook his head. He opened the door that let out into the alcove behind the stage.

The noise was incredible, something Charles could feel pressing toward the front of the room. A wasted, coppery smell hung over the crowd, and a smell of damp clothes and mud so heavy he seemed to taste it in the back of his throat. He moved onto the stage where Mayor Walsh stood with a half-dozen other men. They had their heads close together, conferring. The sheriff was there too, gesturing emphatically and shaking his head in the negative.

Mayor Walsh stepped to the lectern and looked around the vast room. Charles noticed mud on his fine calfskin boots. For a moment, the noise in the hall seemed to grow, then the men began to quiet each other. There was a shout of "Hear him!" and the mayor had their attention.

"Men, we understand there's been trouble tonight. Very serious trouble. Captain Kendall was an exemplary citizen of this city."

"What are you doing about it, Walsh?" someone shouted. A rumble of assent.

"We want to handle this properly," Walsh said. "It's important that none of you go off half-cocked."

"We're not going to swallow this—eye for an eye!" The men cheered. "We're going to get them all," a voice cried, "massacre every damn one of them killing bastards."

It was what they had expected, Charles knew, why the city fathers had hurried away from their suppers and down to the hall, why they now stood in the shadowed recesses of the stage, awaiting a cue, someone to tell them what part they had to play here.

A tall man in the back wearing cork boots stepped onto a bench and issued a long piercing whistle; voices fell and heads swiveled toward him.

"Listen here," he said, his voice almost conversational. "Are you murderers? You want blood on your hands? We've seen that here, before," he said, shaking his head, "and you all ought to know that ain't right." Charles watched several in the crowd drop their heads, but the undercurrent of voices kept on. "We don't have to have that on our conscience," the man said. "But—" He held up an index finger. "But that don't mean we have to keep them heathens in our midst. I say we put them out. Out in the woods, like animals. See if they can get along with the Diggers living out there. No shelter, not here."

This got a vast roar of approval and they took it up as a chant—no shelter, not here, no shelter.

Charles stepped to the front of the stage. There were men in this multitude that he had known for years, men that he saw from his pulpit every Sunday. Neighbors and shopkeepers stood cheek and jowl with men who spent most of their time in the saloons and bawdy houses on 2nd Street. The desire for revenge looked the same on every face. He didn't try to shout them down or quiet them. He just stood, looking from person to person. The chant died out.

"Gentlemen," he said. He was used to making his voice carry, and he made sure they heard him in the very back of the room. "I ask you to listen to me for just a minute here." When he had their attention he continued.

"There's a thing to be done tonight, that's sure. It's going to be up to all of us to determine what that thing will be. Now, I know you don't want to hear this, but what I'm about to say is the truth, and sometimes the truth is a hard thing to swallow." He paused, let another grumble run through them. "The truth is that this thing that's happened, this terrible death of one of our esteemed fellows, was an accident." Their voices began to cycle up again, and the gas lamps on the walls flickered from the energy that moved through the room.

"*Yes!*" Charles roared. The deep baritone of his voice bounced back at him from the rear wall of the hall in a tight echo, and the men stood still, apparently dumbfounded to hear such a voice come from a white-haired man. "A terrible, unthinkable accident," he continued. "But the rank and file in our Chinatown are as innocent of David Kendall's death as I am. He looked across the mass of faces, shaking his head, and lowered his voice just enough to be heard. "If this is a matter of character," he said, "I suggest we show what kind of character we have."

Sheriff Brown stepped forward then. "The reverend is right about this situation," he said. "I'm just as mad as you are, but I'm standing here telling you that I don't know who shot Dave

Kendall." Charles could see that the man's hands shook the tiniest bit, but his voice was solid. "No one set out to commit murder here tonight. I haven't got a single person to pin this on, and I'm not going to have you men tearing up this town." He shifted his weight from one foot to the other. "I'm sworn to uphold the law, and I mean to do so. If any of you start something that violates the laws of this county, you'll be reckoning with me, and with my deputies."

Elias Kent, who kept the books at one of the small sawmills, spoke up from near the front. "Something's got to be done here, Sheriff. Do you mean to tell us otherwise?"

Mayor Walsh addressed him. "Absolutely not, Mr. Kent. Never think it, boys. Justice will be served. But we've got to make this decision with our heads set right. Now, look here, you know these men behind me." The group, dressed in fine coats and clean collars stood like a church choir toward the back of the stage. Walsh motioned them forward. "We have a citizen's committee to help us decide our course. What we suggest is this: we feel, and we believe you'll all agree with us, that enough is enough." Charles flinched inwardly, thinking this would just rile the crowd again. But someone shouted, "You're not running for office here, Tom," and heads craned around to see who the comedian was.

Walsh nodded grimly. "We believe that the best thing for Eureka is the orderly removal of Chinese persons from our midst. All of them."

"Now you're making sense," someone shouted.

"It so happens there are two steamers in harbor tonight," Walsh said. "We propose that the Chinese be compelled to pack themselves up, lock, stock, and barrel, and be taken by sea to San Francisco." He waited and let the idea sink in.

Charles felt a weight in the pit of his stomach. "Mayor, with all due respect," he said, "this is not fair treatment." Walsh turned toward him, clearly nettled at the interruption, but Charles pressed on. "These people pay their rent, they mind their own business and you have no more right to drive them from their homes than you have to drive me from mine."

Someone under the windows began to chant, "No shelter, not here," and the crowd took it up again. The mayor stepped between Charles and the crowd and spoke in his ear.

"You've done your best here, pastor. That's enough now." The look on his face told Charles that there would be no persuading him otherwise; the decision was made. Charles took a step backward and Jacob grasped his arm.

"That's it, Reverend. We've got to get out of here."

Charles took a last look at the crowd and turned away, feeling the mass of men like a monolith behind him. He and Jacob ducked back through the storage room the way they had come in.

They hurried through the deserted streets, hands thrust deep into their pockets. As they walked, Charles explained to Jacob what had happened at the parsonage that afternoon, how he and Lucy and Rose had smuggled Ya Zhen away from Salyer's.

"We thought we were putting her in a relatively safe place today," Charles said. He shook his head. "Now it seems we set the child right on top of a powder keg."

"It's going to be bad."

"Yes."

"Those men are barely under control. They'll shed blood."

"More than likely," Charles said. "Let's get back to the house and decide what's best to do next." They hurried toward the rectory, and the gritty cadence of their shoes on the damp road fell into the silence between them. Over their shoulders, they could hear the voices at Centennial Hall, moving back out into the night.

¤

Bai Lum slipped from the back alley into the Huntingtons' side yard. A dog started barking at the house next door, running along the fence and sticking its snout through broken boards, but there were dogs barking all over town, reacting to shouts and intermittent gunfire. There were occasional whoops that sounded like young men celebrating, which worried Bai Lum more than the gunshots.

Skirting around the carriage house and a half-dozen bare fruit trees, Bai Lum could now see Lucy Huntington in the house. She sat at the table with a silver tea service spread out before her, using a rag to rub furiously at a gleaming sugar bowl. A small caliber rifle rested across her lap. He didn't want to startle her, but every minute that he was away from Rose seemed like throwing the door open to worse trouble. He was nauseated with worry, and it pressed him to take a chance. He took the back porch steps carefully, easing up the sides of the risers. He lifted a closed fist, hesitated and knocked softly, two gentle raps.

"Who is it?" She was already right behind the door, and sounded perfectly calm. *She heard me come up those steps,* he thought, *and knew I was here even before I knocked.*

"It's Bai Lum," he said. We need help." The door opened immediately and Lucy pulled him inside. It was warm in the room and her hands felt hot and strong on his arm.

"Are you hurt, any of you?" She looked out into the yard. "Where are the girls?"

"They're together at my store, with Rose. They were safe when I left them, but it's dangerous for them to stay where they are. A boy saw us, saw Ya Zhen. Knew her."

"Oh Lord." She began to pace the kitchen. "My husband has gone off to try to talk sense to those men," she said. "We'll have to take the carriage to your place. We could bring the girls back here for the night." She moved a few steps toward the door, where the rifle rested against the wall, then back to Bai Lum. "But this isn't the ideal place for them, either."

He felt the time rushing past.

She stopped short in the middle of the floor. "The church." Her face brightened. "There's a room that leads off the sacristy, nothing in it but a couple of old bookcases with baptismal and confirmation records. No one can get to it from the outside, and no one would think to look there."

Bai Lum felt an exhausted wave of dread break over him. Even if they were able to hide for the night, they couldn't stay hidden long. He felt desperate to get back to the store and stand watch, and even more desperate to get everyone into a safe place.

Lucy must have seen the feelings on his face. "I know you're worried," she said. "I am too. But I think this can work. You'll all be out of danger, at least until morning, and it will buy us some time to think."

The back door crashed open. It slammed backward against the wall so hard that the four small panes of glass in its top half shattered. Before either of them could react, three men pushed into the kitchen.

"What the hell are you doing in here with this lady?" The speaker wore rough black work pants. His coat hung open and the buttons on his shirt strained over a huge gut. A small, slender man sporting a bowler hat stood beside the fat man and gripped what looked to be an old axe handle. The third man stood in front and had a big army pistol stuck in his pants. He rested one palm lightly on the butt of the gun.

"How dare you break into this home." Lucy Huntington, herself not much taller than a child, stepped squarely between Bai Lum and the intruders. "This is a church parsonage and this gentleman is my guest." Her white head tipped back to look at the fat man, and she cocked it to one side, appraising him.

Bai Lum stood quietly, but adrenaline made his muscles thrum and the dimly lit kitchen now seemed to vibrate with light and color. He noticed that the gaps between the fat man's shirt buttons revealed not an undershirt, but patches of pasty skin and dark hair. He wished for Lucy's gun, could almost feel its small weight in his hands, but it was behind the broken door, out of reach and useless to them with these three in the breach.

The man with the gun spoke, his voice level and calm. "Mrs. Huntington, where is the girl?"

"What girl?" Lucy managed to sound annoyed by the question.

"Please don't waste my time, Mrs. Huntington. Mr. Salyer's girl. We've come to fetch her."

"For heaven's sake, I sent Ya Zhen back to the hotel hours ago. You've broken my back door for nothing. You go tell Mr. Salyer he'd better send someone around to repair it first thing tomorrow."

"That's a lie," said the big man. "She's lying, Clayton."

Lucy waved her hand as if shooing a fly. "That girl left my house this afternoon on foot, and that is the God's truth—which Cora Salyer already knows, by the way. What happened to the girl after she left here I can't imagine."

The fat man looked toward the parlor door. "Maybe we should have a look around."

"Where's the Reverend?" asked Clayton.

"He's calling on a parishioner." She turned her attention on the fat man again. "I know your mother, don't I?" Lucy stared at him. "Yes, I do. Melinda Fickes. You're Ronald? No, Randall. Randall Fickes, you ought to be ashamed."

Fickes's pudgy face twitched and he looked from Lucy to Bai Lum. "Maybe you ought to be ashamed, old woman, having this sorry heathen in your kitchen when you're home all alone." He pointed at Bai Lum and his meaty hand shook. "There's been a murder done, and for all we know, this one did it." He started to move around Lucy. "You're coming with us, boy, right here and now."

Lucy jockeyed to one side, trying to stay between them, but the man with the bowler hat caught her by the arm. Just before Fickes bore down on him, Lucy slapped the short man a hard shot across the face, knocking his hat off. Randall Fickes reached for one of Bai Lum's arms and Bai Lum pistoned the heel of his hand forward into the man's nose. He felt the cartilage give way with a muffled crunch, and then the man called Clayton leveled a pistol at his face.

"I'll shoot you right now," Clayton said. "If you move you are a dead man." His expression remained bland and composed, as if this scuffle were no more interesting to him than reading yesterday's news. Fickes, meanwhile, bent at the waist and blared, holding a filthy bandanna to his bleeding nose. The bowler hat man had Lucy pressed against the wall, her white hair trailing askew, a red welt rising on her face. Bai Lum started to move, but she held one hand out toward him.

"No, Bai Lum," she said, breathing hard. "Don't do it."

"That's excellent advice," said Clayton. "Listen to the lady now, and don't be rash." He smiled at Bai Lum. "Ready?"

Bai Lum said nothing. He and Lucy held each other's eyes, and she nodded at him, a hard, decisive little nod. She would take care of Rose and Ya Zhen and Shu-Li.

Fickes groaned again. "Mongolian bastard broke my nose." He looked at the gore on his hanky and touched his nose delicately with one finger. "How bad is it?"

"Did I tell you to let me deal with this, Randall?" said Clayton. "Now shut up and let's get him downtown. Walk, Chinaman. Lonny, let go of the lady."

Lonny did as he was told and Lucy moved away from him, smoothing the front of her dress with both hands, as if dusting herself off after working in the garden. Clayton gestured Bai Lum toward the door.

"We need to tie him, Clay," Fickes said in a clogged voice.

"Not a bad idea. Lonny, run out to the carriage house and fetch a bit of rope."

Lonny spat on the kitchen floor at Lucy's feet. "Chink lover," he said, and trotted out the back door.

"Let's go," Clayton said, again motioning to the door with his pistol. Fickes went out, keeping a wide berth between himself and Bai Lum, and Bai Lum followed. He could feel the muzzle of the gun resting lightly at the small of his back, a ghost of feeling that made all the nerves under his skin crawl. As he went, he looked back at Lucy and gave her the same hard nod she had given him.

"Turn around, Chinaman," said Clayton. "You have no business looking at a white lady. And you," he said to Lucy "had better hope that Salyer's girl turns up in one piece."

Lonny came back with the rope and Clayton let Fickes hold Bai Lum's hands behind him while Lonny cinched his wrists. His pulse hammered in his fingertips and the stiff piece of hemp immediately began to rub his skin raw. Fickes pulled him down the porch steps. He stumbled and went hard on one knee against a stone, cried out at the steep pain that shot up his leg.

"Don't you hurt this man," Lucy shouted from behind them. "This is an innocent man, do you hear me? Bai Lum, I'll find Reverend Huntington. We'll get you out of this."

"Rose," he called back to her.

"I understand." She sounded on the verge of tears. They were out in the alley now, moving toward town. He risked a single glance back. She stood on the porch, hair wild around her shoulders.

▢

Rose roamed back and forth through the dark mercantile, holding the broken shovel handle and watching first at the front, then listening at the back. After Bai Lum left, she had bolted the front door and checked the windows, even upstairs.

Byron Tupper's face, so stricken, kept rising in her mind's eye, the way he had turned on Bai Lum, accused him. Shu-Li was asleep again, still wearing Lucy's apron. She had looked alarmed when she realized Bai Lum had gone out. Rose and Ya Zhen explained that he was going to get the Huntingtons, and this seemed to satisfy her. She curled on her bed and fell asleep immediately.

But Ya Zhen was wide awake. She sat on the divan, watching through a slit in the curtains at the street below. The room was so dark and Ya Zhen so still, that all Rose could see was a slender stripe of dim light falling over the girl's cheek, and one watchful eye.

"Have you seen anything?" Rose asked. She stood next to the arm of the divan and looked out the opening in the curtain, too. Other than an occasional shout downtown, the evening had gone almost silent.

"Two men came out of the building across the street," Ya Zhen said, pointing, "and a little boy ran by." Her voice was quiet. Since the encounter with Byron, she had seemed extraordinarily calm.

For her part, Rose felt as if she was going to fly apart, waiting for hell to break loose. When a small clock across the room chimed the quarter-hour, she jumped, her pulse galloping in a thready rush. Bai Lum had been gone only twenty minutes.

"Sit down, Rose," Ya Zhen said. "This is a good place to wait."

Rose dropped onto the scratchy sofa and put her head in her hands. "I wish he hadn't gone out. It's so quiet now."

"Not the little boy. He was pulling a stick across the fence. They love to make noise."

"Yes, they do. Little boys and big boys—they're all pretty noisy." Just then a male voice yee-hawed from some distance. Rose tensed, but Ya Zhen laughed.

"I have a little brother."

It took Rose a moment to process. "A brother. Where is he?" She tried to see Ya Zhen's face, but she had dropped the curtain and was now just a dark shape beside Rose.

"With his mother. Our mother. I see him in dreams." She paused. "He sees me, too, I think." Her voice was light, easy.

"Maybe you'll—" Rose faltered. "Maybe you can see him someday. In life, I mean."

Ya Zhen made no reply and Rose wished she could take the words back. She leaned forward and peeked out again. Nothing.

"I think Bai Lum will come back." Ya Zhen said.

Her voice was so soft, like something Rose might hear inside her own head. She swallowed hard. "I'm afraid to say that."

"Why?"

"Something very bad happened tonight. A man was shot. A wonderful, kind man, with a lovely wife and—" She swallowed a terrible lump in her throat. "He was killed, and it's dangerous for Bai Lum to be outside."

"It is always dangerous." Ya Zhen leaned toward the window again, and Rose watched the faint bar of light cross her features. She was smiling. "Look," she said, pointing up. "The moon."

She looked. Even behind the fog, the half-moon had just cleared the opposite roofline, throwing indistinct shadows across the sidewalk, silvering everything.

Ya Zhen rested her cheek on the back of the divan. "This is a wonderful night, Rose."

The deep shadows around Ya Zhen's eyes and the genuine pleasure in her statement made gooseflesh ripple over the back of Rose's neck. "Wonderful?"

"I make my own choices."

Rose felt as if her own choices were narrowing to a fine point. "You aren't frightened? I'm so afraid, Ya Zhen."

Ya Zhen shook her head. "I can stay here, or I can leave. I can lock the door—" she paused and looked across the road, "or I can run outside and climb into that tree." She smiled again, and Rose was stunned by the relaxed expression on her face. "Right now I am just sitting in this dark room, looking at the moon, and it is wonderful." She sat quietly. "If they try to take me, I will not go."

Rose had no idea how Ya Zhen meant to make good on this vow, but the electric flesh ran up her spine again. She believed her.

In the street, a figure moved out of the fog, directly toward the store. Rose jumped up and raced down the stairs, heart pounding in her throat. She moved as silently as she could to the front windows, gripping the shovel handle so tightly her hand seemed welded to it. Before she could look out, someone rapped on the bolted door, a loud and frantic sound in the high-ceilinged room. Rose dropped the piece of wood with a clatter, but managed not to cry out. She inched toward the window, even as the hard rapping came again. It wasn't Bai Lum.

"Rose, are you in there?" A woman's voice, out of breath. "There's trouble, you have to come!"

Mattie.

Rose threw open the door. In the street, the fog looked almost solid now, the stifled light from the moon illuminating a dense, blank surface. The shifting gray curtain of it obscured everything.

Mattie clutched Rose's arm in a pincer grip. "Thank Christ you're here, I didn't know," she panted. "Rose, they have him—Bai Lum. I think they're going to kill him."

¤

Charles Huntington and Jacob Weimer found Lucy in the carriage house, struggling to hitch Buster to the buggy. Lucy barely paused in her efforts, fumbling with the harness, all the while telling them what had happened with Bai Lum in the kitchen.

"We have to help them," she said, working to adjust a buckle.

Charles took her arm, alarmed by how undone she seemed. When she turned her face up to him, the red mark showed. "What happened to you?"

She shook her head furiously. "I'm fine. It's nothing. But we have to hurry." Her hair was all the way down now and pulled roughly back in a horsetail. He could see that there would be no telling her to stay home.

"Yes," he said, taking the harness from her. "I'll finish this. Get a wrap."

She ran to the house, and Jacob helped Charles hitch Buster, who acted skittish and balky.

"Jacob," Charles said, "I want you home now. This thing has gone off the rails and you should be with your wife and children."

Jacob was silent for a moment, stroking Buster's big head, trying to quiet him. "Reverend, I'm going to get Addy and the children and bring them to the church. The kiddies can sleep anywhere—Addy will make a nest for them." He leaned down and brushed at a streak of dried mud on one pant leg. "Someone might show up, looking for help. It's going to be a long night, I think."

Charles nodded, studying Jacob's tired face. "We'll join you just as soon as we can. Thank you, Jacob."

Lucy hurried in wearing her winter coat, holding a muffler for her husband. Jacob helped her in, and a minute later they were aimed for town again, Charles urging Buster into a trot. The fog made it dangerous to travel fast, but they had to risk it. In the open carriage, they were exposed to the weather. Tiny beads of precipitation clung to Lucy's hair and she seemed to shimmer there next to him. Between the parsonage and downtown, most houses were fully lit, as if every room was occupied and on guard. But the streets were empty—no foot traffic, no carriage traffic—until they reached the Chinatown block.

Here it was chaos. As they passed, a man hurled a brick through the window of Dong Li Ha's laundry and when the proprietor ran to the door, several men shouted at him to hand over whatever laundry he had on hand. The street crawled with men, most in groups of five or six. They roamed back and forth, entering shops and houses, shouting orders to pack up. Several merchants tried to bar entrance to their establishments. Wei Chang was backed against a wall, shaking his head, while a man dressed in a fine topcoat and tie made his point by pushing his finger repeatedly into Mr. Wei's sternum. Some of the Chinese had already begun to pile belongings on the walk, and halfway down the street three young boys, no more than ten years old, had taken someone's household dishes and were throwing them into the road. As the carriage moved through the street, a word echoed forward in Charles's mind, one he had read the year before in relation to problems in Russia. *Pogrom*.

Lucy reached over and grasped his wrist. Her fingers were ice cold.

"Charles, look."

At the far end of the street, a rough gallows. The hemp noose hung in a heavy line from the center beam, swaying slightly. A group of people stood in a horseshoe around the front of the crude construction. Someone let out a raucous shout.

"Do for him, boys!"

There was a murmured response from the spectators, their necks craned to look at three men on the platform. In the center, hands bound before him, was Bai Lum.

CHAPTER NINE

ROSE RAN. Somewhere behind, Mattie called her name, but she did not stop, did not look back. Bai Lum's strong and gracious face filled her mind, the touch of his hands on her feet, the enveloping sensation of his kiss last night. *Please please please.* The words poured through her as her heels pounded the street. She could not even think the rest: *please be alive,* and *I will do anything.* Two more blocks and she was gasping the words aloud. She rounded the corner and the scaffold was right there, people standing three deep around its base. Bai Lum's mouth bled and one eye was swollen almost shut. He stood motionless, the tip of the noose grazing one shoulder. Rose tripped and fell to her hands and knees in the wet dirt of the road.

"No!" She got up, mud streaking the front of her striped dress, palms burning with small abrasions. Heads swiveled in her direction as she tried to push her way through to the front of the scaffold. "Stop this," she shouted. When she got to the steps of the platform, someone grabbed her by the arm and held her. Garland Tupper.

"Let go of me." She tried to jerk free of him, but Tupper held her like a vise.

"That's a dead Chinaman," he said. A weirdly beatific smile spread across his features. "Aw. You love him?"

Coming from Tupper's mouth, the question was grotesque. "I said let go of me," Rose shouted. When she struck at him with her free hand, he caught hold of her wrist. The harder she pulled, the deeper he dug his fingers into her flesh, cutting off her circulation, until she cried out.

Bai Lum made a furious sound through his clenched teeth and one of the men holding him, a fat man with blood on his shirt and what looked to be a freshly broken nose, grabbed Bai Lum's braid and yanked his head back until he was looking straight up.

"Don't look at the white lady," Garland shouted, and the fat man pulled backward until Bai Lum's head cocked at an extreme angle, his mouth open.

"Stop it!" Rose tried to hurl herself toward the steps, but Tupper held her.

"He shot Captain Kendall," Tupper shouted. "My boy saw him. He said so."

"That's a lie," said Rose. "Bai Lum was in the mercantile when Mr. Kendall was shot. I was with him."

"Eye for an eye." It was the other man on the platform. Small and slender, he spoke in a quiet, almost conversational tone. "Isn't that right?" He nodded at the fat man, who released Bai Lum's hair. He grabbed the noose and slipped it over Bai Lum's head.

"You like that?" the fat man said. "Break my nose? We'll see now, won't we." He slapped Bai Lum in the back of the head. The crowd jostled, some pressing forward, others stepping back.

"For God's sake, stop," Rose pleaded. "You know this is wrong."

Elsie Dampler pushed through the spectators, her husband trailing behind her. She pointed at Rose. "Decent folks in town know what you've been doing down here, Rose Allen."

"Decent?" Rose laughed. "You haven't the least idea what decent is."

"You're a whore," Elsie yelled, her large face florid under the hazy glare of the gas lamps. "A whore to a Chinese heathen."

"Look around you, Elsie. Is this decent?" She craned her head, trying to catch the eyes of those nearest her. "Why can't you look at me?" she said. "How will you live with yourselves if you kill an innocent man?" She was shouting now. "Look at me! This is a lynch mob acting on the false testimony of a disturbed boy." Garland twisted her arm. The small bones in her wrist ground together and she screamed, unable to help herself.

"Shut up, whore." His breath was foul with liquor and some darker decay. "Didn't I tell you not to speak ill of my son?"

Then a horse was galloping through the street, a carriage rattling behind it, bearing down on them. People scattered as Buster was reigned up short.

Reverend Huntington was out of the carriage and striding toward them, his face thunderous. His white hair bushed out around his head as if electrified. He mounted the gallows in three large strides. The fat man took several steps backward and fell off the back of the platform, and a few of those watching laughed out loud. But as Reverend Huntington lifted the noose off Bai Lum, the small man put his hand on the butt of the revolver. Charles reached into his coat and drew a clasp knife.

"I'd like to know what the blazes you think you're about, sir," said the man with the gun. He had not pulled his pistol, but his finger was against the trigger.

"You've got an innocent man here," said Charles. He cut the bindings at Bai Lum's wrists. Rose could see raw, livid marks in his skin.

The man drew his gun. "Shoot him," Garland Tupper bellowed.

Charles looked the gunman full in the face. "You'll hang this man over my dead body." With a single fluid motion, he cut the noose off its tether and flung it into the street.

"Shoot him, Clayton, you cowardly son of a bitch. Shoot them both." Garland shoved Rose aside and someone caught her in mid-fall. Tupper bolted for the scaffold steps.

There was a sudden loud crack and several in the crowd cried out or ducked, arms over their heads. Rose flinched, feeling everything inside her go cold. But Bai Lum and Reverend Huntington were still standing. Garland Tupper howled, holding the back of his neck. A thin trickle of blood oozed between his fingers.

"I knew your mother, Mr. Tupper." It was Lucy. She stood up in the carriage, which lent her some height, holding a blacksnake whip. "She was a dear woman, but she neglected something in your upbringing."

Tupper gaped at her, then turned toward the steps again. Rose watched the little woman swing the whip in a whistling arc behind her. In a movement Rose hardly saw, Lucy cracked the whip again, this time splitting the air over Tupper's head.

"If you don't leave now, I will strike you again," she told him. "I believe I can take your eye out, if necessary."

Clayton looked from Lucy to Charles, then down at Garland. He dropped his hands to his sides. "That's enough, Tupper. Salyer didn't pay me to get mixed in with ministers and...and—" He gestured toward Lucy, who had her arm cocked for another pass. He moved to climb down. "Spineless cud," Tupper said. He was still blocking the steps.

Clayton leveled the pistol at Tupper's face. "Not at all, sir. One must simply have the intellect necessary to recognize the difference between advantage and disadvantage. Now get out of my way."

"Do as he says, Tupper." A deputy sauntered over, looking only half interested. "You boys have made your point."

Tupper stepped back, breathing hard and touching the weeping red welt on the back of his neck. "This is the Chinaman that killed Kendall," he yelled. "My boy saw him, damn it."

"Yeah, and we got a dozen witnesses brighter than your boy, each one pointing the finger at some other Chinaman they suspect." The deputy folded his arms over his chest and spat between his spread feet. "Sheriff already filled up the two open cells he had at the jail. Probably got twenty Mongolians packed in there, back to back like sardines. All for the one murder, you follow me?" He stuck out his chin and stared Tupper down. "Move on."

Tupper lowered his head and bulled his way through the thinning group of spectators. They were moving off already, dispersing into the general melee.

Rose pushed her way to the base of the steps just as Clayton came down. His gun had disappeared, probably into the back waistband of his trousers, and he was smiling. Smiling as if leaving some bland amusement, a livestock display at the county fair, perhaps. A harrowing rage filled her, so primitive she felt she could tear his out his throat with her teeth. She crossed her shaking arms over her bosom and held herself back, stared at the ground. He passed so near she could see the raised insignia on the buttons of his coat sleeve. Then he was gone and Reverend Huntington followed Bai Lum off the gallows. Rose approached him; in his eyes was his love for her, and a warning. If she touched him out here in front of these people, it would be incendiary.

She stopped where she was. "Everyone is safe," she said, hoping it was true. "Mattie is with Shu-Li and Ya Zhen."

"Come on," said Charles. "We have to get off the street."

They hurried to the carriage—where Lucy still stood with the whip in her hand—and they climbed up. Bai Lum and Charles sat in the front, Rose and Lucy behind them. When Rose sat down, Lucy embraced her.

"Are you hurt, sweetheart? Let me see your hand." She lifted Rose's left arm and pulled back the sleeve. Her wrist was mottled purple and beginning to swell. Lucy frowned. "Wiggle your fingers."

Charles took the reins and got them moving.

"I'll be fine," Rose assured her. In fact, she could now feel her pulse beating in sick waves that shot from her fingertips to her shoulder. As the carriage raced along the street, Rose looked hard at Lucy. "Mrs. Huntington, where did you learn to handle a whip?"

"Wiggle," Lucy insisted.

Rose did, clenching her teeth.

"She learned that trick from an older brother," said Charles. "When she was no bigger than a minute, her brother Grady made her a little whip of her own and taught her to make it snap."

Lucy still cradled Rose's wrist. "It probably isn't broken," she said. "We'll bind it just as soon as we can."

As they pulled onto the east end of 4th Street, Rose stared at the confusion of people and belongings piling up outside the buildings, and the people, Chinese and white, milling everywhere in the foggy night. She felt terribly hollowed out, as if some vast, black space had opened inside her. She thought about Mattie's parting words when she, Rose, had bolted from the store.

"Mattie said they're forcing an evacuation." It seemed her voice came from somewhere outside the carriage, stifled and distant. "Is it true?"

Charles stopped in front of the store. "Let's get inside," he said.

The door was open, the frame splintered around it. A bag of flour was split open across the threshold. They stepped around gluey piles that had congealed on the damp boards. Inside, Lucy stumbled over something. Even in the dark, Rose could see the entire store was ransacked.

Bai Lum ran for the stairs, calling for Shu-Li and Ya Zhen.

Rose felt rooted in place, afraid to follow, afraid to see no one else here. When she took a step toward the purple curtain, she banged her shin and fell to one knee, bracing herself with her sprained wrist and crying out.

"Wait right there," Lucy said. "Charles, I need your matches." She lit the gas lamps while the reverend wrestled the door closed. The bolt had torn loose when the vandals broke in, so he laid a heavy set of shelves on its side and wedged it across the entrance.

"Bai-Lum!" Rose shouted. "Are they here?"

His voice floated from the top of the stairs. "We're coming."

"Thank God," Rose said, and sighed with relief. Lucy and Charles stood looking around at the wreckage. Shelves were overturned and goods strewn in all directions. Glass was everywhere. Part of a bloody handprint marked the counter, and there was a spatter of blood across the floor. She felt a small, savage satisfaction that at least one of the thieves had been hurt. For there was no doubt thievery had been a large part of what had happened here; it appeared that, for every bit of stock still on the floor, at least three times that amount had vanished. A movement caught Rose's eye and she looked up at the kites, still attached to the ceiling, but mutilated. The beautiful carp hung in long, red streamers.

There was movement in the shadows at the rear of the store, and Rose felt her heart give a lurch. Mattie and Shu-Li, their faces gaunt with tension, followed Bai Lum into the faintly lit storefront.

"Wait," said Rose. "Where's Ya Zhen?"

¤

Byron sat on the rickety back steps of Salyer's, drinking from a half-full bottle he had found in the hotel kitchen, stashed behind a mason jar of pickled cherry peppers.

After Pearl slapped him, he had worked his way over to Chinatown, checking behind the livery and Kennedy's tavern, hoping he might run into Billy Kellogg somewhere. He regretted throwing the gun away. That was stupid. He had panicked like a little boy, only to hear a few minutes later that it was the Chinese who shot that man Kendall. He was stupid about everything! He was stupid about Pearl, who hated him, and he was stupid about the gun, which he needed.

Billy could lay hands on a gun, though, and then they'd get into the Chinaman's store and take care of that man-killer. He'd take care of Pearl, too. She didn't want him, but he'd take her. He'd give her over to Billy, or to his father, maybe. His father had been right about her. A whore. When he was six or seven years old, he'd seen Garland throw a pullet into the circle of a dogfight, just for fun. Byron figured it would be something like that if his father got his hands on the girl out in the street. Let him have her.

When he got to 4th Street, there were people everywhere, moving in and out of shops. Some windows had been broken and glass was scattered across the boards of the sidewalk. A group of men, maybe seven or eight of them, swarmed across a tall platform, hammering planks. It looked like something for electioneering, until one man mounted the platform with a heavy rope in hand. The coil of the noose made Byron's heart skitter in his chest. He drew forward, feeling as if he was walking in a dream, and touched the side of the scaffold. The boards were so newly cut they oozed pitch and Byron's hand came away sticky.

Then an amazing thing happened. Three men came swaggering down 4th Street with that goddamn raping killer Chinaman, him trussed up between them by the wrists. Byron took one look and was wide awake. He charged them. Before the captors knew what was happening, Byron drew back and punched the bastard in the face. He got in a second swipe, right in the mouth, before fat Randy Fickes had shoved him away.

"Get off, Tupper," Fickes said, his voice thick and nasal. Byron could see that his nose was mashed-looking and pushed off to one side, just the way his own was. He thought Garland must be out distributing beatings. "This one belongs to me," Fickes said.

"Like hell," Byron said. "He's the shooter. Mongolian whore master shot Mr. Kendall dead." He panted and rubbed the knuckles of his right hand. "You look a little like me now. How does that feel?" The Chinaman's mouth was bleeding good, and his eye puffing.

"I did nothing." The Chinaman tried to wipe the blood off his mouth, but Fickes yanked his hands away by the rope lead.

"You're a damn liar," Byron said. He looked around at the three captors. "He's the one, he did it."

The smallish man with the pistol stuck in his pants was looking at Byron steadily. "Are you sure about that?"

Byron nodded solemnly. "I seen it happen."

"Well then," the small man said, smiling and gesturing one hand toward the gallows. "Our arrival appears serendipitous."

Things happened fast after that. Fickes and the small man hauled the Chinaman up the stairs, and it was only a minute before a little crowd had gathered. Then a bigger one. Byron stood, looking up at the prisoner with the rope hanging next to him, and a surge of happiness beat through him. When a hand landed on his shoulder he looked around with a big grin on his face, thinking it was Billy, but there was his father, grinning right back. He tried to step away, but Garland held his shoulder with a vise grip.

"What's all this?" Garland said. He swayed slightly and Byron could smell the drink on him.

"He shot a white man," Byron said. He wanted to shrug out from under his father's arm, but couldn't do it without twisting himself around.

Garland stared at Byron, then swiveled his head to look at the scaffold. "Him? The store keeper?" He looked at Byron again, shuffling one foot to keep his balance. "The hell you say."

Byron straightened conspicuously. "I was there. I seen the man fall."

Garland's brow furrowed. "I seen him fall, too. Didn't see you."

Byron remembered then, watching for his father at the opium room. Somehow he had forgotten that moment, Garland easing out into the fog in a swirl of smoke. He forgot firing the gun, the man falling in the street. His tongue felt swollen to the roof of his mouth.

Then Garland smiled. "Guess this is one that won't make the boat, tomorrow, eh?" He let go of Byron and cupped his hands around his mouth. "Do for him, boys!"

That was his chance. Byron ducked off into the crowd. He worked his way around to the back of the scaffold just in time to see the teacher come tearing around the corner, tripping and hollering. If the Chinaman and Miss Allen were here, where was Pearl?

That was when he decided to make a last trip to Salyer's. Now, while people were occupied.

The hotel was dark. He crept around back and let himself in the rear entrance, watching for the old woman; he'd slapped her a good one earlier, and if she saw him here now there'd be hell to pay. But the hotel seemed deserted. There was no light in the small hallway and he had to feel his way along. Pearl's room was empty. He worked his way to the next room. Inside, he nearly gagged on the smell. He could see the outline of the body on the bed, head cocked back and dark hair spread all around her, bedclothes dragging the floor. His knees buckled and he stumbled sideways. She was dead.

He staggered out of the room and leaned against the wall. The floor seemed to tilt under his feet. He remembered the screaming in here this afternoon, remembered waiting in the alley with the gun. The man fell, but they said a Chinaman did it. He had seen Pearl—

she had hit him—but here she was, dead in this bloody room. He wondered if the opium had done this to him. The door was still ajar and the smell was like Cooper's slaughterhouse. Byron fell on hands and knees and vomited, then crawled away from the mess.

He pulled himself up the wall and felt his way to a side door. A narrow stairwell, black as the bottom of a well, took him to a hallway near the kitchen. He poked his head into the dining room; no lamps had been lit, and most of the chairs were set upside-down with their legs in the air. There had been no supper served. Two stoves hulked in the kitchen, their iron skins barely warm to the touch. He rummaged in the cupboards and after a minute found whiskey. He took a long pull on the bottle, then another. He was about to go out into the lobby when he heard someone come in the front door. If he was caught rifling the kitchen, they might take him for killing Pearl. Or for shooting the man in the street. Put him on the gallows next to the Chinaman. He hurried back upstairs the way he had come, clutching the bottle with one hand and feeling along the wall with the other, trying not to thump his boots on the risers. Then he was into the back wing and out the door, not bothering to shut it behind him. The salty tang of the bay filled his nose, and halfway down he sat on the splintered steps. He took a deep lungful, then rinsed his mouth with a bit of whiskey—just a little so as not to waste it. He spit over the banister to get rid of the taste of vomit and the smell of Pearl's blood, and took another long swallow from the bottle. Something pressed at the small of his back and when he reached around, he remembered the storybook, stuck in his belt for hours. He left it there. He didn't need to look at it to remember the story. Another long draft of whiskey and the bottle was close to empty.

"Mrs. Duck was having a party." He pulled his coat tighter around him and rested against the banister. "She wandered far down the lane, collecting bayberries to make her special bayberry candles."

¤

Ya Zhen wondered if she was still visible. She felt that she might have turned into a fog woman, left her body somewhere behind her. Mattie had told them the news, that all Chinese were to be sent away. When the words fell from Mattie's mouth, Ya Zhen felt as if the boundaries of her spirit had pressed right through her skin. Rose had run out the door, and while Mattie stood calling after her, Ya Zhen slipped into the storage room, rolled back the freight door as Bai Lum had earlier, and rolled it shut behind her. She had a knife from his kitchen hidden in her sleeve, its haft gripped firmly in one hand and the slender, curved blade resting against her arm.

The fine, cold mist of fog filling the street washed over her and she walked through the front door of Salyer's Hotel as if born out of the wet night. She had never used the front door before, had never been in the lobby. No lamps burned, but the tall front windows lent enough light to see. She glanced around at the upholstered furniture and potted palms. No one was at the desk. She thought she heard a small noise back in the kitchen, but she didn't care. She walked up the center of the wide, carpeted stairs, making no effort at stealth. She was wet as a fish, her hair clinging to her back. At the top of the stairs, she turned right and went through the door into the back wing. The first room on the left belonged to Wu Song and Wu Lin. It was dark and silent, the door ajar. The narrow hallway was empty, and at the far end the rear entrance stood wide open. The passage was freezing and smelled of vomit. She could hear the ruckus from Chinatown now, voices mostly, but it had an altogether different tenor than the earlier menacing noise of the street mob. Almost celebratory.

In the room where they had kept her, Ya Zhen did not need to put on a light. She went to the bed and set the knife on the floor. She rolled back the thin mattress. At the head of the bed, she found the small wrapped bundle, bound in a remnant of the clothes in which the granny woman had dressed her, years ago. She set the bundle by the knife, then stood and tore a long strip from the bedsheet. This she wound around her waist, creating a heavy, layered sash under her tunic. She stuck the bundle into this sash, picked up the knife, and left the room. In the hallway she hesitated, then went to Li Lau's closed door. She put her ear to it before turning the knob. Inside, the smell of blood was a miasma.

Even in the dark, she could see that Li Lau lay on the bed as she had died, her face turned to the window, bedclothes pulled to her knees and lying partway on the floor. Ya Zhen tucked the knife into her sash and went to the bed. She could not see Li Lau's face, just the faintest suggestion of her features, a curve of cheek and brow. She pulled the top sheet away and tucked a long edge under the girl. She crossed Li Lau's thin arms over her chest and rolled her face down, trying not to see the wide, dark stain underneath the body. Li Lau shifted heavily under Ya Zhen's hands, like a rag doll filled with sand. Pulling the single chair to the bed, Ya Zhen sat and combed the girl's hair through her fingers. When it was smooth, she plaited a snug braid and coiled it at the nape of Li Lau's neck. She rolled the body twice more in the sheet, swaddled it as tightly as she could, and tucked the ends inside the wrapping. When she finished she thought Li Lau looked like an insect waiting to break out into a different sort of life. She rested her hand on top of the mound made by Li Lau's hands.

"Go and see your son," she said, and left her there, far from home.

She retraced her steps, moving silently. It seemed as if the entire sprawling hotel was empty, a dead husk, insubstantial as a dream that blows away on waking.

As she reached for the front door, Clarence Salyer stepped from behind a parlor palm and put one hand around her throat.

"Where the hell do you think you're going?" He propelled her backward until she slammed against the wide banister. His thumb dug deeply into the underside of her jaw and his hand tightened, not yet strangling her, but making it hard to draw breath. "Waltz in and out of here like the Queen of Sheba? That's what you thought?" His breath was all whiskey. He pushed his weight against her and the square frame of the newel post ground into her shoulder blades. He forced one knee between her thighs and pulled back a few inches to fumble at his fly. It gave her enough room to reach between his legs. With her left hand, she twisted his scrotum and clenched it with all her strength. One of his testicles gave way in a terrible silent burst. His upper body arched backward when he screamed.

He was in such pain and the knife was so sharp, that for a brief moment he didn't realize she had cut him. He took a shambling step backward, hands between his legs, and looked down at himself. The gash ran horizontally across his chest at a slight upward angle. His vest and shirt gaped open to reveal the long, pink mouth of skin and muscle that ran from armpit to armpit. Blood began to soak the front of his clothes and run onto his hands, still cupped around his wounded scrotum. It fell in dark splashes onto his shoes and the polished floor. When Salyer opened his mouth to scream again, his eyes rolled back to whites and his knees buckled. He went down on his face at the foot of the stairs.

Ya Zhen stood looking at him for a moment. He didn't move. She could see that he was breathing and that a pool of blood was inching out from under him. She looked at the knife in her hand. It was spotless. The handle balanced perfectly in her palm and its curved blade picked up a glimmer of light from the street. She tucked it through the heavy sash under her clothes and stepped out of Salyer's for the last time. Outside, the wet night closed around her again. She waved her hands through the air, smiling at the way the fog swirled through her fingers. Then she wiped her damp hands on her trousers. On the walk back to the mercantile, she rested her right palm against the slender bundle of her mother's chopsticks, and the knife.

¤

"When I first got here," Mattie said, "she was standing behind Rose." Her face was so devoid of color that her freckles looked like bits of wood ash stuck there. "But then Rose went running. When I turned around Ya Zhen was gone, too. I thought she'd gone upstairs, but I couldn't find her anywhere."

While Bai Lum and Reverend Huntington went to check the back storeroom doors, Lucy tore the broken flour sack into strips to bind Rose's swollen wrist. The two men returned through the alcove. "The back was unlocked," Charles said, "but it doesn't look like anyone tried to get in that way."

"Not when they can waltz in through the front and take everything," said Lucy, securing the ends of the makeshift bandage. "This will help with the swelling," she told Rose.

"We put up a barricade anyway," Charles said. "They'll have to come through the wall with an axe to get in back there now."

"I thought maybe I should go after her," Mattie continued, seeming unable to stop telling the story. She twisted her hands in front of her as she spoke. "But I couldn't leave Shu-Li alone, and then all the noise started down here." She blinked slowly, like someone trying to recall a dream. "We went into the kitchen and hid in the broom closet. They were shouting and laughing, breaking things. I just...I didn't know what they might do if they found us."

"You did exactly the right thing," said Lucy. "If not for you, heaven knows what might have happened."

"We'll go look for her," said Reverend Huntington. "That is, I'll go. The rest of you stay here, together. Stay here, stay safe, keep the door secured. Bai Lum, you're going to need help sorting out this mess and packing some things." He looked at the wreckage strewn everywhere. "I'm afraid it will have to be tonight, too."

"You're saying it's true," Rose said. "What Mattie told me." Her heart constricted; she found Bai Lum's hand, and he wrapped his warm fingers around her cold ones. "They'll try to send everyone away?"

"It's true." Charles ran his hands through his wiry hair and told it all, told them what had happened at Centennial Hall, about the threats and the chanting of 'no shelter.' He faltered and looked away, cleared his throat and tried again. "The two ships will take everyone to San Francisco. They leave port tomorrow afternoon."

"Then we need to get the three of them out of here as quickly as we can," said Lucy. "Bai Lum and Shu-Li, as well as Ya Zhen, if we can find her. We'll load the wagon as well as the carriage and go north tonight."

Rose tightened her grip on Bai Lum's hand. She wouldn't say it now, not with everyone so apprehensive, but she was going with him. If she had to trail the wagon on foot with Hazel dogging her every step, she was going with him.

"First things first," Charles said. "I'm going to look for Ya Zhen. I'll be back as soon as I can."

¤

Lucy and Mattie swept piles of broken glass, spilled coffee and dried beans that littered the floor. Shu-Li picked up larger detritus—unbroken mason jars, tin pie plates, gardening gloves— and piled it all together on the counter. As she moved around the room, weary confusion made her young face look years older. Bai Lum, who was moving intact inventory into the storeroom, had explained to the girl what was happening, and the color had fallen from her face at the words *San Francisco*. A bolt of fabric, silk the color of a ripe persimmon, lay spread across the floor like a red river, covered with footprints limned in dirt and spilled flour; Shu-Li lifted the nearly depleted bolt and stared morosely at its ruined length. The shelf that held the Four Flowers porcelains was overturned, and Rose could see chunks and shards of white and blue scattered everywhere in the mess.

No one spoke.

When Bai Lum came out and gathered another armful of cans and boxes, Rose followed him into the storeroom. There was a bit of light now, a single whale-oil lamp set on a high shelf. He had nearly filled a barrel with items from the front of the store. She watched him fit the lid in place and rap it closed with a hammer. That done, he set the hammer aside and gathered her to him. Her wrist pulsed miserably, but the pain was tangible; it made perfect sense. This other pain, the fear of losing him, was also physical, but feral, deeper than the ache in her wrist, something that snarled behind her solar plexus. Out in the store, Mattie and Lucy conversed, their voices too low to understand. Bai Lum started to hum a tune, so quietly it was more vibration than sound, and it quieted a terrible voice that clamored in her head, howling *What about me?* She made herself stand there, not asking anything, trying not to want anything, perfectly still in the circle of his arms.

"He's back!" Mattie shouted.

She and Lucy were struggling to drag the shelves away from the entrance. Bai Lum hurried over to help. When the door was clear, Reverend Huntington eased in and shut it behind him. He was alone.

¤

Hazel was home.

When she had come downstairs at the Kendalls' and found Prudence lying next to David on the table as if they were tucked into bed for the night, she ran next door for Annabella Briggs. The two of them coaxed Prudence off the table—no small feat—and Annabella finally convinced Prudence to take the sedative the doctor had left for her. Once they'd gotten the poor woman into her bed, Annabella insisted that Hazel go home.

"You've been here all day," she said. "Daniel is at Centennial Hall right now, but I'm sure he'll be home soon. Right next door if we need him." She looked at David Kendall, the beautiful quilt tucked under his chin, and tears welled in her eyes. She went to him and tenderly covered his face, which now had the slack and stiffly-wilted aspect that is the honest countenance of the dead. "Heaven help us, Mrs. Cleary, I don't know how we'll all get through this night," she said.

"Nor I," said Hazel.

Now it seemed she couldn't settle herself anywhere in the house. Rose had said she would bring the Chinese girls here with her, but there was no sign of them. God alone knew where Mattie was, and Hazel couldn't bear to imagine. Things were much quieter out in the street, but this made her more nervous. If things were settling, where were her girls? She walked through the house, upstairs and down, put on the kettle and promptly boiled it dry, smoothed the antimacassars in the parlor, watered her houseplants, stood on the front porch, then the rear porch, and back inside to put the kettle on again. Standing near the stove, watching so that she wouldn't forget the water a second time, there was the smallest sound at the kitchen door—at least, she thought it a sound—and she turned toward it, delighted, her heart and mind flooded with pleasure, absolutely certain that David Kendall was about to sweep in and dance her around the room. In the empty kitchen, with only the tickety whisper of the teakettle, he was here, and not here.

¤

"I couldn't find a sign of her," Reverend Huntington said. "I drove to the waterfront, then up and down every street for blocks and blocks—probably farther than she could ever have gotten on foot this quickly. I even drove past Salyer's, and the place looks completely deserted. Not a light on anywhere." He paused to pull out his pipe and light it. "I didn't see Ya Zhen, but I did see Mayor Walsh and a couple of others that were with him at the hall earlier. Their vaunted committee. Daniel Briggs was there, too. I got him alone and—" He looked at Lucy and shook his head. "This isn't good news, I'm afraid."

"Best tell it straight out, then," she said quietly.

"The coach trails, both north and south, have already been barricaded," he said. "Come first light, teams of men are going out to beat the bushes. They know some of the men in Chinatown made a run for the woods already, and they are almighty determined that not a single one slips out of the net." He looked first at Bai Lum, and then at Rose. "There will be no getting out of town. Even if we had left the minute shots were fired, there wouldn't be a steamship, schooner, or dugout canoe we'd find amenable to letting three Chinese persons aboard to depart for ports unknown." He was quiet for a moment, letting this news sink in. "What's more," he said finally, "they've compiled a roster. Every Chinese person in town, all they can think of, anyway, is on it. The laundrymen, chow slingers, truck gardeners, and tailors." He looked at the torn kites dangling from the ceiling. "The storekeeper."

Rose felt mule-kicked. She went behind the counter, righted the stool and sank onto it.

"There may be some Chinese living around here who aren't on the list, but having a few previously-unknown extras on the boat won't bother the powers that be. What they care about is making certain that those they *do* know about don't disappear. Most of the hooligans we saw rousting folks here tonight were not authorized to do a thing, though I doubt they'll be scolded, let alone held accountable. But Briggs says the committee has marshaled some fellows, tasked them with going place-to-place in teams tomorrow morning, to load goods and escort every living soul out of Chinatown and down to the ships."

"They're going to blame *everyone?*" Lucy said. "Punish everyone and bully them out? That can't be legal!"

"There's no stopping it," he nearly shouted. He smoked furiously, and a wreath of smoke rose around his head. "I'm sorry for snapping, Lucy," he said, "but right now, what's legal isn't worth a tinker's damn in Eureka. The mayor is part of it. Nearly every man of means is conspiring, and the sheriff is willing to enforce. They're pretending this is a reasonable solution, and you can be certain it is going to happen." He put a hand on Bai Lum's shoulder. "It's happening."

They all stood in stunned silence. Finally, Bai Lum went to Shu-Li, who had been shadowing Lucy around the mercantile. He spoke to her quietly, and after a moment she nodded and left the room. "Some of her things were already packed," he said. "I told her to pack everything else. If we have to leave," he said, "then I need to prepare."

"I know it isn't a consolation, Bai Lum, but I'll get a couple of men together and store as much of your stock at the church as possible. When you get settled, wherever that might be, we'll ship it to you."

Someone tried to open the door and they all jumped. Bai Lum moved to the window and pulled the shade aside with one finger.

"Help me with this," he said, pulling at the furniture blockade. "It's Ya Zhen."

Mattie took a convulsive breath and covered her face with her hands.

They wrestled the door open and Lucy grabbed hold of her. "Child, where have you been?" She hustled Ya Zhen inside and looked her over head to toe. "You are wet to the skin and no wrap at all."

"You're here," Mattie said. "I'm so glad you're here." She put her arms around her friend and began to sob; all of them saw Ya Zhen stiffen in the embrace.

Lucy took Mattie by the shoulders. "She's all right, darling, you see? Safe with us. Run upstairs and find her a blanket? Let's get her warmed. Tell Shu-Li."

Mattie nodded and went on the run, swiping at tears with her bandaged hand, the wrapping now frayed and gray at the edges. She returned—Shu-Li right behind her—with a soft-looking brown blanket. The two of them draped it over Ya Zhen's shoulders.

"Now," Lucy said, fussing with the blanket and pulling it snug under Ya Zhen's chin. She cocked her head bemusedly. "Where were you? We were so worried."

Ya Zhen wore the same settled expression Rose had seen earlier, her face now damp and shiny. "For the journey," she said. She slipped a hand under her shirt and pulled out a lumpy bundle wrapped in rough homespun. "I needed my things."

"Do you have everything now?" Lucy asked. "If you disappear again, it may kill us all."

"Yes, everything." She tucked the bundle back under her clothes.

"Now that we're all accounted for, we'd better decide how to proceed," said Charles.

"Of course," said Rose. "Another plan. Planning and plotting all day, and here we are."

Lucy looked astonished. "True enough, she said, approaching Rose on the opposite side of the counter. "Nevertheless." In the low light, her face almost seemed to float above her black dress. "Morning will come whether we like it or not. We can rend our clothes and sit here in the ashes like Job, but it won't stop the clock." She leaned close so that they were almost face-to-face, and no one else could hear. "I can only imagine how much this breaks your heart," she said. "I wish—" her voice faltered and she had to start again. "I'm going to tell you something true: the loss you're feeling, the pain...well, the fact remains that you still have your home here, your aunt. Your friends." Her voice was soft, placatory. "Rose, you're one of the bravest people I know, but for the next few hours, just putting one foot in front of the other is going to take everything in us," she said. "Everything. Can you endure it?"

Rose rested her head on the countertop and swallowed a cry that wanted to fly forward on a wave of rage. She was losing him, losing him in the morning. How was she supposed to act? She felt capsized by the desire to strike someone, anyone, to wreak some sort of punishment. In her mind's eye Garland Tupper—as good a one to blame as any, wasn't he?—was on the gallows, swinging at the end of the noose, his face black, eyes and tongue protruding. She clenched a fist until her bruised and swollen wrist sent a jolt up her arm. The pain brought some focus.

With their choices honed thin as a knife blade, they began—as Hazel had said earlier—to make the next best decision. It would be safest to take Ya Zhen and Shu-Li to Hazel's, along with Rose and Mattie, as they had initially tried to do. For safety in numbers, Lucy would spend the night there, too. Reverend Huntington would stay at the church with Jacob Weimer's family and whoever else may have gone there looking for sanctuary. "In the morning," said Lucy, "Rose and I will bring the girls back here to the mercantile so that you all stay together."

Lucy was right. The night was not going to turn around, no *deus ex machina* would drop from the foggy heavens. Rose could resist, or she could acquiesce—it didn't matter. Everything had already changed. The circumstances had opened an unexpected space. She got off the stool and stepped into that space.

"I'm not going with you," she said. "I'm not going back to Aunt's tonight. I'm going to stay and help Bai Lum get ready for tomorrow."

In the silence that followed, as if on cue, somewhere up the street two men began to shout, and then came the thudding, grunting scuffle of a physical altercation, of blows to the body.

Bai Lum turned to her. "It's not safe here, Rose. You should not stay."

She felt the weight of everyone's eyes, but looked only at Bai Lum. There was blood crusted at one corner of his mouth, and his left eye was now swollen shut entirely. But his gaze was steady, and Rose knew there was only one thing he could say to make her leave.

"Do you love me, Bai Lum?"

Mattie made a sound, a little intake of breath. The almost imperceptible hiss of the gas lamps filled the room. His face was very still. Rose felt the urge to look away, to spare herself, but did not. She clasped both his hands and cast all her bread upon the waters.

"I love you. I've loved you for over a year. And I'm certain that you love me." She paused, drew a deep breath. "Will you marry me?" Then, because she felt as if she was standing in only her underdrawers, and because of the stunned look on Bai Lum's battered face, she finally had to break down laughing. He looked from Rose, who was trying desperately to get her laughter under control, to the Huntingtons, to Shu-Li and Mattie and Ya Zhen. It seemed to buoy him.

"Yes, Rose Allen," he said. "Yes, I love you. I will marry you."

She couldn't manage to make a sound, as though her proposal had used all the words she had left. He leaned down and kissed her cheek.

"Well I'll be," said Mattie.

"Yes Rose Allen," Shu-Li cried, and clapped her hands.

That was all it took. Everyone began to laugh. They hugged her and they hugged Bai Lum. Shu-Li clung to Rose, saying her name over and over, Rose Allen, Rose Allen. Reverend Huntington squeezed her shoulders with his large, knobby hands.

"Will you marry us? Now?"

He rubbed a palm across the plane of one cheek, raspy with stubble so late in the day. "This is dangerous," he said. "For you, especially, Bai Lum."

Bai Lum nodded. "Yes. But already they tried to kill me. Already they came into the store and stole my goods." He put one hand briefly to Rose's face. "They will force me onto the boat tomorrow," he said, "but not tonight. Tonight I am free to do as I please."

Reverend Huntington stood silently, looking at the two of them, then down at the floor. Rose wondered what she could do to convince him—tell him she would stay with Bai Lum regardless, perhaps, which was the truth. Finally, he turned to her. "Are you also sure, Rose?" he asked softly. His clear expression pierced her, his eyes wells of kindness. She understood that performing a marriage like this might ruin his position, not just in this isolated coastal outpost, but into his future ministry, if word got out. Yet his first concern was for the two of them.

"I'm sure," she said, wishing fiercely for her father, and for Hazel.

"Nothing to stop us, then," he said. "You certainly have your witnesses." Reverend Huntington took one of Rose's hands and one of Bai Lum's and held them between his own. Mattie and Ya Zhen stood solemnly next to Lucy, but Shu-Li hurried over to the jumble of things on the counter. She got scissors and took the red silk they had piled there. She ran it through her hands until she found a clean section, and cut out a large square. Beaming, she came to Rose, holding out the piece of fabric.

"*Jí lǐ*, Rose Allen," she said.

Rose looked at Bai Lum. "What is it?"

"She says it is good luck, auspicious." He smiled, wincing a little from the pain in his face. "It is our custom for the bride to wear red," he said to Rose. "Very lucky."

"Of course." She nodded at Shu-Li. The girl lifted the wisp of fabric, standing on tiptoes to reach, and centered it carefully on Rose's head. It fell like a breath over her face, touching just at her shoulders. Rose could see through the fine weave, everything fiery and soft around the edges. The two lamps glowed like small suns.

"Very well then," said Reverend Huntington. "Rose, do you accept Bai Lum as your husband, forsaking forever that which would divide you and nurturing that which will unite you in the eternal mystery of your Creator?"

"I do." The silk puffed out lightly when she spoke. Bai Lum gripped her hand under Reverend Huntington's, and it seemed she could hear the blood coursing through her veins, a thin, silver sound in her ears.

Reverend Huntington asked Bai Lum the same question, and he answered with a resonant, "Yes."

"Lovely. Dear ones, you have made a promise before God and this company. You are husband and wife." He patted their joined hands, and let them go. The whole ceremony had taken less than a minute.

Rose's eyes widened, extraordinarily surprised. *Did I really?*

Shu-Li, who had apparently appointed herself maid of honor, pulled the red veil away, and there was Bai Lum, his beautiful face close to hers.

Yes.

¤

"After we leave, you mustn't go back out on the street. You know that." Lucy buttoned her coat and gave Rose a last lecture.

The door had been cleared; Bai Lum and Reverend Huntington stood in front of it with Mattie, Ya Zhen, and Shu-Li.

"We won't leave," Rose assured her.

"Charles will spend the night at the church and come back for all of us in the morning. We'll bring the girls here early. How is your wrist?" It seemed to Rose that Lucy was stalling her leave-taking.

"Lucy, I'm fine. I'll be fine. Try not to worry."

Lucy nodded, but her face said everything they could not speak aloud. That the marriage was dangerous for both of them. That in a few hours, the town would put her new husband on a ship and put him out to sea like a piece of freight.

Rose touched the furrows in Lucy's brow and smoothed her finger across the lines. "We'll work all those things out in the morning," she said. She leaned close so she could whisper. "You should go now. You're obstructing my wedding night."

Lucy laughed, swatted at her, and—to Rose's delight—blushed. She kissed Rose on the cheek and hurried over to her husband. "All right," she said. "Let's get these girls to Hazel Cleary's so they can finally get some rest."

When the carriage pulled away from the mercantile, Rose and Bai Lum went inside and slid the heavy barricade back in place.

¤

Ya Zhen listened to Shu-Li breathing beside her, deeply and evenly. They were in Mrs. Cleary's bed, a voluminous feather mattress that was like lying in a cloud. Rose's aunt had been tearful and sweet, smothering all of them in bosomy hugs and kissing their cheeks when Reverend and Mrs. Huntington delivered them. Before they could even mount the damp porch steps, she had flung open the door and rushed out, first putting her arms around Mattie and rocking her back and forth, then shaking hands with Ya Zhen and Shu-Li when Mrs. Huntington introduced them.

"I thought Rose was bringing the girls here." She looked around and realized who was missing. "Oh God, where is she now?"

Mattie linked her elbow through Hazel's. "She's fine," she said. "It happens that Rose is not a maiden lady anymore," she said. "Come in and we'll tell you."

Now Ya Zhen lay deep in the glory of Mrs. Cleary's feather bed, her belongings tucked under the pillow and Shu-Li sound asleep. She could hear Reverend Huntington outside, saying goodnight to his wife. She slipped out of bed and went to the window.

Lucy stood at the gate, almost imperceptible in the dark and fog. Reverend Huntington gave the horse a kindly pat on the neck and climbed into the carriage. He put his fingers to his lips and blew Lucy a kiss, then drove away, the clop of the horse's hooves a small and specific sound, like round stones dropped into water. Lucy stayed at the gate for a few moments until her husband drove out of sight and then tipped her face to the occluded sky. The moon, now visible only as a faded hint behind the clouds, still threw enough light to make her features discernible. To Ya Zhen, it almost seemed like the face of a different woman, her expression soft and vulnerable, full of fear and love. She mounted the porch steps slowly, looking every bit her age, and disappeared inside.

The rooftops of Eureka, a crowd of peaks and spires, gables and chimneys, hunched out toward the edge of the bay, all of it swaddled in mist. At the far edge of town, Salyer's Hotel rose above everything near it, the eight-sided cupola standing in stark silhouette. None of its windows was lit. She looked in the direction of Chinatown, but couldn't see those buildings, most of them squatty shacks with rough, unpainted facades and crudely lettered signs. All of the people who had called that place home were strangers to her, including the men who had used her body. In that way, Eureka's Chinese were little different to her than everyone else in town. She was bound to none of them. Somewhere behind those walls were women, a few invisible souls who stayed in because of shame or because their status had literally hobbled them. A woman with bound feet was considered a woman of leisure, who needed only the comforts her husband provided. Tomorrow Ya

Zhen would see them all, every one a refugee now, floating into the unknown.

Back in the bed, she drew close to Shu-Li, relishing the warmth the other girl radiated. She closed her eyes, letting the heavy quilts press her gently toward sleep, and she listened to the small sounds of the other women getting ready for bed: Mrs. Cleary, Lucy, Mattie. The time she had endured at Salyer's taught her not to project her thoughts too far into the future, nor into the past. She chose not to picture much of what might happen in the morning, or what she would do when she arrived in San Francisco. Right here, right now—this was enough.

Ya Zhen sank deeper, and her last thought was of the way the gold threads in her wedding clothes had glimmered on the walls of her mother's home, and of the red veil over Rose's face. She slid a hand under her pillow and cradled the ebony chopsticks.

¤

For a half-hour, Bai Lum hammered shelves apart and nailed the boards across the windows at the front of the store. Rose went into the back and found several empty crates. She fitted as much into each one as she could, and by the time Bai Lum was done securing the windows, she had packed most of what was salvageable and dragged it into the storeroom. Her wrist throbbed heavily; she sat on a wide keg of nails and held her arm to her chest. Bai Lum came through the curtain and looked around at the crates.

"You've done too much." He stood next to her, shaking his head. "I cannot take the store with me." He looked at the way she held her wrist and gestured to the stairs. "We need tea."

She stood, finding it curiously difficult to meet his eye. This is my husband, she thought, my husband. He took the stairs ahead of her, holding the slender neck of the whale-oil lamp. Despite her racing pulse—or perhaps because of it—she had never been so tired, and felt as if she could barely pull herself from step to step. When they turned at the landing, she remembered her hesitation here, the way he had put his face next to hers and breathed her in. It was like something that had happened to someone else, something she'd read it in a book.

In the kitchen, he stoked the fire and she set out cups. He prepared the tea with slow deliberation, and she watched his long fingers in the uncertain light of the lamp. He opened the cold cupboard built into the north wall, chilled by a screened vent to the outside. He retrieved apples and cut them into wedges. These he placed on a plate in front of Rose and sat down next to her at the table.

She leaned her shoulder into Bai Lum's. When she reached for a piece of apple, he picked up the slice himself, put it to her lips. Keeping her eyes on his face, she opened her mouth. The apple was tart and juicy, and the taste of it made saliva squirt from under her tongue. He watched her chew, offered her another. She ate, then lifted a slice to his lips in return. Bai Lum bit the wedge in half, chewed.

"Does your mouth hurt?" she asked. She was nearly whispering. The flame of the little lamp shifted, moving on their faces.

"No. It is fine." He lifted her hand to his mouth, took the rest of the apple from her fingers, smiling.

She felt as if the warm tea was seeping into every small space, every capillary, every hollow inch of her. "You married me, Bai Lum." She put her palms on his cheeks and her eyes roamed across the strong planes of his face. He leaned forward and kissed her. She could taste apple, and salt from the cut in the corner of his mouth.

"Yes, Rose Allen." He pulled her bottom lip gently between both of his, held it for a moment, released her. "*Táng kè.* My love." He breathed the words into her mouth.

She shifted back a little, drank, watched him over the rim of her cup. "What will happen tomorrow?"

His eyes skimmed around the small kitchen as if to take an inventory. "Tomorrow," he said, "I will get on the ship with Shu-Li and Ya Zhen. With everyone."

"With me."

He was silent.

"With me."

"You will come later, Rose," he said. "On another ship. Safer that way."

She wanted to argue, but she knew he was right. He didn't need to say what they both understood: there were people already willing to kill him. She closed her eyes and could see him standing on the scaffold with the noose around his neck, and a shudder wracked her, "I'll get a ticket on the next steamer out," she said. "It might be a week or more, if the weather is bad."

"I will send a wire from San Francisco telling you where to find us."

"Where will you go?"

"There are people I know in the city, probably still there." He lifted her hand and kissed the knuckles. "I will be fine," he said, "and you will be fine."

"What time do you think will they'll raise anchor tomorrow?"

"It depends on the tide," he said. "Probably in the afternoon. But we need to be ready early."

"What do you want to take?"

"My wife is a practical woman. This is a wonderful quality." Rose's hair was slowly but surely falling out of the pins she had ratcheted in when Mattie had gotten her out of bed; Bai Lum smoothed one long tendril away from her face. "I'm going to check downstairs before we sleep," he said. "Will you make us one last cup of tea?"

She moved slowly around the tiny kitchen, stirring the fire, filling the kettle at the pump. It was just past midnight and it seemed as though her exhaustion had shifted, so that she felt not tired but caught in a dream. Measuring tea into the pot, she had the pleasant sensation of moving underwater. While the kettle ticked and simmered, Rose looked out the window. It showed only the back of the building next door. Lamps were lit in the upstairs room, and three people moved behind drawn shades, all men, it appeared. Their shadows first loomed like behemoths and then shrunk to man-size as they went through their rooms, preparing to be turned out. She could no longer hear voices in the street.

She filled the teapot and carried the tray down the hallway, following the lamplight to the back of the apartment.

The room smelled like him, a loamy smell like the deep duff under conifer trees, clean and particular. A small lamp stood on a table beside the bed. The bed, somewhat larger than Shu-Li's was covered with a heavy damask spread, a shade of indigo so dark it was almost black. One small window and tall chest of drawers were draped with polished cotton. He had pulled one of the trunks into the room and it stood open under the window. When she entered, Bai Lum took the tray and set it on the chest of drawers.

"I want to show you something."

On the far side of the room stood an ornate screen, four panels of dark wood etched with symmetrical gilt designs, tendrils and leaves, clusters of flowers and curved branches upon which sat a variety of plumed birds. She followed him behind the screen, and stopped short. Here was a full-sized bathtub, the enamel glossy in the light of a single candle, filled to within a few inches of the rim with steaming water. A square brass table with a glass top stood next to the tub, holding a comb and a slender, corked bottle. Several dried chrysanthemums floated, nearly transparent, across the surface of the bath.

"Oh," she said, amazed at this oasis tucked into the corner of an old plank building. He had arranged it for her delight, and was clearly pleased by her reaction. "How? Bai Lum, how did you do this?"

"The stove downstairs has a boiler," he said. "When the fire is high, it doesn't take long to make the water hot." He moved the pump handle and a stream of water set the flowers rocking.

"It's so beautiful," she said. She ran her palm along the smooth, curved edge of the tub.

"I built it two years ago," he said. "It would be better in its own room, but—" he shrugged, "no room."

All the care he had lavished here. Who would bathe here tomorrow, or next week, next year? Who else would expend such effort on these simple rooms? Tears welled in her eyes.

"Now a wedding gift."

She turned and put her arms around his waist. The firm, silky length of his braid was beneath her hands. "Thank you."

He lifted her chin and kissed her on the corner of her mouth, her eyelids, the tip of her nose. "I will get your tea."

Rose took her hair down. It was knotted and tangled, and when the last of the many hairpins was piled on the brass table, she worked the tortoiseshell comb through the snarls. When he brought the tea, he looked stunned by the wild, coppery abundance of her hair. She stood very still, feeling the cool length of the comb in her hand, waiting for whatever came next.

He put the teacup on the table. Moving behind her, he lifted her hair in his two hands and let it cascade through his fingers. A line of buttons closed the bodice of her dress, neck to waist. He reached around from behind for the button at her throat, slipped it loose, unbuttoned the next, and the next. When the bodice was open, he ran his fingertips down the length of her neck and across her collarbones, just as he'd traced her cheekbones earlier. He slid the top of her dress off the points of her shoulders, and her heart beat so hard she could see the lace at the top of her chemise shaking. She pulled her arms out of her sleeves. He unwound the bandage from her injured wrist. Naked, it was swollen and dark where Garland Tupper had squeezed, and a shadow passed over his face. She touched one fingertip, ever so slightly, to the corner of his wounded eye.

"We're all right. Just...colorful." She smiled. "Will you give me a little time alone?"

He kissed her once more, a brief brush of his lips across her shoulder, and went out from behind the screen. Through the scant space between its panels, she could see him move through the bedroom, from the chest of drawers to the trunk and back again.

She undid the hooks that held her dress closed at the waist and stepped out of the skirt. The front of the skirt, her petticoat, and even the knees of her underdrawers had streaks of mud from her fall in the street. Her right knee was scraped and beginning to scab over. She slid out of her underthings, acutely aware of the air on her skin and of Bai Lum on the other side of the screen. When she put her foot into the warm water, it was wonderful. She sat, leaned back slowly, and sighed. Like being born, she thought, but in reverse.

"There is oil in the bottle, on the table."

She startled at the sound of his voice and sloshed a little water onto the floorboards. "Oil?"

"Smell it." His shadow shifted on the ceiling, a faded blur that grew and receded as he moved through the room. She picked up the little bottle and pulled the cork. Roses. Attar of roses. She breathed deeply and tipped the bottle. The oil broke into small puddles, floated together, broke apart again. She moved her hands through the water in figure-eights, swirling the oil around her. She bent one knee, and a chrysanthemum clung to the inside of her thigh. She took it between her fingers and held it to the light of the candle. She could see the flame through its petals, but there was a milky opaqueness at the center that turned yellow in front of the flame.

"I can smell the roses," Bai Lum said. His voice was soft, near.

"How do you say my name," she said, "where you grew up?" She stroked the flower over her belly and across her thighs until it came apart, the petals floating across the water like small exclamations. She drank some tea, and laid her neck on the curved edge of the tub, her hair hanging to the floor behind her.

"*Qiáng.*"

"*Qiáng,*" she whispered to herself.

"That is the wild rose."

She closed her eyes. Perhaps she slept; when he spoke the water was cooling.

"*Qiángli*, I am bringing you a gown." Bai Lum stepped behind the screen.

Rose's understanding of the sexual act was mostly theoretical, but she wanted him, and thought that would be enough for this night. She stood, and her hair clung to the skin of her shoulders and back. The cool air of the room made her nipples hard as two cherry pips. He stepped to the tub and helped her out, wrapping the robe around her. It was too large, one of his own, and the sleeves fell far past her fingertips. She lifted the sleeve above her elbow, reached in and pulled the stopper in the tub. The water was loud as it drained out through the pipes in the floor and down to the street below. He was smiling again. "A practical wife."

She took his hand. In the room, he had pulled the coverlet back to show the pale bedding beneath. On the table next to the bed, a small white bowl with four cobalt blue flowers painted inside. The lamplight was reflected in a few inches of water.

"You saved it," she laughed.

"To capture the moon."

Rose lay back. He took off his clothes, draped them on the footboard. His skin was smooth and the muscles of his chest and shoulders prominent from years of lifting barrels and crates and sacks of grain. On the bed, he leaned over her and his hair fell in dark curtains on either side of the pillow. The smell of roses was everywhere between them. He kissed her neck, the space between her breasts, ran his hands along her sides until they fitted into the curve of her waist. All her life, her body had been an expected and functional thing. Under his hands, she knew herself to be something else altogether. He stroked the insides of her thighs, rested between her legs, watched her face. He touched her, touched her, all the while watching, until all the boundaries of her body seemed to be dissolving like melting wax. Then there was a moment, a small tearing sting, yes, but that moment she would remember the rest of her life, when she understood there had been a place for him, empty, and then filled.

Deep in the farthest selvage of the night, she woke to hear a sea lion barking and barking out in the bay. Rose turned onto her side, feeling quiet and heavy. When the sheets moved she could smell their sex. He turned in his sleep, too, and she lifted his arm over her, cupping his palm to her breast. He stirred, pulled her close so that his chin rested lightly at the crown of her head. They made love again this way, and this time there was an almost unbearable, coiling pleasure that made her cry out. The cry turned into quiet weeping. Bai Lum pulled her tight to him, still inside her, the curve of her spine against his chest, and she felt herself falling back into sleep, even with the tears still on her face. The sea lion barked again and paused, as if waiting for some like voice to answer.

PART IV

CHASING DOWN THE MOON

We intend to try and vote the Chinaman out, to frighten him out, and if this won't do, to kill him out....The heathen slaves must leave this coast.

—*Denis Kearney, Labor Activist*
Workingmen's Party Speech
San Francisco, December 28, 1877

In the secret chamber of the public heart they were virtually all of one mind, and to be rid of the Chinese by any and all means....As against this sentiment there was no restraint in existence that had any more power than that of an ostrich feather to change the course of the wind.

—*Reverend Charles A. Huntington*
Personal Autobiography, 1899

CHAPTER TEN

DAWN BROUGHT RANKS of low clouds, herded from west to east by a mild onshore breeze. Sunrise lit the ragged bottom of the sky until it was massed with gold and coral and pale lavender, color that reflected off the calm surface of the marshy sloughs that made ingress from Humboldt Bay. The tide was in. It covered the barnacles and mussels that sheathed the pilings at the wharf and deposited whip-like snarls of bull kelp at the high tide line. When the sun cleared Berry Summit, the usual pall of wood smoke that issued continuously from the sawmills along the coast was conspicuously absent, as if it was a holiday. Steller's jays began squabbling in the surrounding trees, and a turkey vulture sat atop a telegraph pole, fanning its massive wings in order to warm and dry its plumage.

In the streets of Eureka, even before the gaslights were extinguished, every wagon and dray in the city limits was pressed into service for haulage.

At six o'clock, someone pounded on the back doors of the mercantile. Rose jerked awake, disoriented. She sat up, heart racing, and looked around the dark room. Bai Lum was already dressed; he hurried to the window and lifted the sash.

"I'm coming," he called into the alley. Someone shouted a response and he closed the window.

"Who is it?" She climbed out of bed and pulled Bai Lum's robe around herself.

"Huntington and some others. They have wagons."

"Go," she said. "I'll be right there."

He pulled her close and looked down into her face. His own was tight and set. She wished she could think of some right thing to say, but she felt so husked out by dread she could only stare at him, mute. The banging at the rear entrance came again.

Watching him leave caused a wave of nausea. She went to the bathtub and worked the pump handle, washed in a few inches of cold water. The smell of the attar of roses still clung to the porcelain. Her dirty clothes were there in a pile; she dressed hurriedly and yanked her hair into a braid, not bothering to pin it up. She re-wrapped her swollen left wrist, now a bilious shade of green-purple. When her boots were laced, she folded the gilt screen and laid it against the wall. In the weak morning twilight, the bed stood askew. She pulled off the sheets and coverlet and stuffed them into the open trunk.

Looking around, her eyes landed on the bowl. Four flowers. Her fingertip made tiny ripples in the surface of the water. She picked it up and drank, then wrapped it in his robe and buried it in the center of the trunk. She lowered the lid, secured the leather buckles, and pulled the trunk out into the hallway. A last glance at the bedroom showed the bare mattress and the empty tub, squatting side-by-side.

The stairwell was dim, but at the landing she could see the sky brightening with intense color. In the storeroom, the large freight door was rolled back. Two men she didn't know hauled what was left of Bai Lum's stock into the alley. They avoided looking at her as they carried barrels and boxes. Outside, Reverend Huntington and Bai Lum shifted the cargo around into two wagons.

"Morning, Rose," Reverend Huntington said. "We've not unblocked the front door yet. Might be best to wait. We're going to hustle as much of this to the church as we're able, then I'll get back here with Mrs. Huntington and the girls. Gentlemen," he called to the two others, "this is my dear friend, Rose Allen."

One man stopped and took off his hat. "Pleased," he said. "Name's Patrick." Blond hair corkscrewed around his face and caught the glow of sunrise colors now radiating into the alley. He set his cap and climbed onto the lead wagon. The other man gave Rose a brief nod as he went by carrying a fifty-pound bag of rice.

"Thank you for your help," she said, but he busied himself at the wagon and did not reply.

Patrick flicked the reins and got the first wagon rolling.

"We'll be back soon," said Reverend Huntington. "Lock it up. Come on, Buster."

Rose and Bai Lum rolled the big door closed on its track and Bai Lum slammed the bolt in place.

He looked around the empty storeroom. "Nothing left to steal," he said. The end of a broken box lay in one corner and he picked it up. He hurled the splintered chunk. The wood slammed into the wall and shattered. She flinched and threw up an arm to shield her face. He turned his back to her, breathing hard. She wrapped her arms around him from behind and put her face between his shoulder blades. The muscles of his back felt stiff as plaster.

He took one of her hands and rested his cheek in her palm. When his breathing finally slowed, they climbed the stairs. Together they brought down the trunks and boxes for his journey. The sound of their feet on the steps, the garish color of the sky outside, and the intermittent pictures in her mind from their night together, all seemed weirdly insubstantial, as if she only needed to take a long nap on her bed at Hazel's to put things back in order. But no, this was real: here was her husband, whose hands had been so sweet and clever last night, piling his possessions, preparing to leave her.

By the time everything was in the storefront, they could hear a commotion of traffic and voices on the street.

He went to the barricade and started to pull it aside.

"No, please don't open it." She took hold of his sleeve.

He gently pulled her hand away. "This won't stop them."

"But it's still early."

He opened the door and stepped out. When she looked into the street she couldn't breathe.

The sidewalks were nearly invisible under piles of goods— boxes, trunks, sacks, bundles of bedding, handcarts filled with vegetables, crated poultry. People were dragging out more even now and wagons filled the street. They seemed to be coming into Chinatown from every direction. Both of the laundries had been ransacked, their windows broken in; articles of clothing and linens lay in filthy disarray on the street. In front of a chow shop, a small dog with swollen teats chewed at a gristled knob of bone. A man came out of the shop with a lumpy burlap bag over his shoulder and kicked at the dog. It yelped and jumped out of the way, but when the man passed, it darted over and dragged the raw joint into the road.

At the top of the street a group of men gathered, most of them well-dressed, all of them white. It appeared that a very few of them were at the center, issuing instructions with a great deal of emphatic gesticulation. Rose and Bai Lum, standing apart by several feet, watched the men break off in small groups and start down the street, moving in the general direction of the mercantile. As they came, they stopped at every door, surrounded people who were still sorting and packing, entered buildings without knocking. They gestured, shouted, hailed empty wagons. They started throwing the piled possessions onto whichever wagon was nearest. A few Chinese men began to protest, trying to assert some authority over their belongings. But the posture of the deposers left no question; they were prepared to meet resistance with force. What was, just now, vigilance, teetered on the razor's edge of violence. They moved toward the mercantile, inexorable.

"We should go inside," she said. Dread filled her belly.

He turned to her. The deep sorrow and love and anger there hit her like a blow. "It won't help now, *Qiángli.*"

Before she could reply, a pair of mules entered the street from the opposite direction, pulling a log sledge. The driver stood on the low platform that skidded along the road behind the team. He brought the animals to a stop directly in front of the store as two men approached from up street.

"Where's your things, boy?" Rose recognized Charlie Dampler, his thin chest puffed out like a cockerel. "We're here to haul your lot to the docks. Time to go, savvy?"

"We are waiting for Huntington," Bai Lum told him. "He'll be here soon."

"Shut up," said the second man. "You're going to the docks, right now. The law is behind this, and we're hauling every one of your yellow asses to the boats." The driver of the sledge climbed down. As they approached Bai Lum, none of them seemed to notice Rose.

"I understand," said Bai Lum. His voice was quiet, reasonable. "We have already prepared. Everything is ready for Huntington."

"That's *Reverend* Huntington," said the second man, "and you better clean your ears out. Get your stuff out here now, or we'll give you a ride without it."

"No, he's telling you the truth," said Rose, still keeping a careful distance from Bai Lum. "Reverend Huntington brought me here to help. We have everything packed. He'll be back any moment."

Charlie Dampler looked at Rose, let his eyes linger on her bosom then run down the front of her. "Looks like you got your dress dirty. That was last night, wasn't it? When you saved your sweetheart here from the noose?" He smirked at her. "I guess you haven't had a chance to freshen up."

The sledge driver grimaced. "You saying this is a Chinaman's whore?"

"Not for long," said Charlie. "You're coming in this wagon now, boy, with or without your goods. Move."

Rose laughed. "Oh, Charlie."

He looked at her, his smug expression faltering.

"Don't you usually *take* the orders?" She stared at him, cocking a half grin. An interior voice warned her off tweaking him this way, but her tongue apparently had its own ideas. "Did Elsie give you permission to be down here so early, all by yourself?" Rose expected him to get angry, but the mention of his wife actually seemed to deflate him further. He stood looking at her, his mouth opening and closing like a fish. The sledge driver, though, was not put off in the least. He moved in on Rose until her back pressed against the wall of the store.

"You have some respect," he said, his face inches from hers, flecking her with spittle. He leaned forward, put his mouth next to her ear and whispered. "That's a white man you're talking to." Rose turned her head, but the driver dragged her chin back around. She tried to pull away, but he had one solid forearm against her shoulder, pinning her with the weight of his body. There was the sound of a struggle, a thudding effort Rose could feel in the boards under her feet, but she could see only the driver's face, his features so close they blurred. One of the mules began to bray. When she tried to cry out, he clamped his hand over her open mouth. She gagged, tried to bite down, but he gripped her jaw, pressing her lips against her teeth.

Then he was gone, yanked away so suddenly she fell forward on hands and knees. When she looked around, Daniel Briggs stood over the driver, leveling a pistol at his face. Rose stood and scrubbed at her mouth with the back of her hand, tasting blood.

"Are you all right?" Daniel asked her, keeping his eyes on the driver.

"Fine," she managed.

Daniel motioned with the gun. "Get up, Creigh," he told the sledge driver. The driver crab-scuttled and gained his feet. "When I sent you over here with the sledge I told you to carry goods. What the hell goes on here?"

Charlie and the other man had Bai Lum bent double over the rail of the sledge. Charlie had his hand on the back of Bai Lum's head, pressing it down at a hard angle.

"Get off him," Rose cried.

Daniel took Charlie by the upper arm and yanked him backward. When he stumbled sideways, Bai Lum yanked himself free.

"I said what the hell are you men doing here?" Daniel demanded. "This was supposed to be an orderly process, getting these people out of here. You all knew that."

"He resisted," Charlie said. It came out in a defensive whine and his already ruddy face colored more deeply.

"And the lady?"

"Lady," Creigh snorted.

Daniel brought the pistol around in a neat arc and backhanded Creigh, catching him on the point of his chin. He kept his feet but had to clap a hand to his face, which started to bleed.

"You're out of a job, Creigh," Daniel said. "Pick up your final pay on Monday."

Charlie repeated his banty rooster routine, looking indignant. "Creigh's right, Briggs. She's consorting with this heathen." He glared at Rose and Bai Lum, who were standing away from the sledge now, near, but not touching each other. He leaned toward Daniel and curled his lip in a disgusted grimace. "Do you take my meaning? She was with him all night."

Daniel looked at Rose, a question on his face. Wagons, piled high with furniture, clothing, trunks, were passing now, white drivers on the buckboards, dozens of Chinese men walking alongside. One old man, his gray queue so thin it seemed almost transparent, hunched over a carved walking stick, shuffling at the elbow of a younger man.

Rose approached Daniel and spoke quietly. "He's my husband."

Daniel Briggs frowned, looking for a moment as if he had not heard her. She watched as understanding changed his face. *This is an expression you will see over and over*, Rose thought, *on even the most familiar faces.*

He shook his head and looked away. "I can't help you," he finally said. "You've made yourself a hard bed here, Rose. I can't help you." Rose reached out to put a hand on his arm, but he moved away.

"You're not needed here," he told Creigh. He moved in on the man and spoke inches from his face. "If I hear of you bothering another woman, I won't call the sheriff. You'll leave town gelded." Then he stepped back and motioned with the pistol. "Get out of my sight."

Creigh shouldered stiffly past, holding his bleeding chin, and stalked upstreet, disappearing into the crowd.

"You," Daniel said to Bai Lum, "are to get your things onto this sledge right now. You're going to the boats."

"Daniel, we really are with Reverend Huntington," Rose said. "He'll be here any minute."

Daniel shook his head. "I have a job to do, Rose. We're not waiting." He looked at Bai Lum. "Understand?"

"Yes," said Bai Lum. "Let me get my things." He went into the mercantile.

The panic had returned, constricting her breathing. She had imagined having time, just a little more time to get ready, to brace herself. To lose sight of him. "Daniel, please."

"You two help him," Daniel said to Charlie and the other man. "Any more roughhousing and I'll get the sheriff down here." They followed Bai Lum into the store and Rose started after. Daniel caught her by the arm.

"Go home Rose. Whatever you've gotten yourself mixed up in here, it's finished. Go home."

Rose pulled her arm free. "He's my husband," she said through clenched teeth. "So tell me, Daniel—where is my home?"

He blinked. Rose felt the anger drain out of her and she shook her head, "I know it's a lot to understand. I only thought—" She faltered, looking up the street at the chaos of wagons and people. "I thought you were a bigger man." She turned her back. When Charlie and his accomplice came out carrying boxes, she ducked into the mercantile.

Bai Lum entered the storefront with the gilt screen under one arm. Light from the high windows bounced off the painted branches and birds and threw moving reflections onto the ceiling. She went straight to him and put her hands on his where they held the screen. The two of them stood that way, not speaking, while the other men came and went under Daniel's scrutiny.

"I'll come to the harbor as soon as Reverend Huntington gets here," Rose said, "and I will not leave Shu-Li or Ya Zhen until I find you there."

His face was stony. "Out there. Did he hurt you?"

In truth, she wanted to find a faucet, to rinse her mouth of the taste of the driver's dirty hand. "No," she said. "I'm all right."

He looked at the door. For that instant they were alone; he put down the screen and touched her face. "You married me, *Qiángli*. This day does not change that."

She opened her mouth to tell him she loved him, but then the men were there, watching. She held his eyes and nodded, just once. He picked up the screen again and walked out of the mercantile.

Rose carried Shu-Li's box to the sledge, ignoring Daniel, ignoring Charlie, ignoring the stream of people and belongings parading past. She stepped onto the rough deck and wedged the little box carefully between the crate of kitchen items and Bai Lum's trunk, the trunk with the Four Flowers bowl buried at its heart.

ロ

They were nearly at the mercantile, but the road was completely impacted. There was no way to maneuver Buster through the standing people and stalled wagons. Finally, Reverend Huntington pulled over and the six of them climbed out to walk. He and Lucy led, followed by Shu-Li and Ya Zhen. Mattie and Hazel Cleary brought up the rear of their small company.

"Keep the girls between us," he told them. "We can't risk being separated, not now."

Shortly after sunrise, Lucy had gone upstairs to wake the girls. Minutes later Ya Zhen came downstairs wearing an elaborate red robe embroidered in gold thread, pulled over the top of her usual dark tunic and trousers. It was deeply creased and had obviously been tightly folded for some time. Her hair was combed away from her face and hung down her back in a black sheet. Lucy laughed out loud; how could she not? The girl was so vivid, and so very much herself.

They moved en masse through the gathered citizenry, Ya Zhen like a vibrant scarlet heart at their center. Lucy was astounded by the number of people on the street. It seemed to her that every soul in Eureka had arrived and now milled around outside Chinatown, many dressed in their Sunday best.

Near the corner, a group of women stood in a loose knot, talking with their heads close together. A child with mousey brown ringlets ran to one of the women and pulled on her skirt.

"Mama, look," she said breathlessly. She pointed at Ya Zhen. "A pretty China lady."

Her mother slapped her hand. "Don't point."

The girl's face pinched as if she would cry, but she only put the offending hand behind her back and stared. As they passed, Ya Zhen smiled at her.

The woman yanked the girl against her legs. "Don't you look at my child, you filthy thing."

Mattie put her arm around Ya Zhen's shoulders. Lucy opened her mouth to make a retort, but Hazel had already stepped aside with her hands on her hips. She looked at the woman as if sizing up a cockroach. "Shame," she said. "What a way to behave. And in front of a child." She turned to catch up with the others, but shouted back over her shoulder as if addressing the crowd at large. "Can't you see these folks are suffering?"

At the end of the block, as they entered Chinatown, Reverend Huntington stopped short, staring off to his right. Lucy followed his gaze and had to clap a hand to her mouth.

It was the gallows. Swaying in a heavy pendulum, a figure dangled from the noose. Its head was cocked at a terrible angle and the feet moved in a slow arc far above the street. It was several seconds before Lucy realized it was not a real body; even so, she shuddered, feeling as if her veins were choked with ice. Whoever built the straw man had made a meticulous likeness of her husband. It was Charles Huntington, hung in effigy. A crude but carefully lettered sign was nailed to the crossbeam: NO REFUGE NOT HERE.

Charles beckoned them. "Come on, everyone. We're almost there." Lucy turned away from the dangling figure, fastening her eyes on her breathing husband.

They pushed through the line of people that flanked 4th Street, threaded between wagons and horses moving toward the docks. Before they had fully gained the sidewalk in front of the mercantile, Rose was there, her face swollen with crying.

"Rose Allen," Shu-Li cried. She started to move around Rose into the mercantile, but Rose caught her arm.

"No, Shu-Li," she said. "He's not here."

"Oh Rose, I'm sorry," said Lucy. "We couldn't get the wagon through the street."

"*Tǎ guō!*" Shu-Li tried to pull away and get into the store.

"She's calling for her brother," Ya Zhen said. She took Shu-Li by the shoulders and spoke sharply. The girl stopped struggling and looked from face to face, trying to understand what was happening.

"Tell her he's gone to the boats already, that he's waiting for us there. Tell her everything will—" Rose's voice broke and she cleared her throat. "Everything will be all right."

Shu-Li sank to her knees. Ya Zhen, resplendent in the red gown, squatted beside her, speaking quietly and rubbing her back.

Hazel wrapped Rose in her arms. "Married, I hear," she murmured. Rose nodded, crying harder.

Reverend Huntington handed her a folded handkerchief from his breast pocket. "What happened here?"

She wiped her face and told them about the sledge, that the men would not take no for an answer.

"Precious Jesus," said Hazel. "Are you harmed?"

Rose shook her head, but couldn't make eye contact. Hazel moved close and whispered in her ear. "Tell me the truth, Rosie."

Rose shook her head. "I'm fine, honestly. One of the men grabbed me, but Daniel Briggs stopped him. I tried to tell Daniel. I said that you all were coming to get us. He didn't hear me at all."

"I'm sorry, Rose," Charles said, "but I'm not surprised. It's a dark day. Listen, everyone, we need to get Shu-Li and Ya Zhen to the boats right now. If we don't, they might be separated. These girls can't travel alone."

Mattie and Ya Zhen got Shu-Li to her feet and Hazel kept her arm firmly around Rose's waist. Charles moved all of them off the sidewalk and back into the street.

He led them west, then northwest toward the harbor, the wind blowing his mane of silver hair around his ears. He reminded Lucy suddenly of the color plate in the center of her Bible, a wild-haired Moses standing before the Red Sea. She held his arm, and they fell in among the rest of the refugees, bound for the pier.

¤

No one could remember later who found Byron Tupper first, lying dead next to the stairs behind Salyer's Hotel. But a crowd had already gathered by the time Cora Salyer heard the news.

She came down to the kitchen just before full daylight and stoked the fire, poured a little milk and made a bit of toasted bread to dip into it, hoping to settle a sour stomach. The hotel was preternaturally silent—no Ivo banging around, no guests stirring, Clarence apparently still asleep. She was not surprised at the quiet after the nightmare of the previous day, and she was glad to have the kitchen to herself. Cora had received the news of the expulsion with particular satisfaction. She knew that Clarence could not keep the hotel in business without the whoring; his tastes had become far too extravagant. Once the nasty women were gone, Clarence would have no choice but to take Cora's father on as a partner, and when that happened things would change. Oh yes they would.

She finished her toast and was carrying her cup to the sink, marveling at the rosy color of the morning outside, when two men came charging in through the back door.

"You got somebody dead outside the hotel," one of them shouted.

With a small cry Cora dropped the cup and saucer into the sink and turned, clutching her morning wrapper at her throat.

"What are you talking about? What the devil are you doing, breaking in here like this?"

"I'm sorry about that, Miz Salyer, but you got a fella dead right out here in the back." The second man stood where he was near the open door, as if he thought Cora would bark at him, too.

"I can't go out there. Can't you see I'm not dressed?" She glared at them. "I'll go find my husband."

"No ma'am, you need to come now. I can't be responsible for this, not with the other trouble going on."

He tried to pull her by the elbow, but she jerked her arm free. "Let go of me, you idiot. I'm capable of moving under my own power."

Outside, behind the hotel, the man was most certainly dead—though he was hardly a man, just a boy, really. Even though Cora had never seen a dead body before, she knew the moment she laid eyes on him. It wasn't the small stain of blood around his head or the strange angle at which his right arm was cocked. There was simply an unmistakable stillness, an absence of being that even one in the darkest maw of unconsciousness does not exhibit. The boy was gone.

"Who is it?" she asked. "Why don't you cover him?" One of the men, shamefaced, fumbled out of his jacket and spread it over the young man's upper body. Before he did, Cora saw that the blood had congealed enough to stick closed the eye nearest the ground, while the other eye stared up at a cloudy angle. She turned away. A small group of people, five or six, had gathered to stare.

"It's Garland Tupper's boy," someone said. "Name's Byron." He held his cap crushed in one hand. "Looks like he fell from the stairs, there." He pointed to the back stairs, and Cora could see that the banister was splintered, one baluster hanging in pieces from the broken rail. "We haven't found his daddy yet, to tell him."

"Garland Tupper?" Cora stared at the man. "He's a killer. He killed one of …one of those upstairs girls. Yesterday." She looked at Byron's body and wondered if perhaps this was no accident. Perhaps Clarence had dealt some justice to Garland Tupper by way of his son. "I guess his chickens have come home to roost, haven't they," she said, meaning both Tupper and Clarence.

At the door she turned. "When you find Mr. Tupper, tell him my husband will have the sheriff on him for murder." She surveyed the small crowd around Byron Tupper's body. "Take that away from here," she said, and closed the door.

It was dark inside, and chilly. Cora climbed the stairs to their apartment. If Clarence was still asleep, she intended to wake him with news of the boy's death, see for herself what his reaction might be. The large skeleton key was in the lock; they tended to keep it there during the day for convenience's sake and remove it when they turned in at night. He must have left it there all night, thinking she'd come in after him. Inside, the curtains were wide open and the early sun poured in, now shifting from pink to gold. So, she thought, he was awake already.

But in his small bedroom—which had been Clarence's office before they had parted matrimonial ways—the striped satin spread was smooth on the bed and the pillows untouched. Cora looked around the tidy room. Her husband was not a man to make a bed or straighten up after himself. He hadn't slept here.

She went to the armoire in her room and dressed with slow deliberation. No matter how late he had stayed out before, getting up to nasty business, Clarence Salyer had always finished the night in his own bed. His habits might be foul, Cora thought, but they were habits nonetheless. She pinned a freshly starched collar onto her dress, laced her shoes, and locked the apartment behind her, pocketing the key. With the whores dead or shipped off, things were certainly going to change, starting today. Cora intended to find her husband and have some answers out of him. But first, she would open the hotel.

She crossed to the wide front stairs and started down, her feet soundless on the dark red carpet. They couldn't afford to miss a bit of business now, even if it was just a few folks coming in off the street for a bite of lunch later on.

Things had changed.

¤

In the woods surrounding Eureka, scores of men thrashed through sword fern and scraggles of wild rhododendron, trampled low-lying sorrel and poison oak, frantically hunting for Chinese that had fled there. Little natural light penetrated the vast redwood canopy, and in the dim morning the forest floor was remarkably open, with the lowest redwood branches well over a hundred feet from the ground. One searcher, an out-of-work tinsmith named Harvey, discovered most of the escapees massed into the burned-out bole of one of the immense trees. Before ten o'clock, all the fugitives had been tracked down and herded back into town, many sporting split lips and swelling eyes. Their captors, jubilant over their success, seemed none the worse for wear.

Sheriff Tom Brown discharged nearly twenty Chinese men from the county jail, where they had spent the night pushed together in three cells. The iron bed frames had been removed in order to accommodate as many men as possible, and they did their best to sleep by crouching against the walls of the cells, trying to stay off the grimy floor. Now, despite a short but vocal protest, none of them was allowed to retrieve belongings from either home or business. Once they were led out into the breezy February morning they were taken directly to the wharf. Those who complained were told it was their own damned faults for getting jugged in the first place. A hastily recruited deputy—perhaps all of sixteen years old—was appointed to keep watch over the whole group until they were loaded aboard ship.

¤

Ya Zhen had not been near the pier since the day she arrived, malnourished and insensible. On the day she landed in Eureka, she hadn't bathed for weeks; her scalp itched with lice and between her legs the skin burned like fire. She could smell herself, sour and rank. Walking from the boat to the room at Salyer's Hotel, she had watched her own feet, looking only far enough in front of her so that she didn't run into anything. It had recently rained and the street was sticky with mud; her clearest memory was of looking at the tracks of shoes, human and horse, moving in every direction.

Today she could not see the road at all, so filled was it with people and goods. It did not matter. She meant to remember this day, and to be remembered. The nearer they got to the water the slower they were forced to move, until finally their approach became as deliberate and stately as an imperial entourage. The breeze coming off the water was a little stronger here where the buildings gave way. It lifted long strands of her hair, blew them back from her face and up off of her shoulders in thin onyx ribbons. The sun caught in the gold threads of her gown, imprinted glimmers of peonies and cranes on the clothing of Lucy and Shu-Li and Mattie. She moved her head from side to side, looking back at the white people lined up to watch her go. Women and men, children, ranked along the street five and six deep. They had fallen curiously silent, gaping at their former neighbors, now exiles, moving past. Ya Zhen sought their eyes, face after face. Their countenances shifted like sand under a sheet of muslin, haughty then repulsed, curious then shamed, women hiding secret recognition under a blank mask, men pulling a pall of indifference over their previous frank hungers. She held each pair of eyes as long as they could bear it, smiled them down in their ranks.

As the crowd near the wharf swelled and their progress slowed, Rose felt as though she might start screaming. The relative quiet was unnerving, just the sound of feet on the road, the creak of wheels, a half -dozen seagulls circling overhead, an occasional cough. To her left, people began to whisper and point at a Chinese woman, one of the merchants' wives who had lived her life in Eureka hidden from public view. Two young men carried her between them in an ornate chair. Her bound feet were nothing but buds at the hem of her trousers, clad in tiny pointed slippers. She hid her face behind her hands and wept quietly.

Rose craned her neck, trying to see around people, trying to catch a glimpse of Bai Lum in the mass of moving bodies. Moments of their night together kept passing through her mind, luminous soap bubbles of memory—the faintly earthy smell of his hair, the angularity of his cheekbones in the candlelight, the smooth skin on his shoulders. Waking in the dark, knowing he was there with her.

Then she saw him. "This way," she said to the others, gesturing to her right.

"Show me," said Reverend Huntington. He craned to see where she pointed.

He stood among dozens of men grouped near the edge of the wharf, taller than most of those around him. At his back, the wind was strong enough to ruffle the harbor with whitecaps and throw a fine salt spray into the air. Two skiffs were tethered to the pier; their slender masts rocked in the swell. Reverend Huntington waved his arms over his head, and when Bai Lum spotted him he lifted his hand in a return wave, relief evident on his face even at a distance.

"Look, Shu-Li," said Lucy. "There's your brother." She and Hazel pointed him out. Shu-Li stood on her toes, holding onto Rose's arm, then burst into loud sobs when she saw him wave.

Ya Zhen once more soothed the younger girl. "*É qǐng, mèi mei*," she said. "Don't cry anymore." She thought of Hong Tai, running after her the day the men took her in the ox-cart. She kissed Shu-Li on the cheek. "You'll be safe now." Shu-Li nodded and wiped her eyes.

Everything had come to a motionless bottleneck. The committee of appointed leaders, backed by their vigilante enforcers, clapped their hands, whistled and called for attention. Sheriff Brown addressed the crowd.

"Listen up now, all of you." Before he could say more, the wind flipped the hat off his head and sent it skittering down the street. Two young boys ran after it and one stopped its flight by leaping on it, driving it partway into the mud. A ripple of uneasy laughter passed through the bystanders. An elderly Chinese man smiled at the boys, but the faces around him were grim, somber as a funeral cortege. The boy returned the sheriff's hat and swaggered over to the sidewalk to stand by his father. The sheriff, holding the muddy hat in one hand, continued.

"So far," he said, "this thing has gone pretty well. Just a little longer and you folks can be on your way." Rose was astounded at his choice of words. As if there was a choice. As if they were going on an excursion by their own free will. She kept her eyes on Bai Lum's face, storing every moment to hold in her heart until she saw him again. *Wait for me*, she thought. *Wait*. She needed to get to him.

Sheriff Brown continued. "What we're going to do here is divide everyone into groups and get you out to the ships on skiffs." A flow of voices passed through the crowd, dispersing and interpreting this new information. The sheriff lifted his hands and waited until he had everyone's attention again. "I know that slows the process down some, and I'm sorry for that. But with this chop," he said, gesturing at the bay, "we can't risk bringing the big boats to the pier." He moved as if to put his hat back on, noticed the mud and instead ran the fingers of one hand through his thinning hair.

"It's important that we continue to keep order." He turned somewhat to look more fully at the white onlookers. "I'm real proud of the upstanding way you folks have conducted yourself in light of how grieved we all are over—" Here he paused, perhaps not wanting to invoke David Kendall's name and stir up trouble he didn't need. "Over the recent events." He glanced at his boots as if deciding whether he'd said enough, and looked again at the crowd massed together in the street. "Let's go ahead and get started, then." He nodded to his left where a group of men stood by, and pointed his hands toward the pier like two revolvers. The men jumped into action.

"Hurry," Rose said. "We have to get to him now." She pushed forward, holding Shu-Li's hand, pulling her along.

Reverend Huntington put an arm around Ya Zhen's shoulders and followed. "Wait right here," he called back to Lucy just before he disappeared into the crowd.

"I have to come!" Mattie said.

He nodded and gestured for her to hurry.

Lucy and Hazel worked their way onto the sidewalk, pushing through a throng of onlookers. The wind riffled through clothing and blew hair back from faces that were charged with curiosity and feral gratification.

When they finally reached a spot where they could see Bai Lum, Hazel shook her head. "I don't know how Rose will bear it."

"We'll see she gets to the city," Lucy said. "We'll find him, and the girls will be with him."

Hazel blew her nose. "From your lips to God's ear," she said. "In the meantime, you and I will be a poor substitute, I'm afraid."

From their vantage point they could see Charles, so tall in the crush of people, following in Rose's wake. The first skiff was already loaded with people and cargo, riding low, water almost to the gunwales. Two oarsmen heaved the craft into the oncoming wind, pointed toward the two steamships sitting at anchor a hundred yards out in the bay.

Rose was within a few feet of Bai Lum, Charles directly behind her, when Hazel pointed into the crowd near them. "What is that idiot doing?"

Lucy squinted. Someone else was on the same trajectory, bulling through, shoving people out of his way. "No," Lucy moaned, "not again."

¤

They had almost reached Bai Lum when Garland Tupper appeared from nowhere.

Before Rose could turn around, Shu-Li screamed. Tupper had Ya Zhen by the throat, shaking her back and forth and shouting into her face.

"What'd you do to my boy?" he bawled, but in his drunken rage Rose could hardly understand him. His face was the color of a boiled beet and spittle flew from his lips into Ya Zhen's face. He looked as though he might sink his bared teeth into her cheek. Ya

Zhen's hair whipped around her as Tupper pulled her from side to side.

"Ya Zhen!" Rose bolted toward them, aware on some level that the crowd had pulled back, staring. Shu-Li kept screaming, trying to back away as Reverend Huntington lurched forward. Rose reached them a split-second before Charles did. Still howling, no real words now, Garland threw Ya Zhen aside. She hit the ground face-first and did not move, the crimson gown belled out on the ground. Mattie fell to her knees beside her.

Tupper pulled his arm around and backhanded Rose. She took the blow on her cheek and ear. There was no pain as she fell against the shifting crowd, just a stunning force that seemed to drive sound out of the day. Large black moths floated into her field of vision and she blinked them away. Even as someone pulled her to her feet, Garland swung around, a line of drool depending from his baying mouth, and punched Reverend Huntington. Rose's sense of hearing came back in pulsing waves that lit her face with pain, and she could detect, in rapid beats, the hectoring voices of the sheriff and other men trying to push into the center of the people, and wagons all around them.

Charles staggered, blood pouring from the side of his face.

That was when Bai Lum reached them.

Tupper saw him coming. He pulled back to throw another punch but in his stupefied state produced only a predictable looping roundhouse. Bai Lum drove into him, Garland's blow glancing off his shoulder. He threw Garland into the muddy road and clubbed him in the temple with one hand, took hold of his throat with the other, forcing his thumb deep into the cleft under Tupper's jaw. The drunken man bucked beneath Bai Lum, digging in with his heels and writhing, clawing for Bai Lum's throat but unable to get a hold. Bai Lum hooked one hand into the man's greasy hair. Teeth bared, he pounded the back of Tupper's head into the ground.

"Stop!" Rose screamed. "Stop it, Bai Lum." She reached for him, feeling the vibrations under her feet of Garland's head striking the dirt.

Reverend Huntington stepped in front of Rose and put Bai Lum into a headlock, yanking him backward. Bai Lum turned on Charles, his lips still lifted in a half-snarl, but then he saw. Saw that it was Charles, saw a weeping, terrified Shu-Li kneeling with Mattie next to Ya Zhen's prone form. And then Rose, he saw Rose, a trail of blood trickling from a cut beneath her eye, her ear and jaw swelling, reaching for him.

Garland moaned and tried to lift his head, but lapsed back, unconscious.

Before Bai Lum could take a step toward Rose, the sheriff and several other men broke through the crowd. Tom Brown looked around at all of them, his eyes wide.

"What in the name of Christ?" He looked at Charles, whose lower face and shirt were covered with blood. "Reverend?"

"The drink," Charles said. He cleared his throat and spat a gobbet of blood and mucous into the dirt. "I believe the drink has finally sent Mr. Tupper around the bend. He attacked these good people, Tom. First the young women," he gestured at Ya Zhen and Shu-Li, "and then Rose Allen. Bai Lum here was simply trying to protect his sisters."

Then Lucy and Hazel pushed their way through. "Charles." Lucy stumbled over to her husband, beginning to cry.

He put his arms around her. "Don't worry, old girl. It looks much worse than it is." He stroked the back of her head with an unsteady hand.

The sheriff looked at Rose, then back at Charles and Lucy. "Why the hell are you all mixed up in this? You ought to be on the walk over there, out of harm's way."

"We were acting as chaperones, Sheriff. Trying to reunite these girls with their brother." He looked over at Ya Zhen, who still had not moved. Mattie was trying to turn Ya Zhen onto her back. Shu-Li crouched next to her, inconsolable.

"Apparently it's a very good thing we were here, too," said Hazel. "Rose, let's see to the girls."

It took every bit of strength Rose had to turn her back on her husband, but she forced herself to look away, went and knelt by Ya Zhen's still form. When she bent over, the pain in the side of her face made her momentarily woozy. Hazel motioned for Shu-Li to go to Bai Lum. Rose didn't watch her go, but she could hear Bai Lum soothing her.

"Ya Zhen?" Rose said quietly. She and Mattie turned her over as gently as they could, and Hazel brushed the hair from her face. There were marks on her throat, but she was breathing and didn't seem seriously injured. "Ya Zhen," Rose said again, and patted her cheek.

Her eyes opened, closed again, then opened and cleared. She winced and sat up. Hazel got behind to help lift her to a sitting position. The sun reflected off the slightly curved edge of a large knife in her hand.

Rose folded her hand over Ya Zhen's and, without missing a beat, Mattie covered the blade with the hem of her skirt.

Hazel shifted her weight to be sure she blocked the sheriff's line of sight. "Put it away," she said quietly, "or you will never make it to the boat. Never in life."

Rose did not take her eyes from Ya Zhen's. She felt the girl's hand tighten on the handle, shaking minutely. Without breaking eye contact, Ya Zhen slipped the knife under her tunic, then held up her hand, the five fingers spread. Hazel let out a long, shaky breath.

"Can you stand?" Mattie asked.

Ya Zhen got her feet under her, swaying slightly, with Mattie and Rose supporting her on both sides. They walked over to where the sheriff stood with Charles and Lucy, Bai Lum and Shu-Li.

"She's going to be all right," Hazel said. "Thank heavens."

"The Reverend says Tupper tried to kill the girl, unprovoked," Tom Brown said. "Is that the way you saw it, Miss Allen?"

"Absolutely. He was screaming and incoherent."

"Hazel and I saw him, too," said Lucy. "From clear over there, pushing to get at them."

Garland Tupper lay sprawled, now snoring loudly. The sheriff gestured at two of his men. "Get him out of here. Drop him in a cell for now and we'll sort his hash later."

Each of the men hooked an elbow under Tupper's armpits and dragged him away, yelling at the crowd of Chinese onlookers to get out of their way. The heels of Garland's big cork-soled boots left an uneven trail in the mud, like the path of two snakes. The people closed behind him, obliterating all sign of his passage.

The sheriff turned to Bai Lum and looked at Shu-Li, still huddled next to him. "You almost got hung last night," he said. There was unvarnished disgust on his face. "Trouble seems to follow you, Chinaman. Maybe I should have let them take care of you when I had the chance."

"You just finished telling this town how proud you are," said Charles. "I don't think you want to finish up here with innocent blood on your hands."

The sheriff said nothing.

"Do you, Tom?"

Tom Brown snorted and looked away. "We've wasted enough time here," he shouted. "Get these people on the boats." He made a curt gesture to Ya Zhen. "Get over here with your so-called brother. You three are on the skiff. *Now.*"

"Come on," Mattie told Ya Zhen. "You're almost on your way." She kept her arm snugged around Ya Zhen's shoulders and helped her to where Shu-Li and Bai Lum stood.

Bai Lum's eyes locked on Rose's and he held her that way, just as he had last night, moving slowly above her in their bed. She let him hold her with his eyes until her beating heart warmed every desperate, desolate place inside her.

"We're going to say goodbye to our friends first," Charles Huntington told the sheriff. "Won't take a moment." He and Lucy stepped squarely between Bai Lum and Rose, and grasped Bai Lum's hand. "You have a place to go in the city?"

"Yes, I'll find a place."

"I don't have to tell you that it will be very dangerous for Shu-Li to be back there."

"Nothing will happen, I promise you."

"My friend," Charles said. "You'll be missed here. I will miss you."

"Thank you, Huntington."

Reverend Huntington embraced each of the girls in turn. "Be very careful. Until we meet again."

"Telegraph when you're settled," Lucy told Bai Lum. "We'll set things as right as we can." She turned to Rose, who seemed rooted in place. "Rose," she said softly. "Are you ready to say goodbye?"

All around Rose, people shuffled, readjusted the loads they carried, waiting only to complete this outrage, perhaps to find a place to stretch out and sleep after spending the night disassembling their lives. The woman with bound feet stood nearby, leaning heavily on one of the young men who had carried her. Two chickens penned together in a slatted crate erupted in short, gabbling contention, and somewhere in the crowd lining the road, a little boy cried *Catch it! Catch it!*

Rose looked at Hazel, and everything she wanted was plain on her face.

"Oh, child," Hazel sighed.

"I have to, Aunt."

Hazel wrapped her niece in a bear hug. "As if I could keep you."

"I'm scared for Mattie," she whispered.

"So am I. But I won't turn loose of her, you know that." She gave Rose another squeeze. "Come on then."

It seemed to last forever, that walk of a few yards. Finally, finally she stood right in front of him. He didn't smile, but brushed his thumb across her unmarked cheek, just as he had the night before.

"Enough," the sheriff barked. "You people get back so we can finish this."

"This is her husband, Tom," Hazel said. "She's going with him."

Tom Brown stared at Bai Lum and Rose, arms crossed over his chest, nostrils flaring like a dog with its wind up.

"For heaven's sake," Hazel said. "Isn't that what you're about here? Getting rid of folks? What's one more?"

Sheriff Tom Brown turned to the man next to him. "Get them on those double-damned boats. After that, the whole mess of them is San Francisco's trouble." He shoved his way into the crowd, shouting at them to line up and get ready to board.

Hazel took Bai Lum's hands. "You take good care of these ladies," she told him. "God bless you all. Rose, I'll write your father."

"I will too, as soon as we get there," Rose said. She opened her arms to Mattie, who stood nearby looking worried and miserable. They held each other.

"I'll try, Rose. Every day," Mattie said. "Honest I will."

"I know," said Rose. "I love you."

The men tasked with loading the skiffs now walked alongside, physically prodding them toward the pier. Hazel took Mattie's hand and pulled her from their queue. Rose linked her arm through Ya Zhen's and shuffled along behind Bai Lum and Shu-Li, who clutched the hem of his jacket like a small child.

And just that quickly, they were leaving. She blew a kiss to Hazel and Mattie then turned for a last look at the Huntingtons, but could no longer see them through the press of people behind her.

The skiff tilted precariously as one after another climbed aboard. Rose took Bai Lum's hand. The rowers began to pull them out into the bay toward the *City of Chester*, the same ship that had brought her here almost five years ago. He lifted her fingers to his lips and kissed them. They moved a little faster when the oarsmen found their rhythm. The prow lifted and slapped the water unevenly as they got farther and farther from shore. The small boat was filled with Chinese faces, some dark, some light, old, young, all men but for Ya Zhen and Shu-Li. *Here are the women in my family*, thought Rose. Everyone in the skiff looked back at the crowd on the pier, the diminishing line of buildings, and the high ridges of ancient forest, trees that put down roots when Christ wore swaddling.

All but Ya Zhen.

Ya Zhen sat next to Shu-Li, eyes forward, staring at the *City of Chester*. Her red robe, torn along the neckline, was so brilliant it was hard to look at without squinting. Her black hair streamed back on the wind as if she was the masthead on the bowsprit of a grand schooner.

Rose leaned into Bai Lum and watched the city shrink as the oars sliced water, creaking in their locks, the intermittent grunt of effort from the men rowing, the liquid thud of whitecaps striking the hull and breaking on the rocks near shore.

Then she saw them. "Look," she told Bai Lum, and waved wildly. Shu-Li saw too, and lifted her hand. Charles and Lucy, Hazel and Mattie had broken through the masses of people who had crowded the shoreline to watch what they pretended was justice being served. These four stood right down at the edge of the bay, Charles up to his pant cuffs in water, his wild white hair blowing around his head.

"I love you," Rose called. "Don't worry."

"They can't hear you," said Bai Lum, lifting his hand in a steady salute.

She knew they couldn't hear. But that was fine. "Eureka," she whispered.

I have found it.

AFTER

March 15, 1885

Dearest Father,

When I was a little girl, you used to tease me to be careful and 'beware the Ides of March.' Remember? There have been some troubles here, as you will see in the newspaper clippings I enclose. This letter brings with it much news of change, but know that underneath it all I am well and truly happy.

I am no longer in Eureka, but living in a small town in the foothills of the Sierra Nevadas. It is called Grass Valley, though we have not seen much grass yet, as the snow has been slow in melting. Since leaving you and Paw Paw I thought I missed the snow, but now I remember why we loved spring so well.

I have other news too, hard to tell, so I'll do it quickly and not keep you in suspense. When I write that 'we' are watching for the grass, I mean my husband and me. I am sorry to tell you so bluntly, but you know how I am when I make up my mind. You needn't worry, Papa. He is a fine man, a widower. We left Eureka during the troubles, along with two friends—young women whom I now count as dear friends. We are making a go of life in the mountains. When our supplies arrived from Eureka, we opened a small store and business is thriving. Though the rush for gold is not what it was in the days of the '49ers' there are still plenty seeking their fortunes and needing to pay for life's necessities.

Papa, when I came west, you said you wished you could come with me. What would you think of a new adventure? We are already making plans to build a house, and will need it done before November. Perhaps you could add your hand in the finish work. We'll also be in need of a cradle.

I must close for now, as the days are short and I'm too tired to write more. Please, Papa, come and see us.

Always,
Your Rose

CHAPTER ELEVEN

Contemplation in the night watches
and at the sun's zenith,
my mind like a barren tree
arrives at the heart of Tao.
Beneath a still sea
fly fish and dragons, unbounded.
A limitless sky
filled only with moonlight.

—*Zhou Xuanjin*, 12th century

Late May, 1885

SHE FISHES NEARLY EVERY DAY. The trout are large here, and hungry. They love stone flies with their long, delicate wings. She slides one onto her hook and casts the line in a lazy curve over the still water under a granite outcrop. Minuscule ripples vibrate out from the dying beat of the fly's wings. The sun makes her feel loose-jointed and sleepy.

All around the valley spring flowers have come up in broad bands of color, visible for miles. The new house is surrounded by brilliant orange poppies and spears of purple lupine. Rose and Shu-Li are forever cutting blooms and bringing them inside, filling tin cans and mason jars. Ya Zhen tells them to go outside and fill their eyes instead and they only laugh.

She pulls in her line, casts it again. She leaves early and hikes high into the hills to reach this spot. Two or three times she convinced Shu-Li to join her, but after they spotted a black bear wallow along the river, a wide swath of grass matted down and festooned with piles of scat, Shu-Li refused to return. Working in the store with Bai Lum is Shu-Li's preference, or helping Rose with the new garden. Ya Zhen doesn't worry about the bears, but she keeps her eyes open.

Finally a hit. Her rod bows and she works the fish patiently in. It's a golden trout, sides smooth and brilliant as melted ore, rosy at the edges. It is the work of a moment to get the hook free. The bait is gone, but she is done for the day and the maturing stone flies are everywhere.

Before they grow wings the stone flies live in the shallows at the edge of the river. Each nymph builds a home, a tiny tubular shell spackled together with bits of sand and small river detritus, even flecks of gold dust now and then. Ya Zhen thinks that her family is like that, too, building something around themselves here. She is learning to work wood with Rose's father, whom they all call *Bà ba*. All over the house there are little cupboards built into the walls with stars and moons, birds and trees carved in. He is letting Ya Zhen help him make a bed for the baby, and as they think and plan he tells her to let the wood give up its secrets. She is learning to listen with her hands.

On the first of May, Bà ba presented Ya Zhen and Shu-Li each with a small chest. A hummingbird is carved in Shu-Li's, its long beak hidden in the drooping bell of a columbine blossom. The top of Ya Zhen's box is inlaid with a tiger, its stripes alternating between maple and red fir, sanded and oiled to a glassy finish. Below is a hidden drawer that slides open if she presses a particular spot underneath. Her ebony chopsticks are in the upper part of the box; she keeps only one thing in the secret place. By the time she goes to bed tonight that little drawer will be empty.

She pulls her knife from its sheath and guts the fish. She lays it with the other three in the basket Bai Lum gave her—Rose calls it a creel, but Ya Zhen has given up trying to fit such a gnarled word to her tongue. She and Bai Lum have long ago stopped translating for Shu-Li, who almost sounds now as if she had been born in California.

Shadows have shifted to the easterly sides of the firs and madrones. If she leaves now she will get back in time to help Rose in the garden before it gets dark. They have been digging and planting and watering for weeks. The plan is to have fresh vegetables to sell to the miners at the end of summer, with enough left over to see the family through all winter.

Bai Lum does the heavy work after he closes the store. One afternoon he caught Rose carting stones out of the way and they had words about it. He lets her do all the talking until, more often than not, she talks her way around to his way of thinking. Then he smiles and tells her he agrees. There are nights when Ya Zhen finds sleep elusive and she hears Bai Lum and Rose in their bed, Rose's soft sounds like a night bird.

Part way down the last of the rocky trail out of the woods, Ya Zhen steps forward and nearly puts her foot on something stretched across the red dirt. Rattlesnake. Some instinct causes her to lengthen her stride and step over it before she even registers what it is. She stumbles slightly, backing away a few feet and breathing hard. The snake, a young and slender animal, is taking advantage of the late afternoon light. It doesn't bother to curl up or shake its tail. Rather, it slides into the long grass on the side of the path and she loses sight of it immediately, as if it hadn't been there at all.

She hurries a little now, though her heart is already slowing. The only thing in the secret drawer of her polished box is a twist of paper holding a small pile of sunflower seeds. They have traveled with her for a long time, from her first home to here, and she has no idea if they will grow. But she intends to plant them this evening on the south side of the house. If they take, she'll save the seeds and plant again next spring.

As she cuts across the meadow behind their home, she imagines it—a vast field of yellow blooms lighting up the hillside, recreating itself year upon year.

EPILOGUE

SIX YEARS AFTER THE EXPULSION

A CHINESE INVASION — This morning the steamer "Los Angeles" arrived bringing 25 cabin passengers & 15 in the steerage, one of whom was a live Chinaman. Shortly after the steamer landed 'John' came ashore & wandered into a blacksmith shop on the corner of 4th & D streets, where he was soon surrounded by a curious crowd of people who let the almond-eyed 'Celestial' know that no Chinamen were allowed in Eureka. The poor fellow was frightened but made his questioners understand that he came here by mistake & that he would return by the steamer. Mr. Albert Backman who was a passenger on the steamer says that the crew & passengers had no end of fun with the Chinaman, who was told they would hang him if he landed in Eureka. 'John' will not stay long in Humboldt. The climate will not agree with his health.

Daily Humboldt Standard
Thursday, September 17, 1891

A NOTE TO THE READER

THANK YOU FOR READING *Chasing Down the Moon.* If you enjoyed this story, there are two simple things you can do to that would mean the world to the author:

First, take a moment to leave an honest reader review on Amazon, Goodreads, or whatever social media you prefer. Your word-of-mouth is invaluable, and helps make *Chasing Down the Moon* visible to more potential readers.

Second, tell a friend about *Moon.* There's nothing better than an enthusiastic, reader-to-reader personal recommendation.

And, Gentle Reader, do keep in touch! Subscribe to my newsletter at www.carlabaku.com. I'd love to hear from you. Subscribing gets you:

1. An occasional email letting you know what's up or what's new. Every couple of months, I'll keep you in the loop with news from the world of words, give you updates on my own new book releases, and other cool stuff.
2. Access to deals and freebies, Advance Reader Copy giveaways of my new books, and more.
3. A small gift: The *Chasing Down the Moon* "**History Happens Sidebar"** has vintage photographs of some of the actual people and places you just read about, plus historical notes about Eureka and what took place there after the Chinese expulsion. Also includes the **Author's Cut: Four short vignettes from *Chasing Down the Moon.*** The Author's Cut will give you a parting glimpse of several of the novel's memorable secondary characters.

Again, many thanks for reading!

Until next time: make peace, share love, read books

In the works from Carla Baku:

AFTER THE PRETTY POX
Book One: The Attic
(Carla Baku writing as August Ansel)

A searing act of bioterrorism. A catastrophic plague.

Most of the human race is dead, and for two years Arie McInnes has been alone, riding out the aftermath of the Pretty Pox, waiting for her own inevitable end.

Hidden in the attic of her ruined home, Arie survives by wit and skill, ritual and habit. Convinced that humans are a dangerous fluke, a problematic species best allowed to expire, she chooses solitude...even in matters of life and death.

Arie's precarious world is upended when her youngest brother – a man she's never met – appears out of nowhere with a badly injured woman. Their presence in the attic draws the attention of a dark watcher in the woods, and Arie is forced to choose between the narrow beliefs that have sustained her and the stubborn instinct to love and protect.

In Book One of this captivating new post-apocalyptic series, *After the Pretty Pox* casts an unwavering eye on what it means to be human in a world where nature has the upper hand, and the only rules left to live by – for good or ill – are the ones written on the heart.

Available July 26, 2016!

ACKNOWLEDGMENTS

A great deal of research went into *Chasing Down the Moon*. The Humboldt County Historical Society (thank you, Jim Garrison) and the Humboldt County Library provided invaluable blocks of information. Thanks also to Professor Gordon Chang at Stanford for resource suggestions. Tara Mayberry of TeaBerry Creative designed the book's beautiful cover.

This novel has had several incarnations, and I'm grateful to a great many people who offered encouragement and suggestions along the way. Molly Antopol, Elizabeth Tallent, Adam Johnson, and David Haynes saw the earliest drafts at both Stanford and Warren Wilson College, and offered fierce, cheerful, incisive guidance. Several chapters were scrutinized by creative writing classmates in workshop; thanks for helping make my words stronger. Libbie Hawker, thank you for that shove off the fence—it worked!

Nancy, Lynette, Geoff, and Jude, the book would have been the poorer without your meticulous attention and gracious input as beta readers. Any remaining errors are wholly mine.

Andy, Jeff, Ben, Luke, and Meredith: you're funny, kind, talented, hardworking, creative, loving, and wicked smart—being your mom/stepmom is the best thing.

For many years, my husband Brian and my best friend Christina Gillen have been an unrelentingly optimistic fan club of two, reading early drafts with enthusiasm and letting me talk (a lot) about the difficulties and pleasures of writing—thank you doesn't begin to cover how much I love and appreciate them. Mister, you are my childhood sweetheart, best pal, and knight-in-shining-armor. I am so lucky.

A special note of gratitude to Tobias Wolff. He listened, and he pointed me in the right direction at exactly the right time.

ABOUT THE AUTHOR

Carla Baku holds a BA in English/Creative Writing from Stanford and an MFA in fiction from the Program for Writers at Warren Wilson College. Her award-winning fiction, poetry, and creative nonfiction have been featured in numerous literary magazines, including *Narrative*, *Calyx*, and *PMS*.

She writes in beautiful Northern California, where she lives with her husband Brian. *Chasing Down the Moon* is her first novel.